KNOT HER GOAL

a novel by

Ari Wright

Published and formatted by Blue-Eyed Books

Knot Her Goal, MVP: Most Valuable Pack Book 1

ISBN: 9798989007240

ebook ISBN: 9798989007233

Cover: Quirky Bird Covers by Staci Hart

This book is for the only person who could spontaneously convince me to write a smutty sports Omegaverse without giving me copious amounts of tequila.
In my defense, there <u>were</u> tacos.

Love you, Kel.
This one's for you.

the cheat sheet

WHAT IS
an omegaverse?

An **Omegaverse** is an alternate universe wherein humans have evolved a biological hierarchy based on three individual designations: **alphas, betas, and omegas.** In an Omegaverse, every person falls into one of those three categories (or "designations") by the time they reach adulthood. Their **designation** then determines certain elements of their physiology, psychology, and physical appearance. The humans in this Omegaverse are not shifters.

Alphas are large, strong, dominant, possessive, and territorial. While civilized, they often struggle with the urge to use force or exert their dominance over others; particularly fellow alphas. Optimized anatomy makes them physically superior in many ways, including reproduction.

Male alphas have a "knot" at the base of their penises. This **knot**, much like the penis itself, becomes engorged when they are aroused and expands to its full size upon completion, "locking" an alpha into his partner. Female alphas have a "lock" inside their vaginas that perform a similar locking maneuver on their partners.

Alphas are biologically compelled to find compatible partners based on individual scents. They also tend to form **packs** with others. Omegas often become the center of packs because they are the only designation capable of creating **bonds** between others. There is rarely more than one omega in a pack. Once a pack bonds with an omega, all of their scents alter subtly. This shift helps protect bonded omegas from unwanted advances.

Betas remain the most similar to everyday humans. They do not have intense scents or the same biological compulsions that alphas and omegas share. Many beta-beta relationships resemble traditional monogamous partnerships. Because they cannot bond among themselves, they often choose to marry instead.

Omegas are smaller and softer in stature, naturally submissive, wary of violence, fearful, emotional, empathetic, and magnetically attractive. Omegas' bodies are built to endure the demands of an entire pack of partners, emotionally and physically.

Omega biology draws alphas in. When omegas are aroused, their bodies send nearby alphas a signal by **perfuming**. Omega perfume is a concentrated hit of their specific scent, intended to lure an alpha to their aid.

Alphas and omegas each have distinctive scents. Their bodies produce these scents at all times, but they are particularly strong when the individual is sexually aroused or emotionally distressed. Alphas and omegas can have very intense, all-consuming physical and emotional reactions to each other's scents. While uncommon, the phenomenon is called **scent-sensitivity**.

Scent-sensitive alphas and omegas are referred to as **mates**. By some twist of fate or biology, they are near-irresistible to one another. Separating from their scent-sensitive mates would cause an omega extreme pain and distress.

Omegas experience **heat cycles**. These "heats" are spurred by the biological imperative to mate/bond with an alpha (or group of alphas) who will provide for and protect them. When an omega goes into heat, he/she will experience intense physical pain unless they are knotted by their alphas regularly. Heats send omegas into a state of limited lucidity that is known as a **heat haze**. This haze makes them extremely vulnerable and unstable.

Omegas can take **suppressants** to lower their hormone levels.

Suppressants help make the pain of heats tolerable for omegas who do not have alphas. Unfortunately, over time, suppressants become less effective.

Unbonded alphas who encounter an unbonded omega can experience **rut**. Rut is a condition wherein an alpha loses his/her mental faculties and gives in to the biological imperative to knot/lock an omega. Rut is often dangerous for omegas.

Omegas **nest** in order to feel secure. An omega's nest should be a soft, round place that feels low to the ground and dark. Omegas take great pride in building their nests to their individual tastes and their alphas' approval. It is their alphas' duty to provide this space and the resources to outfit it.

Courting is the process by which alphas can press their suits with an omega of their choosing. It is generally a task undertaken by the entire pack in pursuit of their one chosen omega.

flag on the play

(content warnings)

Welcome to the **MVP** *omegaverse*

I'm so glad you're here!

Knot Her Goal is the first installment in a series of inter-connected standalone Omegaverse romances.

This series is called *MVP: Most Valuable Pack* because each standalone focuses on a different sport, team, or pack of elite athletes.

This is a why-choose Omegaverse romance. It includes lots of knots, tons of spice, and absolutely no choosing!

If you don't like rowdy alphas, swoony mates, and group sex scenes (including packmates lending each other a hand), this may not be the HEA for you <3

Content Warnings: workplace discrimination, loss of a parent, attempted SA, medical anxiety, age gap/Daddy play, double penetration, dubious consent, past abuse/childhood neglect, mention of accidental pregnancy.

knot her goal playlist

Cruel Summer — Taylor Swift
Bones — Imagine Dragons
POWER — Kanye West
6 Foot 7 Foot — Lil Wayne, Cory Gunz
Hustlin' — Double A-Ron
Welcome to the Party - Diplo, French Montana Lil Pump, Zhavia
Forever — Paper Planes
Trophies — Young Money, Drake
if u think i'm pretty — Artemas
Murder In My Mind — Kordhell
Agora Hills — Doja Cat
I Was Never There — The Weeknd, Gesaffelstein
older — Isabel LaRosa
Killer — Eminem, Jack Harlow, Cordae
Good Riddance — Oceanside, Alex D'Rosso, Badjack
bad guy — Vitamin String Quartet
Why Don't You — Thorgan
Blood // Water — grandson
Tick Tick Boom — Sage The Gemini, BygTwo3
Daylight — David Kushner
Lovin on Me — Jack Harlow
All Of The Lights — Kanye West
High For This — The Weeknd
Made for Me — Chaitha, Sidi
Dreams and Nightmares — Meek Mill
Invincible —Machine Gun Kelly, Ester Dean
New Romantics (Taylor's Version) — Taylor Swift

prologue

YOU KNOW those moments when the stars align? Where the universe is good, the world is generous, and everything just works out perfectly?

Yeah, me neither.

"I'm sorry, Miss Reed, but we're going to have to terminate your employment. Effective immediately."

The bald man sitting across from me has a bumpy head and a sour expression. With his face bathed in the yellow light reflecting off of my employment file, he sort of looks like a lemon. I focus on that to keep from bursting into tears.

Again.

"But my—"

Lemon Head interrupts, his thin eyebrows bunching. "You know the rules for *your kind*. The two-year trial period is still in effect. Therefore, the company is within its rights to terminate your employment without severance or any benefit extension."

Oh boy.

Here it comes.

I do everything to choke down the sob scaling the back of my tongue, but I can't keep the tears at bay *and* keep my lunch in my stomach, so I settle for the latter.

I'm already the girl who ruined the entire executive floor. I can't barf all over HR, too.

Seeing my tears, the middle-aged, middle-management man sighs. As if *he's* the one losing his salary and healthcare. "It's a shame that you had to endure all of this," he mutters, looking away. "Back in my day, you wouldn't have been allowed in the office. This is exactly why."

I don't need the lecture. I could present it myself, at this point.

Omegas are too fragile to handle the stress of a career.

Omegas are too sensitive to handle constructive criticism.

Omegas need too much time off for their heats.

And then they want time off for maternity leave, too?

I know, I know. The *audacity* of keeping the species alive. How dare we?

Still, I thought I'd proven the nay-sayers wrong once and for all when I finished my Master's degree and started working for the only marketing firm in the whole state that would hire an unbonded omega. But even here, at this "progressive" company, it only took eighteen months for me to become a pariah.

As if this whole thing is *my* fault.

My innocence only makes me cry harder.

How did this happen? I did everything right. I did everything they told me to do.

Lemon Head tosses a pointed look at the door, dismissing me. And I want to go. At that moment, I want nothing more than to get out of there and hide in my bed for all eternity.

But I have to force myself to sit up and sniff back my tears. "I need my last paycheck," I tell him, hating how my voice wobbles. "I'm owed for two weeks."

I'll need that money. I'm already living paycheck-to-paycheck. Without this steady income, and the health insurance...

The thought of not having anything to fall back on finally sinks in. I can't quite strangle the whine that builds in my chest.

The beta rolls his eyes and scoffs, going back to his paperwork with a flick of his hand. "Call payroll. That's their problem."

The girl my mother raised would tell this guy to stick it where the sun doesn't shine.

Unfortunately, I've never actually *been* that girl.

So I take my big fat L and scramble to the exit, praying no one notices me crying the whole way out.

chapter
one

Megera

"SO WHAT DID THE DOCTOR SAY?"

I poke at the sandwich on the plate next to my laptop, scowling at the stale bread, my best friend's question. And, you know, my general existence. "I don't want to talk about it."

Denial has become a lifestyle of sorts.

And, turns out? It's not exactly an effective strategy.

Two weeks of avoidance, and I'm still unemployed. Broke. Alone. And edging toward desperation.

"How much do you think I could get for feet pics?" I ask around a mouthful.

Remi squeals, then sobers. "Seriously, Meg. Is it *that* bad?"

Well, it isn't good. I suck in a quick breath to force down a wave of dread. "Two months. Max."

The doctor actually said eight weeks. But... denial.

In this instance, it's entirely necessary. If I let myself think about my upcoming heat, I might actually give myself a stroke.

It will be my first unmedicated cycle. Ever. I've been on a steady regimen of suppressants to lower my hormones to a livable level and pain medication to get me through without any... help.

If losing my medical insurance just meant losing access to the pain management drugs, I could deal. It would be painful and terrifying and all that fun stuff, but I would live. According to my doctor, the same can't be said for going through heat alone without my suppressants.

Remi's gasp really doesn't help my anxiety. On the screen in front of me, my WorkNow inbox stares back at me. Empty.

"What are you going to do?" my friend frets. "You could get really sick, Meg. Or really hurt."

I know she's right. Stories of unbonded, untended omegas going crazy during their heats are well-documented. The thought of stripping all of my clothes off and running through my neighborhood in desperate search of an alpha to climb may sound ridiculous to me now, but that doesn't mean it won't happen once my unchecked heat hormones shoot through the roof.

Remi is right. I can try to chain myself to my bed and ride out the excruciating cramps, but there's no guarantee I won't somehow wander once the delirium sets in.

And a perfuming, slick-dripping omega roaming the streets? Let's just say recent experience has taught me there are plenty of alphas evil enough to take advantage. And even more who simply wouldn't be able to control themselves.

I swallow another whine, doubling over my keyboard and pressing the tips of my fingers into my face. "I know, I know."

Because we're true best friends, Remi and I take turns panicking. As soon as it's clear I'm about to melt down, she's suddenly brimming with optimism.

"You have two months, Meg. That's plenty of time. You'll get a job soon. I just know it."

Hearing the sunshine in her voice would ordinarily boost my spirits. But, now, it just makes it clear exactly how hopeless I feel.

I wasn't always like this. There was a time when I couldn't imagine I'd designate as an omega. My mom was an *alpha*. And since she conceived me with a test-tube from another alpha, I definitely didn't grow up dreaming of the perfect nest or the right pack to share my heats with.

Mom raised me to be independent, smart, and tough. All of the things she was before I lost her.

Since I was only fourteen at the time, I was sorted into the system and lived in group homes until my designation started to come through.

At first, I thought the blood tests were wrong. Government medicine is notoriously mediocre, and everything I knew about myself told me that my recent mood swings and weird urges had to be some sort of teenage fluke.

I could *not* be an omega.

...See what I mean about the denial?

The first time I perfumed, I thought I was hallucinating. If Remi—who was a brand-new omega herself—wasn't there to talk me down, I might have hurt myself.

Poor Rems had to teach me everything. I was totally clueless about how to be an omega. Sometimes, I still am.

Okay; most of the time.

I hate feeling helpless. Weak. I want to be like Mom—independent and badass. Before The Incident cost me my job, I thought I might have a shot.

I still do, I tell myself now. *I will. I just have to suck it up and move forward.* Pulling in a deep breath, I wrap myself deeper into my favorite blanket and click refresh again.

It's okay.

It's fine.

I have two months.

Well. Eight weeks.

OMEGAS NEED NOT APPLY.

Okay, it doesn't actually say that.

But it might as well.

I'm not sure why I'm surprised. We live in a world that's controlled by our stronger, more dominant counterparts. Our very existence reminds them of their greatest weakness—namely, *us*—and brings that weakness right to the surface. Of course they don't want us in their spaces.

Problem is—*all of the spaces* are their spaces.

Including the Orlando Ospreys' headquarters, apparently.

The job on my screen is perfect for me in every other way. The state's premier national football team needs a new social media manager, which is exactly the sort of work I love.

A big, dynamic organization? An exciting field with lots of splashy competition? Cheering crowds and bright stadium lights? It's a marketing mind's dream.

Honestly, even the location sounds perfect. Moving a couple hours away—near the team's facilities—would be ideal after my humiliating ordeal at my last job. Hopefully, two-hundred miles is far enough for no one to recognize me. Plus, Remi and I could see each other more if I lived in Orlando; she works just outside the downtown area.

A quick perusal of the Ospreys' Instagram account tells me exactly why they have a position available. Their marketing is trite and predictable. Their orange-on-black bird logo looks like something out of the eighties. And their social presence feels sporadic, at best.

It's mostly an endless crawl of two types of pictures: the outdated logo and their obnoxiously gorgeous quarterback.

Declan Howard.

Considering I know nothing at all about football, the fact that I recognize him right away is telling. It would be hard *not* to remember the guy, since he's probably the most beautiful person on the planet.

He's also tagged in every Ospreys picture, his all-American good looks grinning up at me.

Declan in a helmet.

Declan in a suit.

Declan being interviewed post-game. Pre-game. Mid-game.

Sheesh.

He *is* a perfect physical specimen. Two-hundred-and-thirty pounds of lean, solid muscle, if his stats are to be believed. He also has a perfectly square jaw, a straight nose, and the naughtiest grin I've ever seen. His head of thick, brown hair and striking blue eyes are just the double-cherries on top of his yumminess.

As undeniably attractive as the quarterback is—especially in those tight pants they wear... damn—surely, there must be other things for the team to advertise.

Don't they have events? Philanthropies? *Other* hot players? Why do they lean so heavily on the fact that this one guy was on *Today Magazine*'s Sexiest Men Alive List?

Twice.

But still.

It doesn't make sense to me until I search the team and pull up their Wikipedia page.

Oh.

The Orlando Ospreys were sold in 2021 to billionaire magnate, Ronan Ash. His all-alpha pack, the Ash pack, also includes the team's star quarterback, Declan Howard; Pro Bowl tight end, Theo Matthews; and the Ospreys' lead physician, Dr. Archer Monroe. Their pack resides in the Orlando area at an undisclosed address.

The page doesn't have a photo of the pack, but it does go on about the team itself, listing their past players, current standings, and a jumble of statistics I don't understand.

I really don't know anything about the game... except the quarterback is the star.

Evidently.

After an hour of research, though, other things start to take shape. The National League kicks off within a week and the Ospreys will play their first game of the season on Sunday. That's a tight turnaround time for whoever they hire, considering it's already Monday afternoon. They must be desperate to fill the social media role, which is perfect for my current situation.

Besides, they clearly need help. I don't have to be a sports expert to know that their feeds are cluttered, their branding needs a refresh, and their recent press is all negative.

There are pages and pages of articles about Declan Howard's "fumbling" performance last year. A poor season that came off the heels of a National Championship loss and a scandalous break-up with some woman named Katrina. I scroll through the pictures, but there aren't very many of them together, and I get bored after the fifteenth snap of her pouting at the camera.

It doesn't matter for my work anyway, I decide, since he's clearly working the whole single-athlete-sex-symbol thing these days.

Besides, if I had my way, he won't even be the star of the social media anymore. The rest of the Ash pack seems non-existent as far as Google is concerned, aside from Ronan Ash's charitable foundation and few select snaps of the dark-haired, scowling alpha winning philanthropic awards.

Yeesh. We'll have to work on smiling for the camera...

Despite the mixed press, I have plenty of ideas for the Ospreys. They need to re-brand and start fresh to shake off whatever funk dragged them down last year. They also need to get into the twenty-twenties and get on TikTok.

I already have some choice influencers in mind for partnership deals. Plus, a locker room full of football hotties sounds like *prime* material for viral videos.

Riding my first burst of true excitement in weeks, I fill out the whole application and carefully re-check my résumé before scrolling down to all the legal jargon slapped above the place for my e-signature.

And there it is. An omega disclaimer.

The thick, carefully-worded paragraph basically says unbonded omegas cannot be admitted to their facility "for their own safety." Something about the number of unbonded alphas who work on and for the team... and the League's rules prohibiting players from taking rut-blockers or any other hormones.

Which essentially means that one whiff of my perfume at the wrong moment would likely cause The Incident Part Two: The Ospreys' Omega Chew Toy.

A flutter of pure anxiety stretches through my abdomen while the rest of my body betrays me, reacting instinctively to the thought of throwing an unbonded, pro-athlete alpha into rut. My nipples tighten. The crotch of my panties grows damp.

So... I guess whichever lawyer drafted their disclaimer *may* have had a point.

But I'm so sick of my designation ruining my life. I'm tired of feeling weak and silly and fragile.

I know I can do this job. If I could just show them I have what it takes...

Besides, even if it turns out that the position or the environment really isn't for me, I'm fast running out of other options. I need health insurance, and I need it, like, yesterday.

My teeth sink into my lower lip while I stare at the clause, debating.

If I could somehow get the job just long enough to get healthcare, I could ask my doctor for a six-month supply of suppressants. That would get me through my upcoming heat and buy me time to prove

I can do this job. Or get a different job where I wouldn't have to lie and hide my designation.

Can I even hide it?

I've heard stories. There are lots of omega blogs that list extra measures we can take to keep our pheromones to ourselves. Another hour of research convinces me that my plan might just be crazy enough to work. The more I read, the riskier and more complicated it seems. But *doable*.

At the end of the day, do I even have a choice? My WorkNow inbox is still empty, apart from this one position.

With my eyes half-shut in horror, I quickly click back into the application and change my answer beside the question asking me to indicate my designation. Then I grit my teeth and hit Submit before I change my mind.

chapter
two

"WE'RE DEFINITELY NOT NERVOUS," Remi chimes, her voice floating out of my car speakers.

The double-layer of scent-blocking, slick-absorbent panties under my navy pencil skirt makes a liar out of her. I pinch the pearly blouse tucked into the tight fabric and pull it out a bit so it billows around my ribs, drawing attention away from the bulky material covering my hips.

Whatever. I'm not here to walk a runway. If their current (pitiful) marketing is any indication, my interview will be a room full of clueless straight men who don't know the first thing about aesthetics. No one will notice a frumpy skirt.

Just in case, I forced myself to wear my highest nude pumps, even though I cringe slightly every time my toes scrunch. I wonder if all omegas secretly hate heels or if that's a 'me' problem.

Exhaling slowly and tamping down the urge to abandon my whole plan, I do a double-check of my scent. It's buried under the industrial-strength de-scenter I sprayed liberally over my entire body. The cloud of fumes almost gagged me, but now I'm grateful I used so much.

I can't take any chances.

Following my GPS, I turn right. A sunny yellow building across the road catches my eye. It's big, with a yard and a picket fence. My face splits into a smile at the sight of it... until I notice the sign over the door.

New Horizons Children's Home.

There's a girl on the front porch, one much too old to be holding the doll hanging from her grasp. I get it, though. It's probably the only thing she has left from whatever her life was *before*. My heart lurches, remembering that feeling all too well.

"Meg?"

Get it together, I tell myself. *There's no time for that shit.*

Shaking myself out of my own head, I paste my panicked smile back on and glance at the GPS. "Yep. Still here. Hold on. It looks like I'm about to turn in."

After one more left turn, I find myself on a wide drive surrounded by man-made lakes on both sides. Huge, magazine-worthy palm trees frame the road leading to an enormous parking lot.

"Um, wow."

The Ospreys' offices aren't crammed into some downtown high-rise or suburban strip mall. No; they have a whole freaking *compound*.

I'm starting to suspect I may have underestimated what a big deal this interview is.

"Tell me *everything*," Remi squeals. "I need details!"

She's been so sweet and supportive, staying on the phone with me for the whole drive. I gulp, my eyes wide while I blink at the scene in front of me and try to come up with a description.

"It's..." *A lot.*

Off to the left, I see fields. Plural. Three football fields slotted side-by-side, their goal posts shining yellow. Behind those, their team training center gleams, all steely beams and silvery windows. Through the glass walls, I make out dozens of alphas milling about the first floor. A shiver shimmies down my spine.

Up in the distance, over several acres of grassy hills and valleys, I spot the silhouette of the Ospreys' home stadium, all twisting metal and glass. Parking garages and other buildings surround it, but I can't make out any of the businesses from what I estimate to be about half a mile away.

I turn my attention down to my Maps app, hoping my ultimate destination is *not* inside that gym or the stadium. Thankfully, the dot pinpointing the address is slightly off to the right.

Which means it must be the scary-looking building looming over me. I bend forward and try not to whine as I crane my neck to take it in.

Yikes.

The Ospreys' ten-story office sucks the sun right out of the sky. It's massive. Imposing. Pure matte-black from top-to-bottom. Even the windows.

I am so out of my league here.

Remi listens to me mumble some lame description, parking my car as close to the building's side entrance as I can get. Just in case I need to make a quick get-away. When I tell her I have to go, she assures me I'll do great and clicks off.

I'm glad she seems confident. Because I'm definitely not.

chapter
three

"WHO'S NEXT?"

I sit at the end of the conference table with my elbows on my chair, hands steepled in front of my face. I'm pissed off. And tired.

Always tired.

Always pissed off.

Theo likes to tell me it's because I'm an old man.

Fuck Theo.

There's no denying it though; I feel my age today. I may only be forty, but our doctor packmate, Archer, likes to remind me that CEOs age faster. Which might be why, despite my usual focus, I simply don't want to deal with this shit today.

Declan has a pretentious saying painted on the wall of our home gym, claiming it motivates him. *No days off.* It might as well be our pack motto at this point. Especially mine.

But an owner's work is never done. Nor is a pack alpha's. There's always some problem that needs handling. Money to burn. Fires to put out.

That's why we need a new social media person in the first place. Last season was a disaster, by my standards. It will not happen again.

The second-to-last candidate in our pile just hustled out of the room, leaving a faint trace of his bitter gasoline scent behind. Archer leans over the glass conference table, plucking up the single remaining résumé. One-by-one, all of the others have gone from the "potential" stack to the "fuck no" pile.

I reach for my phone, growling as I dial our secretary and ask her to turn up our air conditioning, along with the scent-neutralizer circulating through it. I can't even smell the guy anymore but fuck it. I'm balanced on a razor-thin edge today, my instincts prowling under my skin, urging me to fight. Fuck. Dominate.

Useless rut-blockers don't work for shit half the time.

Luckily, in our facility, it isn't a problem. No omegas to tempt my baser instincts means the only consequences will be the effects on my sanity.

"Megera Reed," Archer reads, his free hand curling around the back of his neck as he squints through his glasses. His face furrows. "She's a young beta with a background in omega demographics."

On Archer's other side, Declan makes a derisive sound. "Sounds like an airhead."

Archer glares at him. I recognize his expression from years of being on the receiving end of his lectures. He opens his mouth to knock Declan down a few pegs—which, really, should be my job

—but a timid rap sounds at the double doors on the other side of the room.

"*Come in.*"

Archer pinches the bridge of his nose under his square frames, muttering, "Jesus, Ronan."

He's right. I didn't mean to bark. It should never happen, especially not at work. I know how dominant I am; my bark clobbers most people, regardless of their designation.

Only omegas *have* to obey, though, so there isn't really any *harm* in barking at a beta. It's just rude. And frightening.

I have no excuse, apart from feeling like my insides are trying to crawl out of my skin.

Fucking hell. What is wrong *with me today?*

I decide to leave after the last interview and go for a long run. Maybe all the way to the alpha bar downtown. A rash of willing betas hang out there, waiting for horny alphas. Sometimes, there are even a few omegas.

I usually don't enjoy that, though. As much as I want to fuck them, I also worry about them being out on their own and feel like shit for not being able to take proper care of them after we fuck in a bathroom stall. Plus, their scents are impossible. They cling for days—never quite right, but close enough to torment me and resurrect my guilt every time I change my clothes.

The A/C kicks up, pumping clean, cool air into the room. I notice Archer's shoulders unwind a fraction.

Fuck. Arch, too? If his alpha is riding him as hard as mine is, that means something.

My pack is fracturing.

I don't even let myself think the words, but I feel them anyway. I'm sure we all do.

Even if Archer didn't drone on about designation biology on a regular basis, we're all aware we have problems. One major one, in particular.

No omega.

Alphas in a pack are like spokes on a wheel. Without a center to bind them, they wind up flying off the tire, or tangling... or impaling someone. Eventually, without that middle, the wheel collapses.

Not to mention—no omega, no central bond.

No central bond? No connection between the four of us.

If we had that bond, I would know why Archer's shoulders are up around his ears. I would know why Declan would rather roll his eyes than meet mine. And I would know why Theo is fucking late. Again.

As it is, I smother a frustrated growl and force my attention over to the small woman with blonde layers slipping into the room.

Huh.

There's something different about this beta.

At least, her application *says* she's a beta. She could be an alien for all I know—her scent is so cloaked in a thick fog of chemical de-scenter, I have to work hard to keep from showing disgust on my face. The aerosol edge of it is *acrid.*

Instead, I focus on her appearance, which is infinitely more pleasant. Beautiful, really. If I was still in my prime, I would be all over her. Even if she smells like she just came out of swimming pool full of fruity air-freshener.

Dear God.

This is what I'm expected to work with? People who don't even know how to put on de-scenter without fumigating an entire building?

I snatch the résumé off the top of her application, trying to recall why I selected her for an interview in the first place.

Ah.

I remember now. She has one of the cleanest, most aesthetically-pleasing CV's in the pile. On top of that, she has a Master's from an Ivy League university and worked for one of the biggest marketing firms in the state for the last eighteen months.

When I called the references listed on the application, they were all glowing. Her coworkers liked her a lot and lamented her leaving their company on short notice.

In fact, that was the only negative thing any of them came up with—she quit suddenly. Otherwise, they said her idea to create a marketing division devoted entirely to omegas was a resounding success.

I know little about them as a demographic, but, as a businessman, I have to admit: the idea sounds intriguing. Omegas are, largely, an untapped market.

Until recently, laws restricted their movements within society. They weren't permitted in certain alpha-centric environments unless they were bonded or accompanied by a guardian of some sort.

It took a lot of lobbying from various omega rights organizations to change things. I donated millions to back as many groups as I could. Declan shocked me by matching my contributions, muttering something about most old-school politicians being "archaic knot-heads."

Which... fair.

Changing the laws took some time, but, now, most companies no longer have the option of turning single, unbonded omegas away on the basis of their designation or pack status.

Unless their presence would pose a significant risk to themselves or others—which, unfortunately, is the case for our team.

Still, since omegas have been permitted to enter the workforce, I imagine their buying power has exploded. The thought of catering to them specifically is obvious, actually. I wonder why so few companies have tried it.

When I selected Miss Reed as a candidate, I thought her background might give us a slight edge online. Omegas dominate social media. Behind the safety of their screens, they're free to flaunt their beauty and magnetism.

Alphas want them. Betas want to be them. If we could get

omegas interested in our team over others, it may get us some traction with the younger generation.

Her generation, I note, taking in her fine-boned, youthful features. A quick glance at the application makes me feel like the fucking Crypt Keeper.

She was born in 2000? And she's already twenty-four? *By that math, shouldn't I be* dead?

Archer interrupts my morbid musings, clearing his throat. Behind his square glasses, dark eyes dart between my face and the girl hesitating near the doors. I follow his gaze until mine lands on hers, the big, blue doe eyes blinking. Long, blonde lashes fan her lightly tanned cheeks.

The expression does something to me. My alpha instincts roil, urging me to get up and go over to her.

But why?

Her shoulders suddenly jerk back, straightening her posture. She balls her fists at her sides and marches forward, jerking to a halt at the end of our table before practically throwing her purse onto it.

A cheap pleather sack, I notice. A strange tug of longing yanks at my gut.

We can do better than that.

The odd thought agitates me. What the fuck is my problem today?

Oblivious, she whips a binder out of her bag and slams it open. The graceless movement would amuse me, if I wasn't so confused.

Why is my body straining to get closer to her? And why is she rushing?

Declan leans back in his swiveling chair and snorts, all arrogant ease. "Where's the fire, baby?"

"Fire?" Megera's head snaps up, her expression strangely strangled. Her eyes fly to me and then quickly drop back to her work.

She can smell me? In here?

I have a smoky scent, but it's odd for a beta to catch it. Especially in a room full of scent-neutralizers. Plus, it's rude to point out strangers' individual scents in an office setting.

The beta makes a high-pitched, throat-clearing sound. Her cheeks warm in a fetching blush as she realizes her faux pas and processes that Declan was taunting her. She gives him an unimpressed look.

"Oh. You were kidding."

She's adorable.

"He was being an ass," I correct, cutting Declan a severe look. "Please excuse him, Miss...?"

I know her name. I want to see if she'll correct my assumption that she isn't married. I don't see a ring, but that's no guarantee. Beta-beta couples and same-designation packs usually wear wedding rings if they're romantically exclusive, since they don't have visible bond marks the way alphas and omegas do. But some packs prefer not to.

Maybe she has bites hidden under those prim clothes. Maybe she has her own alpha and her own omega. Maybe they've both bitten her, leaving secret silver half-moons on that smooth, gorgeous skin.

I can't decide if that thought makes me unbearably horny or irrationally jealous.

"Miss Reed," she demurs, still not raising her eyes. "It's nice to meet you, Mr. Ash."

I stifle another smile. "You know my name."

Her nod tries just a little too hard to be brisk. "Yes, sir. I researched the team and your organization to prepare my marketing strategy for you."

Sir.

I would prefer *alpha*. I can work with "sir," though.

Like he can sense my fucked-up thoughts, Archer's head snaps to the side, his features full of surprise. It takes me a second to realize he's impressed with her.

None of the other candidates came in with a prepared

marketing strategy. They all wanted to talk about their degrees, their past work experience and whether this job includes season tickets.

"*You* prepared a marketing strategy?" Declan's voice drips disdain while he flicks his cool eyes up and down her body. "That's cute. Have you ever even watched a game, honey?"

Miss Reed's spine snaps straight again. Her expression wobbles, and I think I might have to beat the shit out of my pack-mate for making her look so stricken.

But, in a blink, she locks her features down, pinning her gaze on our resident prima donna.

"No," she says simply. "I don't watch football. If that's a prerequisite, I'm afraid I'm not right for this job. *But,* if you would rather have someone who understands people and aesthetics and knows how to reinvigorate your fan base instead of some knot-for-brains, who's probably just interested in kissing your butt and getting box seats, then maybe you should give me a chance."

Usually, as our pack leader, it makes me twitchy to watch other people put the guys in their place. I don't even like to watch Coach Henshaw reprimand Theo or Declan on the field.

But this feels different.

For one, she really *is* adorable.

As if she realizes she might not look intimidating enough, she tosses a cocky hip and narrows those big blue eyes at the man who just insulted her, waiting for his retort. Declan stares back at her for a beat, wrestling with his options.

Damn. She really *did* nail him.

Very deliberately, Megera Reed slides her attention from Declan and shoots it toward the door before blinking back to him. Wordlessly suggesting that she may just turn around and walk out the door if he says the wrong thing.

For the first time in a long time, I don't have to bark or snap to get Declan's head out of his ass. He shifts, sitting forward and begrudgingly reaching for the stack of papers she pushed toward us.

Rage shifts in his eyes, his expression seething. But he picks up a packet and starts to read.

And, this time, I *do* smile.

"Have a seat, Miss Reed."

chapter
four

Megera

I HAVE to get out of here.

Now.

How I even managed to last three minutes is beyond me. The second their scents assaulted me, my vision tunneled. My heart's been stuttering in response to so many alphas staring at me...

Smelling so *utterly edible.*

Walking into the interview was like getting hit in the face with all of my wildest dreams. Three exceptionally striking men, sprawled around a conference table. The elegant, dangerous billionaire; a gorgeous Black man in sexy Clark Kent glasses; and one international sex symbol wearing gray freaking sweatpants.

Am I gaping like a fish?

Drooling?

Oh. Em. Gee.

Deliciously Dangerous has on a black suit with an open-collar onyx shirt underneath. It makes his glowing, gray eyes even more arresting. A matching head of short, black hair and stubble covering his wide jaw. The curls of a solid, thick tattoo creep over his sternum. I notice a matching tail of ink wrapped around the top of his left hand.

The man with glasses and a flawless brown complexion has a tattoo, too. I just barely make out a thin geometric pattern peeking out from the rolled sleeve of his white button-down. It ends halfway down his forearm, tapering into large hands with long fingers. Between his loafers, slacks, glasses, and impressive physique, he gives off hot professor vibes.

And then, of course, there's THE Declan Howard.

All my research pointed to quarterbacks being more compact than other football players, but Declan is pretty massive. His shoulders ripple under his black Ospreys T-shirt, his forearms and the black feathers inked over his left bicep bulging when he adjusts himself to glare ice-blue daggers at me.

Well, then.

I just about manage not to drop my jaw to the floor. But the second my eyes adjust to their otherworldly hotness, three incredible scents slam into me.

The mouth-watering aroma of fresh-churned ice cream hits first—vanilla beans and smooth lusciousness. A blend of rich liquor and spice comes next. It's as mysterious as it is delectable—warm layers of bourbon and ginger that somehow elevate the vanilla cream.

Then there's *smoke*. The deep, almost-sweet aroma of a bonfire. Earthy woods, crackling flames. It makes the vanilla sweeter and the spice more pungent.

Thank *God* I am wearing two sets of panties.

The vanilla and spice are too close together for me to tell which scent belongs to which alpha. The bonfire, though... That has to be Ronan Ash. Only a dominant alpha could possibly fill the room with his scent in seconds.

The smell turns darker and sweeter—almost edging into an aromatic incense.

What does that mean?

Is he upset?

Can he see through me already?

Only my desperation—pure and simple—allows me to even attempt to stay in the room. I really *try*. Clamping my thighs together, breathing strictly through my mouth.

I want to whimper, but that won't do. The men sitting in front of me are pure powerhouses. And my mother prepared me for just such a thing. Or tried to, at least.

I have to blaze on.

But that's the thing about going to war with your own body. Eventually, it just shuts you down. By force.

It doesn't take long for me to reach my limit. My body riots, pushing whine after whine up into my gullet until I think I'll vomit from stuffing them all back down.

What's the matter with me? I never acted so crazy with the alphas at my last job. Never even *felt* like the purely emotional ball of hormones everyone seemed to insist I was.

But, here, that feels like *exactly* what I am.

Every little movement, every flicker of their features, affects me. When Ronan Ash catches my chemically altered scent and makes a face, I want to burst into tears. When Dr. Monroe's pretty dark eyes fill with confused concern, my voice almost cracks. And when Declan Howard calls me out for not being a football fan, it's all I can do to keep from snarling at him.

How dare he talk that way to me? He's—

Nothing. He's nothing to me.

Because we are *literal strangers*.

My instincts and my logic play tug-of-war with my brain stem.

Sit down, my heart screams. *Stay right here forever.*

But my mind yanks back the reins.

Leave. Leave now before you perfume and they find out what you are and chase you out of here.

Or hunt me down and catch me.

chapter
five

ARCHER

I KNOW THAT LOOK.

Ronan is hungry. And the cute beta nervously leafing through paperwork is about to be lunch.

For the love of—

Will a single day go by without someone in my pack acting like an asshole?

The woman is here for a job interview. She doesn't need to be ogled or demeaned, but so far that's all Declan and Ronan have done.

It's a toss-up for which seems to bother her more.

Her physiology suggests extreme stress. Her shoulders kink, her elbows flinch, her knees wobble slightly as she lowers herself toward a chair across from us.

But she keeps speaking, outlining the finer points of her pitch while she distributes impressive piles of glossy paper and gives a brief description of the new logo she's designed.

I do a double-take at that, my eyes roaming over her and the new orange-and-black Ospreys' icon in turn. The image depicts our mascot as a phoenix rising from its own ashes. A white silhouette on a black background, emerging from a fiery pit of our team's signature orange.

It's... infinitely better than ours. The artwork is clean. Modern, but with an edge, and some new angles that hold my interest. Great aesthetics; but it's the symbolism that really draws me in.

And she *designed* it? In addition to being a designation demographic expert with two advanced degrees?

She's impressive. Not just her proposed marketing plan, but her professional demeanor, too. Whatever's bothering her, she seems determined to ignore it.

I could use some of that control, myself. I've been tense all day, but her anxiety sends my agitation to a whole new level.

I need to help her. Fix it. Make her feel safe.

A perplexing sensation to have for a total stranger who smells like industrial air-freshener.

But—logical or not—I can't deny the way she draws my complete focus. Even while she does something as mundane as sitting down.

Declan opens his mouth again. I glare at him until he shuts it.

Why is he being such a dick anyway? It's not like he cares about any of the pack's business decisions. He's only here because he expects to work closely with whatever PR person we hire. Since he loves having his face printed all over everything all the time.

It's only been a handful of minutes when Miss Reed suddenly pauses. Then lurches to her feet.

"Uh-umm," she stutters. "I..."

Her wide, blue eyes meet mine first. Surrounded by the delicate features of her face, they look enormous. And full of fear.

Help me.

My brow knots while she flashes me a panicked, beseeching look. It has an instant effect. I push to my feet, too, prepared to hurdle across the room and catch her.

But she takes a step back, trembling harder.

"I think you'll find everything else you need in those packets." She says the words in a rush. "If you like what you see, please let me know and I'd be happy to come back to film some trial content."

Ronan rises, too. His face is like a thundercloud, all booming anger and stormy eyes. "We have an interview now," he replies, his voice nearly edging into a bark. "Please, Miss Reed, sit down."

The almost-command hits her right in her knees. They give out for a split second before she draws herself back up.

"I-I'm sorry," she stammers. "I really should go now. It was nice to meet you, Mr. Ash."

She looks back at me, her eyes piercing right into my center. "Dr. Monroe."

Does she... Am I... Is that my scent spiking? *Now?* Because she *said my name?* Not even my first name, either.

It makes no sense. My pheromones shouldn't spike for a beta woman I don't know. The only reason for them to randomly surge for a stranger would be a scent-sensitive omega. A scent-match. The odds of that are so low they're statistically insignificant.

Declan waits for the confusing woman to address him, wearing a cocky, cold little smirk that makes me want to thump his head. Instead of looking at him, though, Miss Reed ducks her head and runs for the doors.

Leaving me to wonder why every fiber of my being demands I chase her down.

chapter
six

THE BABBLING BETA has already gotten under our pack leader's skin.

Pathetic.

Ronan could at least *pretend* it doesn't make him horny to watch the mouthy little thing insult me and sling paperwork at us. Instead he stares right at her, all intensity and pure alpha dominance, making no secret of the way he adjusts his suit pants.

Over what? *This* girl?

Sure, she's hot. Really hot. Like, *fucking hot*. But I'm not impressed.

Being world-famous and ridiculously rich sort of makes it hard to get excited about shit. I feel like I've done everything. Seen everything. Heard everything. Had everything.

Except that stupid Championship ring.

And, you know, an omega. But that ended in a clusterfuck last time, so I'm prepared to write that desire off.

I want the ring more out of spite than anything else. For months, I've listened to an endless string of commentators lay odds on my talent, career, and future. I'll win to show them all how wrong they've been.

And I owe it to our pack. Especially Theo.

Sure, I know having a strong fan base and good ad funding will be pivotal to our program this year. And, yeah, I know I have ground to recover after the disaster that was last season.

But this girl just pisses me off.

She doesn't belong here. Something about her being in this building, at our facility in general, makes my skin itch.

And she has the audacity to walk out of the interview without so much as saying my name? Seriously, what the fuck is wrong with her?

I expect Ronan to chuck her résumé in the trash the second the door snicks closed. Instead, he pushes aside all the other applications and holds hers up.

"I like her."

A growl slips out from behind my teeth. "*What?*"

Archer nods with the same infuriating calm he always gives off. "I agree. We can talk about it more tonight. I need to get over to the gym; I have a ton of pre-season exams to sign off on before tomorrow."

They both pause to glance at me. Ronan's face issues a challenge—almost a taunt.

Fight me, kid, it says, *I dare you.*

Archer simply sighs, turning weary while he rubs his eyes under his glasses. "Declan, for the love of God, what is wrong? We haven't hired her. We're just going to discuss it."

I don't know what my problem is. This is how we always do everything. The four of us give our opinions, Ronan makes a final decision, and Archer puts it into motion.

It usually doesn't bother me—they've been a pack since they met in college. Their friendship built Ronan's company, got Archer through med school. When they found Theo and me, we were clueless college bums, and they were already successful businessmen in their early thirties.

They rebuilt Ronan's entire empire for us. Took his wealth and funneled it into buying the right team, getting us in with the right trainers. They built Theo and me just as much as they built our pack.

We only ever disagree on personal shit. Specifically, over one woman. One omega. And it turned out they were fucking right, and I was an idiot.

So why do I want to fight them now?

Anger rumbles in my voice. "I don't want her here."

It's fucking wrong. She doesn't belong here.

My alpha instincts are going batshit at the thought of this girl roaming around our building, our gym. Probably filming other players half-naked for fucking TikTok.

"Well I didn't want to watch the team I put fifty-million dollars into tank last year, but here we are," Ronan replies, his cool eyes flickering.

"Because it's my fault I got injured making plays for you?" I bite back, shoving out of my chair.

"No," he yells. "It's *your fault* we lost the title the year before and had to start from scratch last season. Your fault we lost half of our offensive line, which *led* to you being injured."

"I won't work with her," I growl, digging in. "She doesn't belong here."

"*Enough.*"

Ronan's alpha bark rings in my ears like a gunshot, stilling the air around me. Its dominance immediately shoves me into submission. My nose twitches against the urge to bare my neck.

Our alpha sweeps his packet from the beta off the table and starts for the door, issuing one last command on his way past me. "*Get to practice.*"

chapter
seven

Megera

I COME-TO IN THE BATHROOM. Curled into a ball on the floor of a corner stall... covered in a sticky layer of dried sweat, with both pairs of slick-absorbing panties drenched *through*.

Oh eww.

So unattractive.

I survey my surroundings, taking stock. I've sweated off all of my de-scenter, leaving a fine layer of my own natural musk drying on my skin. Between that and the wet underwear, I'm basically wearing a neon sign for any alpha within a mile radius.

KNOT ME. BITE ME.

Definitely not humiliating or dangerous at all.

Luckily my mini-breakdown hasn't alerted anyone to my presence. Yet. An omega having a heat-breakthrough in the hallway would be cause for plenty of fanfare, if anyone noticed.

I can't remember anything after I ran out of the conference room. The sensation reminded me of the haze that comes over me during my heat. It was probably all I could do to get to the ladies' room and curl into a ball.

The doctor warned me about this, dammit. She said my suppressants were going to stop working eventually—that they can only do so much for so long. Not that it matters if I've built up a resistance to the meds, since I can't afford them anymore anyway. Especially after that disastrous interview.

I'm okay. It's okay. I can still do this.

The reassurances I offer myself sound like bold-faced lies, considering I'm currently taking a sink-bath in a public restroom.

Even in complete denial, I can admit: I didn't think it would be this bad. I sort of assumed stories about omegas walking into rooms of alphas and spinning into a tizzy were just exaggerations... or really pitiful omegas.

Joke's on me. Another point for biology.

At least my hormones have settled. I no longer feel like I'm going to wind up streaking naked across the football fields. Now, I'm just exhausted. I want my bed and my pile of cozy blankets. Or, since I'm heading to her place, one of Remi's cozy blankets.

Shaking off the last of my jitters, I stuff the ruined underpants into the bottom of the trash can and wash my hands until they feel raw.

I can't risk any hint of my perfume on any of my exposed skin. Even walking out of the building sans panties will be a huge risk.

But the elevator is right next to the bathroom, and it will let me out right at the side exit to the parking lot. Since I haven't seen anyone else around, I figure all of the alphas on the team are in conditioning, out of the office, along with the coaches.

I should be safe for the thirty seconds it will take to get to my car.

chapter
eight

I'M LATE.

Again.

I really don't know how this always happens to me.

I was eating a sandwich, and then that led to needing a new shirt because of a mustard stain. But my shirts were wrinkled so I had to steam one, and while I was running hot water, I decided to shower...

Whatever. The rest of pack knows better than to expect me to be on time anyway. I'm only prompt for gamedays. And that's because Ronan usually barks me out of the house.

The elevator crawls up to the top floor of our team facility, where all the pencil pushers spend their days. Damn, the thing is extra slow.

Maybe I should get out and take the stairs. But my knee already hurts like a bitch today. No point risking it five days before our season opener. Declan would be so pissed. Arch, too.

Ronan would just kill me on the spot.

Still, my brain pinballs, restless as ever. My tapping foot practically shakes the whole cart.

I'm a big dude. One of the biggest tight ends in the League. It's sort of amazing the elevator can move me at all.

The doors finally roll open, and I start to rush out.

But the world stops.

Oh holy fuck.

Omega.

I stagger back like I've been shot. In a way, I have. Shot with pure fucking adrenaline.

My heart hammers, inflating my cock with each pounding pump. I feel my throat go dry while my mouth fills with saliva, my teeth aching as much as my dick.

Dear *God.*

What is a perfuming omega doing in our building? In our *elevator*? Doesn't she know how dangerous it is for her in a building brimming with unbonded alphas?

With *me*?

The guy currently seconds away from grabbing her plush little hips and sinking his teeth into the gorgeous, perfectly blank line of her throat?

If she notices me at all, she doesn't let on. In fact, she looks flustered as hell. Her hands quiver while she repeatedly brushes them over her skirt, smoothing it like she's worried someone will look at it for a moment too long...

The doors close behind her as she blows out big breath.

Inhales.

And fucking freezes.

Oh shit. Oh shit. Oh *shit*.

She raises her chin and looks up at me. I look back at her and watch her realize what she's done. Watch her gulp down my scent the same way I'm huffing hers.

The mouth-watering aroma of peach cobbler has already filled the entire lift. So delicious—the syrupy, juicy flavor of peaches mixed with brown sugar and butter. *Fucking oh my Goddddd*.

I reach behind my body and grip the steel bar along the edge of the cart, holding on for dear life.

Do not lunge at the omega.

Do not scare the omega.

Do not rut the omega into the doors.

As if she's reading my mind, the little omega falls back into the closed doors. A small whine spills from the back of her throat, the sound absolutely *wrecking* me. My instincts claw at the inside of my chest, demanding I comfort the sweet creature filling my body with pheromones.

Grab her, hold her, fuck her. Knot her deep. Stay forever. Purr for her until she's boneless omega mush. Then bite the fuck out her.

My dick turns to steel, swelling my knot and spiking my scent. Her blue eyes flicker, the pupil at their center expanding.

The sugar-and-butter undercurrent to her scent shifts, from perfectly warm to burned. It's still good, like dark caramel, but the change is enough to knock me back all over again.

She's terrified, I realize, sobering up. *Think about how scary this must be for her. Think about what you would want for your sisters.*

They're both omegas. And I worry about them every day.

Shame cools me off a bit. Just enough for me to control my voice and posture.

"Hey, peaches," I say, flattening my back into the wall. "It's okay. I'm not going to hurt you."

The small woman presses closer to the doors, her hands scrabble against them like she's looking for a handle. It would be cute if her scent wasn't burning by the second.

"I promise," I go on, showing her the way I'm clutching the bar. "I won't move them."

It's weird. One minute, she's clearly freaking the fuck out, her scent swelling and smoldering, her eyes filling, shivers wracking her whole body. But then she just... stops.

Her shoulders fly back, and she raises her head. She blinks and twines her hands together, squeezing them to try to hide her shakes.

It does nothing to change her terrified scent, but damn. The gorgeous girl leaking peachy perfume has some balls.

The thought makes my lips twitch into a smile. Arch says I always smile at inappropriate times. I can't help it, though. The determined look in her eye is as impressive as it is endearing.

"You're one of the players," she says, running her gaze down my body in an appreciative glide.

My chest puffs out. A tiny smirk fills her face. "And you smell like... lemongrass? I never would have guessed that."

A startled laugh blurts out of me. "Lemongrass? No way, peaches. I'll have you know my scent is *citrus*. *Masculine* citrus. Nothing frou-frou like *lemongrass*."

She rolls her big blue eyes and reaches behind her to slap the button for the lobby. She's still shaking. I decide to ride down with her.

For, you know, protection.

"Whatever you say, big guy," she chuckles, instantly refolding her hands, her knuckles white. Her gaze drops to her heels. "I guess I'm no expert, anyway. Since I'm a beta and all."

My eyes round while my brain trips over itself.

A *beta*?

Who the hell does this sweet little snack think she's fooling? I know a perfect omega when I smell one.

But if it makes her feel safer to pretend, that's fine. It's what I'd want my sisters to do if they found themselves in her situation. Omegas have to do whatever they need to do to keep themselves safe. And this girl has no reason to trust me.

Hell, I have no reason to trust *myself*. She smells waaaaaay too good.

I force myself to look in her eyes, reminding myself that she's a person. And she's scared. When our gazes bump, I see the plea shining in hers. *Please, please, please.* Because we both know she isn't supposed to be here.

I would never rat this gorgeous girl out. Even though we have policies against this kind of shit for a reason. I know it's dangerous; if either one of us had some sort of hormone spike, things could get out of hand really fucking fast.

But I know—in my bones—that I won't hurt her. So why not let her have her story? "Sure, peaches. Of course you are."

It's none of my business, anyway. I tell myself that until I almost believe it. Still, as we near the lobby, my muscles bunch and twitch. I hate the idea of her walking out alone, trying to get wherever she's going without an escort.

"Did you drive here or...?"

She narrows her eyes. "Why do you ask?"

Suspicious. As she should be. She looks way too hot in that tight skirt; and her white blouse lets me know exactly what kind of bra she wears... The lacy kind with those half-cups. I gulp down another mouthful of drool.

"Just wanted to offer to walk you to the parking lot. Never know what kind of crazies are lurking around here. Wouldn't want such a sweet *beta* like you to get into trouble."

The omega-in-disguise bites her plump lower lip, speaking around it. "Okay... but hands in your pockets, and you're only walking me to the door."

I nod, making a show of sliding my hands into my joggers, fisting the seams of the pockets. I even flash a smile. "You got it, gorgeous."

Light pink fills her face, her scent edging away from burned sugar. An intense burst of fresh peach swirls into the cart while she perfumes.

Holy *shit* it is good.

It. Is. *Good*.

Oh God.

I have to fight the urge to drop to my knees and bury my head between her thighs *right now*.

Letting all that sweet nectar go to waste is a tragedy. I want to snarl. My balls throb while I choke down the menacing growl and cough to cover it.

"Sorry," she whispers, hanging her head.

My teeth clack together. I hate that I can't touch her. Hate that she has to apologize for something so natural. Hate that we live in such a fucked-up world where people like her and my sisters are constantly in danger.

Hate that, right now, I *am* that danger.

I almost shout THANK GOD when the doors inch open. The definitely-not-a-beta scurries out, needing two steps for every one that I take behind her.

That's biology, too. Her body tells her to run. Let me chase.

And, fuck me, I honestly don't know if I would be able to stop myself from hunting her down if she took off.

Stepping out of the building, leaving her perfume behind us, helps. The oppressive Florida humidity presses in. I hope it stifles my scent. God knows how strong it must be right now.

Fuck the meeting.

I need to go home and take another shower. A long one. With a bottle of lube.

The peachy omega has her keys in her hand one blink later. The lights on a small, white Fiat flash, four spots from the door. I'm relieved she doesn't have far to walk.

I think she'll rush off, but instead she bites that luscious lip again. Her eyes bore into mine, imploring. "So... thanks for walking me. Sorry again about my... new body spray."

Hmm. She wants to pretend her scent is just one of those store-bought perfumes betas use to lure in alphas.

But how can I act like I haven't scented her arousal when it feels like thirty seconds in the elevator with her re-wired my entire brain? How can I walk away when I desperately want to ask her to come to our pack house and let us all take turns *eating her*?

Honestly, I'm so close to the edge, I can't even let myself *breathe* anymore.

She walks away, one last whiff of perfume—a stronger, cleaner one, without all the scent-neutralizers inside to block it—swirling into my face. My nerves snap, my instincts lunging against their binds.

It can't be.

I have to be *wrong*.

But... what if there is a reason she smells like that? A reason her scent feels ten times more concentrated than anyone else's. A reason why watching her back her car out and drive away feels like yanking the sun out of the sky and shattering it on the pavement.

Oh my fuck.

Did I just find our omega?

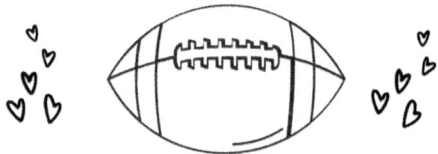

chapter
nine

I'M DOOMED. But at least Remi has a pile of chocolate-chip cookies waiting for me.

The fresh-baked deliciousness blends perfectly with her own omega scent—a smooth, almost-floral caramel. The two sugary aromas feel just right in her small apartment, with its cheerful blush walls and mason jars full of fake flowers.

She watches me shove a cookie in my mouth and makes no comment when crumbs stick to the tear tracks lining my face.

"This is *disgusting*," I sob, wiping at my snotty nose while I cram more cookies into my gullet. "I hate myself."

Rems pats my knee. Her quiet, tiny omega purr starts up. It's a sound I've only ever heard from her; one I'm not even sure I'm capable of making. Since, you know, I'm a biological failure and all.

"I'm so sorry," she whispers for the tenth time, tucking herself close to my side, letting the soft vibrations of her body sink into mine. "Want my favorite blanket?"

From one omega to another, that's better than a friendship bracelet. I sniffle-snort. "That's okay. I'm sorry I came crashing in here like this. I..."

Well, I actually still don't know *what* happened.

"Go through it again," Remi urges, flipping her dark curls off her shoulders and brushing a few cookie crumbs from her tank top. "You walked into the room and you scented them right away?"

I nod, sniffing my blouse again. It's no use, though—there is no trace of any of them on my clothes. Which means the office had scent-neutralizers in the air. Which *should* have made it impossible for me to smell any of those alphas the way I did.

A fact that didn't occur to me until I was already ten miles away from the facility and had breathed enough fresh air from my open car window to restart the logical part of my brain.

"Yeah," I murmur, picking at the hem of my skirt. "I could smell each one *really* clearly, especially Ro—Mr. Ash."

I keep calling him Ronan in my head. As if I have any right to.

"Hmm." Remi pats my arm softly, handing over another cookie. "Maybe their scent-blockers weren't working. Could you smell any of the other alphas working in the building?"

"There weren't any others that I saw," I say around the bite of melty chocolate goodness.

Dang. Remi really can bake. I need to have her teach me. At the rate I'm going, the ability to eat will be the only thing I have left by the time my heat rolls around.

She frowns, her doll-like features pinching. "Yeah, but aren't, like, all the guys who work there alphas? You should have at least gotten a few traces of other employees, even if they were all in the other building at the time. Unless the neutralizer they use is the premium, super-expensive kind. But, then..."

Then I shouldn't have been able to scent any of them at all.

A chill rolls down my back, arching it. "Is there any way this could be related to my heat issues?"

She rolls her head back and forth in a doubtful gesture. "You're not in heat yet. You still have a few suppressants left, and you took your dose this morning. But even if you didn't, I've never heard of an omega in heat being resistant to scent-neutralization. Other than scent-sensitive packs."

Scent-sensitive?

She's told me about those packs before—the ones drawn together by some crazy combination of fate and biology. It's Remi's dream to be in one of those weird "fated mate" situations. But it all just sounds insane to me.

I mean, *c'mon.* An entire group of people—alphas and an omega—that all magically imprint on each other's scents?

And then... *boom?*

Happily ever after?

Remi stares. And stares. Until her insight finally sinks in.

"No." I don't realize I'm saying the word out loud until I can't stop. "No, no, no. No. No. No, no."

She laughs. "Were they old or ugly or something? I thought you said one of them was *Declan Howard*!"

"Yes and he is an *ass*!" I cry, then cover my mouth and squeak, shaking my head. "No, this cannot be happening. It isn't happening."

Remi takes a slow bite of a cookie, chewing deliberately, every crunch calling me a liar. "Why not?"

"Because..."

I scramble for an explanation. True, the men in the conference room smelled better than any others I've ever encountered. Like perfection, actually.

But what about the random player in the elevator? He wasn't

part of their pack. And he smelled soooo good. Even better than the others. At least, once we got out of the building.

Stupid scent-neutralizers.

The other men may have gotten under my skin and caused the demise of my panties, but Elevator Hottie was the original reason for my meltdown. I drove away from him because I knew I had to for my own safety—

But it was *agony*.

And once I got to the first stoplight and realized we hadn't even exchanged names; that I would never have any way of seeing him again, assuming I didn't get the job I'd just walked out of the interview for.

I lost it. The whine that came out of me would have stopped traffic, if anyone had heard it.

Then I started crying like an idiot. Over some *stranger* I only spent two minutes with. Granted, he was unfairly gorgeous and sweeter than he had any reason to be, but still.

I *should've* been afraid of him. He was the most enormous person I've ever seen—easily twice the size of an average man. Between his stature, those light green eyes, his blond man-bun and beard, he looked like Thor's hotter little brother.

An unbonded alpha of that size, scenting my perfume and looking at me the way he did when I first walked onto the lift, ought to have terrified me. For a moment, I *was* afraid. You know, like a *sane* person would be.

But, then, I don't know. He just felt safe.

Kind, too. The way he tried to joke with me and made a sincere effort to show me where he intended to keep his hands.

He was gentle. Not at all what I expected from such a monstrously large man. One who plays a violent sport, no less.

"I guess if it really had been a mate situation, the guy on the elevator wouldn't have smelled as good as the Ash pack," Remi muses, reading my mind. "So maybe your heat is sooner than we think? Or the suppressants aren't working at all anymore?"

Her light hazel eyes glow with disapproval and worry. "You

should talk to your doctors, Meg. I'm super worried about you. What if your heat starts early?"

I whine before I can help myself. The image of going through that ordeal alone and unmedicated is nauseating.

Remi scoots closer, banding her arm around my waist. "Sorry," she mumbles, blushing while she ducks her head and reaches for another cookie.

"It's okay. You're right, anyway."

We crunch cookies in silence for a long moment before Remi's brows tweak. "Didn't you say that the Ash pack has four alphas? Where was the other one?"

I shrug, wishing I'd changed my clothes. My big-girl bra and blouse feel scratchy and too tight. "I don't know. Not there, I guess. Maybe at practice? He's the—something."

A lightbulb flicks on behind Remi's features. She grabs her phone and types furiously, her expression crumpling in concentration until she smiles and flips the screen around.

I choke on my breath, wheezing over the involuntary whimper climbing up my throat.

Her screen displays my lemongrass-scented elevator buddy. All two-hundred-eighty pounds of him. And his sexy man-bun.

"Is this the guy you met?" she guesses, grinning.

"*Yes*," I shriek, amazed. "How did you find him?"

Remi grins. "It was easy. I just googled Ash Pack Packmates and looked under images. This is their fourth alpha. Theo Matthews."

chapter
ten

ARCHER

"WHERE THE FUCK have you guys been?"

Theo rarely sounds angry. Of all of us, he's easily the most relaxed. Which is a good thing. The man is the size of two grizzly bears and could probably beat Ronan in a fight if he really wanted to.

Which might happen right now. Because Theo is standing in the middle of our kitchen with a towel wrapped around his hips and his enormous arms spread three feet in either direction, irate.

The whole scene feels off. He was clearly in the shower when he heard us pull up. There are still water droplets clinging to his blond beard, and his long hair is dripping onto the marble floor... so he must have leaped out and run downstairs for some reason.

And, he's *scowling*.

I can't remember ever seeing that before.

I set my leather messenger bag on the kitchen island, careful not to scuff it on the raw-wood edge. Black stone floors gleam under my feet while the halogens above illuminate wood counters and steel cabinets.

Our kitchen has the same masculine motif as the rest of our pack house. It's all a bit much for me, but this is what comes with Ash Family money.

Oblivious to our packmate's mood—or maybe just apathetic, as per usual—Declan shuffles in behind me and goes straight for the fridge. Can't blame him there. I'm also starving and I haven't spent six hours in conditioning.

Ronan enters last, sliding his suit jacket off and dropping it over one of the metal barstools tucked under the island. He looks distracted, his cold eyes far away, until he lifts his head and sees Theo dripping all over the place.

The temperature around him plummets. "Theo, you're making a mess. And where were you today? We've discussed timeliness. You missed the interviews and your conditioning."

Theo's frown drops into an open-mouth gape. "Are you *shitting me* right now?"

I collapse onto a stool, resting my forehead against the heels of my hands. It's been a hellish day, finishing pre-season exams for fifty players, arguing with Declan every time we're in the same room....

And thinking about the beta.

Our potential new employee.

Very inconvenient, considering I've been half-hard for eight hours from the mere memory of her.

"Guys," I grunt. "Can we not do this tonight?"

Ronan makes a low noise of agreement, slumping next to me, his joints clicking. Stubborn old man. He needs to stretch more.

Theo lunges forward, his huge ham-hands wrapping around the corner of the island until his knuckles blanch. "Are you all messing with me? Is this a joke?"

Declan's face sours as he stabs a fork into one of the dozens of personal-chef-prepared training-macro-approved meals we keep on hand for him and Theo. This one is a salad. He has to be seriously hungry to choose that over one of the filet minion plates. Or maybe just so exhausted he can't even face the microwave.

Rolling my eyes, I force myself up and walk over to the double-door refrigerator, rummaging until I find two steak dinners and throwing them into the microwave. I grab a clean fork and take the salad out of Declan's hands. "Have the steak. I'll eat this."

Next, I slide a small plastic platter of sushi at Ronan. "You need the omega-3s, old man."

Ronan glowers, but starts opening the package.

"GUYS!" Theo shouts. "Can you all listen to me, please?"

Our pack alpha's thick eyebrows bunch while he speaks, not looking up from his plate. "*Stop yelling*," he barks, pouring soy sauce out of a packet.

Dec rips into his steak like a wild dog, barely pausing long enough to hand Theo his. Our always-hungry, normally-happy-go-lucky packmate stares at the food like we've offered him a dead rat. His dismayed expression turns from Declan to Ronan to me, an edge of hysteria creeping into his wide features.

"Arch," he exclaims, green eyes wincing. "Come on, put me out of my misery. Tell me you're all fucking with me."

I swallow a wad of salad. "Theo, we don't know what you're talking about."

He drops the takeout container to the island with a thud before throwing his hands into the air. "*The omega!*"

All the air in our kitchen freezes.

Declan recovers first, snarling, "*What* omega?"

Theo reaches his limit. He doubles over to lean on the island while he groans. I see why when he shifts, exposing the rigid erection tenting the front of his towel.

"Not *again*," he practically whines, dropping his forehead to the countertop. "Fuck me."

"*What omega?*" Declan repeats, truly growling now.

"Where?" Ronan demands, his cold eyes narrowing into slivers of ice.

I reach over and grip Theo's forearm. "We're listening now. You met an omega?"

"She was in—" Theo chokes and groans, his hips stuttering slightly. The towel clings to him. Barely. Things will get very awkward very quickly if he doesn't settle down. Theo isn't known for his impulse control.

He guzzles down deep breaths through gritted teeth. His eyes squeeze shut while he fists his fingers. "She wouldn't want me to tell you where I met her, but I did, okay?" he finally shoves out.

We all parse that for a moment. Ronan scowls ominously, opening his mouth to bark. I knock his shoulder to stop him. If Theo really found a viable match for us, we shouldn't start the whole thing off with force.

"When did this happen?" I interject.

"This afternoon," Theo manages. "She—we—I ran into her, and my body *short-circuited*, I swear to God. I couldn't even go to practice. I had to come home and..." He waves at his groin.

The air is so thick, I swear I could slice it with my scalpel. Declan's stone-still, as if he might crumble. Ronan and I look at each other, both of us wary. I get the feeling we've been thinking the same thing all day, and neither of us wanted the other to know.

"What did she look like?" he asks, rasping.

Theo's teeth grind. His hands flinch. "Little thing. Blonde. Peaches."

Peaches.

He isn't making sense.

Except he is.

Because under the thick layer of chemical cover, the little beta who made my head spin smelled...

Peachy.

chapter
eleven

REMI INSISTS I sleep on her futon.

Apparently, the whole almost-going-into-heat-in-public, possible-life-altering-realization, head-blown-off vibe I have going does not inspire confidence in my driving abilities.

She has a point about me being preoccupied. I can barely stop staring into space long enough to put on my borrowed pajamas or brush my teeth.

Remi goes to sleep early because her job at the local coffee shop starts at five a.m. I end up lying on her futon, missing my bed and worrying about silly things to distract myself from the enormous pink elephant standing in the middle of my brain.

Alphas.

Ash pack.

Scent-sensitive.

Mates?

The one reaction I keep coming back to is... no.

No.

No to *all of it.*

None of this is what I want. Romance has never been on my radar. I spend half of my life hiding, the other half working myself to the bone.

Until three years ago, omegas couldn't even get financing for their own houses without an alpha guardian to sign off on it. I didn't have one of those. So I grew up thinking I would have to save every single penny I needed just to be able to buy a stable place to live. It didn't exactly leave a lot of time for fake-wedding-planning.

Besides, feeling sorry for myself seemed like a dangerously endless wormhole. If I let myself think too hard about how much time I spent alone, I wasn't sure how I would continue to function. Failure is not an option when you're all you have.

On the low coffee table beside me, my phone buzzes. And keeps buzzing. Someone is calling me. I pick it up and hold the screen over my face, watching the words *Private Caller* scroll by.

Is it... could I possibly be getting a call about the job?

A choked squeal catches in my windpipe. Screwing my eyes shut, I swipe my thumb over the screen. "Hello?"

I don't recognize my own voice. It's almost a whisper, for one thing; because I don't want to wake Remi up. But it also sounds way too shrill, somehow.

"Megera?"

I recognize the smoky, rich timbre of Ronan Ash immediately. My insides flip and squirm, my mouth falling open in shock.

Holy—

When I don't reply, he clears his throat. "Megera, this is Ronan Ash. We met earlier today."

"Mr. Ash," I manage. "Hi. I mean, yes, we did. Hello."

I slap my palm into my face.

Oh boy.

A rumbling chuckle fills my ear, tightening my nipples. "You said that already," he points out.

"Sorry, sir," I stammer. "I mean, Mr. Ash. Sir."

Whyyyyy am I repeating things? Gah!

I suck in a burst of oxygen and channel all of my control, summoning some poise. "I apologize, sir. I was about to fall asleep when my phone rang."

"Ronan is fine," he corrects, noticeably quieter. "And I'll call you Megera, okay?"

I bite my lip and speak around it. "It's Meg, actually."

Another smile in his voice. "Meg."

I hear commotion behind him. Is he out somewhere? Or still at work?

Ronan makes a reluctant sound. "My pack is here with me. We'd like to talk to you if that's all right. We can certainly call back in the morning if you'd prefer to get to sleep."

"No," I murmur, glancing anxiously at Remi's door. "Now is fine. Just hold on one moment. I'm staying on a friend's couch, and I don't want to wake her."

I press the phone to my chest as I creep out of the little apartment, into the hallway. It is nice that Remi lives in an omega-only condo complex. They have special security features that mean I can sit in the hallway outside her unit without having to worry someone might walk into the building unannounced.

When I bring the phone back up to my ear, I hear the muttered tones of an argument.

"Hello?"

Their squabble cuts off abruptly. Ronan's outraged voice replies, "Did you just say you were sleeping on a *couch*?"

I blink at the blank wall across from me. "A futon, actually. I don't live in town, so I made arrangements to stay with a friend after the interview."

I decide it's probably best not to mention my inability to drive after meeting all of them. Awkward.

"Is it safe?" Ronan practically barks. "Is she someone you trust? Where are you?"

More angry murmurs behind him. A second later he speaks again, sounding minutely calmer. "What I meant was: if you would rather stay in a hotel, we'd be happy to put you up. It's the least we could do for dragging you all the way to town without realizing we were inconveniencing you."

"I'm okay," I assure him. "She lives in a condo that's specifically for—"

Oh crap. "Never mind," I fumble. "Anyway. How can I help you, Mr. Ash?"

"Ronan," he reminds, still sounding put-out. When I don't reply, he pushes on. "We were hoping to extend an offer to you, Meg. We like your proposed changes and think you would be a good fit for the team. However, we did want to go over a few key details before we bring you onboard."

I clamp my lower lip between my teeth, unsure of what to say. What if he asks me point-blank about my designation? Somehow, lying in response to a direct question feels way worse than checking the wrong box on an application and pretending I didn't read the fine print.

As it stands, the whole thing could just be a misunderstanding. But as soon as he asks and I lie directly... then I'm a liar. And that will surely end any future I might have had with the four of them before I've even considered it.

My mind weighs that fact against my desperate need for a job. *Shit.* This is so not a simple decision, and I have exactly zero minutes to make it.

I wonder if Theo is there, listening. The thought is almost enough to make me whine, but I stuff it down.

"Of course," I finally croak.

Ronan pauses for a long beat. "For starters, we would need to discuss your living arrangements. You'd be moving to the area for this job?"

I nod, then realize he can't see me. Thank God. There's a hole in this T-shirt. "That's correct."

"We will provide an apartment."

He says it like he's checking an item off his grocery list: bread, milk, eggs, a new apartment. I'm so stunned I can't even reply before he continues.

"We can discuss the location in person. You have a proper vehicle, yes?"

I nearly snort at the word "proper." My car runs and all, but it's ten years old and smaller than most people's refrigerators. I don't want him to know that, though.

"I have reliable transportation."

He grumbles. "*Safe* and reliable?"

I mean, there are air bags...

"Yes?"

"We'll discuss that in person too," he replies, and I notice it is in no way an outright acceptance of my vehicle's suitability. He's crafty with his words, negotiating even when he doesn't say much at all. I keep my lips clamped shut, deciding it's better to give less away.

He fills the silence with confident command. "We'll speak more tomorrow. Would you be available to come back here in the morning? We want to see you in action with the team. Assuming that goes well, you'll have to sit down with HR and hammer out the finer details. They'll want to verify all of your information. Date of birth, social security number... designation."

My head is spinning so hard from all of this information, I can't tell if he really paused before he mentioned my designation or if my anxiety is playing tricks on me. He doesn't give me much time to consider it.

"Megera?"

"Y-yes. Sir. Ronan." I cringe, rushing on. "I'll be there in the morning."

"Nine-thirty," he intones. But before he hangs up, his voice drops into a low hum. "Don't make me wait."

———————— ♥ ————————

AT NINE-TWENTY-THREE, I park my car as far from the office building as I can get, hiding it between two big SUV's. You know, just in case Ronan's threatened vehicle inspection has some bearing on my eligibility.

Unfortunately, the rest of me isn't much better off than my beater. Without another change of professional clothes, I was forced to recycle yesterday's nude pumps and navy pencil skirt.

Remi rushed out before the crack of dawn, but I woke to find two pairs of fresh scent-and-slick-absorbing panties laid out on the coffee table for me. She also left her own bottle of de-scenter out, along with a few clean shirts.

My best friend is so much smaller than me; most of her shirts were at risk of popping open when I tried to close them over my chest. In the end, I had to settle for a light pink sleeveless blouse with a bow neckline. Definitely not my style at all, but at least it covers my ta-tas.

I doused myself in her neutralizing spray before and after dressing. Thankfully, whatever brand Remi uses is better than my usual stuff. My peach scent disappears without any chemical residue in its place.

Before stepping out of my car, I check to make sure the smell is still entirely absent. When I'm satisfied, I grab my purse and jaunt toward the office as confidently as I can manage.

There's a man standing on the sidewalk outside the entrance, his head bowed over his phone. My eyes glide over him while I approach, admiring the tight fit of his black joggers and the onyx-and-orange Ospreys T-shirt stretched across his broad shoulders.

He's tall and trim—an alpha, certainly, although maybe one in his mid-thirties. Not a professional athlete, but incredibly fit for a man of his age. A touch of silver graces his temples, peeking out from the edges of his solid black baseball cap. The smattering of salt-and-pepper in his dark hair and close-cropped facial hair is the only reason to suspect he isn't in his late twenties.

As I approach, my focus shifts to the tattoo covering his left side. Bold curls of black ink swirl down his arm before spreading across the back of his hand. I gulp back a thick swallow and move to hold my breath, hoping the alpha won't notice me slip past.

No such luck. He hears my heels scrape against the asphalt and snaps to attention.

Oh God.

It's Ronan Ash.

chapter
twelve

IT'S possible I've gone fucking crazy.

Honestly? I wouldn't be shocked.

After spending fifteen years conducting omega interviews all across the country, searching for the right person for our pack until I literally *couldn't take it anymore...* Maybe I've cracked.

Did Arch ever study psychology in med school? I can't remember. Hopefully he knows a guy or something. Because this woman in front of me? The one who smelled like peach napalm yesterday?

She is now completely scent-less.

Which is unacceptable, because I'm supposed to be figuring out what the hell is going on.

The mysterious blonde lifts her chin. Her blue eyes fly wide as she recognizes me. I bounce my gaze between them for a moment before sliding down her body.

Her missing scent may make it harder to identify her true designation, but it also leaves my mind free to notice every other detail. I can see the place where she clipped a loose thread from her skirt—the same one she had on yesterday. There's the tiny scuff mark at the toe of her heel. She clearly tried to use the bow on her blouse to cover the way the buttons underneath gap across her breasts, but I see that too.

When I meet her wide eyes again, a spark of amusement settles along the curve of my mouth. "Good morning, Miss Reed."

Her mouth closes and reopens. "Mr.—Sir. You're in sweatpants."

My lips twitch up for the smallest second. "That is correct. It seemed appropriate since we're heading to the gym."

Just when I thought she couldn't look more thrown, she manages even bigger eyes. She clearly doesn't want to go into the gym.

Is it because she'll be surrounded by alpha pheromones? Or is it some other issue? It looks like I'll have to figure her out the hard way; by throwing every alpha move I can at her and watching her reactions.

I give her a solid nod, projecting my certainty. "Yes. That's where the team is gathered. They typically trade off between spending half of the day in the conditioning center and the other half on the practice field. They're in the gym first today, due to the weather."

She ignores the clouds swirling overhead, taking my word without verifying for herself, and steps closer.

Intent to follow my lead.

I won't let myself examine exactly how much I like that.

The closer she gets, the more confused I feel. For half a

second, my nostrils flare, almost picking up the edges of a scent. But when I try to inhale it, it's gone.

Meg seems just as muddled. For a long, awkward moment, she stares straight at the V-neck of my T-shirt. Her pupils expand.

"Are you all right?" I snap. My voice is too gruff. Thanks to the bark I'm actively repressing. "You need to tell me if anything we ask you to do makes you uncomfortable."

I must truly be losing my mind. As she looks up at me, I think of a hundred ways I could test this little one's boundaries. And none of them have to do with work.

She suddenly straightens, raising her chin again. *Resilient. Tough.* "I'm perfectly fine. Lead the way."

I nod and walk on, pointing out the different buildings as we go. My offices, Archer's med center. I also give her a feel for the layout of the stadium, explaining that each player has their own locker at the stadium and in the gym behind the practice fields.

Meg nods along, but I notice the tight way she keeps her arms tucked across her chest. Silence stretches taut between us. The tension reminds me that there are things at stake here. My pack is counting on me; I need to figure out who this woman is. And she clearly wants this job.

It takes me way too long to realize she's panting, trying to keep up with my strides—while only breathing through her mouth? It seems that way. Her voice sounds breathy as she asks, "So how long have you had your pack?"

I slow my steps down for her automatically, fisting my hand in my pocket to avoid reaching to touch the small of her back. When I turn and find her gaze on my face, it gets even harder to control myself. She has beautiful eyes.

"Close to fifteen years," I grumble. "Dr. Monroe and I became friends in university."

She does the math and looks stunned. I chuckle. "I'll take your surprise as a compliment."

Her eyes narrow. "But Dec—Mr. Howard is only twenty-seven."

I nod. "Archer and I met Declan and Theo when *they* were in university. We were well into our thirties by then. But we saw their potential, and we knew we wanted to build something like this." I wave at the facilities around us. "It seemed a natural progression for us to form a unit as soon as they graduated."

It's an extremely abridged version of our story, but I'm not sure I want to give her all the gory details. The truth tends to make me look like an asshole. I guess because I was.

But when she looks at me with her big blue doe eyes, so full of genuine interest, I find I can't hold out on her. A sigh floats out of me.

"I met Archer at my first job. It was a smoothie bar," I grunt, remembered vitriol filling my voice. "In our university's gym."

"*You* worked in a *smoothie bar*?" she chokes.

I smile ruefully. "Not by choice. My father made me get a job to pay off a credit card I maxed out and they were the only place hiring."

God, I was so pissed about that. The man who sired me was the very worst kind of alpha and he did just about everything he could to make my mother's life hell. Money was the one—the *only*—thing I could count on him for.

After a while, I started to regard his limitless credit cards and endless cash flow as payment for putting up with him. The day he decided to take his one contribution to my life and hold it over my head was the day I decided he would regret ever fathering me in the first place.

It took a while to figure out how to do that. I wanted to shatter him. It took Archer convincing me, over a few years, that sometimes a blade could be more effective than a hammer.

Making my father's abuse public or ruining my own reputation would only cause temporary damage and indirectly punish my long-suffering mother, Archer argued. He thought I should play the long game. Wait for my inheritance to come in, wait for my father to feel safe passing off some of his holdings as he edged into retirement.

Arch has a mind for strategy and all the patience I lack. His plan was a thing of beauty. It enabled me to systematically take over more and more of my family business, keeping my mom's post-humous reputation pristine while destroying the only thing my father cared for—his legacy.

The day after he officially retired, I liquidated everything he spent decades building.

It was cold. Legendary. The press reported on it for *years*. And the last I heard, my dad was dying alone in the one property I left in his name—the house I vowed never to return to.

Meg pulls me from my ominous thoughts, her face sparkling with mischief. "Did you have to wear a hairnet?"

A laugh staggers out of me. "Absolutely *not*."

She flashes a beatific smile. "Dang. I was hoping there might be pictures."

I glower, knowing it will make her giggle. She shakes her head while she laughs. "Okay, okay. Never mind. So you and Dr. Monroe hit it off right away?"

I must make some sort of face because she cracks up again. "Uh oh," she says. "So you *weren't* friends?"

I scratch the back of my neck. "Yeah, not exactly."

Archer would describe me as a nightmare employee on every level. He constantly covered for me because he actually *needed* that job.

I do still feel bad about that, actually. Now that I'm an adult in the real world, I hate the way I dismissed Archer's repeated reminders that he needed to work in order to, you know, *eat*.

Meg practically bounces beside me. "So...what happened?!"

Her enthusiasm is irresistibly adorable. I heave out a breath and blurt, "I was a dickhead, okay? I obviously know that *now*. But, at the time, I showed up way late for one of my shifts and made him miss an exam. Put his scholarship in jeopardy. Later that afternoon, he walked back into work and punched me in the face."

Meg snorts, nearly tripping over her feet. "He did *what*?"

I wince, realizing that I sound more and more like a joke with every answered question. "He broke my nose."

Meg's laughter makes up for all of my regret. The sound is high and melodic, like wind chimes. She shifts her sparkling eyes over me again. "How did you guys ever become friends after that?"

I find myself almost-smiling. "Well, after we both got fired for having a fist fight, I went to the bathroom to clean all the blood off my face. My nose hurt like a bitch, and I was impressed that another alpha even had the balls to step up to me."

A rarity, even back then. My innate dominance bowls over even the cockiest alpha-holes. I would probably enjoy that power more if I didn't know exactly where I inherited it from.

"So I walked out of the gym, and Archer was standing around the corner, on the phone. I heard him telling his father what happened and asking his dad to send him some money to get by."

Fuck, I still remember that moment so clearly. How devastated Arch was to let his old man down and ask him for money that he knew his family didn't have. It was like a kick to the gut, the realization that another person might not have a place to live or food to eat because of *me*.

I was such an arrogant little prick. Obsessed with pissing off my father and ruining our family's reputation. It never occurred to me that I could hurt innocent people in the process.

Meg looks stricken. "You must have felt so bad."

I nod. "Rightfully so. I had to try to make it right, so I hounded him every time I saw him around campus. Insisted I needed help with my courses and told him I'd pay if he would tutor me. I didn't really need help, but it got the cash I owed him into his pocket, so I didn't give a fuck. That's how we eventually stopped hating each other."

When I told him about my inheritance and what I originally wanted to do—piss it all away in the most egregious fashion—he told me I was an idiot. He said, if he had the money I did, he would do so much more. When I asked him what he meant, he laid it all out on paper. Quite convincingly.

"And then you decided to start the pack?" Meg guesses.

I nod. "We thought we would keep things simple. It was just us, and we weren't ever romantically interested in each other, so we figured we'd try to find the right omega and that would be that, but..."

Humor flashes over Meg's face. "Did Theo and Declan sneak in or something?"

"As if Theo could sneak anywhere," I mutter. "He got *wheeled* in. On a gurney."

Meg's mouth drops open while I go on. "Archer was doing his sports medicine residency at the hospital attached to the university where he went to medical school. The university's football team was having a great season, mostly because of this quarterback/tight end duo everyone kept hearing about."

They *were* really good. Still are.

"It was the last home game of the season, and Theo was injured taking a hit for Declan. Luckily, Arch was there to piece him back to together. He told me that Declan and Theo reminded him of us. Dec was all ornery and spoiled. Theo was easy-going and chill. They'd been friends all their lives. When Archer asked them what their plans were for playing after college, they told him they didn't know. But they both dreaded learning to play without the dynamic they'd developed on the field. It gave Arch an idea."

A brilliant idea.

He called me up that very day and told me he knew what we should invest in. Something we could both work on—him with his sports medicine degree and me on the business side. Something that would horrify my hoity-toity father. Something just pedestrian enough to bring the Ash name down from the lofty heights of high society.

A fucking football team.

It was perfect. While Archer finished his residency, I worked on finding the right team and the right location. We took Declan and Theo under our wing and formed a larger pack, providing a home base of sorts while they went through the draft process and got signed to different teams. It was important for them to cultivate their own reputations for a couple years to legitimize their talent.

By the time we announced that our pack would take over the Ospreys, with the best quarterback and tight end in the League reuniting to captain our ranks, it was the biggest coup in Major League sports.

For one season, everything fell into place. Turned out, all of my years in business school and taking over my father's shit actually accomplished something: the team ran perfectly. Our facilities were unmatched, our staff superb.

And we won.

Game after game. With a near-undefeated first season under our belts, we went to the championship.

But Declan had to fuck all that to hell and back. He betrayed us all. And our pack was never the same.

"This team," Meg murmurs, bringing me back to the present.

"Yes," I confirm.

Before she can ask any more questions, we arrive at the gym. I see the outdated team logo I paid a shitload of money to have etched into the doors and shoot her an exasperated glance.

"I suppose I'll be paying to have that redone."

She smiles widely. "If you know what's good for you."

chapter
thirteen

Megera

RONAN STARES at me for a beat too long, his eyes shifting hotly. A second later, he's back to his cool mask. He opens the door and gives me one last pointed look. "If anyone bothers you in here, *you will tell me.*"

It's horribly rude for him to bark at me. Unacceptable, actually—but he doesn't know I'm not a beta. So I just nod and pretend like his command didn't sock me in the stomach. "Yes, sir."

I ignore the too-pleasant hum that surges through me when I acquiesce to his order. The truth is, as good as it feels, I hate it. It feels like the height of injustice—not only am I smaller and physically weaker than him, my body tells me to *obey* him. Begs me to. In a desperate way it really never has before.

The clang of dropped weights interrupts the odd moment. I inhale quickly, testing the air. It's mercifully clean. I can still scent Ronan, of course, just like yesterday, but it's muted in here.

When the smoke—musky, masculine, woodsy, and sweet— first hit me in the parking lot, it was all I could do not to snap into one of my fits. I had to breathe through my mouth the whole way to the gym, and I'm still praying I don't lose my grip.

But all these other shirtless alphas grunting and sweating? Nothing.

I ignore the way Ronan studies me, as if waiting for some sort of reaction. Instead, I turn toward the enormous exercise floor stretched out before us. Rows of machines, weight benches, and padded floor mats, all in the same matte-black and brilliant orange stretched over Ronan's muscled chest.

With a disappointed sigh, he leads me around the periphery of the room. I force down the skittish impulse to flick my eyes from one alpha to the next, but it's hard. My instincts tell me not to turn my back on any of them.

Ronan's on edge too. The further into the gym we wander, the tighter his shoulders look from behind. I notice him shooting glares at anyone who so much as glances at us.

By the third guy, a confused giggle bubbles out of me. "Is everything okay?"

Ronan's jaw works, and he speaks through gritted teeth. "Remains to be seen. Your plan mentioned viral videos of the team working out?"

"Yep," I agree, digging in my purse for my phone. "They're funny. I have a couple saved on TikTok. Do you want to see them?"

Ronan shrugs. "I'd rather you show me what *you* can do."

I have to stifle a grin. Somehow, I knew he'd ask me that. I already have an account set up for the team; and I saved several viral sound clips to record content with.

"All right," I agree, game. I wave my hand at the floor. "First, we need to pick the hottest guy here."

Ronan's features fill with disapproval, but his eyes ooze heat. "And who might that be?"

My smile feels grim. "That would be Declan Howard."

———————— ♥ ————————

DECLAN HOWARD. *Asshole extraordinaire.*

I regret my request the second Ronan motions for me to follow him.

Still, Declan's attractiveness is an indisputable fact. He's arguably the hottest guy in the whole damn *country*, let alone this gym.

As much as I loathe the idea of starting yet another social media account starring his handsome, stupid face, I reassure myself that using him to get things going isn't the end of the world. As soon as we have a proper following, I won't have to see him nearly as much. Or at all.

We stride into a wide, high-ceilinged hallway. One side is a curved wall of glass. Ronan takes me to a door on the opposite stretch and nods at the window, showing a glimpse of what's inside.

It's *huge*. At least one hundred feet of turf, all indoors. The "room" must comprise the entire center of the building. I see markings on the fake grass to indicate yardage.

"This is where we can usually find Declan and Theo, along with our wide receivers and a few select defense players. Dec likes to run plays for every contingency—he has the defense run down our receivers so he can work on ways around them. Theo practices blocking and receiving."

I know next to nothing about anything he just said, but it strikes me as odd that someone would block *and* receive the ball. When I make a face, Ronan's expression softens slightly. "You really don't know anything about the game, huh?"

I bite my lip and drop my eyes to my shoes. "Um... a touchdown is seven points?"

"Six," he corrects. "Without the kick. Or a two-point conversion."

Oh-kay...?

Ronan steps a bit closer, only inches from my back, and bends a bit to peer over my shoulder, watching as a cluster of shirtless men organize themselves into opposing rows at the far end of the huge room. His voice drops low.

"Watch."

His tattooed arm raises to point out the biggest man in the room. My heart—which is already pounding at my ribs from his proximity and scent—lurches and flips.

It's Theo.

I choke down the whine tickling my throat and nod. Ronan's voice warms, closer to my ear. "Theo's our tight end. It's a very valuable, skilled position."

My voice trembles. "W-what does he do?"

"Everything," Ronan rasps. The word tingles down my neck. "In some plays, he blocks defenders trying to get to Declan to take him down. In others, he breaks away from the defense entirely and acts as a receiver. He has to be stronger than the defenders to accomplish either task."

I only have to watch for a couple moments to see that he undoubtedly is. After a few plays, I'm mesmerized by the way he and Declan work together. The quarterback is light on his feet, always dropping back and setting up his passes with a fluidity that indicates decades of practice.

As beautiful as he is, I find myself wanting to snarl at him.

Infuriating ass.

Watching Theo is much more enjoyable. For one, he's a mountain of a man in tight black shorts and *nothing else. Holy—*

After I've thoroughly ogled every line of his thick, chiseled chest, I can appreciate the way he moves. There's a whomping kind of enthusiasm to it. Whether he's finding holes to get open or plowing his opponent to the turf, he does it with the sort of gusto you just can't fake. In the brief moments when he spits out his mouth guard, I catch glimpses of a wide, bright grin.

There's no hiding the way it makes me smile, too. Especially on one play, when the big guy takes down a defender in one smooth blow and then bursts out laughing.

My chest seizes at the sight. Inexplicable tears block my throat.

Theo.

Ronan hovers at my back, watching me closely. Every bit as captivating as his packmates in a completely different way.

Theo lights up my insides. Ronan *surrounds* me.

There's no other way to describe it. Whenever he's around, I feel him in every breath. Sweet smoke that smothers any uncertainty or fear. Except, of course, the fear of disappointing him.

All of my nerves stand to attention, waiting for the alpha's directives. When he speaks, his voice is a quiet rumble. "Would you like to meet him?"

He doesn't say the word *"again,"* but I hear it in his voice.

Does he know Theo and I met? Did his packmate tell him I'm not really a beta? If he did, why did Ronan ask me to come back here?

Either way, I should say no. Because—even assuming that Theo kept my secret—if I go in there, how will I ever keep myself from *climbing him*?

What if I perfume and blow my cover? Or whine and have a meltdown?

I'm seconds away from both right now. Need beats at my skin, battering the insides of my chest.

Pounding, pounding, *pounding.*

"Yes."

The word is a whisper. There's no way anyone but Ronan heard me. But at that exact moment, Declan Howard's head snaps up. He whips his helmet off and turns, ice-blue eyes flying across the indoor field to find me peering in at him.

Our gazes collide. His entire face contorts. Rage, disgust, and refusal ingrain themselves into every line of his angelic features.

Rejection. That's what his face is doing. Rejecting me and my presence here.

I see it.

I *feel* it.

And that's all it takes to send me spiraling.

chapter
fourteen

ARCHER

BEING a doctor for an entire team of violent, pumped-up alphas has prepared me for a lot. I can re-break bones as thick as my own arm. I can speed-stitch torn skin in the middle of a field while thousands of fans watch. I can even wrestle deliriously-injured players to the ground with a tranquilizer between my teeth.

But when Ronan storms into the Ospreys' med bay with a small, blonde woman hanging from his arms, I realize one thing I have no experience with:

Handling something delicate. Fixing someone precious.

Because that's what she is. I recognize it instantly, this time.

My eyes fly over her slack, feminine features—the barely-there dusting of freckles, the blonde lashes, gently parted rosebud lips— and see her for exactly what she is. Even before I smell the incredible scent emanating from her.

My jaw falls open. A choked noise catches halfway through it, spilling into the sweet, peachy air.

I've read countless articles and studies on scent-sensitivity in packs. The science is undeniable. If alphas and omegas can find true scent-mates, their packs report higher levels of happiness, group harmony, and general health.

After all my research and years studying medicine, I thought I understood. But the second Ronan sets Meg in front of me, and I inhale her unmasked scent, I realize I understand nothing.

She smells the way I imagine my own personal heaven would smell. The sweetest brown sugar; the warm, comforting aroma of buttery pastry; and *peaches*. Good God.

The fresh, lush scent sets off fireworks inside of me—crackling sparks that buzz through my blood. I'm not usually ruled by my alpha urges, but for a moment they practically flatten me. I can't remember who or what I am. Other than this omega's alpha. Hers.

Ronan growls, "Archer. *Help*."

I finally catch up, hurtling into action. My medical training and alpha nature war with one another for a split second. Instincts demand I check our surroundings first, to make sure no one else scents her. I give in to that singular impulse before shoving the rest of them down.

Snapping forward, I pull the stethoscope from the pocket of my white lab coat. I move as carefully as I can, but when I press the implement over her left breast, the thick fabric of her bow blouse impedes me.

Too amped up to be patient, Ronan rips the top open, popping multiple hidden buttons in the process. I start to snarl a warning at him, but the sound dies in my chest when I see the fanatical fear written all over his face.

He feels it too. The pull. The one Theo described. The same sensation that's currently *choking* me. Which can only mean that not only is she *my omega*; she's *our* omega.

It would be the most miraculous moment of my life if she weren't also unconscious.

I take stock of the muted thumping behind her breast and release a harsh exhale. "Pulse is steady. How long has she been down?"

Ronan's movements are agitated. His elbow jerks as he checks his watch. "Eight minutes. I had to carry her from the practice room."

That's two buildings away. A cold trickle of horror drips through me as I consider the route he had to take. "Did anyone—"

He nods, face thunderous. "I put them in their places. No one followed me."

But they could have.

Even though he doesn't say the words, I hear him loud and clear. Meg isn't safe here while she's perfuming like this.

Ronan and I are both exempt from the League rules banning rut-blockers, but it's still incredible that neither of us have lost control. Yet.

When I observe Ronan, I notice his white knuckles stretched over closed fists and the muscle ticking in his jaw while he grinds his teeth. The brim of his hat shadows his expression, but it's one I don't think I've ever seen before. That's saying something after fifteen years.

When I check in with myself, I find my body in complete conflict. The smell of her, the heat of her bared breasts—a thick pulse pounds into my cock, readying me to take the omega with the siren scent.

My head is shockingly clear, though. Concerned only with *her*, but in an entirely different way. What does she need? What would she like? How can I keep her safe?

"We have to get her out of here."

He nods, his jaw wired shut. "Hospital?" he grits.

It's hard to think straight with Meg's perfume filling the air. I shut my eyes and focus, imagining the scene if we carried her into the ER like this. She may be better off there, if the nurses and doctors on staff are all betas or bonded alphas. If not...

"Too risky," I husk out. "She's likely in a heat-spike. We need to take her somewhere safe until it ends."

I gather every blanket in sight and begin bundling her. They won't help much, but any extra layer between us and her soaked panties will help.

"Where?" he growls back, catching on and tucking a sheet around her legs.

Can't keep her here. Can't take her into the offices. We don't know where her friend's apartment is. Any public place is just as dangerous as the hospital.

I raise my eyes to his. "Home."

chapter
fifteen

ASH PACK GROUP TEXT

RONAN

Meg is having a heat-spike. She passed out.

THEO

WHAT THE FUCK

So wait. I was right?

Guys?

GUYS????

DECLAN

I told you not to bring her back here.

Get her out of my gym.

ARCHER

Not helpful, Declan.

And yes, Theo. We're taking her home now.

THEO

I want to leave but Coach is up my asshole.

RONAN

I'll deal with Coach. Just get home.

You too, Dec. Now.

DECLAN HAS LEFT THE CONVERSATION

HAS anyone else ever woken up from an extremely vivid sex dream with their hand down their panties and found a hot doctor standing over them?

No?

Just me?

As soon as my brain comes back online, I fling my hand away from my center. The beautiful man next to me watches while I scrabble into a seated position, gasping on a breath of *the most incredible scent* I've ever encountered.

Well. It's in the top four, anyway.

The rich, smooth aroma of bourbon mixed with the fresh spice of ginger. Two things that would normally intoxicate or energize, but instead, they have an oddly soothing effect on me. I take another deep breath, loosening the claws digging into my lungs.

Was I panicking a second ago?

Why would anyone panic with this beautiful man to look at?

Oh. Right. Because *he* is looking at *me*. And I am currently a not-so-hot mess.

A not-so-hot mess with her *panties out*?! Except—*oh my God* —they aren't even *my* panties.

I glance down and realize with absolute horror that Remi's underwear is covered in tiny, purple kitty cats and rainbow hearts.

Then—because, you know, this isn't mortifying enough—I shriek, "They're not mine!"

Because that's somehow better?

Dr. Monroe blinks, his dark brown eyes creasing in confusion behind his square glasses. He looks down at my crotch briefly, then pauses on my chest before turning back to my face. "I'm sorry, what?"

He's polite. Giving me an out. But do I take it like a sane person?

Of course not.

"THE PANTIES," I practically shout. "THESE PANTIES AREN'T MINE."

Dr. Monroe's gorgeous face leaps in surprise. And for half a second, I think I might actually die from humiliation.

But then he *smiles*. A bright, beaming smile that fills his whole face with some shiny emotion I don't have a name for. A quiet chuckle stumbles out of his mouth.

"Good to know," he says, feigning solemnity. "I was worried. The rainbows or the cats alone would have been one thing, but both together? Concerning."

I laugh, grateful for his kindness. "Is that your medical opinion?"

"Medical and personal, yes." He flashes another grin. His smiles are quick, but not in a flirty way. It takes me a second to recognize the shyness behind them. He isn't used to smiling like this.

That might be adorable, if not for the fact that he just saw my underwear.

Or Remi's underwear. Whatever.

I'm embarrassed to admit that it takes this long for me to realize I am... in a bed?

Dr. Monroe seems to see the exact moment horror hooks its talons into me. His smile fades, and his eyes fill with compassion. Actual, *visible* compassion. When he explains, his voice is concerned but calm. Calm*ing*.

"You lost consciousness while you were on your tour. Ronan carried you to me, but the damage was done. A lot of alphas had scented you." He leans away slightly and clears his throat, looking down at his shoes. "He probably would have called me to come to you, but I don't think he was in his right mind. We had to get you out of there and somewhere safe."

I struggle to raise my head off the pillow below and look around. The all-white room is plush, but devoid of any sort of personality. Off to the side, two French doors hang open, revealing a little balcony surrounded by a lush canopy of palm trees. A mockingbird starts up, harmonizing with the late-summer cicadas. Somewhere in the distance, a fountain or pool bubbles.

"This is our guest room," Archer murmurs. "It seemed as good a place as any to weather a heat-spike."

Our gazes meet. His eyes are somehow sharply intelligent and warm with understanding. I might be swept away by them, if I weren't so worried about what, exactly, he understands.

"You're an omega."

He says it softly, without any accusation or judgment. I squeeze my eyes closed, nodding. "I-I'm sorry. I know I shouldn't have lied to apply for the job, but—"

He hums thoughtfully. "You needed it."

I crack my eyelids open, terrified of seeing any disappointment or anger on his face. But he simply watches me, curious and solemn.

I nod again. "Y-yes. It was—it *is*—not the best situation." I wave a hand at my soaked, borrowed underwear. "Clearly."

His full lips quirk down. "I understand that better than you may think, but you were in real danger there." He glances down at his rigid posture and chuffs. "You still are. I took an emergency dose of rut-blockers, and your perfume has settled, but none of this is *safe* for you, Megera. We would have been destroyed if one us hurt you by accident."

I stare at him and he doesn't waver, looking back steadily. Usually, it's hard for me to hold eye contact with an alpha like this. Their dominance can be stifling. Most of them project it without even realizing.

Not Archer. He sighs and lowers himself to the foot of the queen-sized bed. Purposely putting our faces on the same level so as not to loom over me.

The motion hits my heart like a stray lightning bolt. A low whine leaks out of me before I can stop it.

His entire face softens as he leans in. Ginger spice grows thicker in the air. My muscles go lax everywhere except my core, which contracts painfully. When I set my hands over my lower belly and wince, he tracks the movement.

"What do you need?" he asks, that dark gaze imploring me. "Anything. Say it and it's yours."

I don't know where to begin. So many foreign urges swirl through me. I'm used to avoiding alphas—always skirting around them as carefully as possible.

But these men make me want to reach out and touch. They have me wishing I could offer them things I have no business even considering.

Is this what happens in scent-sensitive packs?

Are we—am I—?

No.

My mind fights every impulse inside of me, struggling for reason.

No, it's not possible.

Remi's doubtful face flashes through my head. Her challenging, direct stare while she asked, *"Why not?"*

I guess she has a point. I know this happens. There are tons of studies on it. Not to mention, all of the scent-matched omega influencers who humble-brag about their mates at every opportunity. I always sort of assumed they were lying. Or exaggerating. But if this whole thing is real and it actually happens to people... *why not* me?

Because you've never been a good omega, and you have no idea how to be one for these successful, high-profile men.

Another pathetic whimper escapes while my mind reels, trying to imagine what that would even look like. Dr. Monroe seems pained by the sound. His perfect teeth gnash in a grimace. He starts to reach for me, but stops before our hands touch.

It makes sense. Why would any of them want to touch me? I must look like crap, and now they all know I'm a pathetic liar, too.

In a flash, the image of Declan glaring at me through the glass door to his practice room sails through my head. God, he *hates* me. It was clear from that one look. The memory alone has me gagging on another whine, barely managing to keep the pitiful sound down.

This is a mess. The most famous football player in the world hates me for reasons I don't even want to understand. His pack acts like they want to eat me and/or commit me. And to top it all off, I still don't have a job, income, or insurance.

Then, there's Dr. Archer Monroe. Sitting next to me, kind and steady. Waiting for me to tell him how to help.

I *want* to. And I'm ashamed of that.

I should be able to handle all of this stuff on my own. I don't want to need any help or comfort or protection. I don't want to be like this.

I don't want to be an omega.

So how could I ever be *their* omega?

After cresting high over my head for the entire interaction, a tsunami of complete overwhelm finally engulfs me. The urge to hide hits hard.

It's the only omega impulse I routinely give in to when I'm

home alone—burying myself under blankets and pretending no one would ever find me there.

That's all I really want to do, now. But I have hours of driving ahead of me before I can get in my bed. Hours spent sitting in wet panties and a torn blouse.

Remember when I said the universe hated me?

Feeling defeated, overwhelmed, and embarrassed, I sniffle. "I'm so sorry," I whisper. "I—This has never happened to me before. Well, aside from the other day, in the interview."

My face flames while I drop my gaze to my lap. "That's why I ran out. I didn't want to put any of you in an uncomfortable situation, but I could feel a spike coming on..."

Archer's fingers are long and cool against my jaw. He lifts my chin slowly, bending closer to put us eye-to-eye.

There's a bright gleam in his chocolate irises. Some excitement I don't understand. "You've never had a spike like this for any other alphas?"

I shake my head, trembling. "N-no. And I—Archer, what's happening to me? What *is* this?"

His handsome smile kicks up again. Completely at odds with the wistful look in his eyes. "I think it may be fate."

chapter
sixteen

I'VE ALWAYS LIKED FIGHTING.

Well. *Needed* it.

Theo calls me "a fighter." Like it's a hobby. Or some sort of choice. He doesn't get that I *have to* push the poison out somewhere.

That's how I started playing football.

Every sports network asks me how I got into the game. I tell them my grandfather played. I tell them my mother bought me a ball for my fifth birthday. I tell them I joined a pee-wee team and discovered a lifelong love of throwing spiral passes.

Basically, I lie my fucking ass off.

Because the truth? It would depress the hell out of everyone.

Nobody wants a weak quarterback. Women won't salivate over the World's Sexiest Man if they know just how fucked up his head is.

Problem is, one can only hide that shit for so long. And I have the sinking feeling my pack is slowly realizing they fucked up when they chose to hitch their wagon to mine.

I see it in the way Theo is staring at me with his mouth hanging open. Like I just suggested we skin a litter of puppies to make a coat.

In reality, all I said was, "No."

Theo sputters. "What the fuck do you mean, '*no*'? Have you lost your ever-loving mind? This is our omega. Our scent-match. She's *perfect* for us."

I roll my eyes, dropping my head back to thump against the kitchen cabinets behind me. We're back where we started yesterday; gathered in a tense circle around the island while we talk about this random woman. Again.

"I *mean*," I growl, staring up at the ceiling. "Who is this person? None of us even know her! And she has us breaking all of our goddamn rules? Lying to get a job at the facility she isn't even supposed to be allowed in? Now she's *in our house*? Driving a wedge between all of us?"

"You're the one doing that," Archer argues, quiet but deadly. "We all agree. The three of us want to court her. *You're* the problem here, Declan."

I hate it when Archer makes sense. Which is always.

Seriously; what the fuck can I say to that? He's right. I am the problem. Just like I was the problem last season when I got hurt. And the season before that, when I blew the championship to hell.

But, like I said, I like to fight.

"How the hell am I the problem when she's the one lying, scheming—"

"*Enough*," Ronan barks. "Meg may have lied, but we haven't even asked her why. Stop accusing her of shit when we don't know the circumstances."

"We have to make sure she knows we aren't mad," Theo interrupts, desperate. "We should make her dinner. Invite her to stay."

The pain creasing his green eyes looks all wrong on him. Theo's the carefree, happy one around here. I don't know how to react to this new, earnest side of him. It doesn't creep me out, exactly, but it makes me uncomfortable for some reason.

I snort at him, "Whipped already? You took one goddamn elevator with this bitch."

Theo's brows drop into an angry V just as a snarl erupts from Ronan, "Declan—*Shut. Up.*"

His bark pins my lungs inside my chest. I go to speak, but everything wads up in the middle of my throat, choking me. Instead, I glare at our pack leader until his returning stare spears me into submission.

Goddamn it.

I'm outvoted, and I know it. Why can't I just let them have this? They can court whoever they want, the same way I did. And they can fall on their faces, the same way I did.

So fuck it, I think. *Let them simp for her all they want.*

Because there's no way this chick is the one for us.

I shove off the counter. "Fine, make her dinner. But count me out."

chapter
seventeen

Megera

"MISS REED, I PRESUME?"

This woman has to be a kick-ass grandma. She just has that look—round, rosy cheeks, a no-nonsense haircut, and the sort of sweet warmth that reminds me of Remi's chocolate-chip cookies.

I'm thankful she's so welcoming because I have absolutely no idea what I've gotten myself into here.

But it seems like *a lot*.

"Uh-um..." I blink, trying to stay cool. "Yes, that's me. I—I'm sorry, I wasn't expecting anyone out here in the hallway."

She smiles widely. "That's quite all right, dearest. I hear you've been through an absolute ordeal today. The boys asked me to show you around the estate and make sure you're comfortable."

If I wasn't so busy smiling at the way she calls a billionaire, a doctor, and two NFL players "the boys," I might have a small panic attack over the phrase "around the estate."

I suppose that's what it is, though. I can tell just from taking two steps into the hall. The wide, white space is perfectly clean and full of natural sunlight. And I'm bedraggled at best.

I've lost count of all the things I'm mortified by: my wet hair, the hodgepodge of men's clothing hanging off my body, my general existence. I didn't have many options, though. I had to shower before I faced the Ash pack and I don't have any spare clothes with me.

I start to back toward the safety of the guest room, but the woman hooks her arm through mine and gives my hand a reassuring pat. "Well you are every bit as beautiful as Mr. Theo described you," she says. "And he described you a lot. I'm Mrs. Fleming, the housekeeper."

The kindly beta woman grips my limp hand and squeezes warmly, sending a rush of calm through me. It's a nifty trick. She clocks the surprise on my face. Her smile turns knowing.

"I have three omega daughters and three alpha sons," she whispers, her tone conspiratorial. "Not to mention all of the grandkids. I've learned a few tricks."

I believe her. She seems to know precisely when I start to panic and has a way of distracting me when I need it most. She talks about the unseasonably mild weather while she pulls me out of the hall and onto an enormous second-floor landing.

Below, the first-floor foyer sprawls at the base of a set of floating steps with a glass railing. It's all modern opulence—black marble floors, thick wood doors, and floor-to-ceiling windows. I open my mouth, but words don't come out. Instead, some choked, squeaking noise slips up my throat while I blink at the woman guiding me.

A hint of sympathy enters her eyes. "The boys can be a lot to take on, I know. But they haven't been able to stop talking about you all week. I know they're waiting anxiously downstairs."

"They... are?"

But this time I manage to at least smile. She pats my arm again, nodding enthusiastically. "Come along, dear. I'll show you."

I follow Mrs. Fleming into the foyer. The floors gleam, polished black stone shining under the smoky glass light fixture hanging from two stories above. Off to the right, there's a huge living room with a luxurious leather sofa curved in the middle.

When I freeze over the threshold, Mrs. Fleming chuckles. "There's a lot more to see, I'm afraid. The kitchen, garage, and pack wing are off the other side of the foyer, but we're going to the lanai."

The *lanai*?

Good lord.

Mrs. Fleming notices the way I tense up and draws to a halt. I can see our destination a few yards away—the back wall of glass folded open like an accordion, revealing the bleached white stone of a pool deck and outdoor entertaining space.

Ronan is off to the side, standing next to a smoking grill. Archer seems to be reading at a glass table.

My heart jumps when I notice that Theo is here, too. He paces around the enormous square pool, waving his arms while he talks on his phone. Mrs. Fleming follows my gaze and grins.

"He's been on the phone with his little sister for an hour," she tells me. "Miss Emma is also an omega. He's asking her for advice on how to make you more comfortable."

I watch him for a long moment, not believing what I'm hearing. But, sure enough, his eyes look wide and earnest while he nods vigorously. As though his sister can hear him silently agreeing with whatever she's saying.

My cheeks hurt. After a moment, I realize it's because I'm smiling so hard.

And the next thing I know, I'm running.

chapter
eighteen

"I'M GOING out of my skin," I mutter, "I swear, Em."

My sister's laugh floats through the phone. "I believe you, but it might take her a while to come downstairs. She's just had a heat-spike in a house full of strange alphas. If I were her, I'd be *hiding*."

I grimace. Both of my sisters have been known to hide in their nests whenever they get freaked out. Only, Meg doesn't have one of those in her guest room. *My poor sweet little peach.*

"What else should I get for her?" I ask, practically begging for advice.

Emma hums. "Well, you guys left her clothes with your scents on them?"

I look around the outdoor kitchen. Ronan silently mans the grill. He's been quiet since I came home, but he nods. Archer is sitting at the nearby dining table, pretending to read some stack of papers. He looks up and offers a nod of his own, confirming.

"Yep."

"Good," Em says. "And she has scent-canceling body wash up there? I know you guys won't like it, but it will make her feel more comfortable if she isn't steeped in her own perfume."

She's right—I don't like it. But that fact barely registers. Meg is all that matters to me right now. "Yeah, she has some."

"And you're wearing your softest shirt?"

I run my hand over the burgundy Henley, checking the fabric. "Affirmative. And Mrs. Fleming is waiting to show her down when she's ready."

"Okay then. I know it's hard to wait, but that's all you can really do, big brother. She'll come out when she's ready. Just don't, like, tackle her."

"I wasn't going to *tackle her*," I lie. Archer smirks quietly. Ronan casts me a quelling glare. "All right, all right. Hanging up now."

The call clicks off. I'm in the middle of my millionth circuit around the edge of the pool when all three of us suddenly pause. My neck prickles.

Even before she steps into view, I know she's here. I can smell her natural scent—not the thick, mind-bending perfection of her perfume, but something equally as perfect. Just less potent.

We're all frozen when she shuffles out from the shadows of the pack house and floats onto the lanai.

Holy shit.

Was she always this *gorgeous*?

Back in the elevator, my brain could only run at half-speed, impaired by the luscious perfume of peaches. Now, I see the way the setting sun hits her shoulder-length layers of golden hair. I notice the sexy flare of her hips and her heart-shaped face.

And when she smiles?

I am *done for.*

Every part of me strains to sprint over and swoop her up. I'm fighting my every instinct when she suddenly skips into a run, launching herself right at me.

Oh. My. God.

This girl.

She is *mine.*

So I take off too, only stopping to brace myself when we're a couple yards apart. I crouch low and catch her, easily absorbing the blow as she leaps into my arms and lets me swing her around.

Her scent—the full, true, *fucking perfect* version I only caught one whiff of last time—swirls around me.

Oh fuck, *yes.* I knew it, I knew it, *I knew it.*

This is our omega.

My omega.

I shove down a territorial growl, rasping around it. "Hey, peaches." My arms tighten around her while I rub my face against her hair, accidentally scent-marking her before I can help myself.

She likes that. Her perfume swells again. My cock jerks to life.

I want to bury myself so deep in her, she'll never get my knot out. Fill her up until I have nothing left. Hold her all night long.

"Big guy," she murmurs, wrapping her arms around my neck, inhaling me the same way I breathe her in. "You want to know a secret?"

I hold her closer. "Hell yes."

She leans up to my ear, her soft cheek grazing my beard. "I think you're the real reason I went back there today," she whispers. "I knew it was dangerous, but I was so scared I'd never see you again."

The watery sound of her voice has me leaning back, tucking one arm under her sexy ass and reaching my free hand up to pet her head. "I would have found you, precious," I promise. "You can count on that."

chapter
nineteen

ARCHER

I'VE HEARD Meg tell Declan off twice. Witnessed the way she makes our moody, short-tempered pack alpha pause and reassess his reactions. Now, just when I think I should have bought a leash to keep Theo from tackling her...

She tackles *him*.

I'm beginning to think she might look perfect in everything. The baggy sweats and oversized T-shirt do nothing to detract from her sweet, sloping nose. Those wide blue eyes with their dark blonde lashes. The cinnamon freckles sprinkled over the apples of her cheeks. Her rosebud lips.

And her *skin*. As smooth and clear as honey.

I feel like I can exhale for the first time in hours as her scent twines around me. It isn't heat perfume; in some ways, it's better. I can still think, but I feel euphoric from our proximity.

I want to drop to my knees and worship her. Wrap her in my arms to keep her safe. Lock our bodies together so no one can ever hurt or upset her again.

As Theo lowers her feet to the ground—very carefully, to his credit—and turns the omega to face me, her glowing smile shrinks. Hesitation rolls over her features, like an eclipse swallowing the sun. She blinks, looking stricken as she stares at my face.

For one horrible moment, I worry I've done something to frighten her. Then her perfume *explodes*.

I choke on a growl. Ronan snarls viciously. And Theo groans like he just came in his pants. Judging from the way he doubles over—and my own aching erection—it's a distinct possibility.

Meg blinks up at me, biting her plump lower lip with a row of even white teeth. "I can't seem to stop that around you all. I'm so sorry."

For perfuming?

As if I'm not elated by it. As if she has any control over her biology.

I know I don't. Especially at the moment.

Or maybe she expects me to be upset about the incident today, the way she misled us. I am—but not for the reasons she must suspect. I'm more upset that our team has to discriminate against unbonded omegas, even though we truly do so with their safety in mind.

It's also concerning that she felt desperate enough to lie and put herself in danger in the first place. After examining the portfolio she provided and re-checking all of her character references, I'm fairly certain Megera isn't reckless or dishonest. Her situation must be dire.

Before I can ask why she's apologizing, she snaps her posture up and exhales harshly. Brazening it out, even though her voice shakes slightly. "Anyway, thank you for taking care of me today."

"Of course. I—"

There are no words. Nothing to say except, *I didn't think you existed.* Or, *I finally found you;* which seem both melodramatic and obvious, respectively.

But her smile only grows the longer I hesitate. As kind as it is beautiful. "I wondered which scent was you during the interview. Bourbon and ginger and spice. It's…"

Her pupils dilate while she leans closer. Allowing herself to drift for only a couple of seconds before she snaps upright again and blurts, "I like it."

I can see her pulling herself back from her instincts. Like a puppy on a leash—she initially follows her senses before some tether yanks her away.

It's disconcerting. Concerning. Confusing.

All of those are appropriate, logical reactions. But I also feel insanely, irrationally *protective.*

A purr roars to life in my chest, as natural as breathing. I should be surprised it springs up so easily; purrs are normally reserved for intimate relationships, and I've barely touched this omega.

I don't care. Meg responds to the vibrating sound automatically, swaying on her feet. "Oh," she murmurs, sounding dazed. "Is that a—"

Before the question can properly horrify me, more perfume fills the open air around us. A warm flush glows over her cheeks. She bites her lip again, peeking up at me through her lashes.

"Sorry. Again. No one's ever purred for me before."

An embarrassed wince flits over her features. She leans forward, as if she doesn't want to be overheard. "That's what this is, right?"

A sharp twinge of pain pinches my lungs as I step closer. "Yes, sweetheart. No one's ever done this for you?"

She shakes her head, whispering, "No."

Her confession appeases some primal, possessive urge inside of me. Which is, frankly, stupid. My brain fares better than my body. Years of medical training kick in, formulating pertinent questions.

How has this omega gone twenty-four years without someone purring for her? Not even during her heats? What sorts of knot-heads tended to her?

An icy avalanche of dismay rolls down my spine.

Has she been alone?

As she sways on her feet, her eyes fly wide and fill with emotion. I see trepidation, but there's also a lot of longing. My chest aches to see it written so plainly on her pretty face.

I hold my hand out to her. "Are you comfortable with us touching you?" I try for a smile as I roll my eyes to Theo. "The big guy forgot to get verbal confirmation."

Meg shoots Theo a fond look, silently reassuring him that she doesn't mind his presumption. She forces a thick laugh. "I'm... not really sure, actually." Her wispy brows pinch. She looks back up at me, shyness returning. "No one has ever asked."

I don't need a pack bond to feel shock echo through all three of us. It's common courtesy for alphas to ask before they touch omegas. Our pheromones affect theirs so heavily, it's only right.

If no one has ever asked her before, she's either been forced or she's been by herself. Based on her confusion, I'm leaning toward the latter.

Ronan stiffens behind me. Beginning what will truly be an epic seethe, I assume; no one broods quite as thoroughly as he does.

Theo puffs up. All action. Ready to rush in and assure her just how much he wants to cuddle her.

I'm cautious. Trying my damnedest to be considerate.

Meg tracks our reactions. She glances down at the way she's clutching her hands together before blowing out a big breath and pushing out more words.

"I'm not very good at this sort of thing. I know I was just

pretending to be a beta, but sometimes I feel like I'd be better off if I were one. All of this alpha-omega stuff... I don't really know the expectations or the rules." Her gaze skirts back up to mine, the blue irises swirling with shame. "I'm sorry."

I hate that we've only been standing here for five minutes, and she's already apologized three times over things that either aren't her fault or are not *faults* at all.

I stare back at her, projecting the steady assurance she needs. "There are no rules or expectations between us. There's only what you want and what you need. Tell us those things, and we will take care of the rest."

She swallows, looking back down at her nails. "I think—" She gives a hard laugh, frustrated with herself. "Is it weird that I *want* you to touch me?"

Ronan shoots me a look she can't see. After years of pre-courting interviews, he's used to omegas having their boundaries and desires all laid out in triplicate. I am, too; every omega in the heat clinic had paperwork.

It's unusual to come across one who doesn't know their own feelings on physical affection since it's something they tend to crave so fiercely. It's actually essential to their well-being, medically speaking.

As I stare down at the perfect, embarrassed woman in front of me, a harsh realization dawns.

She has no idea she's allowed to need this.

"Meg," I say softly. "Touch starvation is a verifiable medical issue for omegas. It can affect their nervous systems, mental health, appetites, heat hormones."

She bites the corner of her lip. "My doctor mentioned that, actually." She ducks her head. "A few times, over the years."

My stomach sinks. How long has she been touch-starved? Has she always been alone? Without anyone to hold her or comfort her?

Fucking hell.

Heats must be terrifying for her. And if her doctor's been discussing touch starvation with her for *years*, hers must be severe. If she were my patient, I'd advise regular nest sessions with her alphas. Daily, or even twice daily. No clothing. Especially close to her heats.

But I'm not her doctor. I'm her—

Mate, my brain supplies. As if it is a fact, the same as the stone beneath my feet.

I see Ronan's gears turning—he's going to interrogate me on all of this later. I'll have to pull a few studies for him to read. We should all be well-versed in what Meg needs.

As soon as I have the thought, I realize: my decision is made. I'm ready to commit to her now. And we haven't even sat down.

That word—*mate*—streaks across my frontal lobe every time I look into her eyes.

It isn't just her scent, as incredible as it is. It's her. The way she looks at me—so open and vulnerable, even though I can tell she *hates* to ask for anything. The way she jumped into Theo's arms and didn't balk at his enthusiasm. The way she makes Ronan slow down and smile.

She's just... ours.

My purr grows deeper. Meg sways closer. I steady her with my free hand, slowly stepping up against her.

"There's nothing wrong with you," I murmur, caressing her back. She shivers, her scent spiking with her pleasure from that one simple touch. "And definitely nothing wrong with wanting us to touch you. In fact, I think we'll all fight for the privilege."

With a deep breath, she gives in and falls into my arms. For a second, I worry she'll feel the erection pressing at my fly and be nervous. But she only snuggles her plush hips against mine, wrapping her arms around my neck and burying her face against my vibrating chest.

Scent-marking me, I realize. I'm not even sure she knows she's doing it, but a swoop of joy soars through me anyway.

Theo comes to hover at my elbow. He's restless, brimming with the same excitement I feel.

It's odd for us to stand close together; alphas like their personal space. But, somehow, with Meg at the center, it feels right.

He palms the back of her head gently, stroking her hair with his massive hand. When her glassy eyes roll up to his, he winks. "Sorry to intrude, precious. Had to get in on all this good stuff. I felt left out."

With a tiny smirk and a cute little eye roll, Meg reaches one of her hands over to squeeze his beard. "If you want me around, you'll have to share, big guy. Archer says I'm a hot commodity."

Theo reminds me of a school-kid convincing his teacher he can behave, zealously nodding at her with wide eyes. "Sharing. Cool. Yup. Sharing is caring. I *love* sharing. You got it, peaches."

Meg's laugh makes me laugh, too. Until a pointed rumble interrupts our trio. Ronan steps in front of me, his laser intensity focused squarely on the woman in my arms.

"Before we all settle in," he says. "We need to talk."

chapter
twenty

I DON'T HAVE a clue what I expected from these alphas.

But it wasn't this.

Put simply: it *cannot* be *this* easy.

My mother's voice in my head tells me not to trust it, reminding me that I need to be tough. Independent. Smart.

I can't deny the connections I already feel, though. Not just with the pack and their scents, but with each of the alphas individually.

I even feel weirdly drawn to asshat Declan, who clearly wants nothing to do with me. I'm more than a little devastated that he doesn't even want to come out of his room while I'm here.

When his face floats through my mind, I find myself stuffing down sobs. My instincts tell me this *isn't right*, that I need all of my alphas.

But, obviously, that little voice is a psycho. These men aren't *mine*.

Especially not Declan.

I'd probably feel much worse about how much their absent packmate hates me if Archer didn't have me cradled against his lean, solid chest.

His rumbling purr soaks into my body. It's everything I've wanted since I woke up on his exam table.

A flood of endorphins soothes every ragged nerve in my body. Being encased in his long, muscled arms, with Theo pressing into our sides, feels like a sudden runner's high. Ginger and citrus muddle in the air. My body relaxes while my mind clears, my insides melting into contented jelly.

But, of course, the Big Bad Alpha can't have that.

Ronan stares at me, his focus so intense I feel it carving into my facial features. The stormy irises I once thought were so cold now seem white-hot. Passion blazes beneath the cool color, turning them from twin interrogation lamps into glowing beacons.

"Y-you want to talk?"

He nods, but his expression stays calm. My fingertips spark as he clasps them in his, bringing my hand up to his mouth. Warm lips graze my knuckles. A burst of slick seeps into my panties.

His face twitches with masculine amusement. "*Can* you talk, little one?"

I probably ought to find that nickname insulting, but I love it. Because I'm a psycho thirsty-AF omega. Apparently.

"I think so," I mumble. I'm really not sure. The amount of perfume I've already produced for them is just embarrassing. Thank God we appear to be eating dinner outside.

Ronan's gaze sharpens, his focus absolute while it skates over my entire body. His chiseled mouth tightens, and his voice drops low. "I need to feed you before I can focus. Sit down."

It isn't a bark—or even a true command. But his insistence has an instant effect. My Omega hears him and wants to *obey*.

With *relief*, might I add.

Without dropping my hand, the alpha leads me to a seat at the center of the smoked glass table on the lanai. Someone has draped soft blankets over it a layered stack.

Was this one of Theo's sisters tips? It's amusing and oddly touching.

The food is the same way. Bowls of colorful pasta salad, fresh fruit, and mixed veggies sit in a neat row. I notice that the plates and cutlery aren't plastic or paper—and suspect Ronan is responsible for the fancy, impractical place settings.

He watches like a hawk as I drop to the padded chair and serve myself a bit from each dish. When I move to lean back, his deep rumble interjects. "I have chicken, steak, and salmon. Which do you prefer?"

I shake my head. My stomach is still feeling wobbly. "I'm all right."

His brows snap down. "You need to eat a proper meal. It will help you recover from your spike." After one breath, he adds, "Please, little one."

If any of the others tried to micromanage my plate, I would snort at them. But there's something about the way Ronan's eyes burn when he watches me—steady and fanatical at the same time.

Like he *needs* me to take care of myself. But also knows, resolutely, that he will ensure I do. Plus, the way he tries his best to mind his manners around me is sort of cute.

I select a piece of chicken.

Our eyes lock, and he nods, granting the approval I don't know I'm seeking until he says, "Good girl."

Should I be at all concerned about the way those two words make me *swoon*?

Ronan helps himself next, loading a plate completely before he settles right beside me, filling the air with his sweet smokiness. When he catches me leaning into the scent, he smirks, his eyes crinkling, and moves a bit closer.

Theo reaches the end of his patience, crashing down on the seat across from me and jabbering excitedly about the food while he fills two plates to the absolute brim.

Archer is more reserved, his demeanor relaxed as his packmate goes on and on. When the doctor finally settles at my other side, he shoots me a conspiratorial smile, translating, "Basically, we didn't know what you liked, so we took a wild guess. Is this okay?"

It's delicious, actually.

Archer brightens at my enthusiastic nod. As he turns to his own plate, his eyebrows furrow behind his sexy glasses. "We'll need a list of all your favorite things."

"Why?" I giggle.

Archer cocks his head at me. "To get them for you."

I blink at him. Why would they get me anything? I'm the lying, pathetic puddle of hormones who ruined their entire day and almost started a riot of unbonded alpha football players. They should probably have me arrested or something.

Oblivious to my shock, Theo grins around a big bite of fruit. "You need some *serious* spoiling, peaches."

My pitiful omega heart squeals at the thought of presents and pampering. But I won't give in. They'll think I'm materialistic if I accept any gifts. Or selfish. I can still hear my mom muttering about "spoiled little omegas" who "sponge" off their alphas' biologically-driven generosity.

And these *are not my alphas.*

Maybe if I keep forcing that thought, it will eventually sink in.

I roll my eyes to hide my conflicted thoughts. "Says who?"

There's a slight awkward beat before Ronan's tattooed hand snakes into my lap, planting itself on my thigh and squeezing softly. "Says *me.*"

Well then.

Seems dumb to argue with a man like Ronan. But the sinking shame in my stomach is hard to silence.

I shouldn't want any of this.

I shouldn't take any of it.

I should take care of myself.

Archer interrupts me scolding myself. "So you don't live in town?" he inquires, neatly carving his chicken into proper bites.

Theo frowns at his food, picking all of the bananas out of his fruit salad. Archer rolls his eyes, taking the slices onto his own plate without comment.

I hide my amusement and shake my head. "I grew up with my mother, a few hours north. Then I moved to Tampa when I finished college and got a job at a marketing company there."

"Your *Master's*," Ronan corrects, muttering. "You didn't *just* finish college, little one. You have a very impressive résumé."

Archer shoots him an annoyed look when my cheeks heat. Ronan hooks his fingers under my chin and lifts my gaze to his. The molten quicksilver blazes. "Be proud of yourself," he murmurs. "I am."

Before I can process why those two simple sentences flip all of my insides out, Theo interjects, a bright glow of hope in his light green eyes. "So you live in Tampa, but you have a friend who lives here, right?"

Hoping that I'll be in town? The thought is so sweet, I automatically smile at him. "Two friends, now, if I count this big, blond dude I met in an elevator."

Theo nods, his features serious. "Sounds like a great guy. Definitely spank bank material."

The start of a growl rumbles in Ronan's chest, but it dies as soon as I laugh and shoot back, "What makes you think he hasn't already been deposited?"

The way Theo's mouth drops open would make a great screen saver. It looks like his brain is short-circuiting. The two older men chuckle, but their scents sharpen, too.

I lean closer to Archer, drawn by the bourbon and spice. When our elbows bump, my neck flames. He offers me his shy smile, both of our gazes darting to Theo, who's still glitching.

I look back into the quiet alpha's dark eyes, whispering, "You're a doctor—do we put him in rice like a malfunctioning iPhone or just hit his reset button?"

Archer's laugh may be my new favorite sound. Warm and liquid, deeper than any I've ever heard. It feels *true*; as though it has to be *earned*. And I did it.

Theo pounds a giant fist into his sternum like he's giving himself CPR. His verdant eyes turn to Ronan. "Dude, I think I'm in love."

I know he's kidding. And exaggerating. So why does my heart flutter like a hummingbird's wings?

Ronan slides his gray gaze over my profile before giving his packmate a sly smile. "I think you have good taste."

And now my heart is *exploding*.

Not literally, thank God, but my face is definitely bright red.

Archer's grin grows—all perfect white teeth and over-full lips. He turns back to his dinner and continues his line of questioning as if we never detoured.

"So you're still looking for work here?"

The innocent question is an unfortunate reminder. "Anywhere, really." I stab a piece of watermelon. "I..."—*don't want to sound like a total loser so I can't tell them the* whole *story*— "manage on my own. So a steady source of income is important."

My face must register the spectrum of unpleasantness roiling inside of me, because Archer suddenly frowns. "If you don't mind me asking—why did you leave your last job?"

Oh *lord*. Am I going to have to tell these grown-up, gorgeous, outrageously successful men I got *fired*? Right now?

I start to panic. And, worse—I'm panicking about panicking. Because this is all so simple and so easy. I *should* be able to handle this. I *have to* be able to handle this. And if I can't...

If I can't then they'll all see me as incompetent and weak and needy. They'll be turned off and irritated. Or angry.

I'll lose this whole thing before it can even *be* a thing. Before I can even admit to myself that I might possibly *want* it.

Suddenly, Theo moves. He practically chucks his plate aside to lunge across the table and scoop me directly into his arms.

The air goes still while he folds me into his lap. Wrapping his arms around me, he squeezes protectively. "Guys," he growls. "Lay off."

I brace myself for the fall-out. After all, if Ronan and Archer didn't think I was pathetic before, they must think so now.

But Theo's lemongrass and blood orange scent lights up every receptor in my brain, the neurons practically chanting *safe, safe, safe.*

He nuzzles his cheek against my forehead, clearly scent-marking me. It's the sweetest form of acceptance. I don't know how to process it, but tension physically drains out of me anyway.

"That's better," he mumbles, cuddling closer. "Your scent was all burned butter. You're back to peaches now, precious girl."

Unlike Archer's smooth, deep timbre, Theo's purr sounds raspy. Almost hoarse, like it's never been used before. That notion gives me more joy than any other single thought I've ever had.

For one insane second, I'm so stupidly happy in our embrace, I don't notice that the other guys are clearly uncomfortable. Archer is still as death, and Ronan...

Good God, he's practically choking me. The sweet smoke I can't get enough of has swelled into something pitch black and completely overpowering.

Don't get me wrong—if I have to go, this is definitely the way to do it, choking on one of the best smells in the universe. I would have no regrets with this kind of erotic asphyxiation.

But I'm guessing the shift signifies some distress on his part. And when I peek over Theo's stacked bicep, I see that I'm right. Ronan looks thunderous.

He and Archer exchange a loaded look that settles him down a little. His eyes are still hot as a forge, but he winces. "We apologize if we made you uncomfortable, Meg. We've just been discussing your situation, and we want to help. We want to talk about the possibility of having you work for us remotely, but we wanted to know more about your situation first."

Theo bends closer and whispers loudly, "They're nosy fuckers."

Ronan's face flickers with the tiniest spark of humor. I like the way it settles in the corner of his mouth. "Yes," he confirms. "Basically."

Archer reaches across the table and gently cradles my hand in his. "I'm so sorry, sweetheart," he murmurs, utterly sincere. "I overwhelmed you."

...*What?*

No annoyance? Or anger? They aren't frustrated with me for being a baby or upset that I was uncomfortable?

They're just... sorry?

With a grumble, Theo reluctantly loosens his vice-grip on my body. Archer is patient. He waits for me to lean closer before standing and pulling me into his own arms, settling back in his seat with me curled on his lap, facing Ronan.

The rolling purr vibrates against my side, smoothing the last of the panic from my body. His hand cups my head. His eyes fly to his packmates' before settling back on mine, the dark color so solid and soothing.

"I hate to ask because I hate upsetting you, but we need to know if something happened at your old job so we can fix it. Was there a reason you had to quit so suddenly and didn't have time to do any research or make any plans?"

There's so much understanding layered into that question, I'm not even sure where to begin. How does Archer sense that something is off about the way I left my last job? How does he know I'm the type of person who would meticulously plan and look up all of my options before making a career change?

I stare at him; this stranger who seems to know me so well

without knowing me at all. Ronan surprises me by interrupting, shooting me a conspiratorial half-smirk. "He knows everything. I hate it."

It's the first little glimmer of—I don't know—*humanity* that Ronan's shown. He has such a *persona*. All the sly humor and hard stares and biting commands and perfect manners. This is the first thing he's said that feels... Ronan.

I love it.

A stupid grin fills my face, along with a burst of contentment in my chest. The combination makes it a hell of a lot easier to turn to Archer and sigh. "I didn't quit. I was chased out."

chapter
twenty-one

MEG'S EYES dart up to mine. Searching for disappointment.

I'm already addicted to the way she looks at me. Wanting approval. Direction. I've given it to her, and I'll give her more.

This little one is going to be *mine*.

Ours.

I can feel it.

And there will be a day when she knows as surely as I do that I'll never hurt her, that she'll never lose me. Until then, I have to be careful.

For the first time in my life, my alpha instincts urge me to tone my dominance down instead of ramping up. Some part of me recognizes how fragile this girl is. She doesn't like for anyone to see it, and she feels like she shouldn't ask for help, for some reason. But it's there. She needs nurturing.

Usually, I'd say that is not me. Let Archer and Theo cuddle her and compliment her. But, I don't know. I feel like I should soften.

Yield.

Only for her.

I catch myself at the end of a snarl, swallowing down the rest. Under her sweetly curved ass, Archer is still as stone. Theo keeps chewing, his teeth grinding as he goes. He pops his knuckles like he's planning to plant them in someone's face.

Meg's big, blue eyes land on mine, gaze seeking. The fact that I know exactly what she's looking for fills me with endless satisfaction.

"This is hard to talk about but you're doing so well," I approve. "Do you want to tell us more?"

I watch her throat work while she swallows, imagining how beautiful the thin skin would look with a bond mark branded there. She hangs her head. "I guess I probably should. I don't want you guys to find out later and—"

Decide you don't want me.

I'm not ordinarily one for subtext, but I can read hers. So can Archer. His arms bring her closer, his purr growing louder. "Sweetheart," he murmurs into her hair. "That won't happen."

Meg's gaze snaps to mine and darkens. She bites her lower lip and tries to talk around it. "I—It was an accident." She sees me note the lie in her eyes and quickly adds, "I think."

Not complete, immediate honesty, but that will take time. For now, she's done well. I'm proud. "Good girl. I know it isn't easy to tell us the truth, but we need to know so we can protect you."

Her cheeks warm under my praise, her body looser. Archer tosses me a small nod.

"So what exactly happened, precious?" Theo chimes, his fists opening and closing. He's pissed as hell. Half of his food sits uneaten—a dead giveaway where Theo is concerned.

Meg lets go of her lower lip, leaving it slightly swollen. Her fingers worry her hem some more. Until Archer notices and scoops her hand into his, massaging it.

I'm sure there's some documented therapeutic benefit of hand massages for omegas. And, of course, he's probably read every paper on the subject.

Whatever he's doing, it works. Meg sighs.

"It's always hard for an unbonded omega to get a good job," she mutters. "And I knew I would need one right out of school, so I did a dual-degree program to get my Bachelor's and Master's together. I spent my whole senior year applying to dozens of places all over the country and networking as much as I could remotely."

I'm already outraged, and we haven't even gotten to the story. It just seems so obviously unfair that she had to work five times harder than I ever would have to get a job she deserved.

"I found a position at the marketing firm," she goes on. "I was the assistant to one of the VP's when I started. An alpha. And he always acted...interested. But he has an omega and a pack, so I just figured he was a skeevy perv who liked to check out unbonded omegas and left it at that."

Archer tucks her hair behind her ear, nodding his understanding. Meg leans into his palm, and something in my chest cracks.

Fuck. It's been a long time since I remembered I had a heart in there.

"I got promoted," Meg whispers, like it's a mistake she made. "To a junior exec. They liked my omega demographic strategies."

"I like them too," I say. "I read your packet, and I think your ideas have a ton of potential. You're very impressive, little one."

Theo winks at her. "Gorgeous *and* brilliant."

Her timid smile warms my bones. And the way she looks up at Archer only makes it better—she already knows he's the shy one. The one who will understand her in that moment.

His mouth curls up in reply, long fingers smoothing her hair back again. "Then what happened, Meg?"

"It was probably stupid of me to take the job," she sighs. "As soon as I did, I was in individual meetings all the time. A lot of them were with my former boss."

She makes a bratty little snort that gets me half-hard. I like her sassy side. I'll like taming it even more.

Jesus, Ronan. Focus.

"I guess people figured he would be nice to me since I spent a year refilling his coffee and buying presents for his omega," Meg adds.

"Dick cheese," Theo grumbles.

Meg blows out a shakier breath. "We were supposed to be working on a scent spray campaign," she says, her voice losing strength. "We were in the conference room. Alone. And..."

She hangs her head fully, her voice under water. I'm vibrating with rage. I feel it rolling off Theo, too. But Archer is the best of us. And he just holds her tighter, waiting patiently.

It works. Meg raises her eyes to his, her face pleading. "I perfumed. In the meeting. I didn't mean to, I just— It wasn't even *him*. It was one of the spray samples they sent us. And I had on professional clothes. Including undergarments to block scent. But I guess he was sitting close enough to sense it, anyway..."

She flinches with remembered fear. "He *lunged* at me. And tried t-to bite me."

The fury inside of me hardens into ice.

"He *what*?" Theo half-shouts. "Oh *hell* no. Ronan, call the lawyers. I'm going to jail for murder."

"He tried to bite you," Archer repeats, nostrils flaring. "Were you all right? Did he hurt you?"

Meg fidgets, toying with her shirt again. "He twisted my wrist and bruised my arm pretty badly before I got away. The real injuries happened after, when he chased me out of the conference room and tried to corner me in a cubicle."

We all snarl. Meg shivers. "He destroyed the whole executive level in his rut. I wasn't focused on anything except getting away, so I didn't realize how banged up I got. The company lawyers claimed they weren't liable for anything because it happened due to my own actions. My own... um... arousal."

She mouths the last word, too embarrassed to say it out loud. I would find that cute if I wasn't about to rip someone's head from their body.

"They lied," I say flatly. "You had every right to sue. And you will, if I have anything to say about it. Forcing you into meetings, alone, with an alpha? Where you worked around synthetic pheromones? It's negligence. I'll gut them."

Wide blue eyes blink up at me. "You... will?"

I nod, the motion emphatic. "If you allow me to, absolutely."

She looks back at her busy fingers, her skin flushed again. "I—I really don't want anything from them. Except maybe my health-care back? Just for a few months?"

My packmates and I trade worried looks. She needs medical insurance, clearly. It's unacceptable to have her worrying like this. I open my mouth to tell her I will give her a limitless credit card right this second, but Archer catches my eye, his expression severe.

Right. I'm a jackhammer. And right now this girl is brittle as glass.

"We can discuss it more whenever you want," I promise. "But for now, we need to get you settled. Do you know where you'd like to stay? We have the guest room here. Or we can get you a hotel room."

I hate that idea—a hotel isn't as safe as our house or her own. But I don't want her to be hours away, and I know she may not want to stay with us. We technically aren't even courting her yet.

"I should go home," Meg murmurs. "I can't keep inconveniencing you all. And Remi—my local friend—doesn't have a ton of room."

All three of us bristle. We look at one another, at a loss for what to say. I stare at Archer, wishing he could read my mind.

I don't understand what's happening. If Meg is really our

mate, we shouldn't have to convince her to stay near us or to let us take care of her. She should be as desperate to take as we are to give.

Arch smooths his hand over her head and speaks gently. "Megera, you feel this, right? You know what's happening?"

She bites her plump lower lip. "We're... scent-sensitive? I think that's the term, right?"

Archer's face furrows with confusion but he nods. "Yes. How much do you know about scent-sensitive packs?"

Meg's head lowers in shame. "Not very much."

Theo looks like his heart is breaking. Poor big guy. He's from a scent-sensitive pack, and it's all he's ever wanted. It has to be a big blow to hear that our omega doesn't even know what she's in for.

Arch tucks her closer to his body and purrs louder. "Mm. Well, I have a ton of research on the subject if you want to read it."

Meg nods against his chest. I rub my forehead. "In the meantime, little one, you should probably stay nearby."

It would be fucking *painful* to have her hours away from us. Not just for us, but for her, too. She might not know it yet, but her Omega is going to freak the fuck out when she tries to leave here tonight.

Meg's fingers tangle in Archer's shirt, and he snuggles her tighter. "I—I think I want to stay in town. I'll ask Remi if she wouldn't mind having me."

Theo smiles at her. "Ask her if you can stay through the weekend! You can come watch our game!"

She smiles back at him. "I can do that... but I'm not sure about going somewhere big and public right now. These heat spikes are getting out of hand."

Fuck. She's right. If she attends as a guest of the team, she'll be in the staff box with a ton of alphas. If I get her and her friend tickets for stadium seating, they'll be sitting ducks. And we can't bring her into our pack's private booth without the press seeing her. If they find out we're courting, we'll have a media frenzy on our hands.

"You can watch the game here," I decide. "We'll set up the den for you and come straight home afterward to have dinner with you. All of us."

Because I will pry Declan's head from his ass if it's the last thing I do.

Meg flashes a smile that's as tremulous as it is beautiful. "Really? You guys don't want to, like, go out or something?"

Theo snorts, rolling his eyes. "Not without you, peaches, duh."

Archer chuckles and snuggles her some more. "How often do you have heats, sweetheart? How do you manage them?"

Typical doctor bullshit, interrogating her. Meg sighs, leaning back to gaze over at the pool while she thinks. "I usually take pain meds, curl up in bed, and wait them out. But I've never had spikes like these in between. Not until—"

She found us. An absurd burst of pride fills my chest. My scent spikes, and hers responds in kind. Peachy perfume winds around all of us. Theo grunts, shifting in his chair.

Meg clears her throat, clearly embarrassed. "Sorry. Anyway. I'm due for an early heat in about eight weeks. I've been on heat suppressants since I was sixteen, but the doctors think they're losing their effectiveness, now. I guess that happens after so many years."

Archer nods, his face solemn. "Yes. Eight years is actually a very long time to be on the suppressants in the first place."

Meg nods, looking tired. "I know. But I've been on my own the whole time, so I didn't really have any choice. I didn't realize just how poorly they were working until this week and all the... incidents. I guess their potency doesn't matter now that I don't have insurance to pay for them anyway. I'm not sure what I'll do when my heat comes."

Imagining her alone, in pain, needing—it takes me to a dark

place. I work to keep my voice steady. "You'll be with us. We'll take care of you."

A spectrum of emotions flies over her face. There's pure, raw desire. Longing and wistfulness. Awe. Gratitude. Doubt. Pain.

"You would want that?" she whispers.

Theo leans forward, slapping his palm on the table. "Are you kidding? That's like, my dream. In life. Seriously, peaches."

He always seems to make her smile. She giggles quietly, turning her eyes up to Archer. When he nods decisively, she looks over to me.

"It's what we all want," I tell her. "What we've always wanted. If you'll have us, we would love to court you until your heat, and take care of you through it."

Light builds and burns inside her blue eyes. Her teeth capture that lower lip again, betraying her uncertainty. She finally mumbles two words, "But... Declan."

Declan is currently the one and only thing standing between my pack and everything we've always hoped for.

Declan is going to get his ass in line, or I'll kick it.

Declan won't stop us from protecting this woman we're all so obsessed with.

"I don't want you to worry about it, baby girl," I tell her. "I'll take care of everything."

chapter
twenty-two

I'VE WATCHED all the game tape six times and gone over the play book twelve.

But it's well past nine, and no one is home yet.

They all rode together to take the omega home. Or to her friend's house. Whatever. I don't care as long as she isn't here.

I lie back on my bed, throwing a football straight overhead. Of all of the bedrooms in our pack house, mine feels the biggest because it's the emptiest. There's a king-sized bed—the upscale foam kind the trainers and physical therapists make all of us sleep on—covered in navy bedding and a walk-in closet that's bigger than any of the guys'.

My Heisman trophy sits on a set of floating glass shelves, illuminated by some magic up-lighting. It automatically adjusts with the light in the room. On nights like this, when I sit in the dark, that damn trophy is the only thing I see. Staring at me. Asking the same question.

Is this the best you'll ever be?

What if it is?

I lob the football back up at the vaulted ceiling and catch it right before it slams into my face. I've been doing that lately, too. Almost like I want it to hit me. Break my nose. Bruise my cheek.

It's an intrusive thought I can't shake. Almost the desire to be... ugly? For the outside to match the inside, at least.

And the inside is currently fourteen different types of fucked-up.

I'm here alone while my pack is out with an omega. Their omega, they claim. Which would, in theory, make her mine, too.

Most alphas wait their whole life to find their missing piece. Most want it more than anything. I know I did, before. So what the fuck is wrong with me now?

I don't know. All I know is that this ball keeps getting closer and closer to my fucking face and I'm pissed as all hell that they're not home yet.

Maybe it's her. The omega.

I knew she smelled all wrong in that interview. I'll be damned if I have that shit in my house, courting my pack.

They're the only family I have. Which is the problem here. Because, on one hand, I don't trust this scheming girl. And on the other, well, I better get over it if the rest of them decide she's ours.

Because after the hell I've put them through in the last two years, I won't be surprised if they choose her over me.

I might not even blame them for it.

There was a time when Ronan knew exactly what this pack needed and did everything in his power to get it. He paid matchmakers. He traveled across the country to meet eligible women. He signed our pack up for every scent-matching service from coast-to-coast and fielded each offer that came through.

Until sometime, about four years ago, he gave up. Couldn't do it anymore. None of us know why, but he went on one of his omega-scouting trips and came home a different man.

Colder. Darker. And 100 percent *done*.

Arch and Theo tried to talk him into trying again. I tried to help them. But once Ronan decided he was done, it was over.

That's when we started falling apart. Without that hope, I don't know. None of us knew what to do.

When we couldn't sway Ronan, we all tried to fix it in our own ways. Archer launched himself into his research and endless lectures. Theo signed up for every online omega-alpha dating service in the universe and went on more blind dates than anyone I knew.

And I...

Fucked everything up even more.

This time, the ball grazes my nose before I pluck it out of the air. And not a second too soon because my door suddenly flies open, and Theo charges, whooping like an oversized baboon.

He crashes onto the bed, belly flopping next to my feet and talking a mile a minute. It's clear from the grin stretched over his face that their evening went well. I don't let myself tune in enough to hear the details he spews. I lob the ball at his head to shut him up, but he just catches the damn thing and keeps talking.

Archer appears in the doorway. He leans against the door-jamb, his expression completely unrecognizable.

Who the fuck is this person? Dr. Archer Monroe is a serious guy. He doesn't smile like a moony asshole with stars in his eyes.

As soon as our gazes meet, the happiness drains off his face. A hard resolve I've never seen before takes its place. "I need one of your shirts."

Of all the things to ask me for, that one throws me. I jerk upright. "A what?"

"A shirt. Or I guess some sweats would work just as well."

There's an unyielding quality to him. I don't know what to do with it. My alpha instincts tell me to challenge him, duke it out. But he seems ready to actually fight me. And I honestly don't know if I want to punch my packmate in the face over a request I don't even understand.

"For. What?" I bite out, kicking Theo off my mattress. He rolls to the wood floor with a loud *thud*, still chattering on.

Archer stares me down. "I'm collecting clothing from each of us. For Meg."

Theo hops up and races out of the room the same way he zoomed in, shouting something about a hoodie for "his precious peach."

Dear *God*. They want to give her their shit? For what? There's only one reason why she would want our clothing. And there's no way *that's* happening.

"No." I glare. "Fuck no."

Archer doesn't blink. "It isn't what you think. We're not building her a nest. Yet."

My head is already shaking before he finishes. He shrugs. "If you don't like it, take it up with Ronan."

I hate how he does that. The two of them formed the pack together. Why does he defer to Ronan even when our pack alpha is being an asshole? Which is most of the time.

Arguing with Ronan is pointless. We're both too stubborn. Archer is easier. So I fire back, "No way. I'm not giving you my clothes. It's you guys she likes, anyway. I'm sure she'll be fine with your stuff for whatever weird omega bullshit she wants."

The flash of anger in his eyes is visible from across the room. "She didn't *ask*. She actually seems very uncomfortable with a lot of her omega urges. She *did*, however, specifically ask about *you* multiple times tonight. Do you know how hard it was to watch her face every time she remembered that you refuse to even meet her properly? For God's sake, Declan, we've been looking for the perfect omega forever, and she's here. She likes us. She wants to know you. Why can't you give this a chance? What is *wrong* with you?"

Everything.

I only have two talents... and I'm better at losing people than I've ever been at football. I guess I'd have a trophy for that, too, if they made one.

"You can't have my shit," I say with finality, turning away. "Now get out."

Archer's footsteps stride off. They sound agitated. Before I even finish glaring at the wall, I hear heavy, measured thumps approaching, along with the scent of smoke.

Ronan.

Right now his smoky smell is devoid of any trace of pleasantness, leaving a choking, ticklish feeling in my lungs every time I pull it in. Our alpha pauses in the open door, waiting for me to turn. But I don't. Can't, on some level.

Finally, he says, "The three of us are scent-sensitive to Meg. We've all agreed to court her. She's coming to dinner here on Sunday night, after your game."

No questions. No concern. Just pure, powerful Ronan. As per usual.

His words rattle around in my mind.

Scent-sensitive.

Court her.

Official.

There is one word none of them have said out loud. One that keeps swirling through my thoughts. I won't let myself focus on it.

I don't bother replying, either. Instead, I get up and walk over to close my door. Since, apparently, it needs to be locked to keep these assholes away from me and out of my goddamn laundry.

When I get close enough, Ronan's hand wraps around my upper arm. Over the wing tattoo I got to signify my commitment to our pack. Our family.

I expect him to squeeze, but he just waits until I turn my head. His storm-gray eyes are as solid and still as Archer's were.

Peaceful. Final.

"This is happening," he says. "You need to get on board, Declan."

I look down at where his fingers wrap around the feathers inked into my skin; his own thicker, curling black pattern layered over the top. They were supposed to be permanent symbols, more visible than bites or bonds.

I rip my arm away. "Or what?"

He looks me in the eye, the sheer force of his will indomitable. "Or else."

chapter
twenty-three

"YOUR BOOBS ARE ABSURD," Remi mutters.

I tug her T-shirt up over my chest, sighing. "If I had my own clothes, I might not look so ridiculous."

She smirks. "Somehow, I don't think they'll mind."

Her eyes trail around her apartment, pointedly flickering to each of the floral arrangements I've received over the week. There are three—one from each of the alphas who have professed their intentions toward me.

Archer's are the simplest—an arrangement of white and pink that came with the very sweetest note attached.

Ronan's are obviously the most expensive—all rare blooms in vibrant colors. They arrived with a pair of delicate aquamarine earrings.

Theo's came just this morning. A loud, orange arrangement of tropical flowers, perfect for an Ospreys' game day. His came with a box of outrageously large donuts.

I swallow hard, ignoring the pang in the chest when I wonder what sorts of flowers or gifts Declan Howard would send. If he deigned to acknowledge my existence.

That seems less likely by the day. He still won't even join our group chat.

After our impromptu dinner, the rest of the Ash pack created a text thread for us and proceeded to keep in constant contact all week. They wanted to know *every*thing. From my day-to-day plans to my thoughts and feelings about whatever topics came up.

They all texted the same way they spoke in real life. Theo sent the most messages, his focus leaping from one subject to the next with amazing speed.

He was also the most entertaining and relatable. I loved how open and guileless his messages felt. He told me how he felt with an ease I admired, actually. Constantly sharing that he missed me, he was thinking about me, and all sorts of sweet sentiments that turned me to mush.

Archer seemed more focused. He consistently steered our conversations back to me, asking question after question. His tone made me giggle—he typed like he was writing a research paper instead of a text and never used emojis. He was very fond of periods and commas, too.

Then, of course, Ronan. He answered the least out of the four of us, but most of his replies actually left me *swooning*. He'd certainly mastered the art of the panty-dropping one liner. And he asked me for photos almost every day.

In their own individual ways, they each made me feel desired and cared for. Even during their busiest week in months.

The League kick-off is a big deal, apparently. All week, the pack raced in and out of interviews, check-ups, fittings, and practices.

I tried insisting they didn't need to have me over after the game, but they all nipped my uncertainty in the bud. In fact, they insisted I come over to watch the whole production on their enormous flat screen.

When my primping time expires, Remi waves me out the door, humming happily around a stolen donut. "Have fun!"

At midday, the drive from Remi's place to the guys' only takes about ten minutes. Ronan said they would all be gone by lunchtime, but promised Mrs. Fleming would welcome me and get me "set up."

When I left on Wednesday, it was too dark to see the outside of their house in detail. Now, my jaw drops as I turn onto the wide gravel drive.

It's a—

I don't even know what to call it.

The word "mansion" seems outdated, but I guess that's what I'm looking at. "Architectural marvel" is more like it. Huge, black concrete rectangles stacked at artful angles, interspersed with walls of tempered glass and white stone accents. It all makes for a luxurious, masculine, absolutely *enormous*... well, mansion.

The dread of complete and total inadequacy rolls over me. My hands shake as I inch my tiny car up the driveway, suddenly wishing I had washed it or something. Parked in front of the gorgeous pack house, it looks every bit as pitiful as I feel standing there in my borrowed blue shirt and shorts.

I convinced myself the guys wouldn't care or even notice, probably. But now that I see how stylish and luxurious their house is in broad daylight, it's all I can do to keep myself from jumping back into my car and driving to the nearest mall.

Where I would have no money to spend.

But still.

The massive, beautifully-stained wooden slab at the front of the house falls open, revealing Mrs. Fleming in her canvas apron.

She waves me up the slate steps to the front porch, a friendly smile on her plump face.

When I get close enough, she pumps my hand in a firm grip, her smile widening. "Miss Reed! So lovely to see you again. The boys can't wait to come home to you tonight."

Come home to me?

Home... here? This insanely gorgeous house? To me? The girl who wears other people's panties?

Does not compute.

"They... are?"

She nods happily. "Come along, dear. I'll show you what they left for you."

She pulls me into the great room sprawling out from the base of the stairs. It's all I can do to keep walking and not freeze up again.

The room features a huge slate fireplace that stretches up to the ceiling. Over the blue flames crackling in the glass grate, a wide-screen television occupies the mantle space. There's one enormous U-shaped couch, all shiny brown leather.

I feel a pang at the emptiness of it all. My stupid omega brain tells me I need to fill the room with soft blankets and fluffy pillows and strong alphas.

Then I see it.

"Oh my God!" A startled laugh bursts out of me. "What did he *do*?"

By "he," I mean Theo. It can only be Theo. Ronan and Archer would never leave me something so insane. And Declan would never leave me anything at all.

Mrs. Fleming chuckles again, watching me pick up the... pillow-man? An assortment of men's clothing, all stuffed with pillows to make a full-sized man. One inhale tells me he's wearing clothing from all three of them.

The extra-long, super thick joggers are Theo's, of course. The crisp, black zip-up jacket smells of Archer's bourbon and bitters.

And under it all, there's a well-worn Ospreys' T-shirt steeped in sweet smoke.

Ronan.

I don't notice Mrs. Fleming slip away until she bustles back in, carrying a big tray of snacks. Every single food I've mentioned liking, actually. Stacked slices of thin-crust cheese pizza, bowls of kettle corn, Oreos, and pretzel bites.

She sets them in front of me without so much as a flourish and switches the huge TV on. The screen flickers to life.

It's pre-game coverage, with commentators throwing around odds and statistics that make my head spin. With a small, knowing smile, Mrs. Fleming hands me a notepad from a nearby side table. It's covered in neat block handwriting—notes about watching the game and a cheat sheet of football terms. I'd bet every penny in my wallet Archer wrote it out for me.

"Now that you're settled, I'll head out. I want to get home before kick-off! You enjoy the game, Miss Reed," Mrs. Fleming says cheerfully.

She disappears within moments. Leaving me alone in this several-million-dollar house like I own the place. I shake my head, reaching for a bowl of kettle corn and settling back into the soft leather.

On-screen, the camera pans over the sidelines of the game, where players gather and stretch. I see that the Ospreys' stadium follows the same motif Ronan seems to prefer for their home and office—matte-black, metal, modern frameless glass. All the seats are gaudy burnt orange, though; I smile, wondering if Theo picked the color.

The cameras snag their focus on Declan constantly. With black smudges under his bright blue eyes, he looks unfairly good. The big, broad shoulder pads under his black-and-orange jersey accentuate his narrow hips and powerful quads. And those *tight pants.* Good lord, they're practically *painted* on.

Is it hot in here?

If he's going to be such an ass, I wish he'd at least have the courtesy to be ugly, too.

"We all know Declan Howard came into this League with all the ammo he needed to become one of the greatest," a commentator intones. *"But since that first season ended in a disastrous championship performance, many have wondered if the Ospreys' stellar performance that year was just a flash in the pan."*

I frown.

Another announcer picks up where the first left off. *"I think most would agree that this is the season for them. Their last chance to come out swinging and show us all that they have what it takes here. Especially Declan Howard."*

They show him again. This time, he licks two of his fingers and grips the football before launching it down the sideline at a staffer in a polo shirt. I notice that all the Ospreys' employees have the same short-sleeved, collared white shirt on. I'm picturing how gorgeous Archer would look in one when I spot the orange logo emblazoned on the ball boy's chest.

The same one I sketched up for them. On national television.

I'm still in shock when my phone buzzes. A text from Ronan.

We'll discuss your payment for our new team logo tonight, it reads. As if they owe me anything after everything I put them through. *Everyone loves it. Thank you, little one.*

The cameras show the team's executive sky box next. It catches Ronan, in his same all-black suit, slipping his phone back into his breast pocket. He watches the field with a stony expression and dark sunglasses over his eyes. The announcer mentions his name, and a little graphic appears under his image, showing his title as the team owner and general manager.

He sees the camera pointed at him and barely flinches. But that one tiny drop of humor settles into the corner of his lips. And I somehow know it's just for me.

Yep. Definitely hot in here.

I keep my eyes peeled for Theo and Archer on the sidelines, although I don't expect to see the kind doctor—in fact, I suspect he goes out of his way to *avoid* cameras if he can.

The Ospreys are playing a team in red and white. I'm just about to check my notes for their name when I see a neon orange sign waving from our sideline.

Peaches, it says, *Check under the couch.*

Theo lowers the poster and smiles broadly. Everything south of my waist turns liquid at the sight of him.

My citrus-scented alpha is an absolute *mountain* in his shoulder pads. His biceps bulge as big as grapefruits while he thumps his chest and then points at the lens, his bearded mouth grinning wildly.

The male correspondent seems unsure how to explain what the audience just saw. He stutters some version of, *"I guess Theo Matthews has someone at home watching. I wonder how that will affect his game."*

Turns out, very well. By the middle of the second quarter, he's caught two touchdowns and made a couple of crucial blocks. The commentators keep saying his name, his stats climbing with every mention.

The game makes more sense to me as the minutes tick by. I can see what Ronan meant when he described Theo's position. If Declan wants to run or throw the ball long, the big guy rushes forward to take on defenders. When Declan calls for a shallow pass, Theo breaks away and fights men off to get open.

I thought it would be hard for me to watch, but with Archer's notes and the constant flashes of the Ash pack, I find the coverage riveting. I forget all about Theo's note until halftime, when they replay the footage of him waving the poster, speculating about the guys and their prospects. I jump in my seat and reach under the sofa.

It's a big bundle of polyester fabric. I shake it out and feel my face split in a grin.

An Ospreys' jersey with the number 01 emblazoned on it. I turn it over to read the name on the back, and my heart skips.

ASH PACK.

chapter
twenty-four

YOU WANT to know how I know this girl is the one?

Because I just had *the game of my life*, and all I can think about is getting home. To my couch.

To the gorgeous woman on my couch.

Of course, she's also the reason I kicked so much ass out there. Knowing she was watching juiced me.

In the locker room, Declan saunters off to go take all the credit for our win while I send a group text letting Meg know we're on our way. I decline interviews and rush through my shower before hustling the others out of the stadium.

Archer and Ronan, anyway. At this point, we're all barely speaking to Dec.

It feels wrong. Especially for me. Problem is—the only thing that feels even *worse* is the thought of not talking to Meg.

I'm the first one into the house, practically leaping out the back of Ronan's Rolls. I fling the garage door open and shout, "Peaches?!"

I hear a squeal and the slap of bare feet on the marble floor. That's so fucking cute, I'm already grinning when she barrels around the corner, wearing the custom jersey I had made for her.

It's the real deal—the same make as the one I wore on the field today. Only, on our gorgeous girl, it's more like a dress than a top. I only have half a second to notice that she's pants-less before she launches herself through the cased opening of the kitchen and leaps right into my arms.

Uhhhhhgnnnn.

Hoooooooly fuckinggggg—

I just spent three hours with three-hundred-pound monsters trying to knock my lights out, but none of them came anywhere near this close to taking my legs from under me.

What the—?

I knew she smelled amazing. Perfect. Like heaven.

But this?

This is *nirvana*.

This is so impossibly *good*, it's going to *kill me*.

My body acts on impulse, gathering the sweet source of my torment up into my chest, purrs rattling automatically.

Peaches clings to my neck. Big, blue eyes lock on mine. My arms are sore as shit but that will never stop me from banding them under her cute ass, balancing her weight against me.

She smiles wide, little hands coming up to hold my cheeks. "I am so proud of you, big guy."

I didn't expect that. The words or the total sincerity of them. She really means it. She watched my game, and she is proud of me.

The air sweeps out of my lungs and doesn't come back. My

chest burns, along with the bridge of my nose. I've never been on the verge of tearing up while my dick is this hard, but fuck it. For her? I'm down.

For her? I'm starting to think I'll do anything.

Our limbs curl around each other in another hug. Her scent hits me all over again, pounding into my blood with a steady pulse all its own.

Before I know what's happening, we both have our faces buried in each other's necks. I can tell she's inhaling me the same way I'm huffing her down, and that makes me even harder.

Shit. My knot is *throbbing* and she hasn't even touched me. We haven't even *kissed*.

That suddenly seems like a huge fuck up on my part.

I should have kissed her in that elevator. In the parking lot. On the lanai.

And I'm sure as hell gonna kiss her right the fuck now.

As long as she wants that.

Her legs cinch tighter, pressing her panty-covered core into my abs. She whimpers, the sound small and desperate enough to snap my last thread of self-doubt.

In one motion, I have my right arm parallel with her spine, my hand cupping the back of her head. The left tucks her hips in tighter, my fingers kneading the soft perfection of her ass while I seal my mouth over hers.

Oh my fuuuck—

She tastes as good as she smells, which just should not be possible. How am I supposed to impress her with my kissing skills when I can't even breathe? The pleasure coursing through me from the soft brush of the tip of her tongue over my lower lip is strong enough to wind me.

This isn't the type of first kiss I imagined. There's nothing innocent about it. My gorgeous girl isn't shy or hesitant at all. She practically climbs me, fisting one hand against the collar of my Henley and another in the man-bun at the back of my neck.

Fuck. Me.

Every time I think I appreciate just how lucky I am to have found her; she blows my mind in a brand-new way.

Our lips rub over each other in wet, dirty glides. When she nips at me with her teeth, I groan, locking her as close as I can without hurting her.

She starts moving her center over my middle, grinding like she can feel the ridges of my abs against her pussy. The thought makes my cock jump.

The hand under her ass slides closer to her core on instinct. I somehow stop myself from reaching for her panties. But when I do, she fucking *whines*.

I've never hated and loved a sound more. It means she needs me and wants me, which is bliss. But it also means she *needs* something, and I'm not giving it to her fast enough. Which makes me feel as close to feral as I've ever been.

I rip myself back, panting while I examine her face.

Tell me what you need, precious.

Anything. Anything. Anything.

She looks almost high? Her pupils are blown, bleeding over the pretty blue I'm used to. A clear, bright pink covers her cheeks. And pure heat radiates from her skin.

Heat.

Heat.

Oh shit.

I feel it a millisecond later—wet warmth, seeping into my shirt, soaking the fabric between her pussy and my stomach. Which means she's probably already drenched her underwear.

Which means I'm about three seconds away from *rutting her into next year.*

Shiiiiiit.

"ARCH!" I yell, using the hand on her head to cradle her against my neck, protecting her ears from my shouting. "ARCH, GET THE HELL IN HERE, MAN!"

"Sorry, sorry," comes a sarcastic mutter. "Was just unloading your gym bag contents into the washing machine before the smell permanently—"

His voice cuts off as he walks into the kitchen from the mudroom. I turn, still clutching our girl in my arms, and shoot him a desperate look.

He understands right away. His nose flares while he inhales, his own eyes dilating behind his glasses before he blinks the instinctive lust away. Or at least tucks it down.

"How long?" he asks calmly, striding toward us. "Was she like this when you walked in?"

Peaches seems oblivious to our conversation. She makes a humming sound and licks a hot stripe up the side of my neck. I grunt while a burst of pre-cum slicks the head of my very hard, very uncomfortable dick.

"She was happy to see me," I reply, my voice tight as I try not to breathe. "I picked her up. We were kissing..."

Arch is careful. He reaches over very slowly, trying not to nudge me any closer to a rut. I'm already dangling on the edge—any aggression or territorial bullshit, and I might try to snap his hand off.

The urge to protect is every bit as strong as the urge to fuck. I want Meg so much it's killing me. The thought of anyone harming her or tearing her away is the only thing strong enough to distract me from taking what her body is offering.

There's also a small, logical part of my brain screaming at me. Reminding me that just because her body is offering doesn't mean *she* is. She might not even know what's going on if she really is in—

Oh God.

We are so not ready for this shit.

"You're doing great, Theo," Arch murmurs. "Keep holding your breath if you're close to losing control. This might be a real heat or it could just be a hormone spike. We need bloodwork to know for sure."

Peaches whines into my neck again. This time, the noise sounds distinctly distressed.

And I am not. Fucking. Having. It.

With a deep growl, I rip her away from Archer's hands. "*No!*"

And, of fucking course, that's when Ronan strides in. He's slipping his phone into his pocket and unbuttoning his collar when he stops short, taking in the scene spiraling out of my control.

His nostrils flare. Gray eyes sharpen. "*Omega.*"

Archer lets out a growl of his own, more vicious than I've ever heard. "*Stay right there,*" he barks, glaring at our alpha. "Theo is on the precipice of a rut, and none of us have Meg's consent. If she really is in heat, I need to take her—"

I hear *take her,* and that's it.

I'm gone.

All my thoughts are replaced by the image of them *taking her away from me.* And I can't deal. I snarl loud enough to shatter glass. And everything goes white.

chapter
twenty-five

ARCHER

THEO AND MEG are completely lost in themselves.

They stand in the entryway of the kitchen, kissing feverishly and breathing in the scents from each other's throats. She's whining, the desperate, high-pitched plea making us all wild. Theo responds instinctively, purring and growling to soothe and dominate her the way she needs.

Honestly? If I wasn't the only mildly-sane man in the room right now, this would be my exact brand of porn.

But I am a doctor, and I want to be this woman's alpha.

So I can't exactly take my dick out of my pants while her safety is still in question.

Not that I think Theo would hurt her. I know he never would intentionally. I also know that he's a very large guy who tends not to know his own strength and has never knotted anyone before. He could easily harm her without ever meaning to—and that doesn't even take into account the fact that Meg isn't in her right mind at the moment. She could snap out of this hormone surge any second and be horrified by the whole scene.

During our dinner on the lanai, I got the sense that she was embarrassed about her omega tendencies. I've read about designation shame. It's rare—most omegas are taught very early on how wondrous their bodies and their instincts are. Rightly so. But some people struggle with their needs and their heart's desires. I sensed that struggle in Meg when she perfumed for one of us or swallowed her whines.

That was the reason I collected clothing from all of us to give to her. I want her to know we love her instincts and all of the omega urges that go into who she is.

Moreover, we will fucking *cherish* them. They are a gift—the exact softness we need to connect all four of us.

Before last week, I'd started to think I would never get to take care of an omega the way I longed to. Now that I have the opportunity, I certainly don't want her to feel bad for allowing me the honor.

Which makes this even more complicated.

I wish I knew her better. Just a few more dates, and I would probably have at least a basic sense of what she would want in this moment.

I know she adores Theo. It's clear by the way she's drawn to him. They've been more physical than the rest of us so far—I think it's just their individual natures and the dynamic they create together. They're both loving, upbeat people. I'm sure it feels natural for them to give each other affection.

So maybe I should just let them?

Fucking hell, why do all of these monumental decisions end up falling to *me*?

Ronan finally moves, shaking off my earlier command. For a second, I'm poised to put myself in his path, but he isn't looking at Meg and Theo. He comes over and plants a firm hand on my shoulder.

"Talk to me," he demands. "What are our options if we can't take her anywhere?"

Something about his grip grounds me. Ever since Meg came into the picture, I've realized how little the four of us touched each other. It seems strange, now. Sure, we've never been romantic or sexually interested in one another, but we're a family. Why were we shying away from physical proximity?

It's helping. The itch under my skin—the one begging me to rip Meg away from the other alpha and keep her all to myself —dissipates.

This is *Ronan*.

That's *Theo*.

These are my packmates, and I care about them as much as I care about the girl we all desperately want to please and protect.

But I have no idea how we do that without hurting her.

Ronan senses my anxiety and squeezes my neck. Hard. "Hey. *Hey.* You know everything about this shit, Arch. I know you know what to do. Think about what you would tell a patient if they asked you what to do in this situation."

He's clearly on the very edge of his control, too, but he's holding on. For her. For us. Because, for all his faults, Ronan is a natural-born leader.

Tuning out a particularly enticing moan and tamping down the burning desire to know what caused it, I close my eyes.

Can't take her from Theo.

Can't let Theo knot her.

Can't do bloodwork to see if this is a real heat or a spike.

Can't—

I eliminate treatment options systematically, until only one remains.

"Easing."

Ronan nods, even though he has no idea what I mean. Behind me, Meg cries out. His graphite gaze flickers to her before snapping shut. His jaw flexes as he grinds his teeth. "How does easing work?"

It takes way more effort than it should for me swallow. "We essentially take the edge off. If it's just a spike, easing will get her through it. If it's a heat, then she'll bounce right back after. But at least Theo will be in his right mind, however briefly."

If Theo wasn't so busy, he'd make some dumb joke about "post-nut clarity." But, in this case, it wouldn't be so dumb.

None of us are going to be able to avoid rut if we try to keep ourselves locked down like this. Maybe with any other omega; but this is Meg. Our scent-sensitive perfect match. She's ours. And every bit of alpha inside each of us is going to fight to get to her.

Better we give our bodies a small taste of what they crave than try to control them and fail entirely.

"We'll go to the living room," I decide.

Our biggest packmate snarls at that directive. I turn and find him glaring at me, green eyes eclipsed by blown pupils and devoid of any semblance of reason. It galls me to offer submission, but I show him my palms anyway. For Meg.

"It's okay, big guy," I say blandly, hoping her nickname for him might help. "No one will take the omega from you. You can have her. We just have to talk about keeping her happy. You want that, right?"

Theo's thick brow lowers, but he grunts.

"Why don't you take her on the couch?" Ronan tries. "Let her ride your knot there. With the leather? We'll never get the smell of her sweetness out."

He knows more about this shit than he gives himself credit for. Which is obvious when Theo's eyes light up, and he immediately hauls Meg into the family room.

Keeping one eye on the pair, he mutters at me, "What now?"

I scratch the back of my neck. "Think of easing as edging, only we let her come as much as we can."

"So, basically, edging for *us*." Ronan hisses the words like he's angry, but starts unbuttoning his shirt. His free hand pulls out his phone. "I'll text Declan. Tell him not to come back here until I give him the all-clear. The last thing we need is his hostile ass walking into the middle of this. You get in there. We can't leave them alone."

He doesn't have to tell me twice.

chapter
twenty-six

"HOWARD!"

My name rings over the locker room bustle. The kink between my right arm and my shoulder blade twinges.

Coach Henshaw doesn't wait for me to reply before he tacks on, "My office!"

Our rookie kicker, DeLuca, sighs next to me. I don't blame him. He missed a field goal during his first game in the League. Though, to be fair, this was a hell of a first game.

The other team was favored to win by a slight margin. No surprise, given my shitty stats last year. Unfortunately, a lot of us used that chip on our shoulder as an excuse not to take them as a serious threat. And the fact that Theo essentially saved our asses is looming over all our heads.

Practice is going to suck tomorrow.

I clap the rookie on the back while I hoist my duffle bag up onto my good shoulder. "You'll hit them all next week," I tell him. "The first time is always the hardest."

Theo would make a virginity joke right about now, but the spot on my other side is noticeably empty. My three packmates bailed as quickly as humanly possible after the final play, leaving me to—once again—do all of the schmoozing and take all the hits from the press.

I can already hear the comments they'll make on ESPN all week. The turnovers I almost caused. My sloppy footwork on a few drives. How I released the ball too quickly.

They'll all lay odds on whether I'll ever get back to the level I used to play at. The quarterback I was *before*—

"Howard! *Now.*"

Ronan would lose his shit if he knew how often this bastard barks at me. Sometimes, I consider telling him, but what good would that do? I'm already the reason we're this clusterfuck. I shouldn't complain when there are consequences.

While I stomp out of the locker room, my phone dings. Reception in our stadium is usually fine, but the showers are at the lowest level, underground. Most of the time, it takes walking into the hallway for my phone to come to life.

There are a few messages from other NFL players and friends —the ones I know well are polite and encouraging... the ones I know *really* well are already talking shit. Most days, their comments would roll right off. Hell, I might even get a kick out of some.

But right now my pack is off courting their mate without me.

My coach is pissed.

And my shoulder hurts.

While I trudge up the corridor, I start to think I might be

going about this all wrong. Maybe I should be home with my family. Trying my best. Wrestling my issues down to give this girl at least half a chance.

My phone vibrates again. A message from Ronan.

Telling me not to come home.

And now I think maybe I'm too late. They've all made their choice—they've chosen each other. And I'm about to lose a lot more than a stupid fucking game.

chapter
twenty-seven

THE ALPHA HAS TOO many clothes on.

I whimper, tugging at his scratchy pants and the layer of fabric under them. Why does he keep making me do that? Why isn't he naked yet?

I'm about to start begging when he walks us into a different room. I can't care where we are. I only care that he's finally using one of his hands to undo his pants and shove them down. As soon as they're out of the way, his big, hard cock springs up and smacks my ass.

Oh my *God*. Why am I still wearing underwear? This is

torture. I want skin-on-skin. A frantic whine builds in my throat, sharp and full of frustration.

"Shhhh, sweetheart." It's the other alpha. The one who smells like spice and sounds like deep, calm water. I want to *drink* him.

"You want your panties off?" he continues. "You want to feel your alpha without anything in the way?"

My lip hurts from how hard I'm biting it as I whimper more, nodding. That's all the big alpha holding me needs to reach down and rip my black boy shorts right through the crotch.

Which is *so. Effing. Hot.*

My pussy clenches on air. A painful pulse echoes through my empty core while fresh slick pours down my thighs.

I hear voices—something about someone sitting down and someone else taking off his shirt for him. I don't care at all because seconds later, the big alpha lowers us into soft leather. And, suddenly, all of his perfect, scorching skin is on display.

I attack it, nuzzling his chest, kissing his pecs, licking up to the delicious warmth of his neck. His head falls back, his hands gripping me harder while he groans.

This is what I was made for. To make this alpha happy. To make him come. He has to mark me with it, then mark me with his bite. So I'll be able to take care of him forever.

But, first, I need him to make this pulsing *pain* go away.

"Please, Alpha," I beg. "It hurts."

There's panic building under my skin, pressing out of my pores. I need, I need, *I need.*

Someone has to *help* me.

"*Omega.*"

The sweet, intoxicating scent of smoke curls around me like incense. It's coming from the third alpha, the one whose voice eliminates all doubt, fear, or uncertainty.

Because I *know*—when he speaks, I obey.

My eyes snap to his automatically. He's positioned behind the alpha I'm on top of, standing just past his massive, muscled shoulder.

Burning silver eyes meet mine, full of possession and lust. Everything I want and need.

"Perfect," he praises, the word a caress. "You're going to grind on Theo's cock for us while we watch. And if you're good, maybe we'll take our cocks out for you, too. Would you like that, baby girl?"

I'm panting with how much I would like that. His face softens a tiny bit, the expression familiar as half of his mouth curls up at the corner. The little piece of humanity he only seems to offer me.

Ronan, a distant part of my brain shouts, her voice distorted, like it's under water.

That's Ronan and this is Theo.

Mine, the echo in my chest corrects. *They are all mine.*

The thought hits my heart, making it flutter while I gush more slick for them. Under me, the one called Theo groans again, his body surging up to connect with my core. Ronan's hand lands on his shoulder.

"*No*," he barks quietly. "You're going to let her use you."

Theo and I both moan at that thought. His big hands frame my hips, positioning my clit right along his thick, steely length. I can't see it clearly from where I am, but I size him with my body, gliding up and up and *up*.

He doesn't end until well past his navel, where the weeping tip of his cock presses into the ridges of his abs. I slide up over those, too, mewling at the texture against my buzzing clit.

Theo's fingertips dig into my hips, bruising. The thought makes me wild. I want those marks. I'll take any he'll give me.

The deep, clear voice rings behind me, sending a thrill down my spine as my fuzzy mind remembers his name.

Archer.

"So beautiful," he purrs. "Work him harder, sweetheart."

The alpha under me pants and moans while I press down. My hips snap forward and back, chasing the electricity humming through my center.

I can't even keep track of the sounds pouring out of me. The air is thick between us, my sweet scent meshing with his herbaceous lemongrass and sharp citrus.

I lick at his pulse, sucking his skin into my mouth. I want to bite him. I *need* to—

"*No, Omega*," Ronan barks. "Be my good little girl and tease him. No bites."

I whine, and Theo snarls. One of his hands flies up and catches a handful of my hair, yanking me closer. The new angle hits me differently, and I scream, the cry reverberating off his wide, straining chest.

With one final roar, his cock jerks under me, shooting thick ropes of white over his entire abdomen, smearing into the bottom of my breasts while I lose control.

The man under me seems dazed, but the one behind me sounds tighter. "Tell me how she feels, Theo."

He sighs, the rough sound as rumbly as his purr. "Fucking heaven," he grits out. "She's pulsing all over my cock. And when she slides down far enough, her pussy tries to grip my knot."

His hands have softened, petting and stroking, guiding me over him faster and faster. "That's right, precious. Grind that gorgeous slick-soaked pussy all over that knot. So fucking *perfect*."

His lips find mine, tongue teasing just so, pushing me into oblivion.

chapter
twenty-eight

THE FOG CLEARS AS QUICKLY as it came over me.

And I would be jumping off the nearest cliff right about now, if I didn't have the world's most gorgeous pussy wrapped sideways around my still-throbbing dick.

Fuck. My knot has never been this big. I can't imagine how I'll ever fit it in her without hurting her.

If she ever wants to look at me again after this.

I gulp down a thick wash of shame as she flops onto my chest, spent, our mess slicked between our bare bodies. I'm already reaching around, feeling for a blanket to cover her, when one flutters down around us. I glance behind me to find Ronan there, tucking the fabric around us with one hand while the other squeezes his cock through his closed suit pants.

An embarrassed mutter comes from the other side of the couch. "Shit."

Ronan moves again, tossing a kitchen towel over to Archer. His pants are around his knees, his dick covered in a thick layer of cum. He promptly sets to work cleaning up and then slips out of the room, murmuring, "Watch her. I'm going to get a thermometer."

Meg snuggles into my neck, sighing sleepily. I watch her every move, memorizing them. Because I know when she wakes up she might not want anything to do with me.

Ronan settles a firm hand on my shoulder. "You did good, Theo."

I shake my head, chagrin swamping me. "No. She was going into heat, and I snapped into a rut. I could have—"

The words choke off. I can't even say them.

Ronan squeezes my neck, making me turn my head. His steel eyes glint. "You snapped into a rut and didn't take her. You didn't even touch her without permission. You thought about her consent, even when you weren't in your right mind. Honestly, big guy? I don't know many alphas who could have done the same."

My hand shakes while I pet Meg's silky blonde hair. "What if she's mad?"

Ronan sighs. "We won't know for sure until she wakes up. But I'm betting she'll be more embarrassed than angry."

Archer strides up, back to looking like a doctor and not a guy who just jacked off watching his packmate grind his dick against a hot omega. He leans over us and presses a thermometer to her forehead, tsking quietly while he nods. Some of the tension perched on his brow disappears.

"Fever's gone," he reports. "It was just a spike."

His dark eyes shift, meeting mine. Some of the worry ebbs, and something new takes its place.

Is he... proud? Of *me*?

"Well done, Theo. You gave her exactly what she needed."

And I know I should be shitting a brick that my gorgeous girl could wake up and slap me right across the face. But here's the thing: I am the pack fuck up. I forget my chores. I'm late for shit. I don't remember where I set the mail or what password I used when I reset the wi-fi. I ruin clothes in the wash and leave puddles on the wood countertops.

So hearing both of my packmates tell me I didn't fuck this up?

It means more than I imagined it ever could.

I press my face against her temple. "She's exactly what I need."

Archer's hand grazes mine as he sets it on top of her head. "Me, too, big guy."

chapter
twenty-nine

I WAKE up pleasantly cool and deliciously warm all at once.

It's dark? Nighttime, for sure. And I'm in my new jersey... without panties.

A quick peek from one eye tells me I'm crashed out in someone's bedroom. The motif is somber—shades of gray mixed with no-nonsense wooden furniture. I can already guess it's Archer's room before I see the medical texts stacked on his desk and the large Vitruvian Man print hanging over it. Somewhere in the distance, a fire crackles; but the delicious smoky smell surrounding me isn't coming from any fireplace.

Ronan.

He's under me. Which means the very solid pillow propped against my back probably isn't a pillow, but another muscled alpha chest.

How did we end up in a cuddle puddle in Archer's bed?

Oh. My. God.

In a flash, I remember everything: Ronan standing behind Theo's naked chest. Archer's sure, steady fingers checking my temperature and my pulse. Theo's green eyes burning with feral need. And then burning with *pain.*

That last memory has me lurching upright, gasping.

Theo. Where is he?

Is he okay? Did I hurt him?

Oh God, I was insane. And after his big game!

I ruined everything!

Ronan's bark is so soft, it hardly even registers as a command, "*Breathe,* omega."

I gulp down air and realize I'm sobbing. Purrs break out all around me, filling the dim, quiet bedroom with three different types of comfort.

"Theo!"

I pick his rumble out of the others and fling myself toward the foot of the bed, where he lies propped up on one elbow. He's blurry from my panicked tears, but I can see that he's shirtless, wearing army green joggers, with his hair pulled back into a loose bun.

I press my palms to his chest, frantically searching for the injury I caused in my hormone haze. "I'm sorry, I'm sorry," I cry. "I don't know what happened to me, but I'm so, so *sorry.*"

Theo's rusty purr deepens, his arms coming around me in a huge bear hug. "No, precious, *I'm* sorry."

...

WHAT?!

He means it. I can tell from his scent alone—the lemongrass is subdued, the citrus so sharp my nose tingles in alarm. But how can he possibly be apologizing to me? I was the one who totally lost it and ruined their entire night.

I try to teeter upright. Theo only loosens his hold enough to let me balance on my knees, sitting up to keep us chest-to-chest. I brush my messy hair back with two hands, blinking at his tortured expression.

He has no reason to feel bad, though. He was perfect. A dream.

I've spent my whole adult life terrified of accidentally sending an alpha into rut. After what happened at my last job, I thought any alpha in that state would be a savage beast hell-bent on his own pleasure.

But Theo didn't even touch me, really. Sure, he held me and undressed us both when I begged him to... but he didn't press one single advantage or take any liberties.

Hell, he could have knotted me and I wouldn't have blamed him, since I was asking him to. Instead, he let me take what I needed and didn't demand *any*thing. I don't even think he barked.

"Are you *crazy*?" I sob, touching his perfect face, trying to wipe his guilt away. "What could you possibly be sorry for? I *attacked* you. I—I lost it. I put you into a rut. I—Oh God, did I actually use you like a human dildo?"

I'm so mortified, I want to die.

Kill me. Please.

But Theo's pained face splits into a wry grin. "You sure did, gorgeous. And it was seriously hot. Even the good doctor couldn't keep it in his pants."

Grimacing, I turn my head to face Archer and Ronan, who both sit against the headboard, look shockingly calm and not at all furious? *What in the—?!*

Ronan is wearing sweatpants. Gray ones, too. The color perfectly outlines his enormous erection while his tight black T-shirt sets off his bulging arms and the bold, sensual lines covering his left side.

As my wide eyes meet his, he cocks that small half-smile I love. It's a little rueful and almost surprised. Like he can't quite believe he's actually happy and expressing it.

Archer seems a bit more wary. At first I think it's because he witnessed me go feral in the middle of their seven-million-dollar kitchen. Then I see the uneasy way he scratches at the back of his neck.

"I owe you an apology as well, Meg," he intones, his deep voice calm and sincere. "I probably should have left the room when I smelled your heat perfume. I knew I wouldn't be able to control myself for long, and I chose to take the edge off for myself. At the time, I figured it would help me think more clearly in case you were actually in heat. But I also admit that part of me simply lost control. I'm so sorry if anything I did breached your boundaries."

Theo keeps hold of my right hand while I reach my left out to Archer, stretching to try to touch his face. He immediately moves forward, his crawl somehow sinuous.

My voice is small. "You liked seeing me that way?"

Archer exhales hard, his nod jostling my fingers as I trace his brow. "You were everything I never dared to dream," he murmurs, his dark eyes piercing behind his glasses. "Every last thing, sweetheart."

He takes my hand and kisses the knuckles before setting it over his heart and the worn Duke sweatshirt stretched across his chest.

I'm still gaping as he goes to work, silently smoothing his palms over various parts of me and gently probing with his fingertips at others. Examining me, although doing it so sweetly I can't help but lean into his purring chest and close my eyes. When he's satisfied, he caresses long lines down my spine for a moment.

"Baby girl."

Soft demand laces Ronan's voice. I blink out of my purr-induced stupor and move without even meaning to.

Because when he calls, I come. Evidently.

Ronan pulls me into his own lap like it's the most natural thing in the world. His sharp silver eyes simmer over my features, reading every tiny nuance before tightening slightly. "We need to talk."

Oh boy.

I get that stomach-dropping-through-the-floor feeling, reminiscent of being called to the principal's office. Only it's worse, because my Omega is frantic at the thought of truly disappointing Ronan.

He notes the tears that instantly fill my eyes and purrs louder. "Relax, little one. I'm not upset."

Unlike Theo's rattle and Archer's rolling hum, Ronan's chest sounds the deepest and vibrates the hardest. The jet-engine rumble resonates inside of me, instantly unwinding the tension in my muscles and unclogging the lump in my throat.

"Shhh, baby girl." He pets my head, his long, thick fingers slowly moving over my hair and cheek in soothing passes. "Daddy's not mad."

That one sentence unlocks some scary corner closet deep inside of me. A place where all sorts of things I never want to look at have accumulated over the years—the little girl who never seemed to do anything exactly right, the teenager who just wanted approval, the woman who craves a man's sincere praise.

All these parts of me that don't know what it's like to truly please someone... but always wondered. Always wanted.

How does he know?

Ronan feels me snuggle closer and smiles into my hair. "You like that?" When I nod, he presses a firm kiss into my temple. "Me too, baby girl. You and I will work that out between us. Soon."

A happy flutter dances in my stomach, spinning and swooping until it smolders lower. I'm still embarrassed and more than a little flustered, but his promise is too tempting. A small burst of perfume rises off me, mingling perfectly with the sweet smoke, spice, and citrus surrounding us.

I open my mouth to apologize, but Theo groans like he just

bit into the world's most delicious dessert. Archer's laugh is velvet as he falls back onto the bed, the motion uncharacteristically carefree.

"Fuck," he says, always so soft and level, even when he curses. "That smell—all of us together—it's like a miracle."

"You hear that, peaches? Absolute fucking miracle," Theo moans, still sounding borderline-pornographic. "And I found you first. Nailed it."

When I giggle, my scent rising, they both grunt before laughing again.

Ronan smirks, his eyes landing on mine. "Seems my pack is as just obsessed with making you happy as I am. You know what that means, little one?"

I smile, my teeth trapping the corner of my lip as I shake my head.

Ronan leans in, his mouth sealing over mine in a kiss that's all dominance. Pure, undiluted power. And just the slightest thread of tenderness.

I'm already breathless when he pulls away. But then he goes and says, "It means you'll be staying right here."

chapter
thirty

MY ASS HAS BEEN KICKED forty-five different ways by the time I park my Bugatti in last available slot in our garage.

I kill the engine, my head falling back against the hand-stitched leather seat. Blinking, I stare up at the dark fabric above while total silence engulfs me. It starts out peaceful, but gradually builds into a sort of static, pressing into my skull.

Fuck.

I'm so tired.

I don't want to deal with this shit now.

So I don't. I shove it all back down into the dank hole it came from and pop my door open. My shoulder shrieks when I hoist myself out of the low-riding convertible, my neck throbbing from the way my muscles lock around the pinched nerve.

Archer is going to be pissed I didn't tell him during the game. Ronan will be pissed I even have a shoulder and the human ability to injure it.

And Theo is probably dead by now, drowned in omega pussy.

I'm going to walk in there, and he'll be all up in my shit, singing the girl's praises. Ronan will give me that disapproving glare he loves so much. And Archer will be quietly disappointed in me, which is almost worse.

Frankly, after the way they banished me from my own goddamn house for the better part of the night, I should be the one pissed off at them.

I'm actually furious with myself for not being angrier. This is my home. My pack. My family. I should be fucking furious that they're choosing some chick over me.

But instead I just feel... alone.

Lonely.

I miss them. The shit heads. I miss them, and I hate them for it. But not as much as I hate myself for it.

My shoes and suit jacket don't even make it into the house. I kick out of the loafers and rip my tie open, happy to see it go after the way it strangled me through a dozen interviews.

Coach was a dick, too. It's to be expected, when someone is at my level and plays a mediocre game. Still, I want to talk to Theo about it. He'll understand. He's been listening to my quarterback bullshit for ten years. Plus, since he plays a position on the other side of the ball, he usually has good feedback for me.

I shuffle into the house, ready to set shit straight with the guys. But there's no one there.

The entire first floor is completely empty. I know because I walk through it, not quite believing my eyes.

The lights are all off. Even the porch lights and the lanai. It's only nine. Why would they all be in bed? Unless...

I rip my phone out of my pants and scroll through a bunch of bullshit to find a text from Ronan.

RONAN

> We have Meg in Archer's room. She's had a hard night and needs down time. It's probably best if you sleep in your own room and keep your shit attitude to yourself.

I stand in the dark kitchen, staring down at the screen. Feeling fucking devastated, honestly.

Outside of the game, the guys are all I have. And everyone knows pro-athletes have a shitty shelf life. Once my football career is over, if I don't have the pack, who do I have?

No one, a familiar voice hisses. *You've never really had anyone. No one has ever wanted you for anything other than your face, your spiral, or your knot.*

Sadness settles in my center like a gut-punch. Throbbing until it starts to seethe. Simmering into the spite I know so well. The type I've used as motivation my whole life.

Fuck them. If they want to choose some random bitch over our pack, then they can have her. Hell, they can have the whole damn wing. I'll sleep on the other side of the house, in a guest room.

Wouldn't want me upsetting the sensitive little princess with my bullshit, right?

The girl must really hate me if she's already pulling the others' strings, getting them to exclude me from shit. Fuck, is that something she would do? I guess I've never actually talked to her. Which is weird, considering how many times a day her big, blue doe eyes and sassy little hip-cock pop into my head.

I've chalked it up to how hot she is, refusing to believe she got to me during that interview. But she did.

I can admit that now, in the dark, alone. The second I saw her, a hum cracked to life under my skin. I instantly knew I needed her *out* of our building. Away from the other alphas.

Away from me?

I assumed so.

But now that I consider it further, that strikes me as odd, too. I've never been an omega-chaser like Ronan or a heat volunteer like Arch, but omegas don't usually *repel* me. Like any other alpha, they generally get my blood pumping in all the right ways.

There's always that urge—the natural magnetism that draws us to them, makes us pay attention, forces us to want to fix whatever ails them. I resent it, yeah, but I'm not *immune.*

All in all, it usually balances itself out. I don't hate omegas. I don't love them, either. They are, mostly, a necessity, for the sake of a pack. A way to solidify bonds, have babies, all that shit.

Heavy, but nothing to send me running in the other direction.

So why did I instantly feel so strongly about *this* girl? The one they're all so obsessed with?

It's more than that. I know it is. Archer's beat on like a drum all week, hammering the correct phrases into my thick skull.

Scent-sensitive.

Scent-matched.

Mate. Mate. Mate.

But how can that be true when she's tearing us apart?

Maybe you were never meant to be part of this pack, that grating voice whispers. *They all belong with her, and you don't belong anywhere. You don't belong to anyone.*

It feels like an anchor is hooked on my lungs. I carry that heaviness in the middle of my chest, moving slow. Shuffling to the other side of the house, my mind spins with images of what my life would look like without the guys, the pack, the team.

The second I hit the living room, a scent strikes me like a paddle to the face. It hits me so hard, I rear back, rocking to my sock-covered heels, nearly slipping on the glossy marble floor.

Holy motherfucking—

I'm sniffing the air like a blood hound, clutching my pec like I might be able to rip my own heart out.

Oh God. Shit. Fuck.

I'm ripping my suit pants off and vaulting over the couch. I'm on my knees. I'm pressing my face into a cushion.

Groaning. Hard as granite. Mouth-watering. Canines pulsing with the need to bite.

So I do. I bite the fucking couch cushion like an animal, my hands fumbling to get to my aching dick and swelling knot. I grip both, jacking myself hard and fast while I lick the slick-soaked leather between my teeth. Over and over.

Fuuuuuuuuuuuck.

It's so good. Too good. Within seconds, I'm massaging my knot, milking it, pumping cum all over the cushion.

Because *I have to.* My scent *must* be mingled with this one. It just *has to be.*

I fall backward, gasping. Horrified. Staring at my cum-covered hands and still-hard cock. Feeling like I want to laugh and cry and rage and *rut.*

A sudden, terrifying clarity washes over me, landing low in my abdomen.

Scent-sensitive.

Scent-matched.

Mate.

Mate. Mate. Mate.

chapter
thirty-one

"ARE YOU SURE ABOUT THIS?"

I smile, hiding the happy expression behind my stainless steel coffee mug. "Yes."

Outside the double doors to my office, my secretary shoots an alarmed look my way. She's been doing that all morning, ever since I waltzed in here in joggers—why put on a suit when these sweats smell like my perfect baby girl?—and left my doors open.

I'll own that it's a rarity. Theo and Declan even had the doors put on hydraulics—their idea of a gag gift, since I am notorious for slamming the door in people's faces. Now I can do it with the push of a button.

But today? Let them look. Let them all see what this girl is doing to me.

I picture Meg's face as her bratty little snort comes through the phone line. "Like, really sure? Or really, *really* sure? Or just kind-of, mostly sh—"

"*Omega.*" The soft bark instantly calms her rambling. My secretary leaps to her feet and flees, no doubt troubled by the rumble in my tone. "I am entirely certain. And so are the others."

We all decided while she napped on my chest on Sunday night —she's ours. We want her to stay. And if we have to use her heat spikes as an excuse to show how good life in our pack will be? Bring it on.

Even if Meg didn't need easing, our new arrangement isn't uncommon where scent-sensitive courting is concerned. Typically, there would be a few more chaperoned outings, maybe a couple weeks of dating before the public courting became private.

But I saw the way Archer watched her every move while we all shared his bed—he's worried about the heat breakthroughs.

None of us will ever forgive ourselves if she needs us and we aren't there. So, since we're already courting, until we can get her body's needs sorted, it just makes sense for her to move into the pack house.

A purely emotional decision I came up with a million practical excuses for: I don't want her driving hours to get to us when her hormones spike. She could hurt herself if she's alone and loses lucidity. She won't have to worry about rent anymore.

I repeat those facts to myself over and over again. Knowing full damn well that even if none of that shit were true, I'd still want her at home.

It made me nervous enough that she drove back early Monday morning, alone. She promised to stay on the phone with her friend the whole time, insisting she needed to at least go back to collect her "dang underwear."

I started to argue that I would send movers to gather her things, but Archer cut in, reminding me of an omega's need for their spaces to be private, and the necessity of keeping their special comfort items with them.

Basically—if I want her to stay with us, I had to let her go get her blankets.

And her dang underwear.

Still, I worried all the way through the morning, shuffling papers around my desk while I watched the guys' practice through my wall of windows. I don't think I even really breathed until Meg called me at lunchtime, chirping about whether she should pack this shirt or that one.

Little does she know, I plan to make her entire wardrobe obsolete. Today.

I've gotten into the habit of calling her each morning. At first, she kept insisting I get off the phone to work. I finally made it clear that getting her and her things to our pack house is my sole objective for the week.

That didn't stop our omega from working, though. Each morning, I find a new email in my inbox. Each contains links to our new socials, potential marketing strategies, and advertising opportunities. Our ticket sales have already improved by fifteen percent.

I've tried to convince her to let me pay her the salary she deserves, but we're at an impasse. She thinks allowing her to stay in our pack house rent-free is an even trade. I think she's in for a surprise when she sees what we have planned for her.

Now it's Friday, and Theo, Arch, and I are practically feral after four days without her. The team had its first away game last night for a Thursday Night Football special. They eked out another too-close victory, but Declan hasn't spoken a word to any of us since. He knows Meg is moving in today, but he's chosen not to comment on it.

Archer's already at home, opening up the omega suite and

airing out the nest. Theo bounced off to practice, promising to make it out in time to greet our girl.

Meg's heavy sigh comes through the line. The sound immediately makes my stomach clench, the urge to root out the source of her distress a sharp knife to the gut.

"What about Declan?" she whispers.

A fresh bolt of pain strikes my chest. I turn and look out at the field behind me, searching the sea of black practice jerseys for twenty-seven—his number. I don't want to tell her that he was gone when we all got up that morning...

Honestly? I've hated not having him around this week. I'm the pack alpha; and when one of us is missing or lost, I—

I *feel* it.

More so now than ever. It's like Meg has unearthed the place inside of me where I keep all my emotions locked away. Because it all just gushes up, now. The worry and regret and self-doubt.

Maybe I shouldn't have told him to stay away Sunday night. Maybe he would have come home and joined in. It could have been a bonding experience for them. For all of us.

Fuck. What if he went out and banged some other woman because I made him feel like he isn't welcome in our pack's house? With our pack's mate?

I know from the rasp in Meg's whisper that she wants him every bit as much as she seems to want the rest of us. Even though he's done nothing to deserve it, his nature calls to hers the same way her nature calls to each of us.

If he went out with another woman, it will hurt her.

"I'm gonna fix it, baby girl," I vow, searching the field again. "Daddy will fix it."

chapter
thirty-two

Megera

"TELL ME I'M NOT CRAZY."

I know I am, no matter what the girl says. Because only a crazy person agrees to move into a house full of alphas she's only met three times.

And only a crazy person would have slept there with them on Sunday night.

And waking up buried between three massive, hard bodies would definitely make a sane person nervous. Not unbearably horny.

In my defense, I really couldn't drive after whatever hormonal nonsense came over me. I still can't figure out how it happened. Was it the pillow-man covered in their scents? Being in their space for hours? The jersey?

Or is it really just... us?

Scent-sensitivity. Mates.

Archer seems to think so. He's also the one who convinced me to stay at the pack's house leading up to my heat. Which really isn't fair. The man is impossible to argue with, always making perfect sense the calmest way possible.

And the plan *does* make sense. After three close-calls in one week, I know I shouldn't be alone. The guys all claim they want to be there for me. Plus, they have Archer's expertise and access to every specialist in the area. There's plenty of space in the house.

A nest, too.

Just in case, Archer assures me.

No one has so much as pressured me to *look* at it, but Dr. Dreamboat constantly reminds me that it's there for me if I need it.

The only obvious issue—that I'll be alone, in a house full of big, powerful alphas—doesn't seem all that threatening after Sunday night. I practically threw myself at them all, and they still kept their hands to themselves and their knots out of me. I know I can trust them. Physically, at least.

The rest will come in time, Remi claims. The stats I googled appear to back her up—99.8 percent of scent-sensitive packs bond within three months of meeting. 84 percent bond within the *first month*.

I'm too embarrassed to tell my best friend that I barely know anything about omega bonding.

I understand it connects the alphas in a pack, routing their bonds through a central mate. For the alphas, those bonds can make or break their pack. Without them, their natures urge them to compete, fight, dominate.

But bonds turn the other alphas in a pack from just that—

others—into a part of a whole. They no longer feel the need to fight because they stop seeing themselves as separate entities.

Which sounds great. For them. Of course, my mother never thought to teach her sure-to-be-alpha daughter what bonding means for an *omega*.

Would I be able to hear them all? At the same time? Hearing Theo alone seems overwhelming, with the way the big guy's lightning-quick thoughts leap around. And Archer may be quiet, but he's also brilliant. I'm sure his mind never rests, either.

Ronan... Ronan scares me. He's such an enigma, and his temper is as icy as it is quick.

What if they get angry with me? Will all of their vitriol funnel right into my body? Will I start to hate myself if they end up hating me?

I don't like to even think about it... but, at this point, I'm pretty sure loathing is the primary emotion I'd get from Declan.

Remi's light laugh flutters through my car. "You are *not* crazy, Meg. They're just trying to take care of you. This is exact what's supposed to happen when you find your mates."

I hear the stutter in her reassurance. I know it has nothing to do with me and everything to do with the undeniable fact that *I'm* somehow living *her* dream right now.

The irony sucks. I never wanted all of this omega nonsense. I just wanted to get a good job and take care of myself. But Remi... she's wanted a pack of her own for as long as I can remember. Scent-sensitivity is literally her greatest wish.

My heart aches, blooming with guilt and vicarious longing on my best friend's behalf. "Oh, Rems," I whine softly. "I'm really an asshole, aren't I? Talking about them so much. I'm so sorry."

"No." She exhales, the sound shaking. "*I'm* sorry. This is wonderful for you, Meg. So, so wonderful. They're everything you need exactly when you needed it most. I couldn't be happier for you. I'm just sad for me, too, I guess."

I flop back against my car seat, pouting at the universe. "This blows."

Remi laughs again, the sound a bit more sincere. "Right?"

"Totally," I concur, flicking my blinker on and leaning forward to scan around me.

Damn. This area is way nicer than I noticed last weekend. I must have been too nervous to really appreciate the copse of oak trees overhead and the charming brick roads.

The guys' house is modern, but the neighborhood is all historic charm, set way back in the most private area of the city's wealthiest borough. I see a few other modern structures similar to theirs, but most of the homes are grand, stately affairs.

I can imagine walking these sidewalks on cool evenings, enjoying the shade and the sound of wind whispering through the leaves swaying above me. It feels safe way back here, away from the bustle of the downtown area and far from any tourist attractions.

Remi and I hang up as I pull into the driveway. Today, the gates are open and I see why—the garage is full of cars.

Beautiful cars.

Holy—

Is that a Bugatti? Lined up next to a Rolls, a Bentley, and a G-Wagon, of course.

I gulp and park my pathetic beater car in the circular drive beside the front door. It seems like they left the garage open for me, but I don't want to be presumptuous. I'm still a guest. And this is not my house, no matter how homey it feels.

As I clamber out of my car and pop the trunk, I hear a noise. One of them is in the garage, rooting around. The wind shifts, carrying luscious vanilla over the breeze.

Declan.

Lord, that smell. I want to lick him like a big swirl of cool, creamy soft serve. My perfume rises right away, drifting up to mingle with his delicious pheromones.

And some hopeless part of me wants to laugh. Because together... well, we *do* sort of smell like peach cobbler with fresh-churned ice cream.

He scents me the same moment I catch him. Electric eyes

snag on mine, the blue breathtakingly clear, even from across the huge driveway. I watch as he fists the gym bag in his left hand, the feathered pattern of his tattoo moving over his muscles. His jaw pops, working, while we stare each other down.

Submit.

SUBMIT.

My basest instincts scream at me. But there's another, clearer voice. And she's *pissed*.

Let him look, that voice scoffs. *Show him what he's missing.*

As if I have so much to work with. *But whatever, girl. I'll give it my best shot.*

I pop my hip and toss my hair over my shoulder as I turn back to the Fiat's boot, hoisting my duffle bag full of blankets and backpack full of clothes out all on my own. I pause like my hoodie is an afterthought, sliding it off and tying it around my waist, flashing the racerback of my light blue sports bra to him as I walk away.

Between my carefully waved layers and the tight fit of my matching powder-blue leggings... it's no main stage show, but it's something, at least. I think.

Who the heck am I kidding, though? This man routinely sleeps with supermodels.

Still, I feel his eyes on my body, burning hot trails of hatred down the backs of my legs. I'm glad he can't see my face because my heart quivers, stinging like it's been sliced. For the millionth time, I wonder why he loathes me so much, and what I'm going to do about it.

Ronan said he would fix it for me, but my instincts skitter at the thought. Declan may be a jerk, but everything in me says he's mine. And I should be the one to deal with him.

I only wish that same instinct had some sort of suggestion for how I'm supposed to *do* that.

For now, I knock on the front door, pretending I never saw the angry alpha glaring at me from the garage. Theo's bounding footsteps give him away. A wide grin cracks over my face as he throws the door open and charges me.

I guess this is our thing now. The second he sees me, he swings me around like a rag doll, and I absolutely love it. Warm, herbaceous citrus fills my lungs, exciting and comforting me in equal measure.

"Peaches," he drawls, plucking my things from me, somehow shouldering it all while he physically carries me inside. "You don't carry *bags*. What do you think I'm here for?"

"To sit around and look pretty," I toss back, sliding down his body until my tennis shoes reach the floor. "Duh."

His grin grows wild, the green of his eyes sparkling. "And let's not forget my talents as a human dildo."

My cheeks flame while a fresh burst of perfume rises. Theo folds me into a soft, sweet bear hug. "Just teasing, precious. You know I fucking loved it. On my death bed, I'll replay you using my knot to get off and die a happy man."

I swear, I never know whether to laugh, blush, or melt around this alpha. I settle for yanking lightly on his beard, shaking my head. "Shameless."

"Is that Meg?" Archer's voice echoes from the second-floor looming above us. "Bring her up, Theo."

My big guy squeezes my hip, still holding my bags over his shoulder with one hand while the other guides me up the floating plank staircase. I notice his bun looks slightly damp from a shower and remember he spent the better part of the day in conditioning.

"How was practice?" I ask, slinging my arm as far around his thick waist as it will reach. "Did you kick ass?"

His smile is perfectly cocky and achingly kind all at once. Just like him. "Had to, precious. Needed to get home to my best girl. Did you watch my game last night?"

I chuckle. He *knows* I did because I texted him a billion times, commenting semi-competently on all of his amazing plays. I also sent him the victory present I'd promised—a racy photo of me wearing the jersey he got for me and nothing else. I know he got it because the dick pic I received in return was nothing short of epic. I almost slipped into another heat-breakthrough just *looking* at it.

"You were amazing, big guy," I tell him, squeezing his middle. "So proud of you."

That's just what he wanted. His smile grows as he gives a contented sigh. "I tried to get Ronan to let me make you another orange poster, but he's all paranoid about press."

The mention of media makes my throat close. I need to get over it, though. There's a gala for the pack's philanthropic efforts next month, and the guys have already asked me if I would attend with them. As much as I want to see all the good they do for the community, I'm also completely terrified.

What if I disappoint them? What if the paparazzi take horrible pictures of me and I become a meme? What if I somehow embarrass or offend Declan even *more*?

Theo interrupts my silent panic. Oblivious, he pumps his brows at me. "We have a surprise for you, peaches."

I blink, thrown. No one has given me a surprise in ten years. Since my mom died, at least. There weren't exactly birthday and Christmas presents in the government's group home for omegas. Remi and I never have extra money to exchange gifts, either. She usually bakes me something, and I mostly just make her crafts.

Before I can squeal or panic, Archer appears on the landing, looking unfairly handsome in a white linen button-down and tan trousers. The light colors offset his dark skin, turning the nerdy professor look into a sexy men's cologne ad.

The ginger and bourbon spice wafting off him soothes me. I step into his arms without a second thought, loving the way he curls his long-fingered hand over my head and holds me to his chest.

"I have something to show you."

With a nod, I let him drag me down the hallway.

God, this place smells so good. Declan may be on my shit list, but I really have missed his scent. It's everywhere I turn in their house. The combination of all four of them pretty much makes it my own personal heaven.

Or so I thought.

Because ten seconds later, Archer opens the door to *actual heaven*.

The suite occupies the end of the long, wide hallway. Taking up the entire end of the floor, it's almost a wing unto itself. Absolutely *sprawling* in every direction.

I freeze on the threshold, scared to enter. Scared it might actually be what I think it is. Which would mean that that door over there isn't a third closet or a second en-suite, but...

"The nest," Archer chimes quietly, winding one arm around my belly. "It has its own separate bathroom attached and a little butler's pantry, as well. We built it that way to ensure we would never have to leave our omega during their heat. Anything we could ever need, there's a place for it."

I want to make a joke about how, with so much space, no one would expect anything less. But my throat is bone-dry, and I'm stifling the humiliating urge to bawl.

The room is beautiful. It has all the modern elegance of the rest of the house, blended with distinctly homey touches like warm wood floors, high, arched windows, and lovely white molding along the domed ceiling. The glass chandelier is pretty, but unnecessary; golden slants of sunset shaft into the airy space, making patterns over the empty floor.

With a gentle nudge, Archer guides me a bit further in, pointing out the spacious reading nook built into a curved pocket, both walk-in closets, and a marble bathroom.

"There's space for a desk over here," he goes on, pointing to the most well-lit corner. "I know you've been doing so much to help Ronan with the social media stuff for the team. This should be a great place for you to work."

Archer goes on, "The bed area is...well, *spacious*. We once discussed sleeping arrangements in the event of our pack finding an omega and pretty much agreed we'd all prefer one main bed, hence all the space. But, of course, it's whatever you're comfortable with."

I know he's telling me all of this for a reason. Obviously. But I can't force the thought of this being my bedroom into my brain. For the love of God, my apartment was the size of the bathroom, here.

It isn't really *mine*, I tell myself, the thought both a comfort and a pang of pain. *I'm only borrowing it.*

I chant the words to myself again and again, especially when we near the nest. For the first time since I arrived, Archer lets go of me, stepping back.

Being a gentleman, I realize. I don't know much about omega stuff, but Remi did teach me basic nest etiquette. I never thought I would need the information, so the memory is fuzzy, but I recall that it's considered disrespectful to approach an omega's nest without his or her explicit invitation.

This isn't my nest, though.

So I nod at the door and peep, "You should open it."

Really, my scent shouldn't even be in this *room*. What if they chuck me to the curb within the week? Then they'll have to have the whole place de-scented for their next omega.

Probably one that knows what to do with a nest this glorious.

Because it really is.

A short set of stairs lead from the entrance to a wide, perfectly round floor. The roof is way lower in here, thankfully. The height feels cozy. There are no windows, but Archer flips a switch and the walls glimmer to life; dozens of small, warm fairy lights line the circular seam of the ceiling.

It has a lot more room than most nests—it might actually be a bit too big, if not for the *massive* round bed built into a cylindrical recess in the center of the floor.

A spark of relief settles in my lungs as I note that the whole thing is stripped. No cushions or mattress. Hopefully, the lack of soft surfaces means my scent won't be too hard to remove, if they need to.

Archer gives the rest of the tour in hushed, cautious tones. I smile and nod along, standing at the edge of the empty mattress crater, hugging my arms around my body to hold myself together.

Finally, he ushers me back out, where Theo waits with eager eyes. I shoot him the best smile I can manage while Archer slowly winds his arm back around my waist, squeezing gently.

"We're so glad you're here," he murmurs, drawing my gaze with a soft grin. "But it's time to go."

"Go?"

"Shopping."

It's Ronan, whispering into the room the same way his scent winds into my nose. I'm so mesmerized by the swirling silver intensity in his eyes, I almost miss his casual outfit.

Dang. He looks *good*. I mean, he's always a beautiful, imposing specimen. But in gray joggers and a tight Ospreys T-shirt, with a matching black cap shadowing his square features?

Ronan senses my perfume, his mouth curving in his signature half-smile. He crosses the empty room and gathers me up against him, pressing the firmness between his legs right into my lower belly. When he cocks his head to the side, the spark in his eye is close to teasing.

"I wish we could stay home and play, baby girl, but we have a bedroom to decorate, a wardrobe to fill..." All humor evaporates until only pure, burning reverence smolders in his quicksilver gaze. He nods over my shoulder. "And a nest to make."

I ARGUE with them all the way downstairs, but it's useless. We are, apparently, going shopping.

When I mention how totally broke I am, their round of low, disapproving growls is punctuated by Ronan hooking his arm around my neck and pulling me into his hard chest. "Don't make Daddy angry. I want to spoil you, and you're going to let me."

Well, then.

Archer is the first one to sense it. He pauses halfway down the plank steps, halting our whole group as he turns to me.

Bottomless eyes roam over my face, a crease forming behind the bridge of his glasses. "What's the matter, sweetheart?"

Me?

What is he talking about? I'm fine.

But as his hand drifts up and presses flat over my sternum, fingers curling gently to the pulse in the base of my throat, I realize I'm actually not. My heart is pounding. My throat is dry. And I feel low-grade nausea tumbling around my middle.

His other hand smooths hair back from my face, searching my eyes with such tenderness and patience, I feel like I might start crying. No one has ever looked at me the way he does. Like every feeling swirling inside me *means* something. And he wants nothing more than to understand each one.

I'm tempted to lie and tell him I really do feel fine. It's almost a reflex, at this point.

I'm fine. It's fine. Everything will be fine.

Except it's not. He's right. I'm uncomfortable.

"Tell me what you need." His voice is so deep and warm, I want to sink into it. Let it lap over my over-sensitized skin and soothe every sizzling nerve.

He rubs his thumb along my cheekbone, his patience eternal. In the end, that's what breaks me. I sense that he will wait as long as it takes for me to come around. Because he truly, honestly cares.

The problem is—I've gone so long squashing down my panic, telling myself I'm overreacting... when I'm ready to actually explain what's bothering me, I find I can't put it into words.

I open my mouth and struggle to speak. Archer watches for a moment before sliding the hand pressed to my chest up around my neck. He squeezes softly, capturing my attention. "Is it the shopping? You don't want new clothes?"

Ronan makes a gruff sound of disgust. I feel it snag a piece out of my heart before I realize it isn't directed at me at all; he's mad at himself. His solid hands cup my shoulders from behind, adding to the comfort of Archer's touch.

"My sweet baby girl," he rumbles. "I should have clarified—there is nothing wrong with your clothes or the way you dress. We love the way you look. We only wanted to get you some gear for gamedays, team events, date nights, the gala we're hosting in a few weeks. And your room needs furniture, of course. We want you to pick anything you want. Decor, clothes. All of it."

Theo presses in, his scent washing over me in a comforting burst of springy lemongrass. "I told them I'd personally prefer for you to be naked at all times," he grumbles, pressing a kiss to the top of my head. "But Daddy vetoed that suggestion."

He always knows how to make me laugh. Even when I'm teetering on the edge of a meltdown, just like that first day in the elevator. I giggle at him calling Ronan "Daddy" and he grins back, his eyes a mix of joy and worry.

His body draws closer and the rest follow. Until I'm packed between three thick walls of muscle. Something about that soothes my omega instincts. I still don't know what's disturbed me, but I know that these alphas are here to handle it.

Archer's long fingers curl around my free wrist, sliding down to weave into mine. "A lot of studies have recorded verifiable health benefits when omegas receive gifts from their alphas. It's proven to increase their serotonin levels and even out their other hormones. It's also a biological imperative for us. We want to provide for you. Our natures demand it."

Everything he says makes total sense. And I know they have money to burn. Obviously. Plus, Remi warned me that proper courting usually involves all sorts of gifts and grandiosity. I felt prepared for exactly this. So why is it freaking me out?

Unless... maybe it isn't. Maybe it's something else.

I replay the last ten minutes, my throat swelling with panic when I get to one specific part. "The nest," I whisper.

Shame rises inside of me. I huddle closer to Archer on instinct. Because... I need to. Because he's the one who will understand. He's the one who loves to understand me.

His smooth, rolling purr greets me as I press my ear over his heart. I feel his fingertips take my pulse where it batters the thin skin at my wrist. The vibrations resonating in his chest snag on a sharp inhale the second he realizes, "You're scared to build a nest."

Gritting my teeth, I blow air through my nose, forcing myself to be honest. Even though part of me is sure they're three seconds away from shoving my defective ass out the door.

After all, what kind of omega doesn't want to nest? Or worse.

But I have to tell them. They deserve to know how broken I am.

"I am scared to build one here," I admit, talking to Archer's chest. "I'm scared I—I've never—What if I build my nest here and then..."

The others rush to speak, but Archer must give them one hell of a look. His arms fold around me, his purr deepening as he hums, "Mmm. I understand. That's a very valid concern, and one we didn't think about. We should all discuss how we feel about that. I can tell you right now that I personally cannot imagine any other omega in that nest upstairs. To me, it's as good as yours. I'd move before I ever took it away from you."

Ronan and Theo's replies collide over my head. "Absolutely," the alpha says, his voice menacingly final. Just as my big guy scoffs, "Oh duh, peaches."

When none of my muscles unwind, Archer still doesn't lose his patience. He kisses my forehead, whispering, "What else, love?"

I snuggle closer to his spiced scent, fisting the back of his shirt. My eyes snap shut as I force out the last bit of truth I have to offer.

"I've never made a nest before, and I don't know how."

There's a horrible beat of silence. I hold my breath, waiting for the inevitable scorn.

The judgment. Confusion. Rejection.

Theo speaks first. Of course. "Why not, precious?"

"I've been on my own. My apartments have been small. I've been alone for all my heats, and I—I guess I thought I didn't need one. Or deserve one."

His thick arm somehow wedges its way between my stomach and Archer's hips while the other slips between the small of my back and Ronan's abs. He squeezes me hard.

"Oh, peaches." Theo sounds sadder than I've ever heard him. "I'm so sorry you felt like that."

It's the second apology he's given me that straight-up doesn't make sense. My head pops up, swiveling to search their faces, trying to understand.

Archer's dark eyes are soft, full of compassion and concern. Theo seems heartbroken, his shifting green gaze full of grief. Ronan looks *pissed*, but in a distinctly outraged way that I recognize—he's angry *for* me, not at me.

We're all so caught up in the moment that none of us hear the footsteps. Or smell the torched vanilla wafting from the landing below.

Declan announces himself with a firm bark.

"*Omega.*"

I have to turn. I don't really have a choice. But I think I want to, anyway, if only out of sheer curiosity.

Now he's talking to me? While I'm a hot mess? Admitting I'm basically defective?

Yes. His eyes flash the word at me, along with one other. *Now.*

I work my way down a step, the elevation putting us nearly face-to-face over the clear glass railing.

And, lord, he's beautiful. I can't seem to get used to it. Every time I look at him, the perfection of his features stuns me all over again.

Bright blue eyes snap, full of fire and fury. He flicks that gaze down my body and back up before leaning onto his heels and crossing his arms over his chest. In an onyx Ospreys' tank with oversized armholes, I see every muscle in his arms, shoulders, and obliques, each one cinched tight.

"Well," he says, smirking as he waits for me to work my eyes back up to his. "Tell me, *do* you deserve a nest?"

Low warnings rumble out of each of the others; but, weirdly, I'm not offended. He isn't taunting me. He's *challenging* me. Seeing if I have what it takes to seize this thing I only just realized I've always wanted. Asking me what I think I'm worth.

At first, it's terrifying. Is he really going to make me say no in front of these men? Will he actually embarrass me like that?

Except, it wouldn't be him, would it? It would be me. Embarrassing myself. Selling myself short. Giving up before I even have a chance to try.

And deep down, something in me snaps. Or unlocks. Instincts I've buried so insistently rush up, speaking for me. "Every omega deserves a nest."

I brace for a cruel sneer or some sort of jab. But Declan simply nods. His eyes spark with something a little bit like pride. "All right then. Let's go, princess."

chapter
thirty-three

GOOD THING ARCHER'S a doctor because Theo's elbow will have to be surgically removed from my ribs.

I swear the asshole stabs me with it every forty seconds. For good shit and bad shit.

I'm on the receiving end of a hard nudge every time the omega does anything remotely tolerable—like playing music in the car that doesn't make me want to hurl.

And every time I say or do anything he considers rude—so, like, every time I speak.

If I wasn't so disgruntled by this whole situation, I might be happy for the fucker. We've been best friends our whole lives, and I don't think I've ever seen his big, exuberant ass *this* happy.

Ronan drives, even though we're all piled into Theo's G-Wagon. The Mercedes SUV is the only car large enough to fit all of us. My Bugatti only has two seats. Ronan's Rolls and Archer's Bentley are both sedans. Meg would be squished between whoever rode in the back with her.

A stab of panic nails my lungs when I think about it. Which is irritating. Because I've decided not to care about her.

I have no desire to watch her suffer or anything. I just don't want to be *hers*. She can have my knot during her heat and shared rights to my packmates. *Maybe*. Other than that, as long as she's safe... I don't really care.

Liar, the voice in my head hisses.

All right, fine. So I care. I care way too fucking much. So much that if I let myself feel it, it might actually fucking kill me.

So I won't feel it.

Which is the same thing as not caring at all.

In a practical sense, anyway.

Still, my heart bellyflops when she trips on her way across the street. Ronan's having none of that, thank God, because she's barely wobbled before he has her over his shoulder, swatting her perfect ass while he carts her to the sidewalk.

"*Careful*, baby girl."

And she *smiles*.

It's bullshit. How come, when *he* barks at her, she's all wide eyes and eager nods and "yes, Alpha"? But for me she's all sass and glares and waving her sexy little body in my face like a banner that reads, *See what you're missing, jackass?*

Archer leads our group toward some boutique. We've already hit two furniture stores. Meg seemed to do everything in her power to avoid actually choosing shit, constantly demurring or deferring to the rest of us.

She eventually gave in, but goddamn. I thought my eyes might get stuck in my skull for all the eye-rolling I did. Surely, this should be simpler. She's our scent-match. Our mate.

For fuck's sake, girl, just pick a dresser.

I swear, if she pulls the same shit shopping for clothes, I'm doing it for her.

Actually, she might look particularly good in that leather jacket. Or the matching pants.

I hate that I know that leather pants are back in style for women, but it's an occupational hazard. I spend way too much time around make-up artists, stylists, and photoshoots. Being on the cover of *GQ* requires at least a rudimentary understanding of style.

At least, that's what I tell myself as I wander the upscale shop, piling clothes into my arms. It's all shit she needs anyway. A few bodysuits, blazers, some shorts. The nineties band T-shirts, I'll admit, are more for my own benefit than anyone else's.

I love nineties music and I'm sure the princess will be confused when she doesn't recognize any of them. It'll make Ronan feel old, too—knowing our omega doesn't even recognize music from his adolescence. So I throw four of them onto the pile.

Thank God I know what I'm doing because the other guys are just embarrassing. Archer looks distinctly uncomfortable, loitering outside the dressing room like an uneasy husband might hover at his wife's gynecologist visit. Ronan sits in the one chair across from the curtain, tapping his fingers impatiently and glaring at his watch like its pace personally offends him.

Theo approaches me after I've deposited my selections on the ottoman at the edge of the changing area. His eyes dart to the others furtively before he lowers his voice, not wanting to be overheard. For once.

"Where were you Sunday night?"

I wondered if they'd noticed. It's almost good to know they did. "Out."

I'm lying again. I slept in a guest room on the opposite side of the house because I didn't trust myself. The scent of Meg's slick made me insane. I spent the better part of the night rutting my own hand, and still woke up hard enough to break glass.

Theo straightens to his full 6'6", scowling at me. The expression looks all wrong on him. With his hewn features, he's actually scary when he glares. "You're a shithead, you know that?"

I shrug, deciding there's no point revealing the shameful truth. "I was told not to come home. Just following orders."

He crosses his arms. "You know I've known you for our entire lives," he huffs. "Why are you bullshitting me right now?"

Because I just about fucked our couch cushion, and it wasn't exactly my proudest moment.

But now I have to know.

"What the hell happened in the living room?" I counter. "It smelled like a porn set in there."

Theo's unnatural expression eases into a cocky grin. "Ah, so you did come home. Knew it."

I flip him off, turning to look at a rack of clothes I missed before. A tight Lycra skirt catches my eye. The nude color looks just right. Not that I've seen very much of the woman's skin.

I haven't even touched her, I realize, my eyes automatically flying over to her changing room.

No matter how stubborn I am, there's a distinct possibility I may give in on that very front soon. The need to feel her body beats like a separate pulse under my skin. Will it erode my pride eventually?

Theo leans closer, whispering, "Peaches had a heat-spike, and sort of... *rode it out* in the living room."

Oh shit. That image alone.

Who was riding who? Was it just Meg on her own, all over that cushion? Or was one of them under her?

My scent rises while I bite down on a growl. He flashes a shit-eating grin. "I know." Then he shakes his head. "I shouldn't even be telling you this shit. You don't deserve it."

"Yeah, well," I sniff, pretending my dick isn't pressing into my joggers. "If she's yours, then I guess she's mine, too. And she and I will have our own... thing. You guys need to get over it."

His thick brows drop while he considers that. A moment later he sighs and raises his hands, palms out. "Listen, yesterday, I would have told you to get fucked because you clearly make her upset every time you open your fat mouth, and you practically rejected her outright. But, honestly? I really don't want to choose between my best friend and the girl of my dreams. And you *did* get her to come out tonight; so maybe you have more of a handle on this *thing* than I thought."

He's giving me the benefit of the doubt, even though I know he shouldn't. He always does. Always has. In a lot of ways, he's the only one who ever did.

I should tell him that, sometime. Maybe.

I know I'll get no such mercy from the other guys. They think I've rejected our scent-match and threatened their chances of successfully courting her.

And—judging by the way they're both mooning as Meg steps out in a dress that doesn't even fit her properly—they'd probably sell me to human traffickers before they let her step in a puddle.

I wave the sales girl over. She's a beta, but young enough that she has stars in her eyes when she looks at me. I flash an extra-wide smile, knowing it will get me what I want.

"We need the next size down in that," I say, gesturing at the too-flowy maxi dress. "In black, not white." Another thought occurs to me. "And loungewear, if you have any. An assortment— all colors and fabrics. I don't care. She needs all of it. And if any are loose matching sets, she'll take two of each. Slippers or socks to match."

The girl scurries off and I nod, satisfied.

There. Omegas like cozy shit. She'll spend way more time in casual apparel than she will in anything for going out. These other assholes clearly have no idea how to shop.

But when I look up, Theo's grin is wider than I've ever seen it.

"What?" I demand. *She needs everything.* "I want to get out of here and you all suck at shopping."

He nods, the motion somehow mocking. "Good thing you're here, then, Vanilla."

… "*What* did you just call me?"

He claps my shoulder, starting toward the others. "I always knew you had a sweet scent, but Meg told me it's very *vanilla*. She asked if that means you're boring in bed." He shrugs innocently. "I told her I wouldn't know."

It certainly isn't the first time someone has made the vanilla joke. Usually, I shut that shit down the old-fashioned way—by proving exactly how non-vanilla I can be.

Fuck. This omega is just begging for a lesson.

chapter
thirty-four

ARCHER

MEG STARTS to flag by the fourth shop.

Unfortunately, it's the most important stop on our trip. While she yawns, leaning into my arm, I mentally kick myself. We should have started here. And we should have stopped to feed her by now.

"Do you want to go home, sweetheart?" I offer, smoothing my hand down her arm.

She must be exhausted. She drove across the whole state today. Packed up all her stuff by herself. Loaded her own car. And Declan had her in and out of so many outfits at that boutique—

always demanding this color or that size—I swore she might finally snap and claw his face off if he shoved one more item through her dressing room door.

According to my research, any one of those things would be an ordeal for an omega. All of them in one day? Our Meg is tough.

Pride mixes with my guilt when she blinks up at me, the motion a little too slow for my liking. She seems to remember she's trying to act happy and perks up a bit. "I'm fine!"

We're in the middle of the premier store for anything one could possibly need for a nest. They have waterproof cushions, covers, sheets, towels, pillows. Dim string lights, neon signs, salt lamps. Sex toys, mini fridges.

Usually, I spend pack shopping trips silently calculating in my head and quietly hiding a coronary. Ronan has never lived without his wealth, and Theo grew up solidly ensconced in the upper middle class. Whatever frugal impulses Declan maintained from his childhood of neglect are a faint memory ever since he got drafted. I'm ordinarily the only one whose skin crawls when I watch them charge our carbon fiber Amex.

I don't know why. We have plenty. Tons. More than I like to think about, actually, between Ronan's inheritance, his company holdings, two NFL contracts, and the salary I earn from my duties with the team.

Still, it tends to bother me.

Not this time.

Because Meg clearly *needs* all of this, and, moreover, I want it for her. Anytime she touches anything with even a spark of interest, I put it in our cart. We've filled three so far.

It hasn't been easy. While I may not have any qualms about how much we're spending, Meg clearly does. She winces and cringes every time she finds something she likes.

These omega instincts—allowing herself to be pampered, pleasured, protected—don't come easy to her. She has to really pause and hone in on them to make decisions. Yet another reason why this should have struck me as exhausting for her.

"Let's come back tomorrow," I suggest, my voice cajoling as I draw her in for a hug. "You've done so well today, love. Too well. You need to eat and rest now."

The more I think about it, the more pissed I am at all of us. For god's sake, the woman had a full-blown mini-heat Sunday night, and we're dragging her around every store in the city?

She's hung in so well, we're almost done. The only thing left is a mattress for the nest. And, for that, I can call the first furniture store and get the specifications for the one she picked for her bed to have a round replica made.

While I consider the possibilities, I run a hand over her hair, my palm catching the slight layer of sweat misting her forehead. Underneath, she's warm.

No, hot.

My shoulders fly back, inadvertently pushing my groin into her abdomen. A thick burst of heat perfume instantly fills the space around us.

Goddamn it.

The others are walking ahead. Declan's the closest to us. I grab the back of his collar, fisting it hard to get his attention. "Go tell Ronan we need someone to box all of this up and deliver it in the morning." I slide my eyes to Meg meaningfully. "We need to go."

I expect him to snap or roll his eyes, but instead they fly wide. His nostrils flare, spine straightening. "*Fuck*. Get her out of here. I don't want anyone else to smell that."

At least we finally agree on something.

Meg protests weakly while I lead her toward the automatic doors and out to the car. Grateful, for once, that Theo always forgets to lock the damn thing.

"I'm really okay," Meg insists. It sounds like she's starting to doubt herself. I don't blame her. By the time we're both situated in the wide backseat, she's burning up.

"We're just going to wait here while the guys check out," I soothe, running my hand over the stretchy, light blue material covering her thigh.

"I didn't finish the list," she whimpers. "You all are so generous, and I didn't even finish choosing stuff."

She swallows her emotions as best she can, and I hate it. It's completely normal for someone in her predicament to be more sensitive than usual. Hell, most alphas and betas would be wrung out after the week she's had. In my professional opinion, she's extremely resilient.

Or maybe just that scared to let us down.

The thought has me gathering her closer. I loathe the notion that she feels the need to impress us or run herself ragged to appease anyone. She clearly thinks this is some sort of trial run, as if the pack will sit down at the end of each day and report on how well she performs.

That sort of uncertainty must be eating her alive. The constant threat of judgment and rejection. I need to figure out a way to make her feel secure.

Her perfect perfume fills the car within seconds. Just like Sunday night— when she's on the brink of a breakthrough, the scent is so *wet*, it almost feels like I could lick it out of the air. My body reacts instantly.

I'm already hard, knot half-swollen. She shimmies closer, her face seeking my throat. My scent. She breathes it deep, marking her own along my neck. Satisfaction pours through me.

My omega inhaling *my* scent. Leaving hers on my skin. A primal sort of possession rocks my core, leaving me even harder.

"Archer—" she starts, her voice wobbling as she licks my pulse.

I groan softly. "Tell me what you need, sweetheart. You can have anything."

She stammers, trying to tell me what her body is already communicating. Her left leg hooks over both of mine, planting her firmly in my lap just as the driver's door opens.

"Holy *fuck*."

Ronan's hiss barely registers. I'm losing my grip on our surroundings as Meg climbs me, her small hands clamped firmly on either side of my jaw to draw my mouth closer to hers.

"Heat-spike," I manage to grit out.

Then her lips are on mine, and I'm *gone*.

Every fact I memorized, all of the easing techniques I studied; it all evaporates, leaving my instincts firmly in control. They take the wheel, my Alpha snapping forward to meet her.

I'm not in complete control, but I'm not in a rut, either. I know because I'm vaguely aware of the others bickering in the background.

Declan is outraged. "He can't have her here! Someone could *see* her!"

"Agreed," Ronan growls. "But she needs easing, or she'll be in pain."

Theo's practically panting. "We need to get in the car and get the fuck home. I can tell y'all from experience, there's no way Arch will be able to stop right now. We have to *go*."

He's too right.

My hands move without my permission, stripping Meg's hoodie off. Her blue irises narrow to thin bands around blown pupils. She drags them down my body, a soft whine in her chest.

She wants skin.

I start to unbutton my shirt right away.

"I'll drive. No one talk to me or let her whine again. If she's in distress, I'll lose my shit and I have to focus."

Ronan starts the car. I'm just aware enough to note Theo's broad outline filling the passenger seat Meg's currently leaning on, trying to shimmy her leggings off her body. Declan slides in beside me, holding his breath while he blatantly stares at her exposed skin.

Judging by the strength of the scents in the small space, all of us are borderline feral. Declan's is especially potent, though I can't tell if it's his response or his proximity.

The car moves, and the last sane part of me breathes a sigh of relief. The windows are tinted—as long as we're whipping past people on the highway, no one will be able to see our omega writhing in my lap.

Now that I know she won't be exposed, the final piece of my consciousness releases. My brain goes off-line, urges overwhelming me.

I fist her hair, bringing her mouth down to mine. She moans at the tug, licking along the seam of my lips.

Fuck, she's so goddamn gorgeous. I've waited a lifetime for this woman. And she's here, needing me. Urgency lashes at my control.

"Archer," she cries, her pelvis bucking forward, humping the open air between her soaked panties and my bare chest.

I grab her hips, working the sodden fabric down to her knees, then pulling the whole bundle off one foot. Without the clothes stretched between her thighs, her stance widens. Her hot, wet core presses down onto my rock-hard member.

The pressure is exquisite, heat searing me through my trousers. I grunt, pressing up as much as I can in the confined space.

Her muscles are exhausted. They tremble on top of me, the quivers deepening with every roll of her hips against mine. By the time she's worked herself into a steady rhythm, her whole body shakes. I growl, frustrated I can't make enough space to take over properly.

Declan appears at my elbow. His body is coiled to spring, but a certain somber weight in his gaze keeps me from reacting territorially.

When he sees me see him, he nods. A gesture of respect. "I won't take her. Just grab her hips and hold her up higher. I have an idea."

Meg whimpers as I lift her off my lap and cup her plush, perfect ass in my hands, maneuvering her spine into the back of Theo's seat. Luckily, his car is custom-built to accommodate his height—there's plenty of headroom for Meg as I push her higher, until my face is level with her pussy.

The view is somehow as beautiful as it is obscene. Her lips are perfectly pink, swollen, and glistening in the low glow from passing street lamps. I could stare all night... until a shaft of light hits her thighs, revealing the trails of slick dripping down to her knees.

Good fucking—

"Lick that slick pussy, Arch," Declan grinds out. "Or I will."

That time, I snarl, marking my territory loudly while I lunge, lifting her soaked flesh to my lips.

Fucking hell.

I thought the smell of her was heaven, but *the taste—*

I'm not breathing. I don't want to. I just want to inhale this glorious slick until it fills my entire body. I want our scents to be so enmeshed, I can't tell where her sweetness ends and my spice begins.

"God, they smell so good together," Theo gasps. I hear a zipper rending. "Dec—tell me what's happening."

I realize I've completely lost myself in Meg. She's grinding her slit all over my face, and I'm just letting her. Breathing her.

At Theo's request, I feel Declan's hand land on the back of my neck. He squeezes, the grasp reassuring. Like he knows I'm so lost in the pleasure of our omega and the pain of the erection throbbing along my thigh, I can't even do what I need to do.

His hand presses me closer, angling my head down slightly. "Arch is about to lick Meg's sweet little pussy. Is that what you want, princess? You want this alpha lapping up your slick?"

Meg moans sharply, her hands falling to my head and scratching my scalp. I curl my tongue between her labia, reaching back to rim the ring of muscle flexing around her opening. I glide up to her clit next, my cock straining when I feel how swollen it is. I roll it between my lips and lick both sides before sucking at it gently.

Her strangled cry matches the noise that catches in my throat when more slick pulses out of her, drenching the fingertips curved around the backs of her thighs.

"Fuck, she's so wet, and he's barely touched her," Dec narrates, hoarse. "Her pussy is clenching so much, the muscles in her stomach are tightening. You want to see my knot, baby?"

Meg nods frantically, her only answer a high-pitched squeal. I feel Declan shift, the air growing thicker as he releases his cock and starts stroking with his free hand.

Fuck me, the scent of all of us. All of our arousal building and banking. My hips start snapping up and down, doing the only thing I can with both of my hands holding our precious omega. The friction of my inseam chafes my throbbing dick, but I'm too far gone to care.

"Look at your alpha, baby," Declan rasps. "He's so gone, he's trying to fuck the air with his pants on."

Meg's answering whimper edges dangerously close to a whine. Ronan growls a warning.

"I want to see him," she pleads. "Please, Alpha, I want to see your cock."

I want to take it out more than I ever have in my life, but I can't risk fumbling her. She's all sweat and slick and the softest skin I've ever felt. If I move my hands, I'm afraid we'll lose our precarious position.

"Gotta hold you, sweetheart," I rumble, swirling my tongue in a figure-eight over her clit. "I'll be fine."

She moans, pressing her swollen pussy lips closer. "I wanna s-see. P-please, Alpha."

Shit.

She doesn't understand what I'm saying. Her haze is too strong.

Declan shifts again; his hand drops from my neck to my left thigh. He taps the same courtesy motion as before. Telling me he's there and not a threat to me.

But his fingers don't stop on my thigh. They drift inward. My aching cock jumps, desperate for any contact. Any relief. I hiss at the burn of my swollen head rubbing against the rough fabric of my pants.

"Please," Meg cries, tears streaming down her face while she grinds faster and faster against me. "He's hurting. I can't—I can't take it. Help him. *Please.*"

Theo practically blows. "Did she just—oh my *fuck*, I'm definitely in love."

Declan's shoulder nudges mine carefully. "Want me to take it out?"

Dear God, yes. Anything. Please.

I nod, molding my lips around our omega's slick, puffy clit and lapping at it. She moans the same second Declan gets my fly open. I groan in relief as he sticks his hand in, moving with a no-nonsense sort of determination.

My dick springs free a second later, so hard it almost reaches Meg's thigh. I feel the heat rolling off her. When I slide my tongue into her opening and ease the tight muscles open with a quick flick, a fresh burst of slick dribbles down onto my erection.

"That's it, baby," Dec croons. "Gush all over his cock. It's big, right? So perfectly hard for you, too. I can see his knot throbbing. I bet he's dying to rub that slick all over himself right now. I know I want to put it on myself."

His words make her even wetter. Meg pants, her next plea breathless, "Take it. Use it. Please, Alpha. I want you to smell like me."

Declan's shiver echoes through me, his thigh pressed along mine, his pants bunched there. "Can I?" he asks me, reaching his left hand over.

A bolt of fear streaks through me. I want him to have as much of her as he wants; I want her to have what she wants, too. But I'm so close to coming, I'm worried I'll blow all over his hand if he grazes me.

If my mouth wasn't so busy, I'd grit my teeth. As it is, I manage a slight nod and brace myself, doing everything I can not to focus on the way my cock tingles, my pulse pounding so hard I swear Dec will feel it in the air between us.

I pull my mouth back when I feel his cupped hand slide between her thighs. He groans loudly, taking his handful of slick back to his dick, working it harder, squeezing his knot on every pass.

Envy burns through me for one insane moment, then I'm back in pained bliss, sucking on our beautiful girl's pussy. She's so close. I can feel it in every stuttering roll of her hips.

"Fuck, look at that. You're making Archer's cock so messy, baby," Declan pants.

"Touch him," Meg begs. "Stroke his cock for me."

All of the air in the car evaporates. For the longest second of all of our lives, no one breathes. Then I hear Theo curse softly.

And Declan's right hand lands back on my thigh.

His knee bumps mine, the gesture just casual enough to ease the tightness squeezing my lungs. He only says one word, "Yeah?"

If I could reach down and curl his hand around my dick for him, I would. I would do anything, right now, to feel Meg's slick gliding over my shaft.

"Yes," I exhale.

Meg moans loudly, tipping her chin down to watch as Declan wraps his hand around my cock.

chapter
thirty-five

THROUGH THE HAZE, I only understand a few precious pieces of information.

One—a very sexy alpha is licking my clit like he'll die if he stops.

Two—another very sexy alpha is sitting next to him with his hand wrapped around his thick, gorgeous cock, stroking himself in the sorts of slow, erotic pulls that I know have to be for my benefit.

Three—the second alpha just reached over to do the same to the man who's currently working his tongue into my pussy.

Someone behind me makes a choking sound. "Jesus, Dec. Arch. *Fuuuuck.*"

I can't remember who he is, but he's clearly coming. I don't blame him, but I do wish I could thank him for reminding me who's under me.

Archer is the beautiful man with his face pressed into my center. And Declan is the one stroking Archer's huge, dark cock.

My mouth drops open while I stare, unable to feel anything except awed, explosive desire.

Declan smirks at me, his eyes fixed on my face. The expression is cocky and goading. Like he jerks his packmates off at my request every day.

"You like that, princess? You like watching me stroke two hard cocks at once?"

He twists both of his fists, biting his lip while Archer groans loudly. Declan's eyes dance. "He likes that. Should we find out what else the good doctor likes? Give you a head start next time you want to play with this fat alpha cock?"

The sound that comes out of me isn't human, but I don't feel human anymore. I'm an animal, lost to my instincts and urges, gasping while Archer works my clit in earnest, pressing and roughing at it with the flat of his tongue.

Declan leans his torso back, straightening his arms to tug both cocks in slow, hard jerks. Archer's moan catches in his throat this time.

I gush slick over his lips, bearing down. I'm going to come. Declan knows it. He's teasing both of us with it, knowing I'll try to hold out as long as I can so I'll get to watch him longer.

The thought pisses me off. My body is on fire. I need this alpha to make me come. I need to feel his release splattered all over my skin.

And this asshole is toying with us both.

"Harder," I cry. "Stroke him faster."

His hands slow again, tugging them both until Archer grunts.

Declan's smirk blossoms into a crooked grin. "Make me, princess."

I don't think. Can't think. My hand flies off Archer's head and whips Declan across the face.

His head snaps to the side. When he turns back, his eyes flash and darken, the pupils blooming. "Fuck, yes," he hisses, working both cocks faster. "Hit me again."

I obey instantly, striking his other cheek. He roars, all fury and pleasure. His chest heaves while he teases his knot with expert squeezes.

Beneath me, Archer moans. I glance down and see Declan's fingertips massaging the swollen mass at the base of his huge cock, too. They close back into a fist a second later, tugging hard and fast as more slick drips down into our mess.

Archer's hands glide inward slightly, his hold shifting until the tips of his fingers are at my entrance. He presses two into my squelching heat and pulls my whole clit into his mouth at the same moment.

All of the tension pulling at my center releases. I scream, grinding into his face. The sound sets him off. A thick slash of cum hits the bottom of my ass.

"That's right," Declan pants. "*Come.*"

It takes me a moment to realize he's talking to both of us. His fingers tighten on Archer's shaft as it jerks in release. "Come all over her, Arch. *Fuck.*"

Declan erupts. With both hands full, he has no choice but to paint the front of his tank top, shooting thick white ropes all over the Ospreys' old team logo.

While Declan slides his hand out of his packmate's lap, Archer licks the last tremors of my orgasm from my body and bands his arms around my hips, hugging me while he buries his face against my belly. Shaking.

Declan reaches behind himself to yank his shirt over his head, cleaning his hands and his cock with it. When he's done, I silently hold out my hand.

With my haze burning off, I remember he doesn't like me. Not at all. I'm half-expecting him to fling his shirt in the opposite direction just to spite me.

Our eyes meet, his pure blue fire. I don't know what he sees in mine, but his expression softens slightly. "Here," he murmurs, and reaches over to quickly wipe me down, too.

It isn't sweet or romantic, but at least he's thorough and not too rough. Not rough at all, actually.

When he's finished, I let myself collapse into Archer's lap. He catches me, cradling me close, purring before I've even set my cheek over his chest.

Declan watches us, his face more open than I've ever seen it. When Archer's gaze flits over to his packmate, Declan acknowledges the glance with his signature smirk.

"Guess you owe me," he shrugs. Archer laughs, the sound startled but relieved.

Theo twists in his seat, looking from Declan to Archer. "You two fuckers are *so* having my car detailed."

chapter
thirty-six

ASH PACK GROUP TEXT

THEO CHANGED THE GROUP CHAT NAME TO
MEG'S KNOT COLLECTION

DECLAN

Classy.

THEO

I know, right? I was going to go for Meg's Bag
of Dicks, but I thought this sounded better.
Also for your consideration: Meg's Knot-heads
and Meg's Bitches.

DECLAN

Was "Meg's Pathetic Simps" taken or
something?

ARCHER

All are accurate. Though, Knot Collection has
a certain gravitas.

THEO

Did Archer just make a joke?

RONAN

I can't always tell.

DECLAN

He's just confused. Meg snatched his soul
straight out of his cock.

THEO

Nah, bro, pretty sure that was you.

DECLAN

knife emoji you're welcome, assholes.

RONAN

It was a good show.

Would anyone object if I brought her with me
to watch the guys practice today? The offices
should be empty.

ARCHER

With us*? No objection. Only my insistence
that I be with her at all times while she's at the
facility.

RONAN

We both will be. I don't trust any of those
assholes.

DECLAN

You mean our teammates, trainers, coaches,
and doctors?

RONAN

Assholes, one and all.

THEO

Fuck em

But not, like, literally, Dec. Save that shit for
the pack.

DECLAN

You wish, big guy.

I HEAR the omega's light footsteps pad down the stairs.

She clearly thinks she's stealthy, leaping quickly from one foot to the other and pausing at the base of the back staircase, leaning out slightly to search the kitchen before she sighs in relief and steps down onto the marble floor.

I watch from my seat in the breakfast nook, tucked between the wall enclosing the steps and a curved collection of windows, drinking the last of my coffee.

Declan and Theo just left for practice, bickering over which car to drive since Theo's is currently dubbed "The Splash Zone" and Declan hates taking his Bugatti out on the brick roads.

Archer's slept in. I can't remember the last time that happened.

I expected Meg to do the same. As soon as we got home last night, she jumped out of the backseat and raced into the house in nothing but panties and her sports bra, calling out something about needing to sleep.

I paced outside her guest room for a while and debated going in. But it was her first night staying in the house since she agreed to court us. I didn't want to crowd her, no matter how much I hated having her in the guest room instead of the pack wing.

A situation I've already remedied with calls to the furniture and nesting stores. Each assured me all of the things for her suite will arrive before dinner.

As I observe silently, Meg scampers across the floor to the coffee maker. Between her halo of messy blonde hair and her beautiful bare face, she looks like a fucking angel this morning. Thin silk pajamas only add to the effect. I recognize the white loungewear set from the boutique we visited last night. One of the others must have hung it on her door this morning before I got up.

It's only been a couple of weeks, but I'm beginning to understand everything I've ever read about omegas and pack cohesion. Already, I find myself appreciating the other guys more and more. Every time one of them thinks of her before I do or gives her something I can't, my respect for them grows. I'm proud of how caring Archer is; how nurturing Theo's turned out to be. And Declan...

If jerking off his packmate isn't teamwork, I don't know what is.

"Good morning, little one."

Meg jumps when she hears me, her blue eyes as wide as saucers. When she finds me grinning at her, she quickly brushes a few loose strands of hair off her face.

"Oh. Good morning."

She shuffles over, head bowed. I don't understand her posture or her expression. Why is she slinking around like this? Was she hoping no one would see her?

I set my coffee on the table as she folds herself into the bench seat across from me. Every motion screams her discomfort.

What do I do?

This isn't my strong suit. Emotions and uncertainty both make me twitchy.

"The offices are empty since it's the weekend; it should be safer for you. I was going to ask if you wanted to come in with me to go over all of the new marketing materials you created this week."

"Oh," she says again, blinking her beautiful azure eyes. "I forgot all about that after... everything."

I feel my mouth quirk up, along with an eyebrow. "Are you embarrassed, little one?"

Meg's face flushes pink. Her fingers twitch around her coffee while she sinks her top teeth into the side of her lower lip. "Me? Embarrassed? About the—the—"

She's so cute. I fight a bigger smile, not wanting to taunt her. Setting my coffee aside, I start slowly leaning across the tabletop. "I'm referring to the living wet dream that occurred in Theo's car."

Meg's eyes darken. She skirts them down to where her fingers clutch her mug.

Fuck. I'm making this worse.

Where the hell is Archer?

I stare across the breakfast table, watching my pretty girl shrink in on herself. How can I convince her that all of us are fine with what happened? Better than fine. Ecstatic.

What went down between the three of them in the backseat last night is everything we've ever wanted. She's already mending rifts and bringing us together. Effortlessly.

She's such a gift. I spend most of our time convincing myself she's actually here. The fact that she wants all of us even a fraction as much as we want her is a goddamn miracle.

And who taught her to be ashamed of this shit anyway?

She was made to be cared for and worshipped, exactly the way Archer and Declan did last night. Why is she so embarrassed about that?

My instincts rise up, urgency snapping through my blood. "Come here."

Her unmarked throat works over a swallow. When she's within reach, I pull her sideways onto my lap and wrap my hand around her jaw.

Our eyes lock. Her pupils bloom and contract, reacting to the threat of meeting an alpha's gaze head-on. Something catches in my chest; the nag painful and unfamiliar.

I don't want her to be afraid of me.

Everyone else is. I know that.

I didn't start out my life as an alpha endeavoring to be the most dominant, intimidating asshole in any room; but the older I got, the more my dominance grew. And grew. Until it clobbered everyone.

Even me.

The thought of this sweet, gorgeous girl feeling any fear when she's in my arms fucking guts me. My instincts war with each other—the part of me that needs to be powerful in order to keep her safe versus the part that needs to make her happy.

It takes a few minutes.

Then, very deliberately, I lower my eyes and tip my head to the side, bowing it slightly.

Submission.

I don't think I've ever offered it to anyone else. There were a few times when I was *forced*...

This is different.

It's the first real thing I've offered her.

Her shaky little gasp sinks into my center. "Ronan."

She drops her head to my shoulder, nuzzling our faces together. The motion is so sweet, I can't breathe for a moment. My gaze follows her every move, absorbing the way she takes my submission and offers her own version back to me. Because, in the end, she needs me to be in control.

It's heady, knowing I can offer this queen my crown, and she'll just put it back on my head.

She doesn't want the power. She wants me to hold her.

My purr starts up, rolling through us both while I nestle her closer. "This is the way it will be between us. When you need something, you'll come to me. When I need *you*, I'll come find you." I run my lips along her ear. "Either way, we'll both come."

Meg shivers lightly, a nervous giggle catching in her throat. "I was starting to think you didn't like me like that."

That thought slams into my forehead, but won't sink in. How could she ever think that? I've done nothing but worry and lust after her since I set eyes on her.

Seeing my dismay, her plush lips quirk in a small smile. "You've hung back," she peeps. "In the living room last week, and then yesterday, when you decided to drive..."

She swallows and ducks her head. "I thought maybe you just didn't want me that way. Or maybe I turned you off because I was so... crazy."

I grip her chin firmly, angling her face toward mine, forcing her to look into my eyes. "You have nothing to be embarrassed by, baby girl. Both of those nights were the hottest I've ever experienced. And even if we weren't all salivating at the mere thought of touching you, our feelings for you will never change because you have needs. You need, we provide. Period."

I lower my lips to brush hers. "You need, *I* provide. Got it, baby girl?"

Meg's swallow sounds sticky. "Yes, Alpha."

My cock is abruptly, painfully hard. I grunt while I shift her. "*Alpha* is good when I'm inside of you or about to be. Otherwise, it's *Daddy* in private, and whatever else you'd like to call me in public. All right?"

Her eyes darken again, this time for a completely different reason. "Yes, *Alpha*."

She's teasing. Daring me.

I snake my hand up to her throat and grasp it, tightening my fingers just enough to let her feel it. It's a test, to see if she's really as ready for me as she thinks she is. Her pupils yawn wide while sweet succulence bursts from her core.

Goddamn. It's *perfection*. I kiss her forehead, muttering against her sweet-smelling skin. "I can't tell you how much I want you. I've waited more than twenty years to find you, baby girl, but I'm a lot to take on sexually. I don't want to scare you by coming on too strong. You have to trust me before I take you. Because when I take you? It will be possession. And it will be permanent. Do you understand?"

Perfect peach perfume rises off her skin while her eyes fix on mine. She nods slowly.

And slides down onto her knees.

My mouth might drop open.

Some blend of amusement and insecurity fills her fine features. Her lips quirk into a sassy little smile, but her eyes are meek. Her fingers brush my belt, a silent plea.

She wants to please me. Submit to me.

The satisfaction that blooms inside of me is unlike anything I've ever known.

Deeper.

True.

I make short work of my pants, freeing my cock for her. "Is this what you want, baby girl? You want to suck this cock?"

Something hot and wild slides through her gaze. "I want you to show me how you like it, Alpha."

Goddamn fucking hell.

I pet her head, radiating the approval she needs. "Good girl. I'll show you exactly what I like. And, once you've finished your breakfast, Daddy will take you to work with him."

The shy version of her smile reappears. She kisses my inked thigh, subtly scent-marking in a shy, hesitant way. I swear my cold, dead heart grows four sizes in two seconds.

My cock twitches. She parts her lips, offering her mouth again. "Yes, Alpha."

Her supplication is beautiful. The way her lashes sweep over her gaze. The tremor of anticipation in her voice. The softness of her fingers, stroking eager, gentle lines down my length.

I shift closer and spread my thighs, giving her plenty of room to slip between them. My voice turns to gravel, husky from the surge of dominance and lust I hold in check. "Take the whole thing into your mouth."

Meg obeys without hesitation. Her pillowy pink lips slip over my girth, stretching to take me in. When the back of her throat squeezes around the pulsing head of my cock, she gags. I grunt and gently grip the nape of her neck to pull her back.

"I'll make sure you breathe," I tell her. "You don't have to worry about that."

I say the words, knowing she won't take them at face value. No one ever has before. Which makes sense, considering I'm basically telling the girl I'll decide when she breathes; if she breathes.

Who would trust someone else with something like that?

Turns out—*Meg would.*

And she trusts *me.*

I've never felt more aroused or more alpha than I do in the next moment. The moment she takes me right back into her throat and gazes up at me, her eyes soft and wet. Two crystal pools of trust.

My grip tugs her back just as a sparkling tear trickles out of her eye. Unable to help myself, I bend and lick it off her cheek, murmuring praise into her temple.

The second I settle back, she dives for my cock again. I let her work her hot, wet mouth over it again and again, feeling my balls draw tight every time she allows me to block her breathing.

"Look how perfect you are," I rasp, finding her hand on my thigh and guiding it to my knot. "Can you squeeze Daddy right here? I want to feel you around my knot when I come in your mouth."

She moans, the sound a soaked vibration around my erection.

A growl rips out of my heaving chest. "Do you want to swallow your alpha's cum, little one? Pump that knot for me and I'll give it to you."

Her next cry is high and desperate. The pads of her fingers stroke the swelling knot at the base of my cock, sending shivers up my back.

My thighs strain. She watches the way my tattoo moves over the muscles and doubles down, sucking me harder and faster. Her free hand slides between my legs and finds my sac, rolling my aching balls between her fingertips.

"Fuck, you're so good for me. I'm going to come. You want it, baby girl?"

She nods around me seconds before I lose it, spurting onto the velvet warmth of her tongue. A keening moan sails up her throat as her eyes fall shut. Pure rapture fills her face.

From my taste, I realize. To her, I taste as good as I smell.

The thought is enough to make my dick give a final, feeble jerk. Meg releases it, sitting back on her heels, staring up at me while she pants quietly.

For a long moment, I just look at her. It's all I can do. Just gaze back and wonder *how in the ever-loving fuck* I've gotten so lucky.

When I reach my hand out, she puts her cheek in it. I stroke her face, her neck, her nape. The truth slips out of me on an exhale. "I love it when you look like this."

Her lips curve. "Like what?"

I smile, hauling her up into my lap. "Like *mine*."

chapter
thirty-seven

MRS. FLEMING IS GOING to give me a serious Cinderella complex if she keeps leaving outfits out for me.

She must have talked to Ronan about going to the office, because when I get back up to my temporary guest bedroom, I find a garment bag hanging on the door. Inside, there's a casual-yet-polished outfit, perfect for hanging off Ronan's arm at work without, you know, actually being an employee.

After showing me exactly how he wants me to choke on his cock, the pack alpha also fed me a whole omelet and a side of fresh fruit. By the time we finished breakfast, Ronan was already late.

To save time, I leave my hair in messy waves and set to work on a decent make-up routine. The skirt in the garment bag is tight and shiny—a nude fabric that matches my skin tone and hugs every inch from my navel to mid-thigh.

With a blouse, it might be a passable secretary's outfit; but with the artfully faded Nirvana T-shirt and black velvet platforms Mrs. Fleming left with it, the whole thing takes on an edgy, effortlessly sexy vibe. I tuck the front of the loose band shirt into the tight skirt, the way I've seen countless (much trendier) girls do it on TikTok.

There is a *scary* assortment of accessories strewn over the top of the guest room's dresser. Like, wow. Twenty pairs of earrings, a pile of necklaces, a few handfuls of rings. And there's still a small mountain of unpacked boutique bags on the floor next to it.

Mrs. Fleming is probably planning to unpack all of them in my —the *suite.*

I tamp down an instant flair of longing and its accompanying swirl of fear, fiddling with a set of gold stacking rings and a matching tangle of chains for my neck. Still, with every little piece I add or adjust, I can't help but think that this is all temporary. It could all be gone by the end of the day.

Like I was never here...

I don't realize I'm sinking into an anxiety attack until I'm shocked out of it. By sunglasses, of all things.

There are eight pairs lined up in a row. Most are black—mirrored aviators, boxy pairs, trendy goggle-like sets. A couple of wire-rimmed gold and silver cat-eyed shapes.

And the pair that splits my face in a wide grin.

They're perfect. Oversized heart-shaped lenses, surrounded by shiny orange plastic.

Osprey colors. Cheap. Kitschy. Adorable.

Theo.

He clearly had no idea how to contribute to the rest of my wardrobe, but snuck these in so I would still have a piece from him.

Because he wants me to know he tried. Because he wants me here. And because, somehow, even when he isn't in the room, he always knows when I need to smile. And how to make me.

With a goofy grin, I balance the heart-shaped sunnies on top of my head and leave the rest behind.

❤

I **FIND** Archer waiting for me at the bottom of the floating stairs.

Half of me expects some awkwardness from him after last night. But he smiles broadly, the flash of his perfect white teeth especially dazzling behind his full, dark lips. His voice is as calm and deep as ever. "You look gorgeous, sweetheart."

He extends a gentlemanly hand, helping me down onto the polished marble floor. I note the over-stuffed leather messenger bag slung over his shoulder. His eyes gleam as he explains, "Research."

I feel myself brighten. I love research. Specifically anything to do with demographics or psychology.

While we walk out of the front door and lock up, I ask him which studies he's carting around. When he hears my genuine curiosity, his brows lift.

"Pack dynamics. Omega hormones and nutrition. Alpha parasympathetic pheromone responses. Bonding benefits." He lists the incredibly personal—and, honestly, heart-flutteringly sweet—topics with a distracted air, and then pauses, as if he's afraid to ask, "You... *like* research?"

I nod so hard, my sunglasses almost slide down. "How can you not?" I retort, frowning at the thought of someone *not* being interested in learning the secrets of the universe. "I did a lot of statistical data analysis for my Master's. Are your studies peer reviewed? What sorts of sample sizes did they work with?"

Archer's mouth drops half-open. It's the second time this

morning one of these alphas has looked at me like that. Before I can get too self-conscious, a glossy black Rolls Royce pulls around my tiny car, stopping right in the center of the circular drive.

Ronan—looking effortlessly cool in his all-black suit, slides out of the driver's seat and comes around. It takes me a moment to realize he's only gotten out so he can grab me by the hips and lay a scorching kiss on me.

When he pulls back, his quicksilver eyes swirl. "That outfit is fucking perfect, baby girl. Ready to come to work with Daddy?"

I smile, nodding over at Archer. "You might need to do CPR first. I think I broke him."

Ronan raises a thick winged brow, the expression as cooly gorgeous as the rest of him. And his car.

"Twice in twenty-four hours? A record, little one." He claps Archer's shoulder, shaking his packmate. "Breathe, Arch."

With a sharp swat to my behind, Ronan opens the back door of the car—which, of course, swings to the left instead of the right, because... why wouldn't it?

I marvel as I climb inside—midnight leather and plush onyx carpeting fill the spacious interior. The stitching is thick, metallic silver. Like his eyes.

Behind me, I barely hear Archer's shell-shocked whisper. "Ronan—she likes *research*."

And for the first time since we met, our alpha *laughs*.

chapter
thirty-eight

CRINGING, I listen as Coach hands Declan his own balls.

Fuck. I know Dec isn't up his usual standards, but he's still, you know, *the best fucking quarterback* in the League.

And, really, the issue on that last play was more the offensive line's fault. They know his shoulder gets tweaked. They should be protecting his right...

On the sidelines, Dec has his hands on his hips and his head bowed, nodding while Coach yells. My shoulder pads thump against my body as I jog over.

Fuck, it's hot. September in Florida is already miserable—but in full gear, running around, not to mention I weigh more than any other guy here.

The second I hit the sideline, an assistant hands me a water bottle. I toss him my helmet like I would toss a valet my keys. "Keep her running for me, kid."

Coach turns, his bald head already bright red from the sun beating down; or maybe the way he was just beating down Dec. I really can't tell. Either way, his mouth opens wide to shout some more—

But a beautiful burst of peachy perfume winds its way over the humid air.

Declan moves first, his head snapping up, body turning at the same second. He's already moving, ignoring the way Coach yells his last name. I pat our boss's shoulder and follow my packmate. "Sorry, Coach!"

She's at the far corner of the stadium, where the locker room tunnels empty onto the turf. I spot her standing between Archer and Ronan, both of their bodies angled protectively. I realize why when I feel the utter stillness on the field behind me. Sixty-something alphas all frozen dead in place.

Because they can smell her, too.

Was I tired before?

Not anymore.

I sprint my ass over to her as quickly as I can, smiling at her shriek when I rush her right off her feet. I spin us around while I kiss her, rumbling my appreciation for her taste against full, glossy lips.

Part of me hopes she leaves her lipstick all over my face. That's better than war paint, in my opinion.

"Good morning, peaches." I finally stop turning us, banding my arms tight around her little body.

If she cares that I'm covered in grass, sweat, and hard plastic pads, I can't tell. Her legs and arms twine around me as far as they can. She leans back, her beautiful face knocking the wind right out of my chest. Wide, blue eyes sparkle fondly while she smiles my favorite goofy grin. "Thank you for my sunglasses, big guy."

My heart expands when I spot the orange hearts nestled in her hair. I knew she'd like them. And I'm fucking hopeless with clothes. *Although...*

"I think we need to get you matching panties," I muse.

Her smile widens. "Only if you get some orange-heart briefs to wear for games."

Oh *fuck* yeah. That's a great idea. I'm about to agree to our deal when Declan snarls, "Give her to me."

Meg and I both turn; me scowling, her casting him a quelling look. Until we see his face.

The blue in his eyes is down to a thin ring, edged out by his expanding pupils. His jaw grinds, ticking. For one horrifying second, I think he's snapping into rut. Then I see the way he watches Meg's face, reading her emotions. He's still fully in control. He's just...

Wild.

I wait for Meg to give me a little nod before handing her over, placing her in Dec's waiting arms bridal-style. The second he has her, he forgets the rest of us are there, except to mutter, "Watch my back."

Ronan's already on it, charging around our pack and heading for the team and Coach. He'll head them all off, but Archer follows just in case.

I step up, facing the field, shoulder-to-shoulder with Dec, my eyes scanning behind him, warning off anyone who might try to approach us. This seems important—it's the first time he's ever wanted a moment with Meg—and I don't want one of these other asshats to ruin it.

Once I see Ronan pointing to the training center and Coach's jerky nod of agreement, I relax. The other guys are going to go to condition. The field starts to clear while they make their way to the tunnel on the opposite side of the stadium.

All except the kicker, DeLuca, and his beta ball boy. He has to stay out here to practice kicks through the up-rights, but I'm unbothered. The rookie is a good kid. And he isn't even looking at my girl.

Declan is.

He's holding her in his arms, and just... staring at her.

His jaw pops while he grinds his teeth, eyes narrowing slightly while they rove over her whole body, right down to the chunky shoes dangling off her dainty ankles.

It's insane how different all of our relationships with the same woman are. When I think about how she's possibly juggling all four, my head spins.

For me, she's a gorgeous sunbeam. Fun, wily, warm. Effortlessly supportive and reassuring when I need it. Even when I don't *know* I need it.

With Ronan, it's the opposite. *He* supports *her*. Directs her. He seems to need it, that dominance of his demanding her surrender. And she gives it to him willingly.

Then there's Arch, who's been dying for someone to take care of. I think he craves softness. Connection. She's definitely all of that with a side of sweet sex appeal. After last night, I think we all know exactly how gone he is.

All of us, really.

Including Dec.

For fuck's sake, the guy gave himself and Archer a dual handy just because she suggested it. That's the closest to being in love I've ever seen the knot-for-brains.

But he's stubborn.

But so is Meg.

He glares at her, and she glowers back, her own scowl tinged with an amusing dash of *what now asshole?* Not at all intimidated, the way she might be with Ronan.

No, for Dec, *she's* in charge.

And he hates it.

Or, maybe, he hates that he *doesn't* hate it. I can't tell. But he watches her like she's the air he breathes—air that slowly poisons him.

Poor fucker.

He finally unseals his jaw. "Are you all right?"

Meg crosses her arms over her faded Nirvana shirt. And I know if she was standing, she'd have that sexy little hip cocked at him. "Why wouldn't I be?"

He inhales the scent from her throat. "You smell nervous."

Huh.

I don't catch the slight edge to her scent until he mentions it, mostly because it's so crazy-subtle. Just a *tiny* pinch of sour? Not exactly. More like the peaches I love so much are just a bit unripe. Firm, with a bite, instead of her usual syrupy succulence.

I don't like it, but I'm not riled by it. It's just a small shift; a normal emotion, nothing painful or overwhelming. My gorgeous girl is entitled to her feelings, like the rest of us.

Well, Dec doesn't agree. He looks ready to dismember someone.

She blinks at him, some of her sass dissipating. "I'm fine. This is just a lot. I helped Ronan with a whole new social media strategy, and now I'm out here. I've never been around so many unbonded alphas."

Declan growls, "*You shouldn't be here.* Ever. I don't want you here."

His voice rings over all three of us. I bristle as Meg rears back from his ugly words. Her scent turns, burning completely. My chest swells. I stuff the urge to deck him and step over to snatch her away.

He tries to lunge at me, but a snarl unlike any sound I've ever made snaps out of my mouth. "*Fuck off*, Dec," I roar, cradling Meg in the crook of one arm and wrapping a protective hand over her head, shielding her ears between my hand and my chest. She shivers anyway, hearing the echo of my rage under my jersey.

I reach up and unfasten my shoulder pads, letting them fall as I step back from my dickheaded packmate. He stands with his fists balled up, breathing hard behind bared teeth. "*Give her back to me*, Theo."

Meg clings to my body, cowering from the bark. I feel it arrow down my spine and impale my center. For a moment, I want to listen. But my own instincts seethe, rebelling.

I square up to him, covering Meg's head again. "I said: *fuck off*, Dec."

The bark knocks him back a step. He absorbs it, our dominance too evenly matched for either of us to overpower the other without our fists. Something I refuse to attempt while my gorgeous girl is so upset.

She whimpers and tucks her face closer to my neck, shaking. Declan watches the motion and freezes. His eyes flash while he swallows. And backs off another step.

"Get her out of here," he grunts, dropping his eyes to his feet. "Just—get her away from me. *Keep her away from me. Please.*"

He says "please" instead of "now." That's the only reason I listen. Turning on my cleats, I hold Meg tighter and head for the closest exit—the tunnel behind us.

My purr springs to life while I mutter to her. "Ignore him, precious. He's all bent out of shape about a bunch of shit that has nothing to do with you."

"I wish I could ignore him," she replies, the words watery. "I don't *want* to want him, I just—do."

It must hurt her so much every time he rejects her. I hug her closer. "I know, precious. I'm sorry he's such an asshole. I'm going to talk to Archer and Ronan, and we'll..."

Well, I don't actually know. But we'll get his ass in line. Somehow. Come to think of it, there's a bunch of shit I should probably tell the others about Declan's life before college football.

I don't even think I'm supposed to know all of the details, though. If I went running my mouth about the shit his mother put him through and the way his father was, he might never forgive me.

The last thing this pack needs is *another* rift.

Meg fists my jersey and tugs until I meet her wet blue eyes. Maybe she can read my mind and the conflict there, because she seems to settle my internal debate for me.

"Don't," she begs softly. "We can't force him to change. I want him to come to me on his own, when he's ready. Not because he thinks he has to. Or because he thinks I'll take his pack if he doesn't."

Take his pack?

What the fuck?

There's no way Declan thinks that's even a possibility. He's *pack*. And, even before all this shit, he was my brother. As good as, at least.

She smooths her hands over my dirty, sweaty face, the touch sweet. "Let me deal with it, big guy. I'm okay. Thanks for sticking up for me, though." She throws in a crooked little smile. "That was hot."

I huff a laugh, marching us toward the locker room. On the fly, I decide to get my shit and do my conditioning at our home gym. I also decide I'm taking that jackass's Bugatti to get there. His vanilla ass can walk home.

We're totally alone down here. The other guys will be working out for at least two hours. I'm sure Ronan and Archer are waiting at the gym for me to turn up with Meg. When Declan stomps in without us, they'll assume I carried her off.

I send them a text telling them I have her in the locker room, and I'm taking her home because of Declan Dickhead. I put the message in the group chat so he'll see it when he gets his phone later.

Ronan immediately erupts in all caps while Archer calmly asks after Meg. That's his only focus—is she okay? Does she need him? Can I make sure she's comfortable until they get back for the night?

Meg's eyes are closed, her face pressed into the scent of my throat. I seat us on one of the changing benches between walls of glossy orange, extra-wide lockers. They're more like individual mudrooms, really. And mine is, of course, the messiest one in the whole damn place.

"I told the guys that I carried you off to ravage you," I joke, hoping she feels up to playing with me. If she isn't, I'll tell Archer to come.

She cracks another smile, her eyes still relaxed and shut. "Oh boy. Is Daddy mad?"

"Not at us," I reply, smiling back. "Should we give him something to be pissed about? We could tee-pee his office. Or the Rolls."

Her blue eyes flash open. "That car is *way* too beautiful to desecrate."

I snort in pretend offense. "Excuse me, but you seemed to have no issue redecorating *my* car."

She shrugs playfully, her expression full of false innocence. "Well, yours isn't a Rolls."

"Oh-ho," I crow, my fingers finding her ribs, tickling. "I see how it is, peaches. Should we not even bother with a Mercedes for you, then? Straight to a Ferrari?"

She giggles and gasps, squirming around in my lap. "Theo!"

By the time I'm done, she's breathless, straddling one of my thighs—because, in that skirt, she actually *can't* straddle both.

Guess I'll have to take it off.

chapter
thirty-nine

THEO IS predictable in the absolute best way. The second I come on to him, he's on his feet, towering over me and the lockers, kicking off his cleats and socks.

His wide grin is just cocky enough to make my belly flip. "Got a locker room fantasy, peaches?" he teases, rolling his jersey up his abs with a suggestive slowness. "Or did you get all of those out of your system in high school?"

It's one of those weird moments when I suddenly remember —*oh, yeah, we don't* actually *know everything about each other*. My teeth catch the corner of my mouth. "I didn't go to high school, actually."

Theo frowns, pausing mid-strip. I shrug one shoulder, trying to sound casual. "Omega, remember?"

He pulls off his jersey, revealing the manliest torso in existence. Wide, long, entirely covered in muscle, the lines dusted with the same dark blond hair that makes up his beard. He throws his jersey in a careless, distinctly-Theo way, scratching his chin thoughtfully.

"My sisters are omegas. They both went to school. Did your parents not want you to?"

I open my mouth, the whole story stuck in the middle of my throat, aching to come out. But I don't want to tell it under fluorescent lights, surrounded by the faint aroma of a few dozen alphas. And I'd really rather tell them all at once, so I don't have to do the whole thing multiple times.

"I didn't have an alpha brother to kick ass on my behalf," I return.

Theo's grin is like the sun. It warms my face, my bones, my heart. "Very glad I'm not your brother, peaches. I'd much rather be your alpha."

He bucks his hips toward me, the motion teasing. "Does your lack of high school romance mean you don't know how to unlace these pants?"

"Afraid not," I laugh, my hands reaching over to snap the waistband. It's frightfully damp. Just how much do these guys sweat, anyway?

And why does it smell *good*?

Theo watches me pull my hands back, bringing both close to my face on instinct. His brows quirk up. "Yeah?"

I nod, my eyes widening. Perfume rises off me while I shift, my panties feeling as damp as his waistband. "Can I take them off?"

It's weird. Theo and I have already been buck-naked with each other—in the living room, on full display, nonetheless—but, really, neither of us were *there*. He was in a rut; I was in a spike. We wanted each other but we couldn't really *be* together.

This is different. I'm still aroused. Judging by the mondo bulge running more than halfway down his thigh, so is he.

But this time, it's us. It's a decision, not a foregone conclusion. And there's something sweetly awkward about that.

He feels it, too. I can tell by the shy edge of his grin. "You can always take off my clothes. No matter what. Forever."

I smirk, swallowing a gulp of hesitation. "Show me how to unlace them."

His thick fingers meet mine, skimming reverently over my knuckles while his green eyes swirl. "Here? You sure?"

The scent of blood oranges gets stronger. My bottom lip pulls while I bite it. I wiggle in my wet panties, clamping my thighs to stave off the throb between them. I can't deny that the thought of this big, sexy football player taking me in the middle of the locker room is doing something for me. "Could we?"

He nods, swallowing. "The team will be in the gym for two hours, and everyone has lockers over there, too. We'll be alone here."

Our fingers brush and tangle together for a brief second, squeezing. It's our first moment alone since we met, and I can tell he feels that every bit as much as I do.

Theo slowly guides our hands to his waistband. "There's a buckle here," he shows me, tugging a concealed flap to reveal the silver sliver. I unhook it.

"Then you sort of flip the front down..."

He does. His happy trail is entirely visible while he points to the laced placket inside his pants. I hook a finger into the knots, pulling them free before I run the back of my finger down the line of hair leading to his groin.

He exhales, the sound wobbling. "You're a natural, gorgeous."

I hook my hands into his waistband and slowly pull it down, only pausing to glance up for final approval.

There's a seriousness to him I've never seen before. His eyes burn green, but he frowns, the expression confused. "Are you sure?" he asks again. "This will be your first time with one of us. You don't want one of the other guys?"

My heart squeezes.

This big, beautiful man—the only one who recognized me for what I am. The only one who's been completely sure about me from the moment we met. The easiest one to fall for, by far.

He deserves everything good, but he doesn't seem to know it. I skim my hands up his sides, relishing the way he shudders under my touch.

"I want you to be first," I tell him, then flash the smile I know he loves. "Finders keepers, big guy."

My fingertips find his happy trail again. He makes a noise between a chuckle and groan, bending to hoist me up. "If you insist, precious."

Within seconds, I'm up against the lockers, my skirt rolled around my belly, his pants forgotten on the linoleum.

His sweat smells divine. I rub my cheek into the crook of his neck, mixing our scents, wanting more of his herbal citrus on me. He growls, the sound all sex. "Look at my gorgeous girl. You like me smelling like you, peaches?"

I nod, licking at his pulse. It jumps, and I feel that thump echo in his cock, the thick shaft slapping the back of my thigh. I squirm closer, wanting my panties gone.

"Mmm," he inhales the perfume and slick pouring out of me. "Fuck me. I'm pretty sure I'm the luckiest bastard in the world."

My brain feels sluggish. Not in a heat-spike way; more like a slow-building, buzzing high. From his scent, the purr rattling in his thick, perfect chest. The way his green eyes soften when they catch mine.

A small smile touches his sculpted mouth. "I think we need a redo."

Before I can ask, he discards my panties and positions his huge, hard erection against my bare pussy. I gasp and quiver, the feeling of his soft skin and solid girth heavenly against the throb at the top of my thighs.

"Theo," I squeak, unable to keep from rubbing against him. "You're so—"

Everything, really.

Thicker, harder, wider, longer than I remembered.

So *perfect*.

I suddenly understand what they're all on about, constantly complimenting my pussy. If I'm even a fraction as perfect as this alpha, I won't argue with them about it anymore.

My fingers weave into his damp hair, tugging hard to pull myself up and over the thick crown of his penis again and again. Theo groans into my neck, licking and sucking the thin skin. The tease of his teeth scraping *right there* has me desperate in moments.

"Please," I beg, moving faster. "Please, Alpha."

His hands move from under my thighs to brace my hips against the cool metal door at my back. He seals his mouth over mine, both of us moaning as our tongues slide together and our bodies strain to get closer.

He breaks away, panting. Theo presses our foreheads together, his eyes searching mine. "You want my cock, precious? Does this pretty pussy need me to fill it up?"

I moan again, nodding frantically. "Please, Theo. I want you. Please."

He doesn't need any more provocation. With strength that makes me want to gush, he lifts me slightly and slams me down onto his length.

We both cry out. My head falls back. Everything in my middle clenches, grasping the exquisite thickness pressed into every trembling muscle in my core.

Theo goes to work, drilling into me with long, slick thrusts, deeper than I thought possible. His knot teases me with every pulse.

"Can't knot you here," he grinds out, panting. "So use it to rub your sweet little clit."

I can't stop my body from obeying, grinding the spot that aches for him into the swelling knot at the base of his cock. He keeps thrusting, stopping every few pumps to let me bear down and buck against him.

"Theo. *Theo*," I moan, breathless. I know I'm about to lose control. The next time he pauses and—

He grips my bare hips and rubs me along the enormous knot one last time, hitting both sides of my clit until I clamp down on his cock and come.

"*Fuuuuuuck*," he sobs, hissing in my ear while slashes of his release erupt inside of me. He hugs me closer. "*Meg*."

My arms squeeze around his neck, the grip strangling. He kisses my cheek, nuzzling along my jaw as his hands soften, stroking me sweetly. A low, softer purr takes the place of words as he holds me, letting me hide my face against his shoulder.

We stand there for a long moment. Theo just strokes my hair, seemingly unconcerned with his nudity.

Eventually, the words I know he needs to hear make their way to my lips. I press them into his cheek, whispering, "I'm glad it was you. Then and now."

Theo sighs, the sound as uncharacteristically quiet as his voice. "I'm glad it will be you, always."

chapter
forty

"SHOW ME THE BLUE AGAIN."

Remi frowns through my phone screen, tilting her head at my closet. I hold the skirt of the beaded ice-blue gown out for her perusal. A crease appears between her eyebrows.

"Is it formal enough? You have to wear gloves right?"

Ugh. Don't remind me.

"The black is more elegant," she decides.

I almost snort. "Even with my boobs out?"

We both look at the deep V-neckline on the shimmering silk gown. A smirk twists my best friend's lips. "It's called a bra, Meg."

It would have to be one hell of a contraption to keep me covered while also blending into this dress, but she has a point. Plus, Mrs. Fleming is basically magic. The day after I mentioned not having anything appropriate for the guys' annual charity gala, two stunning evening gowns appeared on the back of my closet doors. I'm sure, once I choose one, the correct undergarments will somehow end up there as well.

Part of me is ashamed to admit how quickly I've gotten used to this sort of pampering. After years of completely taking care of myself, it should feel odd to let these alphas dote on me. But, in the two weeks since I moved in, their attention has started to feel natural.

I thought it would be difficult to balance so many men, but it's been pretty seamless so far. Theo and I like movie marathons —evenings spent on the couch with unholy piles of junk food. Most of the time, we don't finish watching the movie. We end up all over each other instead.

The mornings are Ronan's time. We usually have our coffee together before he either hauls me into his lap or carries me to his study, where I work on marketing stuff for the team while he does *literally everything else.*

I mean, seriously. The man is brilliant and tireless and impressively aloof. You'd never know, while he's hammering whoever is at the other end of the phone, that I'm propped on his lap with his fingers strumming my panties.

Archer's claimed my afternoons. He gets home from the Ospreys' facility around three and usually shows up at my doors shortly after, carrying an afternoon snack and whatever research he's currently immersed in.

Officially, we spend the three hours before dinner reading. Unofficially? Archer makes it his personal mission to treat my touch starvation with massages, cuddling, and an endless stream of kisses.

... And then there's Declan.

Who has made avoiding me into another sport he excels at.

We haven't spoken since he rushed me off the field. As one day of silence lapsed into three, then five, now nearly fifteen… it's clear that whatever insanity led him to stake a claim to me that day was stupid territorial alpha nonsense and had nothing at all to do with actually wanting *me*.

Which is *fine* because the others all want me plenty.

There's a knock on my door and I spring up to answer, bringing Remi with me. She laughs. "Uh, Meg? You don't have clothes on."

I glance down at my white cropped tank top and the matching high-waisted panties. It's about as close as I get to actually dressing around here these days, but I don't want to tell her that. I'm still trying to be sensitive to the fact that I somehow found a pack when she's the one who's always wanted one.

"Good call. I'll throw a robe on and text you later?" I half-lie.

Her smirk tells me she doesn't buy my line about the robe for a second. "Mm hmm. Tell Archer hi from me."

She clicks off and I see she's right—it's after three, so the alpha at my door should be my sexy doctor. The warm scents of bourbon and ginger clouding the air confirm her assumption.

While I hurry to the double doors, I do one last check around my suite. The space turned out beautifully. Sheer white curtains on flat gold rods; a modern oriental-style rug in ivories and charcoals; mirrored mercury glass tables; a matte gold-and-white desk; an enormous bed trimmed with dove linens and framed by a dark gray velvet headboard that takes up half the wall.

And Archer's favorite spot—the double-width chaise chair tucked among the corner of blank bookshelves.

He snuggles me into it every day, holding me against his side while late-afternoon sun slants over the lounger. It's become our little ritual—a slice of the peace and quiet we both crave.

He looks particularly good today, wearing one of his white button-downs rolled up to the elbows. The contrast against his rich brown skin is striking, and the way he wears it shows off the thin lines tattooed on his left arm.

Theo explained the significance of their tattoos to me one night. They each have one on their left arm, a different pattern for each man. Like his personality, Theo's is the most chaotic—a dizzying mix of bold tribal patterns.

Ronan has the thick, black curls that resemble smoke. His is the largest, the piece extending from the middle of his chest to the tips of his fingers. I happen to know the sensual curves also continue all the way to the muscles stacked around his thighs...

I've never seen Declan's tattoo up close and personal, but plenty of magazines have immortalized it in print. A series of shaded feathers start on his left shoulder and extend down to his elbow. Like an angel wing. Or an osprey's, maybe; though I'll probably never know what goes on in that guy's head.

True to his nature, Archer's ink is the subtlest. It took me a couple of weeks to figure out that the branch-like lines aren't a grid or some sort of geometry—they're meant to be a map of his veins. Leave it to our doctor to use his pack tattoo as some sort of anatomy lesson.

Arch flashes a shy smile as white as his shirt. "Hi, sweetheart."

I stretch up to kiss his cheek. "Hey! Remi says hi, too. She was just on the phone."

I'm still not used to how much my moods affect Archer, but it's undeniable; he brightens when he hears the happiness in my voice. "Did you extend our invitation to the gala? We'd all love to meet her."

I try not to pout while I shake my head. "She has to work. But maybe I can make us all dinner soon?"

He loops an arm around my waist and tows me toward our lounge chair. "Excellent idea. I'll do the grocery shopping and help you cook. Just tell me which night and what Remi likes to eat."

A familiar ache spreads through my chest. The feeling that I could never deserve this man and all of his kindness. I tuck my face into his chest to hide the emotion welling in my eyes. "Okay. Thank you."

Archer arranges us on the chaise, setting aside the bag of pastries and stack of papers in his other hand. He gathers me into his chest, purring. "You don't need to thank me, sweetheart," he murmurs. His hand comes up to cup the back of my head, and he flashes a small smile, fingering the two buns on either side of my crown. "I like these."

I chuckle. "They were for Ronan this morning. He likes the space buns." *Gives him something to grip while I'm on my knees for him.*

Archer raises a brow, teasingly solemn. "Dirty old man."

"Mm," I confirm dryly. "So very dirty."

Archer's hand skims down my back, settling over the waistband of my panties. The scent of ginger thickens into a haze of spice, sending a dizzy rush through my blood.

"Can't say I blame the guy," he mutters. "You always look so damn beautiful."

Of the three of them, Archer has spent the most one-on-one time with me, but he's also been the least sexual. The current is always there, between us. Shifting and churning. He's just such a complete gentleman.

For the first time, it occurs to me how much he's holding back. He may be a doctor and a scholar, but he's certainly no less alpha than the others. I can feel the strain in his muscles while he anchors me securely into his side. He has better self-control than Ronan or Theo, but he still wants me every bit as much.

Why is that so *ridiculously sexy*?

I snuggle closer, knowing my perfume must be stronger than it was a moment ago. Archer stiffens for a moment before he clears his throat and reaches to the side.

"I brought you some new research today," he reports, voice gravelly. "About omega purrs and barks."

Shock derails my dirty thoughts. "*Omega* barks?"

Archer's smile is fond. He loves teaching me things. I suspect he just loves sharing knowledge in general, but there seems to be some particular appeal to guiding me, specifically.

His free palm smooths down the back of my neck. "Yes. Omegas can bark, too. In very special circumstances, and usually only if one of their alphas or children are in danger."

I deflate a little bit, taking the study from him. "Oh."

He hears my disappointment and taps the pages clutched in my hand. "The barks may be rare, but they're also more powerful than any alpha's. The second an omega uses his or her bark, anyone within earshot will immediately listen—alpha, beta; doesn't matter. It's fascinating."

It really is. I flip through the first few pages until I happen upon the segment on purring.

That one, I knew about. Remi once explained that omegas will sometimes purr for their alphas if they're particularly distressed or injured. I imagine it probably comes in handy for cooling tempers.

Archer watches me carefully, his eyes tracing the way my teeth sink into my lower lip. "You know," he starts, his voice low and cautious, "If there's ever anything you have questions about, you can ask me. I won't tell the others what we discuss. I promise."

Shit.

Has he finally figured out just how little I know about being an omega?

I stare into his kind eyes, waiting for the disappointment. Or, at the very least, irritation. But compassion swells in his dark irises. He brushes his lips along my brow.

"Ask me," he whispers. "I want you to."

I press my lips into a tight line, considering. If I reveal how clueless I am, won't he be appalled? If I don't, will I ever get such a perfect opportunity to ask him questions again?

His purr deepens. A clear ploy to relax me.

A very effective ploy, it turns out. "I... I guess I've been wondering about—"

Bonding.

The word is right there, balanced on the tip of my tongue.

But I chicken out and substitute the very first thought that comes to mind.

"—double-penetration."

Oh. My. God. Kill me.

A surprised chuckle rumbles beneath my ear, but otherwise Archer doesn't seem scandalized. His scent deepens as he hugs me closer. "Hmm. I guess that would make sense, with all of us slobbering all over you constantly."

I appreciate the self-deprecating joke. He slips a hand over my side while he goes on. "If you ever wanted to try that—which is not a requirement, or even an expectation—we would thoroughly prep you for it. Although, during heat, your body will be prepared for us with very little effort. You'll produce enough slick to make the whole thing fairly easy. *If* that's something you want to explore."

The stern tone of his voice is both comforting and confusing. "Is that... not something you guys would like? Sharing me?"

Archer strokes his fingertips under my chin, tilting my head back. His eyes are warm and electric. "I can guarantee, any of us would give anything just to *witness* that. You'll probably have to referee a fight over who gets to go first."

A shaky giggle quivers out of me. "H-how does that work with—"

"Knots?" He raises a brow, gracing me with a flirty grin. "During heat, our knots will release much faster than they normally do. It's our bodies reacting to your needs—you'll need more knots, so we'll adjust to give them to you."

My throat feels thick. The idea of all of them servicing me, their knots and cocks at my disposal...

I cringe at the burst of perfume rising off me. Archer grunts quietly, shifting under me. He grips the long bulge along his thigh and holds his breath.

After a long exhale, he goes back to stroking my spine. "Have you ever taken a knot before, sweetheart?"

I try to burrow my way into his body as I shake my head, hiding my face and the shame splashed over my cheeks. "No."

His whole body goes taut again. I feel him forcing himself to relax. "That's okay. We can work up to that before your heat. There are ways to practice."

"Like what?" I ask, sounding small.

The strength of Archer's spice is making me woozy. I hear him bite back an instinctive growl before he speaks.

"I'll show you, if you'd like. But ask me your other questions first. I'm not sure how focused either of us will be after the knotting lesson."

A giddy flutter flips my belly. Pure excitement provokes my next question. "Is there any other prep I should be doing for the heat? Like, physically?"

He nods. "There are workouts to help get your endurance up. Of course, we'll always be there to make sure you're not overtaxing your body. I'll monitor your vitals and hydration the entire time. But some stretches and a light cardio regimen leading up to the nesting phase may be a good idea."

After showing me a few stretches on his phone, I ask him about what happened with Theo the night he snapped into a rut and why it hasn't happened since. Archer explains that my heat perfume increases the likelihood of ruts for them but assures me that prolonged access to me will help them avoid losing control.

It's like immersion therapy essentially, which makes sense— ever since Theo and I started being physical with each other, he hasn't edged close to another rut. And I know Ronan likes his time with me in the mornings for many reasons, one of them being that it helps him satisfy his Alpha so he can stay in control of his impulses.

According to Archer, bonding helps, too. Apparently, bonded alphas and omegas get on similar cycles—when an omega spikes, her alpha's chances of hitting a rut spike as well.

Of course, he notices the way I shrink down when he brings up bonding. A somber frown pulls at his mouth. "Not that I ever want you to feel pressured about bonding," he adds. "I probably shouldn't have even mentioned it. I just want you to have all the facts."

I nod, swallowing around another new lump in my throat. "It's okay. I—I do have questions. About bonding. About how it works for omegas."

The look he gives me is complicated. There's a surface-layer of surprise—because, let's face it, I should really know this stuff—and a bit of horror? Like he can't believe whoever raised me was so negligent.

Little does he know that person was *me*.

Below all of his dismay, I see concern. And steady resolve. "I'll tell you whatever you want to know, sweetheart."

For a long moment, I struggle, not knowing how to ask him to explain literally *everything* to me. Luckily, his emotional intelligence is unmatched. It only takes a beat for him to recognize my overwhelm and take over for me.

"Bonding would make you the center of our pack," he murmurs, voice soft. "You and Ronan would bond first since he's the pack alpha. Then the rest of us would follow. It can be done one-by-one or all together. But basically, once we bond, we'll all be tied to you. In you. *Through* you. You'll be able to feel what we feel. We'll be able to feel you, and each other, to a lesser extent."

He sees the flicker of fear on my face and hums. "It sounds like a lot, I know. But, from what I understand, the bonds aren't intrusive.

"It's more like... You'll have access to a chamber—a round room with four doorways. Only, instead of doors, the passages are covered by curtains. We can leave our curtains open and let whatever goes on inside each of us flow freely between our chamber and yours. Or we can close that curtain, mute everything down to a hum until someone waves their hand through and asks permission to come inside."

I find it's easy to imagine. When he sees I understand, he goes on. "There are also mental techniques for temporarily sealing the doorways. That's helpful for people like Theo or Declan, who need absolute focus during games and such."

The idea of Theo trying to keep his feelings to himself makes me smile. "So, for the most part, I'll be immersed in most of your feelings most of the time?"

Archer laughs quietly. "No. The bonds aren't that all-consuming. Maybe at first. But eventually, they just become part of us. Think about..."

He mulls for a moment, searching for an analogy. "Your palm, for example. You walk around all day and don't think twice about it. The sensation of air hitting it, the feel of your phone in your hand. You don't think about it, until you *do*. Then, when you focus on that one area, sensations come through. Bonds are like that."

I see what he means. My palms tingle when I focus on them, prickling with awareness. But normally? I forget the nerves are even there.

I smile. "That seems amazing, actually."

He grins back. "It is. *You* are. Bonds are only possible through omegas, sweetheart."

I cock a teasing smirk. "My superpower, huh? Along with taking tons of knots."

Instead of laughing, Archer's face grows intense. "As many knots as you want," he vows.

He wants me. I can feel it. But he's still such a gentleman.

I rise up onto my knees, sliding one across his lap until I'm straddling him. "We should practice, then," I mumble, bending to kiss his throat. "I want you to teach me."

I feel him swallow hard. He runs his hands over my sides, settling them on my hips. "This is the perfect position," he rumbles. "I can purr for you. You can ride my cock and take as much of my knot as you want. I'll rub it against your clit and tease your pussy with it."

A whine slips out of me. Archer shushes me softly, trailing his hand over my backside and finding the crotch of my panties. One long finger strokes along my folds, gathering slick.

He growls into my crown. "Goddamn, Meg. Is all of this for me?"

I nod, raking my teeth over his jaw as I confess, "Your lessons turn me on."

He hums, thoughtful. "Then I think you'll like this one."

Archer snaps into action, kissing me soundly. His muscles tense, holding himself back to go my speed.

But that bitchy, demanding voice in my middle isn't having it. She says, *fuck that*.

And the next thing I know, I've ripped his shirt open.

Archer rears back and runs his eyes over my face. The second he sees the frantic need in my gaze, he *snarls*.

The sound is pure alpha—demanding, possessive, and *aggressive*. I moan as it rolls down my spine, arching my back and settling into the pool of wetness between my thighs.

Archer reaches over and rips my tank top off, watching with dark, hungry eyes while my breasts bounce into view.

He crushes our chests together while he kisses me, licking into my mouth. An empty pang tweaks my core. I grind my body into his, already panting for the feeling of his skin. "Please, Alpha. I need you."

Archer sinks his teeth against the soft part of my shoulder, pinioning me in place while he shucks his pants and rips my panties off.

Yes. *Rips them off*.

I gasp, biting him back, wishing I could break his skin. He chokes on a groan, gripping my hips hard and positioning my slick center over his huge cock. I feel it throb against the thin skin of my thighs, sending tingles down my legs.

I squirm against him until his fingers fist the back of my hair, digging into the roots, tugging at the buns. "Let me teach you," he commands.

Another surge of pure arousal tightens my inner muscles. I

whine for him, begging without words.

"Good omega," he rumbles, dropping his eyes to my slick core. "Push up onto your knees."

I obey, noting that I'm just barely tall enough for this position to work. His cock is just so *big*—the biggest of all of them by far. I have to stretch up a bit to situate the swollen head against my opening.

His large hand presses into the space between my hips, his thumb stroking the swollen bud at the top of my sex. Fresh slick pours out of me, soaking him.

He grits his teeth, chest heaving. His eyes lock on mine, deep pools of adoration that somehow also project his calm, steady dominance. The combination is so very Archer, it makes my chest ache.

"Go slow, sweetheart," he orders, the command reverent. "I want to feel every inch."

His thumb picks up a circular rhythm while I work myself down his length. The stretch is incredible, filling places no one else has ever reached. I whimper when he's fully seated, his hot, pulsing knot splitting my pussy lips wide open.

He curses, rolling his hips and using his free hand to cup my breast. "Perfect," he grinds out. "You're so *perfect*. Bounce on me, sweetheart."

I can't help myself, gliding up and down his length as fast as I can manage, frantic from the feel of him swelling deep inside me. The purr in his chest gets rougher with every breath, turning into a serrated pant.

Just when I think I can't take any more, he tilts his hips and bends me forward. The pounding knot at the base of his cock rubs against the bottom of my clit at the same moment his thumb swipes over the top. I buck into the sensation, coming before I even realize what's happening.

Every muscle in my core seizes around him, clenching rhythmically around his girth. When he only grows harder, the tension inside me starts building all over again, every nerve singing louder.

Archer purrs at my whine. "Yes. That's right, sweetheart, come all over my knot. It's so fucking hard for you. It wants to be in that sweet pussy, filling it so perfectly for you."

I tense around his length, waves of pleasure rippling through my veins. My alpha palms my ass, fingertips pressing down until I sink lower. The first fourth of his knot slips in before he pops me back off.

It's the kind of ecstasy that's so good, it hurts. I *scream* while he sloughs out another groan. His big dick flinches inside of me while he bares his teeth, gritting back a climax.

"Again," he demands, still somehow soft and completely in control.

I obey, slipping down until I think the pressure of his knot against my pussy will break my brain. He sinks a bit deeper this time, stretching me more.

I cry out, shuddering. He goes on, tugging me lower and lower, until every thrust pushes half of his knot into me.

It isn't long before he loses control.

The hands clutching my ass get rougher, working me into sloppier thrusts of his hips. When I score my teeth along the side of his neck, he gives one final buck and roars his release.

My body responds to the hot lash inside of me with another climax. This one moves through me in a slow, languid roll, warming my blood.

Archer tucks me into his chest, purring deeply and murmuring praise into my lopsided hair. "I've never felt anything so incredible. Never come so hard in my life. You took my cock so well, sweetheart. Perfect omega. So good for me."

I melt into him, scent-marking his bare chest and feeling him nuzzle his own scent against my temples. My body gives a final clench around his as he shudders and slips out of me.

I hide my small smile against his shoulder and snuggle closer. "So, I passed my first knotting lesson?"

His grin is practically audible. "A-plus."

chapter
forty-one

MEG'S KNOT COLLECTION

THEO

> Does anyone know what color peaches is wearing tonight?

ARCHER

Why? Are you getting her a corsage? Because I already ordered a white one.

RONAN

Shit. I ordered a red one.

THEO

> Fuck I ordered an orange one but I was trying to match my bowtie to her dress.

DECLAN

You're all idiots, her dress is black.

ARCHER

How do you know?

THEO

> Did you, oh I don't know, TALK TO HER?

DECLAN

no

RONAN

And we're* the idiots?

REMEMBER ALL those times I worried I wouldn't be enough for the Most Valuable Pack?

Yeah, turns out that was an intelligent instinct.

The swanky space stretched out before us holds five-hundred of the most glamorous people I've ever seen.

Black tie?

Pfft.

Not for them.

These people wear *white* tuxedo jackets, the women elbow-length gloves. Together they form a sea of swishing silk and shimmering jewels that's almost as dazzling as the room itself.

The venue is a modern, artsy take on a classic hotel ballroom. Checkerboard-style floors that gleam, flat white walls displaying an assortment of art, opulent floral arrangements dripping with fat, snowy orchids, tables covered in gold place settings, and spotless linens.

Our group huddles just out of sight on the second-floor landing. We purposely had Ronan's driver bring us around the back of the hotel instead of walking the red carpet situated at the front.

Archer adjusts his perfect black bow tie and frowns at me

softly, concern clear in his dark eyes. "You feel good about the plan, sweetheart?"

I know I should, but my stomach suddenly feels like one of those fifties Jello molds—all wiggly and green.

Theo slips his arm around my middle, his white jacket brushing the elegant cut-outs banding my waist. He rolls his eyes and snorts. "It's *her* plan, Arch."

He has a point.

When Ronan and I went over the night, I was the one who decided to forgo the red carpet full of press in favor of making our entrance directly inside the ballroom. Our first appearance as a committed, courting pack feels monumental—I suggested doing so in front of our hired event photographers instead of random paparazzi on the sidewalk. If anything, this gives us more control over which pictures go to print.

God forbid the tabloids run one of Declan sneering at me the way he currently is.

Looking like a bad boy prince with an attitude problem, he lounges in the shadows of the hallway behind us, leaning on one white-coat-clad shoulder. Half-leering, half-glaring at me, he downs whatever is left in the tumbler of liquor he pilfered from our limousine and simply leaves the glass on the floor beside his polished dress shoes.

"Buck up, princess," he grunts, brushing past me. "Isn't this what you wanted? All of our balls on a silver platter? What a happy occasion."

Ronan turns away from the event planner he's liaising with and shoots his packmate a loaded look. "Declan, we talked about this."

It doesn't surprise me that our pack alpha has laid out individual expectations for all of us. He spent all of breakfast holding me in his lap and going over every last detail with me, wanting me to feel prepared.

And I should.

I know this is the annual gala for the Ash Trust, which funds all the philanthropies the guys' support. Each has their own cause within the umbrella of Ronan's inherited wealth, and this event is their best opportunity to get pledges from other donors.

I wasn't shocked to hear that Declan routinely wins the most funding. *Of course*, everyone wants to back the most famous player on the team. And, *of course*, he would have a shitty attitude about the whole thing despite the undeserved generosity.

Ass.

His cause is probably some stupid bullshit like research on erectile dysfunction. Or surgical enhancements for cheerleaders.

I channel my frustration into forced confidence, standing up straight and flashing a smile. "I'm ready."

The asshole extraordinaire rolls his shoulders back, jaw ticking. "Then let's get this over with."

He offers his arm without glancing at me. I sigh and loop mine though it, resisting the urge to pinch him.

This was my idea, too, I remind myself. If the guys really want to make a statement about courting me, I know there's only one way to get all the thirsty women to take me seriously; I have to walk in on the arm of the group's best-known, most-unobtainable member.

I smooth my black-gloved hand down the wispy fabric of my gown, wishing I'd let Ronan call in professional hair and make-up for me. Then, maybe, I'd look like I belong next to this man.

The others crowd around us, each making final adjustments to their own appearances. For a second, I have to swallow down the urge to whine. I know this is polite society and all, but I hate that I can't scent them properly here, with a truckload of neutralizers in the air and each of us carefully covered in de-scenter.

"You have to look like you like me, remember?"

Declan's mutter refocuses me. I tilt my head and offer him a blinding, fake smile, hissing through my teeth. "Better?"

His nostrils flare as his eyes slide over my front, from the deep-V of my gown to the black pearls fastened at my blank throat. They land on my painted red lips. "You'll do," he grumbles.

Ronan thwacks the back of Declan's skull. Theo chortles while Archer reaches for my free hand and weaves our fingers together. I offer him a much more genuine smile that he returns with pure warmth.

"You look perfect, Meg."

I try to replay those words in my head as we move down the ballroom staircase and step onto the polished floor. The room seems to turn on its axis, reorienting around us. There's a short hush before the guests break into uproarious applause.

I truly do smile, then. Seeing these amazing guys get credit for all their brilliance and hard work gives me a giddy rush. Archer's lips graze my cheekbone while Theo steps up behind me, snaking his hand around my side.

Camera flashes erupt on three sides. One second, I'm trying to decide where to look—and the next I'm spinning, falling into a dip as fluid as every other move Declan Howard makes.

He catches me in his opposite arm, his magazine-worthy grin more blinding than the flashes filling the air. I only get half a breath into my lungs before he bends to take my lips, completely stealing the rest of my air when I gasp.

His mouth moves against mine, insistent.

Dare I say... *desperate*?

He kisses me like he's been waiting a hundred years to do it, and he'll only get this one opportunity.

Is it possible he... *wants* to kiss me? That seems impossible, given the way he acts, but heat trickles into my core either way. My silk-covered fingers slide against his lapels, looking for purchase. Wanting to pull him closer for some insane reason I'd rather not examine too closely.

The crowd goes *wild*. And I realize—*oh.*

This isn't about me. He wants their money. Their approval.

I'm nothing more than a prop for him right now.

Our first kiss—gone. Lost to this room of strangers, rabid for gossip.

It *hurts*.

So badly I can't control the whimper of gut-twisting pain. I'm about to shove him back—cameras be damned—but he ends the embrace just as suddenly as he started it. In a blink, I'm back on my feet, being spun right into Ronan.

He catches me, our gazes connecting. Whatever he sees in mine sends a spark of fury through his. Without a word, he tucks me against his chest, playing the gesture of comfort off as a public display of affection.

I know no one else will hear his purr over the din, but I do. It blurs the edges of Declan's actions, making the whole scene just palatable enough for me to do what I need to do and walk forward with the rest of them.

We have a whole plan, I coach internally. *Just remember the plan.*

After making our entrance with Declan, I'm supposed to spend the first hour of the event on Ronan's arm. He has numerous high-profile business contacts to shake hands with and having me there facilitates the necessary introductions. By the end of the hour, it feels like I've met every billionaire on the Eastern Seaboard.

The dinner portion of the evening belongs to Theo, who claims the seat closest to mine at our table. He spends the meal feeding me bites of his food while stealing pieces of mine. With his arm along the back of my chair and his fingers stroking the nape of my neck, it's hard to stay upset. I'm grateful he's there to make me laugh and block me with his big body.

Especially since everyone is *staring* at me. Quite rudely, for a room full of so many proper, wealthy people. There's one old man in particular who outright *leers* from his place at the bar. Every time I pause and take note of the number of eyes on me, shivers roll down my limbs.

Archer's warm palm skims over my thigh under our table. "Are you cold, sweetheart? We should have packed a shawl for you."

Theo immediately moves to wrestle his jacket off, but I stop him, smirking, "You can't take off your tails, big guy. Daddy will be mad."

It was Ronan's one pack rule for the night; no undressing. From his place at Archer's right side, Ronan casts me a dark look promising all sorts of delicious punishments for my impertinence. It reminds me that—before all of the evenings' mixed feelings—I was truly hoping tonight might be the night he decided to take me.

They've all been considerate. They know taking on four alphas is a lot, and no one wants me to feel overwhelmed. But I feel ready for more.

Assuming this whole night doesn't go up in flames.

It seems unlikely by the time our plates are cleared. Ronan excuses himself to wheel and deal. Declan never even made it to our table—he's been camped out at one of the bars across the ballroom with a large group of admirers. They lap up every word he says, collapsing into laughter on cue.

"This is why he does the speeches," Archer grouses, bending to murmur in my ear. "Apparently we're the only ones who know what an ass he is."

"I feel privileged," I smirk. "Time for a dance?"

Throughout all our planning, that was Archer's one request for the night—a dance with me. Little does he know, I have plans for a whole lot more.

His brows lift in surprise. He flashes me the shy grin I adore. "If you're up for it."

I bend down to his ear and tug his hand. "It's a start."

chapter
forty-two

BEFORE THIS PACK, I had a pretty shitty life.

The first ten years were hell. The second ten were worse. Without Theo and his family taking me in, sometimes I think I would be dead.

Maybe I should be. My mom always thought so.

Anyway.

I know what true fear feels like. The deep, visceral kind that grips your guts and yanks them up your throat. The sort you want to vomit up, just to get them *out*.

It's been years since I felt like this.

I almost forgot how much it sucks.

My stomach seethes as I wait beside the stage at the front of the ballroom. It's annoying. I didn't expect to be nervous; I've delivered the remarks at this gala for three years in a row, not to mention all the bullshit interviews I do.

Public speaking isn't new for me, but this speech will be. It's the best I could come up with, after weeks of feeling guilty as fuck for the way I'm treating Meg and my inability to get my shit together.

I've felt like shit ever since that day on the field. After that little blow-up, it took days for me finally admit that I might really care about her; her safety, her feelings. I just don't know *how* to care about anyone the way she needs me to.

And the whole thing fucking terrifies me.

She at least deserves an explanation. And since I can't seem to *talk to her* like a normal person, I decided I'd talk to everyone here.

I know it isn't logical. But, somehow, sharing what I went through as part of a speech to raise money for others is less personal than sitting Meg down and giving her my whole fucked up history one-on-one.

And if this is the only way I can give her the context she needs to understand that none of my bullshit is her fault? Fine. I'll do it.

It's called a grand gesture or some shit.

She didn't seem to enjoy the first part of it, though, when I kissed her during our entrance. That move felt a lot cooler in my head. It wasn't until she tensed up that I realized it was a mistake.

I wanted to claim her beyond a shadow of a doubt. Now, I wonder if maybe Meg isn't the kind of person who needs big public displays. Maybe she would have preferred that I scent-mark her in private, where she would know I wasn't doing it for any reason other than to make her feel wanted.

I would know all of this about her, if I wasn't such a stubborn dick.

Now it's too late. I already fucked up the kiss, and the speech written on the notecards in my pocket is the only one I have. So, I guess I'm going for it.

It's time, right? I have to get better, somehow. Or I'll lose them all. Or they'll lose Meg. At this point, I can't decide which would be worse.

Something painful pulls in my chest as I watch the way Meg dances with Arch. He spins her out and twirls her back. When he rubs his hand down her back, she visibly trembles from delight.

Jealousy joins the riot inside of me, along with a hefty dose of shame.

I haven't really touched her yet and she's literally fucking touch-starved. What the hell is wrong with me? I could have held her hand in the limo. Or sat next to her at dinner. Or just fucking asked how her day was. Am I seriously such an angry, obstinate asshole that I'm neglecting an innocent omega who's literally ill?

I'm fucking this all up.

I'm fucking this all up.

Meg likely hates me. My team has barely hung in for our first three games. Now I'm standing here, going along with my own stupid plan instead of trying to figure out what our omega really needs from me.

Does it matter? that voice inside of me hisses. *It's not like you can actually give her anything worthwhile.*

Because my heart is a shredded fucking *mess*, and Meg deserves better.

For a second, I consider running over to the dance floor and asking for her hand. Holding her close. Inhaling her hair and scent-marking her cheek and just... being hers. *Trying* to be hers.

But I still have to give this fucking speech.

The MC cuts the music and directs everyone back to their seats. Ronan appears just long enough to clap me on the shoulder. He strides up the steps and takes the stage to introduce me. In the process, he announces that we've raised fifteen million dollars for the charity of choice. Which is mine.

I'm about to take my cue and walk up to the podium. But a flash of tawny red catches my eye.

I turn just in time to catch sight of her, slinking around the edge of the room. She sets her empty wine glass on a bar and flashes me a look over her shoulder. Those light brown eyes send me hurtling into some of my worst memories. I watch as she very deliberately looks right at Meg.

And then flashes me a razor-sharp smile.

Oh fuck no.

Ronan is waiting on stage, watching me like I've lost my mind. But I don't care. I won't let her get to Meg. Not before I can.

chapter
forty-three

I'M HAVING AN OUT-OF-BODY EXPERIENCE.

Thats the term for feeling like your head is going to float away and the very real possibility you might throw up on someone's $1000 shoes, right?

As I watch Declan turn away from the stage and follow a woman out of the ballroom, I don't know if I'm closer to throwing up or screaming.

What is he *doing*?

We had a *plan*!

He doesn't have to bite me or bond me. He doesn't even have

to touch me. But chasing after another woman while we're in the middle of a public event? The same event we just used to launch my relationship with his pack?

I mean, I'm not stupid. I've always assumed he was engaged in some form of fuckery or another.

He's *Declan Howard*.

And God knows he doesn't want anything to do with me.

But he seriously couldn't have waited until the end of the evening? He had to publicly humiliate me?

A rumble starts to creep through the crowd. People turn to look at our table. To look at *me*.

I know what they're thinking. It's what I've known from the moment I woke up in these alphas' guest room: I am not enough for them. Not omega enough. Not refined or alluring enough. Not even enough to merit fidelity for a three-hour gala.

I think back to the way Declan kissed me when we came in—leaving absolutely no doubt that I belonged to him. Why did he do that if he had some sort of side piece around?

Was it all just to humiliate me?

How much more of this can I take?

At least a little bit, I tell myself. Because I may be getting better about honoring my instincts, but I'll be damned if I run out of here in tears.

It's nice that my years of emotional denial have actually come in handy, for once.

People murmur and titter, but I keep my head up and my eyes dry, breathing slowly through my nose and imagining I can smell Ronan's smoke, Theo's citrus, and Archer's spice on every inhale.

Archer's eyes are on my face as I force myself to sit up straight, strangling the whine building in my throat. His fingers wind into mine, squeezing hard enough to help me stay grounded. Theo shifts, his large frame blocking me from view.

Onstage, Ronan ad-libs a quick speech about their founda-tion and ends the evening by thanking all of their guests. I know there's supposed to be a second portion of dancing, but I'm no longer in the spirit.

Archer senses my mood and has the car pulled around while Ronan makes his way back to our table. Our alpha's eyes are molten silver, burning with rage, but when he sees my face, they instantly change, glowing with pride. He silently offers me his hand and pulls me up against him, kissing me in front of the entire room.

Twenty minutes, and a lot of handshakes later, Declan is nowhere in sight as the guys guide me into the back of the limo. We settle onto the bench seats. Because I rode between Ronan and Arch on our way to the venue, I scoot into Theo's side this time. He instantly cuddles me into his big body and drops his face to my hair.

For a moment, there's total silence. I can feel each of them thinking. Seething. Regretting.

It's odd. After spending weeks constantly worrying that I won't measure up, their collective silence should totally freak me out. But it doesn't. After a moment, I realize that I can sense their moods so keenly, I know none of their negative feelings are directed at me. If anything, they're all mortified that their pack-mate just put me through that.

I want to reassure them, so I force out words, even though my voice sounds small and frayed. "I thought of a charity."

All three of them look at me, brows furrowed. Ronan speaks first. "For what?"

I try for a wobbly smile, meeting each of their eyes. "For me to support. Everyone in the pack gets to pick one right?"

Their collective relief is palpable. Archer's brows draw up in shock. Theo exhales hard and nuzzles me harder. Ronan's lips quirk into a half-smile. "That's right, little one. Anything you want."

For a moment, I hesitate. I always planned to tell them about my mom when we were all together. After tonight, I doubt Declan would care either way.

And...

I want them.

All of them.

But I want them to know me before we commit to each other that way.

My fingers tangle in my lap and I stare down at them. "I know I never told you guys... but my mother died when I was fourteen."

The backseat grows even more silent than it was before. I push on while I still can, forcing a sad smile. "She was an alpha. Like you guys. She loved her career too much to find a pack of her own, so when she decided she wanted a baby, she did it by herself."

I force a strained laugh. "I was supposed to be an alpha, too. The doctors—I think they select for that sort of thing, genetically. But I guess their plan backfired, because two years after my mother passed, my designation came through."

My eyes find Archer's. "That's why I don't know about nesting or touch starvation." I turn to Ronan. "And why I always had to work so hard to be on my own."

I lean back to see Theo's face. "It's also the reason I couldn't go to high school. I had no guardian, and the government doesn't take responsibility for unbonded omegas once their heats start. No college will, either. I finished my entire education online."

Archer's eyes fill with compassion. He leans across the space between the limo's leather benches and bends to kiss my hands.

Ronan's otherworldly focus falls on my face. "Would you like to start a special school for omegas without guardians? Or a scholarship fund?"

Theo interjects, "Fuck it, we'll do both."

He always makes me laugh at the most inappropriate times. I slap a hand against his chest, chuckling. "Maybe eventually, big guy. But for now, I think I just want to start small. There's a home for abandoned children right across the street from the Ospreys' compound. I lived in a house like that, when I was a teenager and I just... for some reason, I feel like I should start there. I've noticed it every time we drive past, but I don't remember the name."

Another silence falls, this one strangely heavy.

Ronan is the first to answer again. "It's called New Horizons."

I narrow my eyes, casting him a questioning look. Archer sighs, drawing my attention. "We know the name because that's Declan's charity."

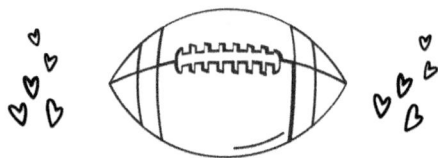

chapter
forty-four

I DON'T REALIZE I've never been in love before Meg until I'm holding her in my arms, watching her rest her tear-stained face against my shoulder.

Fuck, she's so beautiful. Brave and tough and more resilient than anyone I've ever met. After what she's just told us, I want to spoil and protect her every day for the rest of her life.

She can have anything she wants. I'll get it for her. *Be* it for her.

We stand in the foyer as the limo pulls away. Archer locks the door and Theo shucks his jacket. Meg sniffles and looks at the blank space where Declan should be.

"I'm—God, I'm so *sorry*. I feel like it's me. Like if I was someone else, he would like me, and then your pack wouldn't be *breaking*."

Her last word cracks, along with the battered, black organ inside my chest. I tighten my hold on her, pressing her body into the deep purr rolling behind my sternum.

Our eyes meet again. I can feel mine burning when I reply, "I never want you to apologize for this again. You are beautiful and brilliant and sweeter than any of us deserve. You have nothing to apologize for."

"But I'm—I—"

Tears splash down onto her black gown, soaking into the silk. I shift so she can wrap her legs around me, pressing one hand to the back of her head and running the other down her spine.

"You're okay, baby girl," I husk, guiding her face to my throat. "Daddy's here. Daddy's here, now."

Her control fractures. She sobs into my neck, the sound of her sorrow drawing Theo and Archer to her. They close in on us, each offering their own purr. Hands stroke, arms brush.

It's doesn't matter. We're a pack. And this is our omega.

When she starts to settle, I pet her head in slow caresses. "That's it, baby girl," I whisper. "Tell Daddy what you need."

She looks up at me, exhausted and vulnerable and shy. When she skims her nose under my ear, her tongue lightly traces my pulse. I squeeze her as tenderly as I can. "Good girl. That's exactly what you need."

"All of us? Upstairs?" Theo asks, already moving.

Archer follows almost as quickly. "Upstairs. All of us."

——————— ♥ ———————

THEO SHOVES the double doors to her room open, and Archer goes to close them behind us. Meg stops him, her arm limp while she reaches over to brush his sleeve.

"Leave it open," she whispers. "In case Declan comes home."

God. No one will ever convince me this isn't an angel.

Declan's done nothing but reject her, and she still wants to leave the door open for him. Literally and figuratively.

Her words hit all of us hard. Theo especially. He squeezes his eyes shut and exhales before striding up to us, his hands framing her face and turning it away from my neck. He stares right into her eyes.

"I know I say a lot of shit, precious. And I know I've made jokes about this. Made light of it. But I mean this more than I've ever meant anything: I'm so in love with you, it's insane."

Meg laughs weakly, raising her arms up to him. I hate letting her go, but I love watching the way she gives to all of us. All of the things we each need, she offers without hesitation.

Theo slings her into his big body, carrying her the rest of the way to the bed, laying soft kisses all over her face. Eventually the kisses become more enthusiastic, until they both laugh as they fall onto the huge mattress.

Meg keeps her hands on his face, holding it while she gazes up at him. "I love you too, big guy. Finders keepers?"

Theo grins at their inside joke. "Always."

Archer steps up next to me. We have a moment where we both just watch, absorbing everything we have. Everything we made. Everything we found.

"We're doing this," he says out loud. Not a question because he knows my answer and I know his.

"She's ours," I confirm. As far as I'm concerned, it's done. "Anything she needs."

Archer snorts softly and begins unbuttoning his shirt. "Pretty sure you'll like this first part."

Fucking our omega?

Hell yes, I will.

I start unfastening my belt and kick off my shoes. Archer sends me a quelling look. "We need to ask about her boundaries. She's never been knotted before. We should be mindful of that."

I can't remember the last time I knotted an omega who had never taken one before. Possibly never, considering all of my omega sexual encounters took place in the back of a bar.

Perversely, I wish Declan were here.

He's the only one of us who's ever had an actual relationship with an omega. Yeah it was shitty of him, but still. He has experience.

Archer should, too, theoretically. Between his former volunteer work at heat clinics and his medical training. But I can tell he's still reeling from everything Meg just told us, not to mention everything that happened at the godforsaken gala.

And Theo's a knotting virgin.

So, yeah, probably best for us to ask Meg what she wants.

By the time Arch and I are down to our boxers, Theo has the gown off our omega, his own clothes are long gone. She's stretched out beneath him in a strapless bra and plain black panties. All effortless sex appeal.

I prowl to her from the side of the mattress. My voice drops into a commanding tone. "Before we do anything, it's important for you to remember that you have all the power in this bed. In this *house*. Got it, little one?"

Her grabby hand snags my waistband and pulls me closer. My cock jerks to attention while she eyes it through the fabric, biting her lower lip. "I think I like it better when *you* have all the power."

Theo slides down her body and rests his face against her belly. Meg threads her fingers into his hair as if it's the most natural thing in the world, her eyes still locked on me. Theo hums in contentment, closing his eyes.

Archer takes the place on Meg's right, lying on his side to face her. His glasses are on the nightstand, but he seems to be faring pretty well without them. His eyes track every small flicker in her features, absorbing them all. Sensing he's worried about her,

Meg's free hand stretches over and curls around the side of his jaw, stroking lightly.

I'm in awe. I could watch her all day.

And she isn't even naked yet.

"We need to talk about your limits," Archer murmurs, bending to press his forehead into her temple.

With a sigh, Meg's gaze falls from mine. She looks across the room, biting her lip again. "I haven't had a ton of sex before you guys. Only a few times, with betas. There wasn't really... much to it."

Theo snuggles closer to her bare skin. "So there isn't anything you want us to avoid?"

Meg's focus flies back to me. I bend closer, skimming my nose along her throat. "Tell me," I say softly, nipping at her neck. "Tell Daddy."

Her eyes darken, more peachy succulence filling the room. But she still looks embarrassed as she tosses looks at all three of us. "I just... don't want this to be weird. I've obviously never been with a pack before. I have no idea how these things work, and I don't want to cross any lines or make any of you do things you aren't comfortable with. Like what happened in the car a couple of weeks ago..."

Archer nods, listening, even though I know he's dying to interrupt. When she trails off, he presses a soft kiss to her lips, gently biting the lower one to release it from her teeth.

"All of us loved that," he tells her, running his mouth along her cheekbone. "We know we'll get time alone with you and time to share you with each other. None of us feel weird about that, sweetheart."

Meg blinks back up at me. "S-so, you don't mind, like, touching each other?"

All three of us repress chuckles and snorts at her question. Sweet baby girl. It's clear she's never even watched a video of pack sex online before.

"We all talked about this before because we assumed those

things would happen if we ever found you," I explain. "We may not be romantically attracted to each other, but being intimate with our omega as a pack is something we've always wanted. We want to do anything and everything we can with you—that will necessitate touching each other and getting off together. I know I'm good with that. Guys?"

"I agree," Archer says.

Theo gives an evil laugh. "Bring it on."

He rolls his hips, and Meg squeals, giggling, "Theo!"

"Plenty more where that came from, peaches. You've got three alpha cocks here, now."

Archer hums, fighting a smile. Trying to be serious. "Which brings me to my last question. We will take it slow, but we need to know: how do you feel about knotting? Or being penetrated in multiple places at once?"

A tidal wave of perfume erupts from Meg's body.

Oh *fuck*.

I clutch at her comforter, gripping the silk in my fists so I don't tear her away from Theo. It would be too easy right now since he's busy gliding his lips over the waistband of her panties, moaning in the back of his throat.

Meg skims her hand along Archer's face again. "You'll help me learn, right?"

He's losing control, too. His voice rumbles with a slight growl while he bends to kiss her again. "Absolutely. Of course I will."

That's all our bases covered. And our omega is squirming between the three of us, writhing in her sheets. Filling the room with her mouth-watering perfume.

There's really only one question left.

"Who's first?"

chapter
forty-five

I'M STARTING to realize that living with these guys for three years didn't teach me nearly as much about them as a few weeks with an omega has.

For example, who knew Archer could look so annoyed while also sporting a boner the size of my forearm?

Okay, not really.

Maybe the size of our *omega's* forearm...

He cuts Ronan a look and huffs an irritated breath out of his nose, ignoring our alpha's question. His long fingers skirt the edge of our girl's face while he catches her gaze.

"Do you want to get in your nest, sweetheart?"

Oh shit. We're going *there?*

None of us have been in the nest yet. She keeps the door shut. I'm not even sure any of us have seen it. A cringy image of red suede cushions and neon hearts floats through my brain.

Dumb thing to worry about. Meg would never design something ugly after making her bedroom so stupid beautiful.

Underneath me, she tenses up. I kick my purr to the next level and go back to ghosting my lips along her panties. I'm pretty sure they're the scent-blocking kind, which is crazy, given how strong her scent is right now. This whole room is going to *drown* in peach perfection as soon as I get them off...

Focus, Theo.

Meg's voice sounds smaller. "I—It doesn't feel right to me."

Every time she shares these types of things, she looks like she wishes she could shrink down into nothing. It made no sense to me, before. Omegas' instincts are the gold standard. Their intuitions are what make packs work.

Her needs bind us together, give us a common purpose. Her urges help keep us all on track. We literally *need* her to share this shit.

If she says the nest isn't right, it isn't right.

Done.

Archer nods, his face full of caring compassion. How did I never notice he's such a good listener before? It's all I see every time I watch him with Meg.

"Is the room not the right size or shape?" he asks, tucking her blonde hair back. "We can look into remodeling it immediately."

"Or is it the stuff we picked out?" Ronan guesses. "You were in a rush and heading for a heat-spike. No one would blame you if you changed your mind and wanted to do it over again. In fact, we'd insist."

Meg bites her lip and looks down.

At me.

Me?

I'm the one she needs right now? She thinks *I* can fix this?

It's hard to get used that after being the fuck up around here for so long. But, for her, I'll try just about anything.

On my elbows, I army-crawl up her luscious body and bury my face into her boobs for a brief, glorious second. Just to make her laugh. Mostly.

After a tiny giggle, she's quiet again. I hoist myself up until I'm hovering over her, face-to-gorgeous-face. Big blue eyes fill with pleading. She blinks and sucks her lips behind her teeth, sending a quick glance to the open doors.

And I just know.

Dec.

"You don't want to get in the nest without Declan," I translate, my brow lowering. "It doesn't feel right to you."

She blows out a shaky breath. "No, it doesn't. The first time we all—*you know*—in the nest. It should be all of us, I think."

I look at the others, seeing Ronan's solid jaw and Archer's serious eyes. Knowing they'll agree with me even before I open my mouth. "Then we'll wait for him before we all go into the nest with you."

Archer has an opinion on it, probably something to do with her needing her nest for her upcoming heat and all that jazz. As far as I'm concerned, we can figure it out. After this.

I bend closer to Meg's face, widening my eyes. "But for now, I think we should tell Daddy and the good doctor your little secret."

For a second, she looks confused. Then she feels my fingertips skirt the edge of her underwear. A tiny grin flashes over her face.

"Hmm. You figured it out, so I guess you should do the honors."

Mm.

Best girl ever.

I can't help the grin stretching across my face as I yank Meg's panties off with one sharp tug. The sweet, juicy miracle that is her scent instantly explodes, easily ten times more potent without the special fabric covering her core.

Archer's mouth drops open, his pupils expanding like mushroom clouds. If he had a reset button, now would be the time to press it. I think we might have actually broken his brain.

Ronan, on the other hand...

He *roars*.

The sound is unlike anything I've ever heard—and I've played a violent sport entirely made up of alphas for a fucking decade.

This isn't a sound of anger or dominance, though.

It's pure, feral possession.

Need.

Our alpha's control has finally snapped.

chapter
forty-six

I SHOULD BE AFRAID.

The old Meg would be terrified.

There's a massive, tattooed alpha looming over me, brimming with the kind of dominance that normally makes my head swim.

And Ronan is *intense*.

The laser focus of his silver stare. The way every muscle in his chest and shoulders pumps, full of fight. The curling black ink winding down his left arm—almost as thick as the sweet smokiness smoldering off him.

By all accounts, I should be petrified when he rises onto his knees and damn near tackles me into the headboard.

But I'm not.

I'm safe.

His large, hard frame lands on top of me. His face immediately goes to the curve of my neck, lips open over my thrumming pulse. And all I feel is safety.

Teeth graze my throat, harder than any of the others have dared. "You're *mine*," Ronan growls, licking the scrape away. "*My* omega."

Archer and Theo both tell me to follow my instincts, that they know better than any of us do. And, right now, mine tell me what to say.

"Yes, yours," I soothe.

Tingles skirt down my arms when I press my palms into his bare back. He's so ridiculously fit. And there's so *much* of him. Under his trim-cut suits, with all their carefully tailored lines, it's easy to miss how muscular he is.

Not now. I feel each twinge and tweak in every hard slab covering his shoulders; his sides; and even, um, *lower...*

My greedy touch under his boxers seems to snap him back to reality. A bit of the fog clears from his gray eyes, leaving that silver intensity I know so well. His mouth pulls into our secret half-smile.

"Take them off, omega."

I shove them down immediately.

He doesn't need his bark. Pure command laces every soft syllable. Especially when he bends to press his lips to my ear.

"Which knot do you want first, baby girl? Tell Daddy and I'll get it for you."

I'm compelled to answer him, but I don't have the answer. Which one do I want first? It's an impossible choice.

I feel myself start to spiral. Archer's deep voice cuts through the anxiety, smothering it in a thick blanket of dark velvet. "The only wrong answer is ignoring your instincts, love. Let them pick for you. None of us will be upset."

His hand cups my calf, massaging gently. Theo sounds surprisingly placid when he takes my other foot, adding, "We'll *all* be with you the entire time, no matter what. You get whatever you want, precious. And we're all damn lucky to give it to you. That's how this goes."

Still on top of me, Ronan radiates approval. He's proud of the way the guys treat me. His satisfaction oozes out of him. My chest aches as I absorb it.

Basking in his intensity, I smooth my hands over the sides of his face. Taking in his masculine beauty.

Something in me clicks.

I want him first.

I have no idea why I do. I just have to have him. He's the one I need.

Me... and my Omega.

I don't like to think of the instincts and urges that essentially ruined my life as their own separate entity. But, really, they sort of are.

The Omega is in there, whether I like it or not. And it's actually kind of scary how sure she is about her choices.

I touch Ronan's thick, slashing brow, following one silver thread mixed into the black. "Can it be you, Alpha?"

His pupils bloom. The solid length pressed into my belly turns to *steel*. If steel had a hot pulse at the base.

Ronan's hand snaps up, his grasp just the right side of domineering while he clasps his fingers around my jaw in an iron grip. "Perfect girl," he growls. "Your alpha is so fucking proud of you, telling me what you want."

He drags his teeth over my pulse again. A small whine builds in my chest until Ronan's purr vibrates into me, dissolving it.

"Theo," he murmurs into my skin. "Have you gotten to taste our omega yet?"

Theo makes a sound of pure longing. "Not yet."

Ronan rolls onto his side, tucking my face into the crook of his shoulder while his chest rattles on, keeping me boneless. He nods at Archer. "Wanna help, Arch?"

My long, lean alpha slides into my other side, his chest pressed in tight. His deep, smooth purr combined with Ronan's is enough to melt me into mush.

The feeling is indescribable. I have two strong, warm bodies boxing me in, surrounding me in a type of intimate security I didn't know existed.

Ronan uses his hold on my jaw to turn my head, sealing his lips over mine in a filthy, fucking sort of kiss. Archer bends his head and nuzzles his nose against the hardened point of my nipple. He bites softly through the thin bra covering me and makes a sound. Ronan somehow interprets it perfectly.

As one, they prop me up just long enough to whip the bra off before settling me back between their bodies. Ronan takes my mouth again, his growl slipping into me when he presses his large, tattooed hand over my bare belly and spreads his fingers wide, feeling my skin.

"God, Meg," Archer mutters, returning to his place at my breast. "You are so beautiful."

Now totally naked—*holy muscled blond mountain of manly goodness*—Theo hums his agreement, crawling up the mattress. "She's the most gorgeous girl ever."

His calloused fingers skim over my knee. "And so fucking *sweet*." He runs his lips up my thigh, moaning. "*Precious*. I might come all over the bed when I taste this pussy."

Archer hides a smile against the swell of my tit. Ronan breaks our kiss just long enough to toss out, "Don't even *think* about it."

The moment unwinds something inside of me. The last piece that has been clinging to propriety, secretly suspecting this will ruin everything, falls away. Because even like this, we're all still... us.

Which is exactly what I never knew I needed.

I twist closer to Ronan, deepening our kiss. Meeting the

possessive plunges of his tongue with licks of my own. His growl builds into a smothered snarl, echoing in the back of his throat while he moves his hand to my nape, tugging my hair to angle me as he desires.

Archer nips at my nipple, sending a tingly shiver down my back before moving to the other one, unbothered by pushing his head between Ronan's chest and mine. When he traces the puckered bud with the tip of his tongue, I arch from the sensation.

Theo's control snaps. He lunges up with a rumbled roar, which quickly turns into a pained groan.

I don't realize how much slick is sliding out of me until I feel Theo's biceps brush between my thighs, spreading them wide while he props himself on his elbows. There's no friction between his taut skin and my softer flesh. He glides right up to his ultimate goal.

My entire core tightens. He tilts his head and seals his lips right over me. He feels so good—the heat of his tongue, the slight prickle of his facial hair against my bare skin. I cry out, ready for more.

Faster, harder.

Now.

But Theo isn't moving yet. When I grind my hips up, a desperate noise sloughs out of him.

Archer hums his way across my chest and reaches down to pat Theo on the shoulder. "I know, big guy, I know."

Part of me wants to believe they're putting on some sort of show for me. I can't actually taste *that* good to them, right?

Wrong.

Theo *dives*. Like he's never eaten anything before. Like he didn't even know he *could*, and now he's suddenly discovered the most incredible delicacy of all time.

He's ravenous and completely unpredictable. Biting the seam of my thigh, slipping his tongue into me, sucking my clit. Then he's lightly biting my clit, sucking at my opening and licking slick off my thighs.

I can't tell what he's going to do next, and it keeps me on the sweetest edge of ecstasy. So close to coming, I scream and buck, my whole body straining upward.

Archer's touch is soothing. His palm caresses my side and my breasts. Ronan's kisses only add to the inferno Theo's building, every muttered praise and scrape of his teeth pulling the tense bundle in my center tighter and tighter.

My fingers find the sloppy bun at the back of Theo's head and *pull*. He growls against my core. "You ready to come for me, precious? Gonna drench my face with more of this sweet slick?"

Two thick fingers spear into me, the roughened pads pressing up and in, rubbing the spot inside that throbs harder with every passing second. Mindless, I sob and yank his head up to my clit. He lets me, running his closed lips over the swollen bud before sucking it into his mouth and lashing me with his tongue.

All of the sensations collide. Archer's teasing, sweet touches; Ronan's dirty kisses; the figure-eight Theo draws over my pulsing clit. Every muscle in my middle pulls taut until the tension explodes.

My vision dips.

My insides turn gold.

When I float back into my body, I find Theo collapsed between my legs, his expression blissed out, floating on a different plane of existence. He's panting every bit as hard as I am. All of them are, actually.

And, worse—I'm still in desperate *need*. My pussy clenches, the pulse painful without anything to fill me up.

Too late, I realize Theo teased me, using his fingers to push right where a knot would. Prepping me. Pushing me.

Oh, he's going to pay for that later.

Right now all I can do is mewl, the noise dangerously close to a whine. Ronan's eyes snap to mine. "Tell me what you need."

I don't know if it's my scent or the situation, but his alpha energy is *off the charts*. I've never been surrounded by this kind of dominance.

The focus.

The force.

Goosebumps prickle down my spine. But it's excitement, not fear.

My alpha is here. He's going to take care of everything.

"You, Alpha."

His control snaps. I watch it recoil, the silver of his irises receding. "That's goddamn *right*," he grits.

With one yank, he has me on top of him. He rolls, pressing me into a clean, dry portion of my enormous bed, leaving the other two alphas behind.

I don't have time to worry about that. Because Ronan rears up between my spread legs, his entire body straining toward me while he grinds his jaw shut. The softest bark slips from between his bared teeth.

"If I'm too rough, you will tell me."

He snaps a glare in Archer's direction. His next order is a hundred times harsher. *"Watch me. Stop me if you need to."*

I'm listening to my instincts much more easily, now. They speak right into my heart, filling my chest with certainty.

He's scared, I realize. *He's on edge, and he isn't used to losing control.*

He doesn't trust himself, but I do. I wrap my fingers over the curls of ink covering his thick forearm and pull gently. "I need you, Ronan. Please, Alpha."

My plea softens the hard edges of his expression. He falls forward, dropping onto his hands like he's been struck, his head hanging between his shoulders.

I watch him gather himself, dragging air into his lungs for a long moment. When he crawls up to me, there's a solemnity in his eyes that brings tears to mine.

He sees them and nudges at one falling drop with his nose. "Shh. Daddy's here. I have you."

His arms curl around me, lifting me into his warm skin. We

kiss again, this time slower. He draws it out, working his hand between us to cup my slick core.

The gesture is possessive. Demanding. And, as his fingers curl inward, teasing my pussy, so *hot*.

"Mmm." His lips twist into half a smirk. "Good girl, so ready for me. Perfect omega."

The tip of his finger rims the clenching muscles at my opening, and I keen. The sound sends a bolt down Ronan's back. His eyes flash, wildness returning. He snaps forward, sinking the first third of his cock into me before he has to stop.

He's just so *thick*. I know I'm built to fit him, but what if that part of me is as broken as every other omega piece turned out to be? The shameful thought makes everything in me tweak tighter, blocking him.

Molten quicksilver scalds my soul while he stares into me. I feel a bark build inside of him. An order to relax, probably.

It would be well-meaning—he doesn't want me to hurt. And, if he gave the command, I know I would do everything I could to obey.

But instead, he flicks a look to the left. "Arch."

My quiet alpha comes over to us, setting one hand on Ronan's shoulder and smoothing the other over my head. His dark eyes are somehow pure light. Joy and pride and tenderness. "Hi, sweetheart."

There's no helping the way my scent spikes at the love resonating in his deep voice. Archer senses it and smiles. "Does your alpha feel so good inside you, beautiful?"

I nod, the motion only a tiny bit panicky. The hand on Ronan's shoulder tightens, staying him.

"The first time can be nerve-racking," Archer acknowledges, brown eyes brimming with empathy. "I promise, we're going to make you feel so good. All of us would do anything for you. What if Theo and I put on a show for you while Ronan works his way into your perfect pussy? Would you like that?"

Theo appears on my other side, running his hand over my

hair. It still smells like me. Some primal part of my brain likes that. I turn my face into his touch, and his whole face softens.

"Love you, too, precious," he whispers.

A wicked gleam bleeds into his green irises. "You gonna let Arch torture me? That's a dangerous game. I don't think I can watch you take Daddy's knot without coming all over these luscious tits."

A possessive growl slips out of Ronan. His gaze is a forge. Pure cold fire. It's taking every ounce of his power to hold himself back.

I don't blame him. I can feel the way my body pulses around the tip of his cock, the muscles alternatively trying to pull him in and squeeze him out. He grinds his jaw tighter. Archer's fingers dent his shoulder.

"Easy, Alpha," he murmurs. "No one will take her. We're going to help her take *you*."

Ronan grunts his agreement, silver eyes spearing mine again. I see something dark move through them. My hand stretches out automatically.

"It's not your fault," I tell him. "It's me. I'm—"

Broken. Scared. Not a proper omega. Not good enough for such a pure, potent alpha male.

Ronan's eyes scan my face, reading it. He reels back onto his knees, pulling my hips up with him. The change in angle seats him a bit deeper inside me. We both groan.

Our alpha works into me slowly, rocking forward with circular motions that stretch me around his thickness. By the time Archer has his boxers off and kneels across from Theo, both poised over my body, Ronan's almost down to the wide root... and the knot swelling there.

It's hard to remember to feel anxious when I see the two bare, perfect cocks hovering over my torso, though.

Theo's feels familiar at this point. His dick is perfectly proportionate to his size, which makes it massive. The head is a ruddy red, already slick from his excitement. The knot, which I've only felt with my pussy lips—a wide bundle at the base of his impressive length—visibly grows by the second.

Seeing Archer up close is an entirely different experience. Declan wasn't teasing when he said Archer is *big*. A long, fat alpha cock, complete with thick veins pulsing up the sides and a gloriously huge knot.

Geez.

I need to learn some pussy stretches.

My hands drift up without permission, stroking along each, sizing them up. Theo makes a choked grunt when I brush his knot. Archer inhales sharply, his exhale a little shaky.

"That's right, sweetheart," he encourages, touching my cheek. "These are all yours. You touch them whenever you want."

Curling my hands into fists, I grip both and tug toward their heads, my hands meeting in the middle. Ronan watches the motion with a hungry stare.

"Touch their knots," he directs, all husky dominance.

I follow the lines of their erections to the swells at the bases. Theo's body quakes as I brush soft fingers over them both. Archer smothers a moan deep in his throat, purring over it.

Our alpha is back on his game, orchestrating everything effortlessly. His hips start to glide backward, dragging his length over every live wire inside of me. I cry out, my hands automatically gripping Theo and Archer harder. Their knots jerk under my fingertips.

"Knead them," Ronan orders, his teeth flashing. "Hard."

A loud breath scrapes out of Archer. Theo bites his lower lip, watching while I writhe around Ronan's cock. I press the pads of my fingers into their swollen knots and massage the way I saw Declan do it during our car ride.

"God, you're so good at that, Meg," Archer husks out, his hips swaying forward.

Theo's head falls back, gasping. "Gonna need someone to jerk me off or I'm going to do it myself."

Slick gushes out of me, soaking Ronan. He grunts, fucking

me in earnest now. Archer watches me soak our alpha and raises his brow, speaking around pants. "You like that idea, love? You want to watch your alphas jack each other off?"

I whine. I can't help it. Ronan's weighty thickness is tugging on every sensitive spot inside of me, rubbing me so perfectly I feel like I'll die from the pleasure.

The sound makes all three of them feral. Archer grabs Theo's cock and grips it with a hard downward pull I'd never dare to attempt. Theo's groan melds with Ronan's growl, the masculine noises echoing off the high ceiling. A second later, Archer joins in, sloughing out rough sounds while Theo twists his brawny, calloused hand around his packmate's huge, dark cock.

I'm past the point of thought. My hands just move, sliding down and wrapping around both knots, squeezing them.

"Meg, yes," Archer praises, pounding his cock into Theo's hand.

"Fuck, baby," Theo groans. "Just like that. Our good fucking girl knows exactly how to handle her alpha's knots."

I whine again, beyond desperate for... for... Something. Anything.

*Every*thing.

"Please," I whimper.

Ronan hears me and moves in a circle, pushing forward the same second he stretches me down. A scream tears from my throat. His knot presses into me. There's a split second of sting before he's in—

And it's *bliss.*

The heavy swell presses into every secret spot I didn't know I had. And just when I think there can't possibly be anything else to hit? He expands. Stretching me, finding new nerves inside of me for his knot to touch.

It's so good, I cry. Tears stream out of the corners of my eyes while I sob, calling out his name. Ronan, Alpha, Daddy. Probably words in several languages I don't even know.

Ronan is *gone.* Snarls rip from his chest, each one serrated with an edge of pleasured pain. "*Omega*. I've never felt anything so fucking *good*. You're mine. *You. Are. Mine.*"

He senses he only has seconds before we're locked together. His hips work faster, the sensation rough and slick and smooth and tight all at once. Stroking every buzzing nerve inside of me, grinding into my pulsing clit with the friction of our bodies.

We both moan. His fingers dig into my ass, pulling me as close as he can before his knot locks us down.

Archer and Theo are riveted. Their mouths hang open while they both stare at the place where Ronan's body disappears into mine. They work each other faster and harder, pulling one another over my body, dripping pre-cum down onto my belly.

I've forgotten I have their knots in my hands until Theo's suddenly inflates. My fingers tighten on instinct, pushing him over the edge.

"*Fuck*, Meg. Arch. Gonna *come*."

Archer twists his wrist, directing the hot gush of cum from Theo's cock, shooting thick, white ropes onto my breasts.

The feeling of being covered in my alpha's release, watching his face while Archer finishes him off... My core pulls tight, muscles clamping on Ronan's cock and knot, soaking both as I tip over the edge *again*.

This time, it's a flash of white heat. I arch up off the bed while Ronan growls like an animal and spurts inside of me.

Archer watches us both fall apart before he loses himself, too. More hot semen lands on my belly. The scent of his spiced ginger mixes with Theo's grassy citrus, sinking into my skin. I hope I never get either smell off me.

And, for the first time, I don't care how weird that is.

chapter
forty-seven

ARCHER

MEG SLEEPS peacefully in Ronan's arms, their bodies still locked together. The room is calm, apart from three quiet purrs and the occasional sigh from the beautiful woman wrapped up between us.

I've never seen this look on Ronan's face before. He bends his neck to glance down at her every three minutes, his expression flickering between loving concern and visible pride.

When he realizes I've caught him, he gives me a smirk. "I think I'm pretty much done for."

Meg snuggles closer to his chest, unconsciously drawn to his voice. It's so sweet, my heart aches. "Me too. I'd bond with her this minute."

Theo makes a dreamy sound completely at odds with the six-foot-seven-inch mound of muscles lying behind Ronan. "Think she'll want to do a ceremony? Or maybe do it during her heat?"

I remember our conversation earlier this week and smile fondly. "She thinks bonding ceremonies are awkward. She's apprehensive about displaying all that sexual tension in front of other people."

Ronan hums. "Just as well. Ceremonies take time to plan and I'm not sure I'll make it through her next heat without bonding her. I wanted to bite her today. Once her perfume spikes and her heat haze takes over..."

He shakes his head, unsure of himself. After a moment, he surprises me by meeting my gaze. "Thank you," he says simply. "For helping me stay in control."

My brows draw up. Ronan is good at a lot of things, but expressing gratitude isn't one of them. "You're welcome."

Theo rolls up onto his elbow, shooting me a wide-eyed look over Ronan's inked shoulder. "You'll help me during the heat, right, Arch? I don't know what the fuck I'm doing, and I don't want to hurt her."

Ronan actually lifts his arm to pat Theo's. Reassuring him. "You'll do fine, big guy."

If I was a surprised a minute ago, now I am shocked. "Of course I can help if you want me to," I add.

Theo's green eyes glow as he gazes down at our omega. "I really don't want to play that fucking game tomorrow," he mutters.

Ronan snorts. "If I could have told Past-Theo that, in the future, you'd be *complaining* about starting as a tight end against a division rival, you would have punched me."

Theo grumbles, "I'm *complaining* about the fact that we can't take our girl with us." He looks me, ever the optimist. "Or... can we?"

I grimace. "She could be in a box with Ronan and I, maybe. If she feels one-hundred-percent up to it." I turn to our leader. "I don't think I should wander far from Meg. You and I can keep her in a skybox. With security."

Ronan agrees with a gruff nod. I picture the conversation explaining this plan, wincing. "And when Meg asks why we're suddenly not working and just hanging around her like we're waiting for a bomb to go off?"

He shrugs, the motion hindered by the beautiful girl in his arms. "We tell her home games are fucking miserable in September, and we're the bosses, so we get an air-conditioned box that happens to cater her favorite foods."

She'll see right through that.

Ronan's purr deepens, a crease forming between his brows while he stares at our omega. "Is it normal for her to sleep this long?" he asks. "I know she's never taken a knot before but I didn't mean to take this much out of her."

I settle closer to Meg's back. She seems so tiny. Delicate and precious. I nuzzle into her hair, breathing the scent of all four of us to keep myself calm while I admit, "I don't think she's sleeping well. Without..."

"Declan."

Theo says his name in a tight, guilty voice. Ronan and I glance at each other, feeling his pain. If either of us were the one jeopardizing all of this, I know it would be a lot harder to take. We were friends before we were a pack, just like Dec and Theo.

"She wants him," I observe, doing my best to keep my feelings out of my voice. "Despite all his actions, I believe he has feelings for her, too. I don't understand why he won't let himself."

Theo's whole body cringes. He ducks down behind Ronan, obviously ashamed to speak up. "...I think I might know why."

Ronan fights back a bark. "Tell us."

"I shouldn't," Theo mumbles. "It's, like, some deep vault shit. He blacked out once after a game and told me while I was trying to get him into our dorm and hoist him into his bed. Then he puked all over my shoes. I don't think he even remembers that I know."

I sigh.

This is the tough part of being in a pack. Loyalties to each other versus the group as a whole. In a perfect world, the pack would come first for all of us. But it never feels good to betray your family, even if you're speaking to other members of that family.

"If you can't tell us, we understand," I hedge. "I just don't know how to help him. Or her. She needs his scent in this bed, Theo. She needs him in her nest. All of us, together. And when her heat starts, if he rejects her..."

There's no way she'll be in the right headspace to bond. Ideally, we would do it at the end of her heat, when she's lucid enough to enjoy it, but can still enjoy the health benefits that come from completing a bond while she's at her peak.

We have to fix this.

"Peaches," Theo whispers, looking at her over Ronan's shoulder again. His eyes go soft while he traces her cheekbone. Then they turn to solid green stone, swinging back to me with blazing determination.

"Dec's mother was an omega," he says, the quietest I've ever heard him. "She was into some fucked up shit. Drugs and stuff. His dad was a random alpha-hole who bonded her accidentally during a rut. They hated each other, I guess, but she got pregnant. She wanted money to... you know. But his dad barked her into submission, forced her to carry Dec to term and stay clean while she did."

Blood slowly drains out of my face. I knew Declan didn't have any relationship with his parents and always spent holidays with Theo's pack growing up. I had no idea his mother *didn't want him.*

"I don't know what happened when he was little, but he told me his dad left when he was five. Couldn't handle his mom's constant partying, issues, and drama. But they were bonded, right? So even though they were apart, she could *feel* everything he did. And whenever he'd sleep around, she would fly into, like, *rages*. Beat the shit out of Declan. Lock him in his room for hours."

My stomach churns. "His father didn't come back for him?"

Theo blows out a deep breath. "Never. I met Dec in second grade and I never heard a word about his dad coming around. By then, his mom was living on welfare. She wouldn't give him up because she needed the money she got for him. Not that she ever used it on him. He would come to school dirty, hungry, and mad as hell. He got in trouble for fighting all the damn time."

Theo's eyes glaze while he stares at the wall, remembering. "My mom was a chaperone on one of our field trips. She saw him, and it broke her heart. I remember her crying on my dads' shoulders about it later that night. The next day, one of my dads showed up for dinner with Dec in tow. Said he found him sitting in a park next to our school and asked if he had anywhere to go for supper." A sad smile curves his mouth. "I've never seen a kid eat so much."

He blows out another breath. "When you guys met him, he was a cocky, talented quarterback. But you didn't meet that angry, lonely kid. I watched him take all of his anger and make something of himself. He used all that shit he went through to fuel him. It made him the best there is. But..."

It also broke him.

"You think he hates Meg because of all this?" Ronan asks, frustration and dismay thick in his voice.

"No," Theo snorts. "I think he hates how much he wants her. It probably reminds him of his dad and what he did, losing control and bonding like that. And, I mean, there's probably some deep psychological shit about his mother being an omega and rejecting him and telling him he shouldn't even *exist*... and now, this sweet omega... It's gotta be fucking with his head."

"So this is why he wanted us to build that home for abandoned and abused children," I murmur, recalling how adamant he was. Half of his first year's salary went to building that place.

"You know what's fucked up?" Ronan mutters.

Other than everything?

"What?"

He sighs and looks down at Meg. "They're sort of perfect for each other."

chapter
forty-eight

MEG'S KNOT COLLECTION

RONAN

Declan, where are you?

ARCHER

Are you coming home tonight? We need to set the alarm.

THEO

Dec, come on man. Don't do this.

We just want to know you're ok

By the time I get home from the longest fucking day of my life, I've done what I do best:

Worked myself into quite the helpful rage.

Fuck me, fuck them, fuck this. I don't need any of them. I definitely don't need some omega brat running my life and ruining my career.

I don't care what these other motherfuckers are doing.

I don't care that it's nearly one a.m. and none of them are in their own rooms.

I don't care that this whole hallway smells like sweet-soaked *sex.*

Muttering pissy insults under my breath, I shuffle into my bathroom and start up my rain shower. It doesn't matter that I washed off for the gala—I have to get the scent of Meg's pheromones out of my nose before I go to sleep or I'll have a whole different problem.

My shoulder tweaks when I reach for my soap, my mood plummeting from dark to black.

Hell.

If it isn't better by tomorrow, I might have to have Arch wrap it. Which would piss him off since I haven't mentioned the old injury to him in months. Not to mention, I'm not exactly his favorite person at the moment.

Plus, if I show up for game four with my shoulder taped, I might as well slit my wrists and stick them in a tank full of under-fed piranhas.

We've been winning. Barely. But our position for the season is precarious. Every sports network is already laying odds against me on a daily basis. I'm not sure how much longer Ronan can feed them the line about last year being a "rebuilding year." I don't know how much longer people will believe that our first season wasn't a fluke.

It would help if Coach wasn't hell-bent on his latest strategy. Like, my guy, I'm twenty-eight, not twenty-two. All these rushing routes? Pulling the O-line forward to make room for me to try to *run* the motherfucking football? Is he trying to *actually* kill me?

I'm going to get nailed into the turf tomorrow.

And when I do, who will care? No one in this house. Can't say I blame them there.

The shower doesn't help.

My anxiety follows me into my bed, gripping my lungs in a vice. I roll from one side to the other, pummeling my pillows every few minutes.

It's useless. I'm wired.

Maybe I'll feel calmer if I can get my shoulder unlocked.

With a pained grunt, I hoist myself up and throw on the first pair of sweats I touch, deciding to go down to the gym and stretch for a while.

Ironically, I'm too tired to even look at the stairs. I take the elevator tucked in the back corner of our pack wing, holding my breath while I walk past Meg's double doors.

I don't need to fuck her mattress the way I almost humped our couch cushion.

I'm half-hard from the *memory* of her slick. And the way it tasted second-hand when I licked her off my fingers that night in the car...

No.

I ruthlessly tamp all my feelings down and march out of the elevator.

We built the house from the ground, up. Literally—Ronan had a special environmental report conducted to get permission to dig a two-story basement under the three-story house.

One basement floor is just full of bullshit. Storage, security monitors, a movie theater we've literally never used. An in-law suite, which is sort of ridiculous considering we don't *have* any in-laws.

Aside from Theo's folks, none of us have anyone else. Archer's parents are gone, Ronan's disowned him, and mine... For all intents and purposes, I'm an orphan.

I know what it's like not to have a real home. Nowhere to go if everything falls apart. Nowhere to return to if the world defeats you.

It creates a special sort of pressure. Whatever stakes you thought were high? Double them. Because failure is literally not an option.

That's why I had my favorite motivational slogan spray-painted on the wall of our home gym. *No Days Off.*

Because I don't have any other choice.

It looks good, though. Ronan may be equipped to purchase the best of the best, but his taste doesn't extend far beyond all-black-everything. The wall of multicolored neon spray paint and block tag-lettering adds a lot to the otherwise-dark space.

We spared no expense on the whole floor, filling it with every piece of equipment on the market and all the extras, too. There's a sauna. A shower big enough for ten. Special padded mats for stretching and floor-work. A small boxing ring. An ice-bath. Not to mention the Olympic-sized pool we have upstairs.

Right now... all I see is shit I stand to lose.

None of this is mine. It's *ours*. We all built it together. If I'm the one defecting, I won't keep any of it.

And I don't deserve to.

Sorrow—the bitter, bone-deep kind—floods through me. I

swallow it, bracing against the cold prickle in my gut. Waiting for the forced fury to chase it all away.

The second the rage hits my blood, I feel better. Warmer.

Perfect. Now I can work.

I barrel into the gym, not questioning the bright lights until it's too late.

Because there's one very sexy omega ass bent up in the air.

THE MIRRORS along the back wall offer every possible view of the gorgeous woman doubled-over, reaching to touch her toes. I see the crown of her head—all messy blonde, slapped into a floppy bun. The high flush on her higher cheekbones. The sweat soaking into her orange sports bra. And *that ass* in tiny black Spandex shorts.

She arches her arms in a graceful swan, fluid in her stretches. Her legs are toned and lithe, hamstrings flexing while she parts her feet and bends toward each of her sneakers.

If I wasn't so busy staring like an *idiot*, I would have realized; all this sweat, plus her pre-heat pheromones—

Urgh.

Haaaaa—ooooly shit.

I inhale her scent and a *snarl* cracks out of my mouth, splitting the silence of the gym in half. Meg whirls, yanking earbuds out of her ears.

The not-insane part of my brain—tiny and useless as it is—notices the old-fashioned corded headphones and makes a note that she needs new ones.

The over-the-ear, noise canceling Bluetooth kind would look cute as hell on her.

And honestly—what the fuck, brain?

That's all you've got? Buy her new shit?

We have a *situation* here.

Namely, me. About four seconds away from ripping her cropped Ospreys' sweatshirt in half and knotting her into next July.

I speak through grinding molars. "You need to leave."

Fuck, how many times have I told her that?

Leave. Go away. I don't want you here.

Does she know I'm only doing this because I don't think I can control myself? Does she hear the fear under the viciousness?

For a second, I feel like shit. Her face falls. Surprise evaporates, leaving the purest hurt in its wake. A tremble moves through her. She turns her head slightly, like I've slapped her.

It's almost enough to make me backpedal. But then she lifts her chin and nails me with the fiercest glare I've ever seen.

Her eyes *burn* blue. Her feet plant in place. "*You* need to leave," she snaps back, cocking her hip and tossing her head. "I was here first. I haven't worked out today and you have. So if you can't stand to be in the same room as me, then *you* can be the one to admit how pathetic you are and *leave.*"

The fucking audacity.

I growl, "This is *my* house, brat."

Her hands go to her hips. "Yes. It is. But it's also Ronan's, and Theo's, and Archer's. By that logic, this gym is only one-quarter yours. So pick a corner and stay there, asshole."

She waves her hands around her body. "*This* is my corner. We'll call it Theo's. Or maybe Archer's since I'm only down here to do the exercises he recommended for my heat."

I growl in frustration, resisting the urge to breathe through my nose again. Meg's blonde brows lift, her stare pointedly unimpressed. She doesn't care that I'm baring my teeth and fighting the urge to rut her. I don't even think she's noticed. It's like I don't register as a threat to her at all.

Why doesn't that infuriate me?

Why does it—dear God—*amuse* me?

For the love of fuck. Do I think this sassy little brat is *cute*? Is her attitude... *turning me on*?

No. No, that has to be her scent. Because—*shit*—it is perfect. Perfect on a new level of perfection. So flawless, I don't even have the proper word in my vocabulary.

Succulent. Bright freshness, rolled in brown sugar. Golden. Like her.

It rewires my central nervous system. Burns itself into the deepest fibers of my mind.

I make a mistake I've avoided thus far; I let myself imagine what it would be like to give in. If I licked that sweat off her neck... If I rolled in her sheets until they smelled like both of us... If I wallowed in her sweetness and didn't feel afraid...

Mistake.

MISTAKE.

My cock twitches to attention, the room filling with my body's answer to her hormones. Meg freezes. Her stance goes from confident to brittle. She blinks repeatedly, her chest rising and falling faster with every breath.

"Declan," she chokes. "Your *scent*."

I realize she's never smelled me like this. In the car, she had Archer right under her and Theo at her back. Plus, I had clothes on. Now, it's just me. And I'm only wearing sweats.

Hell, I can scent my own arousal. It wafts off my chest, trying to tell the omega to come to me.

I blink to clear my vision, but the edges blur. My throat feels thick. Tingles tickle my fingertips until they flinch.

No.

It can't be.

I *won't let it be* a rut.

But my blood heats to boiling, inflating my knot with hot pulses that seem to shoot straight from my cramping heart to my throbbing groin.

I've dreaded this feeling for as long as I can remember. This madness is what ruined my life before it even started. I would do anything not to feel it. Especially after what happened last time.

It can't get any worse. I'm in the sound-proofed basement, alone with a perfuming omega. She has no suppressants in her system. I have no rut-blockers.

She smells fucking *edible*.

And she hates me almost as much as her body wants me.

Maybe more.

It can't get any worse... until it does.

Her wide eyes lose focus, the black at their centers expanding. Her perfume spikes *hard*. So rich and full and thick, it's almost painful to inhale the urgency of it.

She *needs*.

My entire being screams to provide whatever she requires. I know I'm losing control. I feel it slip, slip, slipping through my fingers.

Fingers.

I reach out and grab the nearest weight machine, gripping it with all of the fervor I want to direct at the omega luring me straight into hell.

"I'll go get one of the others for you," I grit, not breathing. "You need—"*Can't say it. Can't even* think *about it.* "You're spiking. I'll get Arch."

I start to turn away, but my brain is soup.

Why am I leaving?

Where am I going?

Why am I holding my breath?

I breathe. My mind blinks off-line.

Behind me, I hear a whine shrill enough to break glass. It has claws. They dig into the spaces between my ribs, ripping hooks that make me turn around.

Omega.

I charge.

chapter
forty-nine

"MEG."

I really don't want to open my eyes, but the voice speaking to me sounds distraught. It seems rude to ignore it. Also, it would probably be good for me to know where I am?

My eyelids are lazy, so I use the lag time to mentally retrace my steps.

I woke up feeling itchy and too hot with all that manly manness in my bed. I got on my phone and looked up the workouts Archer suggested. Realized I'd look like a clown trying to do them in front of the others for the first time. And then I decided to sneak down to the gym and practice not looking like a dork while doing burpees.

Declan.

He came in, we were arguing, his scent spiked. Then mine did and... oh no.

Sure enough, I open my eyes and find Declan's infuriatingly gorgeous face looming over mine.

We're still in the gym. I see the ridiculous *No Days Off* mural behind him. I wince, my eyes fluttering against the stinging brightness of the lights overhead.

"Shit," he mutters and stretches. Something tugs inside my body just before he settles back over me, hovering on his elbows and using one hand to mess with his phone. Within seconds, the lights above us dim. He grunts, dropping the phone and panting while he hangs his head dangerously close to my chest.

My *bare* chest.

I jerk up onto my own elbows, gaping at the way we're arranged. Declan is on top of me.

And sooooooo naked.

Just... naked-naked. Not a stitch to cover any of his eight-pack abs or his broad, sculpted shoulders or anything below his chiseled hips.

The same hips pressed insistently into mine. So close that I'm forced to wonder... where his penis is? Because there's no way it's between us, with the way we're locked together—

Locked. Together.

Oh. My. GOD.

We're knotted.

"Meg," Declan says again. I whip my head back to look at him, ready to chew his face off, but his expression stops me cold.

He's *agonized*.

"Meg," he breathes, shimmying on his elbows to brush tentative fingers over each of my temples. "God. Are you okay? Did I hurt you? Should I call someone?"

He seems so upset, I can't help but wonder if he has a point. I stretch both of my legs around his, trying to find some hidden injury. But all I feel is his knot, pulsing deep and wide inside me. And how slick I am around it.

"I—I think I'm okay."

He isn't convinced. His frown deepens, blue eyes scanning my face. "Your head. Did I hit it when I tackled you? Are you dizzy or nauseous? What about a headache? Concussions are serious shit, Meg. We should call Archer. Or an ambulance. God, they need to check your whole body. X-ray everything. Or an MRI, even. *Fuck.* I could have hurt you or bitten you or—"

I reach up on instinct, slapping my palm over his lips. His horrified panic melts into an owlish look that almost makes me laugh.

"Hey. Breathe. I'm okay." I try to make a joke. "Luckily, it seems you lived up to your nickname and were pretty vanilla."

My hand falls from his stubbled jaw just in time for me to catch his glower. "This is serious, Megera. I basically just assaulted you."

Is that what happened? Because it doesn't really feel that way to me. And the way he's locked inside of me... well, based on that and the smell in here, I'd say we attacked *each other*.

"You have to believe me," he continues, rasping. "I didn't mean to do this. I *never wanted to do this*."

His words hit me harder than his body did. They're sharp little daggers, flicked right into my diaphragm. Each one dribbles cold poison down into my abdomen.

He never wanted to knot me. Didn't intend to ever lower himself to this level.

It hurts. And I'm surprised. Partly because... how can I really be shocked after everything he's done? Especially after tonight.

But to hear him say he *never* wanted to be this close to me, while he's still *in* me...

My throat closes while tears sting the bridge of my nose. "I— Okay. I'm sorry."

I close my eyes, not wanting to witness the disgust in his once he sees me crying over him. He mumbles another curse. The fingers resting against my crown tighten around a clump of hair.

"Shit. Fuck. Meg? Don't cry. *Stop crying.*"

The bark hits me, but it backfires. The swell of panic from not being able to follow his command on the spot just pushes out more tears. His voice jumps up an octave. "No! I didn't mean to bark. You can cry. I don't care."

He doesn't care.

It's the truth, isn't it?

For weeks, I deluded myself into thinking he might come around, twisting all of his words and actions to give myself some scrap of hope. But he's gone and made things crystal clear, now.

Why doesn't he just stab me in the heart next time? It will be quicker and a lot less messy than *this.*

I squeeze my eyes shut, sobbing soundlessly into the back of my hand while he tugs at my hair and growls some more.

"No! Shit! I mean, of course I care! I guess. A little, okay? Obviously. *Obviously,* I fucking care! You happy? You whined *once* and now we're literally locked together. Your scent electrocutes my fucking *soul.* And I've been basically hiding from you in my own home because I was terrified I would go into a rut and hurt you. So, yeah, okay, I care. But please. Stop crying."

I try to. I gasp and struggle to stop the tears. They only come harder, raining down into my sweat-crusted hair.

After a long moment, Declan sighs, his body deflating on top of mine. He uses the motion to rock us into a quick roll, putting himself beneath me and gathering my wet face against his throat.

"Hey." His voice is warmer. Soft. "Shh, it's okay. You're okay."

My confusion makes me cry harder. He wraps his solid arms around my entire torso, cupping the back of my head with gentle pets. "I'm here. I have you."

At first, I think he clears his throat. Then I hear it—the quiet, unsteady threads of a hesitant purr. I rub my cheek between his pecs, trying to get closer. Hear it better.

He immediately gets louder, the raspy rattle rising up into me. I whimper and his lips graze my forehead. "Is that good, baby?"

His fingers clamp around the back of my neck and begin kneading the muscles. His purr gets deeper and stronger until I'm fairly sure he's the loudest of all the alphas in the pack.

I feel like my brain is unplugged. Almost like it isn't there at all.

My body reacts without consultation. All sorts of omega nonsense comes up. Whines, whimpers. I nestle closer and closer, scent-marking him, kissing his neck.

Declan doesn't flinch. He holds me hard and purrs so steadily. By the time I realize my face is dry, I'm half-asleep, floating in knotted, vibrating bliss.

The alpha under me starts fussing with my hair, his fingers untangling, smoothing it down. The longer we lie together, the more he relaxes, the muscles beneath me slowly losing their rigid tension. When his shoulders drop back to the mat, he hisses.

I catch the way his electric eyes flicker to the left, a vaguely annoyed pout tugging at his lips. A realization hits me.

"You're hurt."

Declan instantly stiffens all over again. His teeth snap together. "I'm fine."

But my crazy omega ass can't take him at his word. Low-grade panic tingles through my stomach, turning it into a sick seethe. And I know—*I know*—he's lying to me. And himself, probably.

My hand flies up. He tries to shift away, but there's nowhere for him to go with my body on top of his and his knot holding us together. I find the injury about an inch south of the place where his left shoulder meets his nape, my fingers gently probing the muscle and sinew. It's hot, like the tissue inside is throbbing with painful inflammation.

I gasp, "Oh my God! This must hurt like crazy! What are you doing working out when your shoulder is like this?"

Declan grunts, reaching up to pluck my hand away. "It's. Nothing. Drop it."

My knotted haze is a thing of the past. Outrage fires my blood. "No! You're injured and you haven't told anyone? That's just— stupid! Dangerous! *Reckless*, Declan."

His jaw flexes and his eyes flash before he suddenly rolls us onto our sides.

His *right* side, of course. Because the left one is *injured*.

But he's also way smarter than I ever gave him credit for. Because instead of starting a full-blown shouting match while his knot is locked up in me, he starts purring again and pulls me into his naked chest.

"Don't be upset," he mutters, almost petulant. "It's just a tweak, okay? Normal bullshit. Archer will stretch it out for me before the game tomorrow, and I'll be fine."

His voice drops back into the soft one I've never heard before tonight. "I don't want you to worry about me. Okay?"

Damn these alphas and their warm muscles and their perfectly-scented skin and their *purrs*.

I can't *think*.

It's worse than being barked into submission, in some ways, because I literally cannot be upset when he holds me like this. But I do manage to sound a little bratty while I snuggle closer, grumbling, "What do you care if I'm worried? After tonight, I thought it was pretty clear where your priorities lie."

Declan huffs out a sigh. "Because I embarrassed myself by walking away from my speech so I could chase my ex out and keep her from upsetting you? Trust me, I wish I knew why I care enough to do something stupid like that. But I do."

Oh.

Wow.

My brain stumbles over that information. He only went after her to keep her *away* from me? Do I believe that?

I don't let myself think about it for more than a millisecond because I'm afraid I'll have another meltdown. Instead, I focus on the curiosity niggling at the corners of my mind. It's as good a distraction as any, since we're literally stuck here.

I lean back and watch this face carefully while I ask the question that's nagged me since I googled famed quarterback Declan Howard weeks ago.

"Is it me? Because I know you've dated other omegas and —*obviously*—had a pretty serious relationship with one."

His angelic bone structure seems tighter, somehow. The blue irises staring back at me darken while his teeth grind. "It's a long story."

I toss him a dry look and wave at our genitals. "I've got time."

The tiniest flicker of amusement sparks in his eyes before he sighs, long and loud. He slumps all the way onto his side, his temple hitting the mat beneath us. Defeated, he lets his eyes drift shut.

"Her name is Trina."

USA Daily said Ka-trina.

My Omega hates that he uses a nickname. But whatever. I can deal with that hoe's irrational snit to get this whole story sorted out. I shove my instincts into their deep, dark hole and listen intently.

"She was a nurse," he goes on, then smirks with his eyes still closed. "I *thought* she was a nurse. We met at a charity thing. When Ronan burned all his dad's shit to the ground, the only piece he kept up and running was their family foundation. They built hospitals, funded underprivileged schools, and all that. He and Arch agreed it would be fucked up to dismantle it, so they let it continue running. We all make appearances for it when we have to. That weekend, a bunch of sick kids wanted me to teach them to throw a football, so I was at one of the hospitals we fund. That's when she approached me."

The hairs on the back of my neck wave to attention. "There aren't many omega nurses who work in big hospitals," I murmur. "The environment is chaotic, and most doctors are alphas. Too much risk, especially if heat hormones spike during a life-or-death situation."

Declan's jaw hardens as his eyes snap open. "That's what Archer said when I told him. It pissed me off at the time. We'd all just moved into this house, the team was thriving; we were *ready* for our omega. And here I found one with—"

He hesitates. I shoot him a glare. "Just say it."

I get a hint of that cocky smirk I have such a toxic love-hate relationship with. "Well, I started to say 'I found one with a good scent,' but then I *breathed* and remembered what *you* smell like. Compared to *this*, she was like... a Glade Plug-In."

But I'm a freaking masochist, apparently, because I have to know. "What was her scent?"

He sighs again, this one a bit growly with annoyance. "Banana cream?"

I instantly get a flash of Theo scowling at the banana on his plate during our first meal together. Ronan also refuses to eat them, blaming Banana Blast trauma from his smoothie bar days.

The enormous bubble of relief in my chest makes me grin. "The guys would have *hated* that."

Declan frowns, clearly confused by my lack-of drama. "They did. Well, Theo *really* did. And Ronan wasn't keen either. Archer agreed to a date, but he wasn't into it. You know him, though, keeping the peace. I also think he wanted an omega the most out of all of us. Someone for him to be soft with."

I roll my eyes at that description of Archer's devoted attention —his desire to care for and cherish another person in a way most people would never humble themselves to. Especially this alpha.

"You're such an ass."

Declan smirks again, but his eyes are somber. "I know that."

Something about the look has me reaching up to comb his hair off his brow. "Then what happened?" I whisper.

His shrug is deceptively casual. But I see the tension gathering between his eyebrows.

"It was clear she wasn't a match for our pack. And, honestly, I knew I wasn't feeling the things I should have been feeling if she was *mine*. We only went out for a month before I broke things off with her. But she came back a few weeks later—"

The anguish in his eyes reminds me of the moment I woke up. Like he's pleading for me to forgive him before I even know what he's done.

I raise my eyebrows, urging him to finish his sentence.

But I never could have guessed the word that falls from his lips.

"—pregnant."

chapter
fifty

I DIDN'T KNOW my knot could deflate so fast.

Some combination of reliving this horrible fucking story and the stricken paleness of Meg's face instantly shrinks me down. She doesn't notice at first, frozen at my side.

My instincts roil inside of me, rebelling against this whole thing. Her swollen face, the red rimming her crystalline irises, the sweat caked into her roots, fingertip bruises I don't remember leaving on her arms and legs—it's all *fucked*.

My omega shouldn't look dirty and exhausted and scared. I should keep her clean and safe and happy, always.

I should be fixing this, but instead I'm making it all worse.

Like I always do.

That's *all* I ever do, lately.

She needs to hear this from me before she accidentally hears it somewhere else. But now I realize how many mistakes I've made, rushing into honesty without thinking.

I should have waited until she could have her other alphas nearby to comfort her. I shouldn't have told her right after knotting her for the first time. Especially since it was a fucking accident, and I rutted her.

Shit. Fuck.

But it's too late. I can't stop now.

Meg's voice comes as a numb, ragged whisper. "You have a baby?"

Her body catches up to her brain. She scrambles away from me, and her scent *burns*.

FUUUUUUUUCK.

I bolt upright, ignoring the painful tug in my shoulder. "*No!* God. No."

Meg starts crying again, more silent tears streaming out of her raw eyes and dripping down her cheeks. She stumbles as she tries to put her shorts on backward. I lunge up to keep her from falling into a rack of free weights, but she shrieks like my fingertips burn her.

Forcing myself back a step, I shove my hands into my hair and grip it to keep from grabbing for her. Desperation is like a living creature, burrowing a pit into my stomach.

"Meg. Listen to me. *Please.*"

She finally gets her pants on and clutches her top to her bare chest, sobbing openly. "You aren't telling me anything!" she cries. "Except that you liked another omega enough to —to—"

She makes a pained sound that hits me straight in the black hole where my heart should be. "And she got *pregnant?*" Meg continues, her eyes full of the most honest, heart-wrenching betrayal I've ever seen. "You were with her during her—her —*heat?*"

God, the *regret.*

It hurts. It's nausea, a dry mouth, and lungs that don't remember how to expand. Panic, guilt, and a manic sort of help-lessness.

What do I do?

What *can* I do except continue my suicidal stream of honesty? "It wasn't her heat," I rasp. "She was on suppressants. It was—"

Still wrong.

It was still wrong. Because it wasn't *Meg.*

I don't have the wherewithal to figure out why what I did suddenly seems so obviously fucked up. At the time, I told myself it was no different from Archer volunteering at those clinics. No more shameful than Ronan's bar hookups.

But that's all just fucking *wrong.*

And I was wrong to think any of it. Looking into Meg's eyes right now nails that particular truth into my middle.

"I'm sorry," I say. Because it's true. Nothing else has ever been this true. "Meg. I'm sorry I ever did that."

She shakes violently, tremors visibly moving over her. Her palms press over her ears while her eyes fall shut, squeeze more tears out. The shrill whine that escapes her shatters the breath in my lungs.

"Don't apologize to me now! Just tell me the rest of what happened so I can—"

Leave.

She wants to leave me.

Didn't I know that this would happen all along?

I expected it. I've been waiting for it. Preparing myself for it by refusing to get close to her.

So why is this *gutting* me?

I know I have to finish the story. She has a right to that, at least. I force air into my tattered lungs, my chest heaving.

"She came back around and told me she was pregnant. She told me it was mine."

Because she somehow knew about my past. The bitch knew, and she figured out that the best way to get me to turn my back on the pack and choose her would be to pretend I'd knocked her up. The same way my dad carelessly impregnated my mother.

It would have worked, too. I can still recall the crushing, leaden weight of responsibility I felt. The determination to not repeat the past.

I almost didn't exist. My mother told me every day how much she wished I didn't. I knew I would never be able to live with myself if Katrina got rid of my child... or raised it with the kind of loathing my mom shoveled at me for sixteen years.

The words stick in my throat, burning. I swallow the story down, opting for the short version so I can let this scared, heart-broken, beautiful omega get the hell away from me and all my poison.

"Archer never trusted her. He insisted on running the tests himself. He figured out she wasn't actually pregnant right away. Then we found out she wasn't really a nurse, either. Everything she told me was a lie, but even with all the shit she made up, she had me by the balls. All she had to do was open her mouth and keep lying, but to a reporter. Ronan had to pay out for a non-disclosure agreement."

It was too late, though. She'd already done interviews, posing as my scorned "ex." The media circus that followed was chaos. Our pack bonds frayed into thin threads. I was so distracted by it all that I blew the biggest game of my career.

Because—of course—it all went down two weeks before the National Championship.

"I saw the pictures," Meg whispers, her voice cracking. "When I looked all of you up, there were some photos and her name on articles, but it was *years* ago, so I didn't read any of them. I just never imagined—"

She just never imagined that her mate would be such a piece of shit.

I dip my head low, taking the words she doesn't say. I don't have any other choice. And now I have to say the thing I should have explained the day she turned up.

"Do you understand now?" I rasp. "*I'm* the problem here. I can't love you because I can't love anyone. I won't trust you because I can't even trust myself. I'm a broken, fucked-up mess. The only thing I can do for you is win some stupid football games and leave you the hell alone."

A full minute ticks by and I don't care. Just like I don't care that I'm standing here naked, baring my neck in submission.

She can have my submission.

Because she'll never have me.

God knows, if I had anything to give her, I would. Right now, I would give her whatever fragments of me she wanted.

But she's too good for that.

She waits for me to lift my chin and meet her eyes. They're dry, now. Still red; but dry and steady. She's strong, this girl. I have so much respect for that.

Especially when she straightens her spine and turns to go.

"Then leave me the hell alone, Declan."

chapter
fifty-one

ARCHER

I WAKE up with Ronan's alarm, reaching over the omega sleeping between us to punch his arm. He grunts and rolls. I hear him fumble for his phone. Whatever he sees on it gets him up and off the mattress, sweeping out of the room.

It's gameday, my mind supplies.

Usually, I get up the second I'm awake, but I have no motivation to move. Not with Meg looking like an angel in the golden morning light bleeding through her sheer curtains.

Theo sleeps at my back, his quiet snores hitching slightly when Ronan closes the bedroom door behind him. Meg's eyelashes flutter, just a little. Barely enough for me to see that her eyelids are an angry, irritated red. Alarm jumps in my chest. Leaning back slightly, I take a closer look at her.

That's when I realize—she smells... wrong. Or *right* actually. More right than she ever has before. The peachy scent of her perfume isn't just entwined with my spice, Theo's citrus, and Ronan's smoke. There's also—

Vanilla.

For a second, I'm elated. Concern quickly replaces the feeling when I see that she's bundled up in a mishmash of our discarded clothes. Plus, her skin is pale, her face slightly swollen.

I brush my lips over her forehead, checking for a fever she doesn't have. Meg leans up into the contact, moaning quietly and shimmying closer. Even in her sleep, she hesitates, as if she wants to be near me, but isn't sure she would be accepted.

Or maybe it's not me she's thinking of at all, based on the new scent on her skin. Perhaps she wandered off to find Declan in the night and got a fresh serving of rejection.

His scent seems a little too strong for that theory. It's more likely they both gave into the pull between them, and he freaked out afterward. That tracks with everything I know about Declan, in light of the story Theo shared with us last night.

I'm going to insist he sees a therapist. His mental and emotional well-being are every bit as important to this pack as his physical health. He needs to realize that we need him whole in every way. Not just his throwing arm.

But there's nothing I can do about it right now except comforting our omega. I ease her into my arms, cuddling her as close as I can. She burrows her face into my neck, inhaling with a soft smile. "Mmm, Archer."

I grin at the ceiling. "Hi, sweetheart. How did you sleep?"

Her smile cracks into a grimace. "Not so good."

I hum as though this is actually news to me, rubbing my palms down her back. "Sleeping skin-to-skin with us may help settle your Omega a bit. Any particular reason you got up and put on clothes?"

She tucks her face down, hiding from me. "Uh...mmm... nope," she squeaks, lying horribly. "No. I was, uh, cold?"

She has to know that's a ridiculous claim. She had me plastered to her front and Ronan wrapped around her back. Even after his knot released her, his Alpha wouldn't. He spent the rest of the night unable to stand being more than a few inches away from her. She had to brush her teeth in his lap.

It's a common reaction for an alpha after knotting his omega for the first time. I ignore the tiny pinch of jealousy snapping at my lungs and focus on my relief and happiness.

She let us all be with her last night, and it was perfect. She took our pack alpha's knot. She told Theo she loved him.

She's really ours.

Which makes her *mine*.

So why is she lying to me right now?

"Hmm," I reply, the sound wry. "Cold?"

She seems to understand that her invented rationale won't hold water. "Or—well, actually, I—umm..."

Not wanting her to struggle, I pet her head in soothing strokes, purring lightly. "You don't have to tell me, sweetheart. Are you all right, though? Last night was a lot."

She snorts. "You can say that again."

"Last night was a lot," Theo parrots, joking sleepily. He grunts and turns toward me, holding out his arms with his eyes shut. "Share, Arch."

I roll my eyes, but tuck Meg into a quick flip. She giggles quietly as she lands between us, stretching over to kiss Theo's scruffy cheek. "Hi, big guy."

He smiles without cracking an eyelid, utterly content. "Hi, precious. Mmm, you smell so good when you smell like us. Come here."

His big, brawny hand grips her thigh to tug her closer. I'm the only one looking at her face, so I see the pain tear across it before he feels her stiffen. His eyes finally fly open, anxiously scanning her.

"What? Where does it hurt?" He shimmies closer to her, smoothing a palm up her hip. His gaze lands at the apex of her thighs. "Fuck. Did Daddy's knot make you sore, precious?"

She winces. "Sort of?"

I know it isn't the whole truth, but I'm guessing she doesn't want to rat Declan out to his teammate hours before they have to play a game together.

It doesn't work. Theo's eyes snag on her forearm. She's wearing his T-shirt, and it's huge on her, but we can still see the faint purple smudges marring her smooth skin.

I lurch upright, examining them closer. Shame lashes through me. "Meg, we—"

Her hand lands on my face. She shakes her head. "It wasn't you guys. It was Declan. He and I... hashed some stuff out last night."

Theo's expression is pure thunder. He sits up behind her and gently lifts her into his lap, cupping her cheek. "He bruised you?" Theo asks, staring into her. "Tell me what he did."

"He didn't mean to." She shakes her head some more. "He was in a rut and I spiked and we just *collided*. Honestly, I don't remember it at all. But I woke up knotted with him and he was freaking out. He wanted to call an ambulance."

I can tell it's true from the shape of the bruises. They're smears, not solid ovals. Anyone trying to injure her would have left clear fingerprints behind. These seem more like smudges.

Theo still looks enraged. I set my hand on his shoulder. "We can watch the security tapes, Meg. If you'd like to know what happened."

Her eyes bug out. "No! Please. I just want to forget it ever happened. Honestly, to me, it *feels* like the sex part didn't even happen."

The sex part? What other part was there? And why did she end up crying so much?

Meg sees the questions in my eyes and shoots her gaze over to Theo. Reminding me that he has to perform later today. She smiles at him, the motion weak. "Anyway. I'm fine. I just need some extra rest, I think. Can I stay in bed?"

Theo leans his forehead against hers. "All day, if you want, peaches. You don't have to come to the game at all. Stay in bed. Get one of these knot-heads to play hooky with you."

She laughs softly. "No, no. I want to go to your game! I just need a long morning nap. But I'll be there, big guy. Promise."

He kisses her softly. "Tough girl. I love you, precious."

"I love you," she whispers back, then grins at him. "But you better kick some ass for me today."

chapter
fifty-two

NOT SURE HOW this asshole thought he would avoid me when *we're on the same damn football team*, but whatever. He's an idiot because despite him leaving the house this morning without a word to anyone, I find him within five minutes of arriving at the stadium.

Grabbing the back of his shoulder pads, I yank him up from the bench where he's tying his cleats. The locker room is so full of big guys avoiding glimpses of each other's junk, no one even notices when I haul Declan's sorry ass into the tunnel and slam him into the wall.

The more I think about those bruises marking Meg's arms, the more pissed I get. I can tell from the look on his face—he knows exactly why I'm glaring.

It isn't the sex part.

If I found out he finally gave in and gave our sweet little omega a good time, I would be bouncing up and down. But fucking her rough right out of the gate isn't right.

He hasn't built any trust with her. He hasn't given her any affection or made a connection. He basically used her and sent her back to her bed, unwashed, with marks all over her. Expecting me to do all the cuddling for him.

I mean, I *did*. But still.

He glares back at me, pouting. Acting like he doesn't understand even though I *know* he does. The little shit.

I shove at his shoulder until the hard, white plastic knocks into the cinderblock wall. "Talk. *Now.*"

I hate this aggressive horseshit. Always have. Unfortunately, sometimes, knocking Dec around is the only way to get through to him. He spent his whole childhood taking hits. It makes sense that's what he responds to now.

God, that's fucking depressing.

When my hands slip off him, he pushes himself up, almost at my eye level but not quite. No one is.

"I'm sure the little princess cried on your shoulder about it all night," he jeers. "You don't need to hear my side."

"You don't *have* a fucking side!" I shout. For a minute, I have to concentrate on not decking him. I shoot air out of my nose, doing my best not to recall all of the times our girl has gone out of her way to give him the benefit of the doubt. Because then I'd have to strangle him.

Instead, I narrow my eyes, taking in the pissed off expression on his face and all the turmoil just underneath it.

He's so angry. *And I get it.*

But not as much Meg would.

"You know what's *fucked*?" I continue. "Of all of us, *she's* the one who could understand you the best. You keep pushing her away because of all your bullshit, the same way she tried to build walls to protect herself. The only difference is *she's* strong enough to try to overcome everything she went through. And you aren't."

Blue fire fills his eyes. His brows slam down. "I don't even know what you're *talking* about."

"I know you don't!" I yell. "Because you have your head so far up your own ass, you can't even *see* her. How amazing she is. After everything she told us last night—"

He thinks I'm talking about him but I'm not. Still, he demands, "What did the brat tell you?"

Fuck. I'm not known for my impulse control. And this is no exception. Some higher part of my brain knows I should probably wait and let Meg tell him herself, but I'm so tired of all of us tiptoeing around each other. The truth needs to come out.

"It wasn't about you and whatever bullshit you two got up to. This was earlier. On the ride home. She asked if she could get involved in the foundation. She wanted to donate more money to your project—the children's home."

His face falls slack for a moment before he remembers to snap it into a sneer. "Why the hell would she want to do that?"

I grit my teeth and glance around, making sure we're totally alone before I lean in. "Because she *lived in one*, Dec. Her mom died when she was fourteen. No one ever adopted or fostered her. She lived in a group home just like the one you built."

He rears back like I just hit him. Some dark desolate thing sinks into his expression. He swallows it... and then this asshole gnashes his teeth at me.

"Stop *telling* me this shit. I don't want to hear it! Especially not before a fucking game."

I slap his shoulder back again. "I don't give a fuck what you want anymore. You snapped into rut and knotted her without ever even *smiling* at her. You're acting like a piece of shit. You're acting like your dad—"

Ah fuck.

I told you, I have no impulse control.

We stare at each other. And I can *see* the second he knows that I know.

We never talked about that night he got wasted and spilled all his shit. Now I realize he didn't really remember it and hoped I didn't, either.

But enough is fucking *enough.*

Our girl, our pack, our lives are on the line. I'm not blowing this.

So, I swallow my anger down and try to meet him where he's at. "Do you want to talk about that shit? I figured that what happened last night would be hard on you. Considering everything."

I might be ready to put my personal feelings aside for the greater good, but this shithead is *not.* He shoves me with both hands, the motion knocking me back as much as the vicious look on his face.

"*Fuck off,*" he growls. "It's done. She decided last night. She's *done.* So whatever stupid fucking fantasies you had for our pack? Forget them." His lip curls up. "Should be easy for you to do since you're such a dumbass."

I've known him our whole lives. I know his fear is like a bear trap around his ankle, and he's really not much more than a desperate animal right now. Taking strips out of me to protect himself.

Weeks ago, I would have let it go. Walked it off. Gone out onto the field and taken his hits. Let him be the hero.

But I keep hearing Meg's voice in my head. Telling me I'm smart. Telling me I'm sweet and fun and kick-ass and strong.

Telling me how proud she is.

Reminding me what I'm worth. Every damn day.

So, *fuck this.*

I snort. "You know what, Dec? Since I'm such a dumbass, who knows?" I shove him back one more time before turning away. "I might forget to cover you."

chapter
fifty-three

Megera

SOMETHING IS WRONG.

It's wrong, wrong, wrong, wrong, *wrong*.

But I'm new at this, and I suck at it, so I have no idea *what's* wrong.

I look down at the outfit Mrs. Fleming left out, searching for any clues as to why I feel like I'm about to hurl all over the Bentley. It's another edgy, cute-but-sexy, cool-but-don't-touch-me sort of vibe. I have to admit, after seeing the woman in nothing but capri pants and aprons, I never would have expected this sort of style from her.

But it looks good on me, I guess. The leather-like leggings feel sleek and durable. With the stretchy bottoms tucked into thick-soled black booties, I feel like I could go on a spy mission if I had to. The Ospreys shirt half-tucked into the pants clearly belongs to one of the guys. I can't tell who because it's been washed—but my Omega isn't having a shit fit about it because I currently have Theo, Ronan, and Archer's scent markings on my throat.

Even though it doesn't smell like one of my alphas, the black cotton tee is soft, with faded orange letters and cut-outs where the crew neck and sleeves used to be. It would look weird with a regular bra, but whatever black, lacy bralette magic I have on works. Plus, the leather jacket I grabbed to cover my bruises also masks most of my exposed skin.

A little make-up, some hair texturing spray... and I look just fine.

So, what is *wrong*?

Archer and Ronan clearly don't feel it. They sit on either side of me, both lost in their phones. Ronan's buzzes every fourteen seconds, and Archer has been typing up a detailed list of instructions for his subordinates for close to twenty minutes.

To keep myself from reading over his biceps, I opt for checking him out. He's in work clothes—a pair of black slacks that highlight his height, and a spotless Ospreys polo that makes his dark skin glow.

I don't often think about how good-looking Archer is—mostly because he's usually so busy wowing me with his kindness and his brilliance, and there's only so much a girl can obsess about at one time. But as his eyebrows furrow over the square rim of his glasses, it strikes me that he has a bone structure almost as perfect as Declan's. And better lips for sure.

He finally hits send on his email and catches me staring. A stunning, white grin stretches over his face. "Come here, my love."

I ignore the ridiculous *squeeeeee* in my heart at him calling me "his love." Or I try to. Pretty sure the fact that I perfume a little bit might give me away.

His smile takes on a crooked air, telling me he absolutely knows exactly how he affects me. Long-fingered hands easily guide my legs over his lap, swiveling my butt on the plush leather seat.

My eyes flit to the driver chauffeuring us. I'm not used to having someone else in the car, but Ronan assured me it's standard for gamedays and other big events. His driver has been with him for decades, apparently, and the partition is up... so I'm sure having my legs in Archer's lap is no big deal.

But I'm still fighting that voice in my head that tells me this is rude and a little bit pathetic. After all, I spent the better part of *a day* in bed with this man. Why does my body still crave his touch so much?

Archer reads my face, his eyes filling with understanding. "It's okay, Meg," he murmurs. "Your touch starvation is advanced. You need a little extra affection and it's our privilege to provide it for you. In fact, I'll miss it when you want your personal space back."

My cheeks heat. A weak smile pulls at my lips. "You'll be sick of me by then."

Archer shakes his head firmly. "No. I will be even more head-over-heels for you than I am now—*and* even better at showing you."

He kisses my hand and gently sets it back on my lap. "I honestly cannot wait for your heat."

An image of my sealed-off nest pops into my mind. I swallow a bolt of panic, my voice tightening. "Are you sure you want to—"

Ronan zeros in on the topic of conversation. In a blink, his phone is silent and in his jacket pocket. "None of us have ever been more sure of anything, omega," he replies, brokering no argument. "I had to arm wrestle Theo to get the rights to your first orgasm."

Archer chuckles, glancing to his left. "And you *lost*, old man."

Ronan flashes a rare grin. "Yeah, but I'm the boss. So I *always* win."

I flick my wrist to smack him with the back of my hand, tutting, "Spoiled."

A careful sort of silence balloons in the backseat. Archer clears his throat, speaking carefully. "We wanted to ask because we weren't entirely sure... How do you feel about the nest issue after last night?"

Ah. So they think I might still change my mind about Declan. I told Archer that he and I had decided to step away from each other indefinitely. But I guess I haven't exactly been the most stable or reliable lately.

Ronan senses a shift in my mood. His brawny hands cup my shoulders and guide my back into his chest while he tilts our way, effectively stretching my body out between theirs without ever undoing my seatbelt.

"You've done nothing wrong," Ronan murmurs. "Whatever you feel is right for the nest is exactly right. "

"And that could change every day," Archer adds, the matter-of-fact tone of his voice reassuring. "Which is why we will always wait to be invited in."

I nod, but the taut feeling in my chest just keeps tweaking tighter.

Our alpha's deep, jet-like purr vibrates into my back, unlocking the tension around my spine. "Relax, baby girl," he directs, sliding his touch down my arms. "Shhh. Daddy's here."

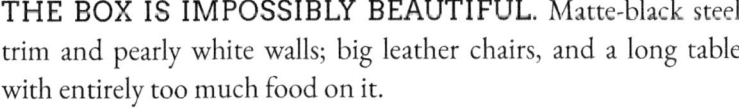

THE BOX IS IMPOSSIBLY BEAUTIFUL. Matte-black steel trim and pearly white walls; big leather chairs, and a long table with entirely too much food on it.

Archer pauses to turn a dial beside the entrance. The muted

voices of commentators filter through the speakers built into the ceiling—just loud enough for me to hear what they're saying when I tune in.

Which I may not be doing...

Ronan's eyes are still hot on my back as he shuts the door behind the three of us and locks it. An excited quiver starts in my belly, but he pauses when he sees me facing the buffet—which, curiously, only contains my favorite foods.

"Are you hungry, little one?" His palm pets the back of my head and I shiver with pleasure, my perfume already ridiculously strong in the small space.

"Let's feed you properly first." He drifts around my body, moving in the sinuous, smoke-like way that is distinctly Ronan. He looks over and locks his quicksilver eyes on mine. "It irritates my Alpha when I think you're hungry."

Archer is on it, already filling a plate with sticky short ribs, mini mac-and-cheese bites—and of course—some stir-fried veggies. He adds a second piece of Texas toast, though, so I decide to let his obsession with my vitamin intake slide.

Ronan leads me to one of the plush, over-stuffed leather chairs lined up in front of a window overlooking the stadium. The view is incredible. We're higher up than most of the fans, but we can see every part of the field. Between that and the close-up coverage flickering on the wide-screen television hanging above the buffet, I feel like I might actually have a prayer of following the play action.

If my alphas let me, that is.

Ronan fills the place beside me, reaching over to feed me bites of toast from his own hand. His other palm continues stroking the back of my head. His eyes spark with pride while he watches me swallow.

Lord.

The obsessive, possessive edge to his gaze is definitely stronger today. Maybe because he knotted me last night? It seems optimistic to think he could possibly look at me like this forever.

Surely, my novelty will wear off soon and these incredible men will all come to their senses, right?

Maybe *that's* what's wrong with me today? I'm just... anxious about how much they're starting to mean to me?

Convinced this can't possibly be *real life*?

Archer seems determined to prove the exact opposite. He slides into the chair at my other side and instantly slips his hand into my lap. Long fingers knead at my thigh while he eats his salad wrap one-handed, watching the sidelines and flicking his focus over to me every few moments.

They both try their best to keep the atmosphere light—keeping our conversation easy, refilling my plate twice, smirking at me when I half-heartedly protest a *third* helping of garlic bread. But as soon as the players line up on the field for kick-off, a charge snaps through the skybox.

We all lean forward, watching while the opposing team scrambles to catch our punt. It's a good one, apparently. Ronan quietly comments on the kicker's rookie status, grumbling while he admits that "the kid" was a decent addition to their roster. Archer is much kinder, listing the new guy's stats with a magnanimous air.

I find this pattern continues while we watch the first quarter unfold. Ronan is grumpy, complaining about every tiny mistake and frowning when the officials make calls against us. Archer, on the other hand, seems optimistic. He shrugs when plays go awry, smiling loosely.

It takes me a while to realize that he doesn't actually care who wins. He only tenses when one of our players is slow to recover from a nasty tackle. I hear the way he holds his breath until the man is back on his feet, waving off the medical staff gathered along the sidelines.

I'm so focused on trying to absorb the ins and outs of the game and my alphas' moods, it takes me a while to return to the niggling sensation that something feels... *off*.

By the time I realize Ronan is *scowling* at the field, there are just a few minutes left until halftime and we're down by ten points. I lean closer to Archer, hoping he might explain what's going on.

"Is something wrong?"

He pauses for half a second, cocking his head and watching the players line up for another down before he replies.

"It's unusual for Theo to miss blocks," he murmurs. "Usually he's so overprotective, I have to tell him not to tear himself up guarding Declan. But today he's just..."

The words trail off as the players below snap into action. I train my gaze on Theo, watching while he absorbs a hit to his shoulder. At first, it seems like he's really blocking the defensive player trying to shove past him. But then he lets his body roll to the right before backing off entirely.

Allowing an enormous linebacker to hustle through the gap and *plow* into Declan.

I spring to my feet the second the player makes contact.

And then I sprint.

I hear noises behind me. Shouts, snarls. I don't care. I only know I have to get down to the field *immediately*.

It's funny. All the fighting I do to keep my omega instincts in check, all the times I was secretly so proud of subverting them— that all seems like a joke now.

Because this? *This* is a proper instinct, and I have no prayer of even slowing myself down long enough to parse it.

I don't know why I need to streak down ten flights of stairs, knocking much bigger, scarier people out of my way. I have no idea why it doesn't occur to me to explain myself to my other alphas. I'm not even in my own brain as I shove past a door clearly marked for staff only and race through the tunnels Theo showed me after practice that day.

My heart hammers as I force my way past a row of armed, enormous guards, ducking to slip between their legs and burst out of the team's tunnel.

Onto the field.

chapter
fifty-four

ARCHER

MEG IS FAST, but I'm faster.

I close in on her as she darts past our security. Behind me, Ronan roars at the guys, forcing them to make a path so we can follow our omega.

My mind races as fast as my feet, wondering what the hell is happening.

Is she spiking?

Or having some sort of episode?

The first thing I notice as I sprint onto the field behind her is silence. The solemn sort of quiet that doesn't have any place in a football stadium. Unless, of course, someone is severely—

Hurt.

It all makes horrible, perfect sense seconds later. My staff are gathered in a tight circle on the field. Coach is hollering at a referee. Theo's fighting four of our biggest offensive linemen, trying to force his way back out onto the field to be with the man crumpled in a heap on the turf.

Declan.

I'm only ten steps away from Meg, almost close enough to reach out and grab her arm. Part of me is relieved that every player on our team is on their feet, standing to watch the scene unfold; they're blocking our omega from running right into a hornet's nest of stressed-out, amped-up alphas.

I should have guessed Meg wouldn't take that, though. She's proven, over and over, how tough she can be. How much backbone she has when she needs it.

"Move!"

If I thought the stadium was holding its breath before, I was wrong. One bark from our little omega and every alpha within fifty yards is stone-still.

I've never heard an omega bark before. Turns out, it's every bit as effective as the literature suggests. Immediately, the men blocking her path scatter out of the way, their eyes wide.

One of the right tackles scents her first. A growl rips up his throat, freezing Meg where she stands.

Fuck!

I start to run for her again, but she suddenly turns her head, fixing the guy with a glare unlike any I've ever seen. Her teeth flash on an answering snarl. *"Stay. Back."*

And... no one moves.

Not even me.

By the time Ronan catches up and shoves me forward, releasing me from our omega's command with a bark of his own, Meg is out on the field.

chapter
fifty-five

SOMEONE MIGHT ACTUALLY FUCKING die if Declan doesn't get up.

And it might not be me who kills them.

It may be *Meg*.

Our omega is fierce. She practically runs over every huge alpha in her way, barking commands at them as she goes. By the time she drops to the turf and lands on her knees, I'm fairly certain I'm the only alpha on the field who isn't rendered immobile by her orders.

Grabbing Theo by the back of his jersey, I yank him out of his stupor. "What the fuck happened?" I demand. "Where were you?"

Green eyes wide and frantic, he looks from me to Declan and back again. "We had a thing before the game, and I—"

My glare shuts him up. I don't want everyone else on the sidelines to hear him admit he purposely missed that block. There'd be hell to pay.

Desperation flashes through his gaze. His voice lowers into a tense mutter. "I swear to god, Ronan, I didn't mean for him to get hurt. I thought they'd just sack him a couple times and then—"

I growl my warning this time, "*Enough.* Meg is going to be devastated if he's harmed, Theo. *Devastated.* Did you think about her *at all?*"

I know he did.

He thought about her so much he couldn't keep his anger to himself. I understand that; it's the real reason I'm laying into him right now. I'm pissed as fuck, and he's an easy target.

The stadium squirms silently while a stretcher is brought out to the field. Meg stays at Declan's side while they roll him onto it. Archer approaches us, keeping one eye trained on our omega the whole time.

"It's a concussion," he reports, grim. "He hasn't woken up since he took the hit."

"But he *will*," I insist, fisting Theo's jersey to keep him from running off onto the turf. "Right?"

Archer sighs, cleaning his glasses on his shirt before turning his focus back to Meg, lingering on the way she holds Declan's lifeless hand.

"She's the best thing for him right now," Arch says, somehow sounding even more somber. "Which might be the worst part of all of this."

chapter
fifty-six

I WAKE UP SOMEWHERE WEIRD.

It's—well, not *weird*. Weird would imply that it's bad. And this is... nice.

Like, *really nice*.

The pillow under my cheek feels fuzzy in a way that somehow does not annoy me. Surprising, since every part of my body currently throbs in pain. My head feels like a broken egg. Were my brains scrambled on a hot slab of pavement?

My eyelids flicker, sending a sharp dart of pain through my

frontal lobe. I groan, cringing down into whatever soft surface I'm lying on.

Goddamn it.

What the fuck did I do?

"Shhh," a soft voice instructs. "Don't try to move."

Something near me shifts. And then I hear it, the sound as quiet as a whisper. A tiny, humming purr.

The gentle vibration of it numbs the pain in my forehead. A plaintive groan scrapes out of my throat. My body automatically tenses to move closer, but a shocking burst of pain seizes me before I manage to shuffle onto my side.

The sweet voice sighs, interrupting the even-sweeter purr. "Don't make me bark at you again, Howard."

Some weak, distant voice in my head tells me that, under normal circumstances, this particular girl scolding me would make me hard. Right now, though, I'm lucky I can even feel that my dick is still attached to my body.

Small mercies or whatever.

When I go limp again, the purr restarts and moves closer. Until I'm pretty sure I would be staring at a familiar omega's rack if I opened my eyes.

That thought seems like as good a reason as any to check my vision. Ignoring the agony that rips through my skull, I crack one lid open just far enough to confirm that, yes, there are tits hovering next to my face.

Beautiful, bare tits.

Another pathetic sound escapes me when my cock twitches, highlighting exactly how sore my abdominal muscles are. Meg hears the pained cross between a moan and a cry. Her eyes flash down my body to where I have a semi.

And then she laughs.

It's a quiet, gentle thing, just like her little omega purr. But, damn if it doesn't make me harder.

"Now that you're *awake*," she says dryly, "I can tell you that this is most definitely karma biting you in the butt."

I manage to swing my gaze up over her naked chest, to her pinched face. "Sorry about the nudity," she murmurs, glancing away. "It's supposed to help regulate your body temperature. I tried putting a blanket on you, but you hated that. And my Omega was freaking the fuck out at how pale and cold you looked. When I called Archer, he suggested I try undressing us both."

Nothing she says makes any sense. I open my mouth, only able to gasp out half a word through the pain in my head, "Wha—"

Soft fingers smooth over my brow, halting me. "Shhh. It's okay. You got hit during the game. You have a concussion. Archer gave you an IV with pain meds and fluids to keep you stable, and we got you home. He said you needed low light, no noise... and me."

Defensiveness raises her voice an octave. "*He* said that, not me, okay? He said that having your—having *me* here with you would probably help you stabilize faster."

I get my one eye open again, slowly rolling it to check out our surroundings. It *is* dark in here. Darker than any room in our house that I know of. Almost like the walls are covered in black velvet.

"Where are we?" I croak, letting my eyelid droop shut again.

Meg sighs. Her voice is apologetic. "The nest."

This time, I manage to open both eyes. The shock of her reply bolsters me long enough to get a decent look around.

If I had the capacity, I'd berate myself for being dense as fuck. The comfortable cushions, the soft lighting, the fabric covering the walls. *Of course* this is a nest.

More than that, it's *her* nest.

I see it, now.

Meg is *everywhere*.

The touches of gold and dove gray that match what she chose for her bedroom. The way they blend with the sumptuous midnight color she selected for her cushions.

The walls have a slight sheen to them—rich onyx velvet inlaid with gold lines that reflect the twinkle lights strung overhead. It's comfortable and beautiful. Classy and elegant, but still inherently sensual. Practical, too, I would imagine, with all these dark fabrics to hide any messes.

It's a weird thing to think about, but my brain is foggy and halting.

Definitely concussed.

Eventually my echoey thoughts remember that none of us have ever been in here before. The notion that she broke her own rule to give me somewhere comfortable to rest sends a different sort of pain rebounding behind my ribs.

"You brought me into your nest?"

She bites her plump lower lip. "Sorry. I know you're probably pissed."

I hope the look I give her is enough to tell her that the only emotion I currently feel is gratitude. "No. Not pissed."

Her blue gaze searches my face. Some of the tension leaves her as she offers a small smile. "This feels familiar, huh? One of us waking up completely out-of-it. The other one assuming they're going to be mad."

I sigh, giving up on eyesight as a gut-clenching roll of nausea grips my stomach. "It's a shame," I pant. "In another life, if you'd invited me into your nest, I would have been worshipping at your feet."

I hear the hurt in her silence and internally curse myself. I open my mouth to apologize but she moves away.

"I'm going to go tell the guys you're awake," she whispers. "Archer wanted to move you to your room as soon as you were. He's worried about having the two of us in here."

After the shitshow that went down in the gym, lying next to her while she purrs seems distinctly tame. "Why?"

"Your scent," she replies, small. "He's concerned having it in the nest will upset me when my heat starts and you're—"

Not here.

Because I'm a selfish piece of shit who rejected her to save myself. Then let her reject me in order to save *her*.

From what?

My past? My own tendency to fuck shit up?

It should maybe be concerning that a concussion has made me *more* introspective.

I peel my gritty eyelids open again, watching while Meg reaches for a wispy silk robe lying along the rim of the nest. Silent tears track down her face. So quiet, I never would have known about them if I hadn't opened my eyes.

That suddenly seems like an appropriate metaphor for this whole mess.

I need to open my goddamn eyes.

My hand fumbles, reaching for hers without grace or strength. But, still, she takes it, wrapping her little fingers over my palm to give me a reassuring squeeze I don't deserve.

But fuck me and what I think I deserve.

What about *her*?

I hold fast, keeping us connected until her gaze meets mine. "Meg, do you want me in here for your heat?"

Her brows curve up. Her mouth pinches open. And for a moment I think—I really *believe*—she'll say no.

Because of course she will. I've done nothing to build trust with her. I've never given her any sort of affection that wasn't motivated by guilt or lust. I lost control and rutted her while we were both essentially unconscious.

Why the hell would this sweet, perfect omega want a knot-headed asshole like me around her when she's at her most vulnerable?

But then she answers. A single hushed word. "Yes."

The look on her face would be enough to wind me if I weren't already gasping. She looks so sad. So sure she's about to be rejected once again. It hits me then, like a ball of lead to the chest —or maybe like a linebacker to the head.

Meg genuinely *hurts* without me.

She *cares.*

The one question that springs into my mouth is sickening. But I have to know. The words come out as a weak whisper.

"Why, baby?"

Her hand shakes in my grasp, her words wobbling. "Because you're a part of them, Declan. And I love them."

She ducks her head, hiding her face as she adds the single most devastating thing anyone has ever said to me. "I want to love you, too," she murmurs. "I wish you would let me try."

chapter
fifty-seven

ARCHER

MEG EMERGES FROM THE NEST, tugging her robe closed
and pulling the door shut right behind her.

My heart aches subtly, pumping longing through my chest. I
hate myself for it, but right now I'm jealous of my semi-conscious
packmate. He's the only person she's let into that nest since the
day I showed it to her.

The envy quickly morphs into a whole host of other, more
aggressive feelings when I see our omega mopping under her wet
eyes.

To my surprise, Ronan is the first one across the room. He

bends to the side, putting his face level with hers and wrapping both hands around her jaw. "Baby girl," he whispers. "Come here."

When it comes to her own comfort, we're used to Meg fighting us at every turn. But, this time, she melts right into our pack alpha's chest and starts to sob against the collar of his shirt.

I'm frozen, halfway between the loveseat I was pretending to read in and the scene unfolding in front of me. When Theo doesn't bound up from his perch on the edge of the bed and insert himself, I turn to find him bent in half with his head in his hands.

He hasn't stopped apologizing since we left the stadium. I know he feels responsible for Dec's injury. Now he probably feels like our omega's distress is his fault too.

Meg keens softly, her hands clutching at Ronan's shirt. He purrs, a deep sonorous sound. "Shh," he soothes. "Daddy's here. I've got you."

I edge up behind our omega, carefully pressing my own purr into her back while I gather her hair off her wet cheeks and drop my face to her crown.

Her body shakes harder. I know I'm a doctor, and it's impossible, but I swear my heart physically cracks.

"Sweetheart," I whisper. "Tell us what you need."

She sniffs and sobs, "I just want him to let me *in*. I—I—"

The words won't come. Meg glances up at Ronan's solemn face before turning to me. Her eyes fill with fresh tears along with the slightest glimmer of hope, begging me to understand.

And I do.

She loves him. She doesn't know how or why, *but she does.*

I don't blame her for being confused. All Declan has done is make her miserable. It must be confusing to have such strong feelings for him after all that.

For a split second, it stings. So far, Theo's the only one she's professed these feelings for. I know it's wrong to compare. All of us will have different relationships with her. Different moments. It's the way it's supposed to be.

I work hard to shove down my less-honorable reflexes. Meg is so sensitive to the way her feelings and instincts affect us. If she thought any of this hurt me, she would be extremely hard on herself.

"You need him, too," I supply, avoiding the word she clearly doesn't want to say. I press a kiss on her forehead. "That's what makes you so perfect for us."

Pain draws her features tight. "I told him how I feel," she whispers. "Maybe that isn't good for him right now. I didn't mean to do it, but it sort of just came out and—" She swallows hard. "He said he needs some time. He can't think right now. But he asked me if he could stay in the nest for the night. Is that okay?"

Ronan and I glance at each other, brows raised. It isn't our place to decide who goes into her sacred space, ever. He looks back down at her. "We don't know. *Is* it okay, little one?"

Meg blinks, absorbing his meaning. Her lower lip trembles. "It isn't mine," she breathes, so small and quiet I barely hear her. "Not really."

I almost jerk back from the shock of her words. My mouth drops open, ready to assure her that the nest is totally and irrevocably hers.

Ronan's growl cuts me off. His fingers flex around her nape. "*What* did you just say?"

It isn't really a question. He clearly heard every gut-wrenching word. Meg shakes, and I shoot him a glare he ignores, staring down at the woman between us with his singular intensity.

"I-it isn't mine," Meg repeats, every word quivering. "It won't belong to anyone officially until you're all bonded. And I don't want to ruin that for all of you."

I don't know if I've ever seen Ronan so focused. My hackles rise. Protective instincts surge through me as a slight snarl vibrates in my throat, warning him.

He snaps his gaze to mine, flexing his dominance until I feel like my lungs won't expand. Thankfully, he looks away first, fixing his absolute attention back on Meg.

I'm half-expecting a bark of some sort. But instead, his voice drops low.

"Do I need to bite you right here, right now?" he rumbles, eyes flashing white-hot. "I will, Megera. I will sink my teeth into your pretty neck, and then I'll get on my knees and beg you to bite me back. I would rather wait until I'm inside of you, tied to you, holding you, but if a formal bond is what you need to know that everything in this house—your nest, your room, your alphas; *everything*—belongs to you, I will take you *right fucking now.*"

For the first time since the incident at the game, Meg's perfume rises. Clear, bright, and beautiful. She gasps, panting when Ronan refuses to release her from his stare. The gray there rolls like a thunderstorm, but his fingers seem gentle while he brushes them over the sides of her face with reverence that echoes through my middle.

I didn't expect this part of finding our omega. I knew I would have all of this for myself—I never anticipated how beautiful it would be to watch the other guys fall just as hard.

Love in its purest form, unfolding right in front of me. All day, every day.

The room holds its breath, and for a moment, Meg looks up at our pack alpha, reading his face. When she finally speaks, the words wobble with wonder. "Y-you want to bond with me?"

All three of us—even miserable, left-out Theo—immediately answer. "Yes."

Our beautiful girl's perfume swells, its brightness sharpening into the sweetest blade. Cutting into my center, carving out my pride. I want to go to my knees for her, beg her to let me pleasure her.

Unfortunately, we're in the middle of a pivotal moment here.

I turn her gingerly, waiting for her luminous blue eyes to land on mine. "What do *you* want?" I murmur.

Our gazes trace over one another. The smallest, cutest smile twists her pink lips. "You," she whispers. "I want you, Archer. Your brilliant mind, your careful hands, the way you listen. I want all of those things forever."

She doesn't say *I love you*, but why would she need to? She's just given me so much more than that.

She stretches up and kisses me, melding our mouths just long enough to leave me winded. With one last flash of her smile, she turns to Ronan. The look on her face is nothing short of rapturous.

"And you," she breathes. "The way you defend and protect me. The way you provide for me like it's as necessary to you as air." Her mouth tilts impishly. "All of our games, and the way they really aren't games at all."

I've never seen the look on Ronan's face before. Soft and electric at the same time. He seems to pause, his eyes sketching over her face like he just doesn't know what to do with the strength of his feelings. He settles for pressing his forehead to hers, sighing. "Goddamn, Meg. You have me."

Meg leans up just long enough to tease his mouth with hers. A second later, she turns in our arms, facing the bed.

Theo is a wretched specimen. Bent over his spread knees, breathing hard, still wearing his grass-stained game gear and covered in dry sweat. His hair is matted into a bun at the back of his neck. He scrubs his hands over his face again and again. I see the moment Meg realizes he's crying, too.

She goes to him, floating down to her knees. Her small hands slide up his chest to cup his jaw.

"And you, Theo."

His head snaps up, disbelief and guilt covering his features. "Meg, I fucked this all up so bad today. This is all my fault. I can't believe I was so *stupid*—"

To my surprise, Meg nods. "I'm mad about what you did today," she tells him. "But that doesn't mean I don't love you. It doesn't mean I don't want you just as much as I want them."

Her smile is a tremulous, warm thing. "You're my big guy. I want your excitement and your optimism. The way you want me and accept me even when I'm at my absolute worst. The joy you give to everyone you meet. There's no one like you, Theo." Her grin grows. "Besides, finders keepers, remember?"

Theo makes a choking, gasping sound, ripping Meg off the ground and crushing her to his chest. "Fuck," he exhales. "I thought you would hate me for this."

Meg smooths her touch over his hair, not caring how sticky he must be. "Never," she vows, sweet and quiet. "Never ever, big guy."

Theo moves to kiss her carefully, giving her plenty of time to pull away. When she doesn't, he tenderly brushes his lips over hers. "Tell me again," he begs, squeezing his eyes shut.

Meg scent-marks his cheek with hers, the gesture more touching than any words. *I choose you*, it says. *Even now*. "I love you, Theo."

He visibly shudders. She gives his beard a tiny tug until he meets her eyes. "You must be hungry. We'll have dinner in an hour, okay?" she says, her voice soothing. "Archer can order something that will be easy on Declan's stomach. Ronan will get a statement out for the team to let everyone know Declan is recovering. Go start my shower and I'll come wash you off, baby."

He nods, swallows thickly, and then walks off. I watch him go, catching Ronan's silver eyes as I turn. He stares at Meg with an odd look on his face. It takes me a moment to realize she's just put him out of a job, ordering Theo around and deciding when the pack will gather for a meal.

A flush colors Meg's cheeks when she reaches the same conclusion. She gapes at Ronan. "Oh. Sorry. Sir."

I laugh. Ronan flashes me a glower that quickly cracks into a half-smile. "I guess our omega has finally figured out who's really in charge around here, huh?" A swell of pride fills his face. "Smart girl."

chapter
fifty-eight

I WAKE up with the memory of Meg's hands washing me at the front of my brain. Only twelve hours later, and I already know we created a core memory under the steamy spray.

The way she beamed up at me. Her soft, sweet touches. The kisses I stole from her lips until she giggled.

Both of us were too wrung out for sex. It was almost better that way. We both needed the connection more than we needed anything physical.

After she scrubbed every inch of my body, Meg listened while I told her about my fight with Declan. She held me under the water, letting me bend almost in half to rest my face against her shoulder. It was easier for me to talk that way, spilling my tears of shame against her neck instead of all over her face.

When I finally got it all out, she hugged me for a long time. Long enough for me to believe that she meant what she said—she was mad about I did. But she still loves me.

It was the best shower of my life; and when we both came out, all pink-skinned from an hour under the hot water, the guys had dinner laid out on a big tray in the middle of our bed.

Meg slipped away just long enough to take Declan his protein smoothie and came back seconds later, not lingering. He was asleep again, she reported, equally dejected and resigned.

I could tell Archer felt some type of way about Dec hogging the nest, but he didn't complain. Instead, he spread our omega out in the center of the bed after I cleared all the dishes away. He and Ronan took turns massaging her and getting her off with their mouths.

They wouldn't let her worry about them, and I didn't either. Instead, I watched, burning yet another core memory into my gray matter.

And I mean... *fuck*.

Even our *worst* days are incredible. Together.

We all slept in the big bed again. Ronan spooned Meg's back while Archer held her against his side. That left me to lie between peaches' luscious legs and nuzzle her belly.

But I guess our girl is a ninja because when the sunlight hits the tangled bedsheets and wakes me up, I find an empty crater between the three of us. Some instinct pricks the back of my neck, and I turn to the right, seeing the nest door cracked open, the lights turned off.

Which means Declan is gone.

And so is our omega.

chapter
fifty-nine

I KNEW something was wrong before I opened my eyes. As soon as I saw my nest door cracked open, I was fully awake and worried.

Where did Declan go?

Would he leave?

It took some serious maneuvering to get out of the bed without waking anyone up. I decided to crawl over Archer, knowing he usually sleeps the hardest of the three alphas. Something about good men with clear consciouses sleeping well at night, right?

The thought made me smile the tiniest bit while I tripped into the flowy, pale-pink loungewear Mrs. Fleming somehow left out for me.

Lord. What time does the poor woman get here every day?

She even laid out a pair of slippers I've never seen before. Beautiful ivory fluff adorned with pearls, crystals, and a bit of feather plumage that somehow looks cute instead of ridiculous. I slide them on and scurry downstairs, worry creeping back up.

The house is silent. I have to remind myself to breathe while I dash from the base of the floating steps to the kitchen. All of my anxiety rushes out on a harsh exhale.

Declan is here.

He sits at the island, simultaneously looking like total shit and an absolute *masterpiece.*

His skin has a pale gray cast to it. There are dark purple smudges under both of his eyes and over the bridge of his nose—bruising from the impact of his helmet. His usual preening posture absent, he huddles over a mug on the island.

Yeah, he looks bad. But, on the other hand...

Dang.

Has *anyone* else ever been *this* handsome?

Morning light doesn't help. It illuminates his sandy brown hair and highlights the pronounced cut of his angular jaw and matching cheekbones. With all the golden sunlight, his blue eyes glow.

And that's just his *face.*

The rest of his body is bare, aside from a pair of tight navy boxers. I take a moment to run my eyes over every single slab of muscle, memorizing the flex of his calves, his quads, his obliques, and traps. He would be perfect, if not for the bruises blooming all over him.

Those don't stop my body's reaction, though. Perfume spins off me and I wince, knowing he'll snap and glare at me any second.

Instead, he simply turns his head and lets his eyes drift over me for a long beat, lingering on my curves and my bare neck. I can't really complain, though. I just ogled him *thoroughly*.

I'm still frozen, waiting for his usual lash of rage, when the scent of vanilla sweetness wafts over me.

Oh.

Oh wow.

I blink, my brain slowing to a sluggish roll as I try to process how insanely good he smells and why it's so much better than I remember. It takes entirely too long for me to realize that his face is calm and smooth, lacking any trace of animosity.

Oh, I think again. *This isn't a new facet of his scent. This* is *his scent. The way it's supposed to smell when he isn't stressed or angry.*

Which he has been, every day, for weeks.

It's an incredibly sad realization. It also sends a warm tingle through my heart. Because, if I thought his scent was perfect for me *before*... this is a whole new level.

Fresh peach perfume swells to fill the kitchen. I bite my lip, embarrassed, still waiting for his rebuke. But his demeanor doesn't change, aside from a slight spark in his eyes and the twitch of fingers around his mug.

He opens his mouth to speak. I prepare myself to cringe back from whatever vitriol he'll spew—

"Good morning," he murmurs.

... good morning?

GOOD MORNING???

What the—

He waves his hand at the island, indicating the kettle sitting on top of a trivet and—oh my God—the *bouquet* beside it. "I boiled water for tea, if you'd like some," he adds, still quiet and even. His blue eyes flash back to mine. "The flowers are for you."

Declan Howard drinks *tea*?

And he got *me* flowers?

My mouth hangs open. I inch across the black marble floor, hands shaking while I touch the soft white petals bursting from a dark crystal vase. And I have no idea where or how he would have gotten them at this hour.

Seeing the question in my face, Declan gives a tight shrug and a lopsided flash of what I can only describe as a pussy-melting grin. "I stole them. The lady next door has a whole flower bed in her front yard."

I can't help it; I gape like a fish. Imagining Declan Howard, basically naked, sneaking into the neighbor's yard at dawn to filch flowers for me?

Does. Not. Compute.

But he isn't done absolutely flooring me.

His warm fingers slide along my jaw and up to the hollow under my eye. "You look like you got some decent sleep," he muses, honest consternation in his gaze. "I'm glad."

When I can't manage to close my mouth, he smirks and presses under my chin, doing it for me. "I'm also glad you seem to like my selections." He nods at my silky pajamas. "Those look perfect on you."

Wait. *His* selections? "Mrs. Fleming leaves these out for me," I sputter.

He cocks a brow. "Yeah, but who did you think arranged the outfits and told her which ones to put out for specific days? In case her capri pants weren't a dead giveaway—she's not exactly a fan of Lycra and leather."

I'm stunned, blinking stupidly. "Why would you do that for me, though?"

His teeth flash in a grimace. "I had to manage the urge to take care of you somehow. And... maybe I wanted to feel like you had a little piece of me with you every day. Even if you didn't know it."

I smile down at my slippers. I should have known my clothes were way too boujee to be the work of anyone else in this house. All of this luxury and attitude? It screams Declan.

His face relaxes when he sees mine. He reaches up to brush my hair back again. "Did Ronan and Arch take good care of you last night?" he asks, still full of genuine amusement. "I could hear you. It gave me some excellent dreams. Where was our big guy?"

Our.

That one little word cracks my heart wide open. I swallow the lump of emotion suddenly pushing up my throat. "He was there. He hung back, though. I think he still feels really, really guilty about what happened on the field."

Declan listens intently to every word, never once rolling his eyes or grinding his teeth. The humor leeches away from his features, leaving him serious but not angry.

"I don't blame Theo," he says. "I'll talk to him when he gets up, okay?"

When I do nothing but nod mutely, he sighs and runs his thumb over my lip to pull it out of my teeth. "Seriously. I don't want you to worry about this, princess."

His mean-spirited, taunting nickname for me. Only... it isn't. Because pure sincerity radiates from him while he stares into my eyes.

Still, I shoot him a suspicious look. "Princess, huh?"

The corner of his mouth quirks, and he tucks a strand of hair behind my ear. "That's what you are, isn't it? Our princess?" He leans closer, eyes heating. "Or do you prefer 'queen'?"

This time, I actually balk. "Exactly how hard did you hit your head?" A terrible thought occurs to me, and I gasp, "Oh my God, Declan, did you fall down this morning and crack your skull all over again?"

His sexy grin flashes, but his eyes turn sad. "No."

I blow air out of my nose, feeling weirdly frustrated. My hands go to my hips. "Then what is this, Declan?"

He takes in my posture with another of his wolfish smirks. It fades away while we stare at each other. "This is me," he says. "Trying. Letting you try, like you wanted."

And then the infuriating man inclines his head. Like a dare.

Your move, baby.

For a second, I'm frozen from shock. I don't know what to do to return these little slivers of hope he's giving me. But he waits patiently, offering me time to tune into the intuition that helped me get down to the field when he needed me most.

Maybe... maybe I actually *do* know what to do.

I slide around the island, coming to stand right by his side. Like this, our faces are level. I slip my hand up his feathered tattoo, finding the hard knot on his shoulder. It didn't escape my notice yesterday that he played through the pain instead of alerting Archer to the issue.

As gently as I can, I press the pads of my fingers into the lump and begin to work it loose, following the hard cords of muscle up to his nape and over to the sharp ridge of his shoulder.

He shoots me a slightly pissy look that I ignore. A terse grunt hefts out of him, followed by a low rumble a moment later. I carefully move closer until my breasts pad his arm, and his head lolls forward on a moan of pained pleasure.

"*Meg*," he sloughs out. "Fuck, that's good."

His scent is better than ever, creamy vanilla so sweet my mouth waters. I bear down a bit harder, giving deeper pressure until the pinched muscles start to loosen. When I push my thumb and forefinger along the tight traps at the back of his nape, he rolls his head toward me, tucking his temple against my collarbone.

Declan pauses there, breathing hard. Waiting, I think, for me to accept this new kind of affection. This vulnerability he hates to show.

I get it.

We're alike that way.

My left hand comes up, cupping his cheek to encourage him. Running my fingers back into his hair, combing through it. His next moan is plaintive. He moves with sudden decisiveness, snatching my hips and pulling me between his flexing thighs.

Chiseled lips latch onto my clavicle, sucking lightly as I add my second hand to the first, spreading my massage over both of his wide, hard shoulders.

"Baby," he mumbles softly, burrowing closer, nipping my

neck before releasing a groan that tightens my nipples. "You feel like heaven."

His scent, his voice, the feel of his rough hands clutching my hips—I perfume again. *A lot.*

Declan groans, his fingers slipping under the hem of my shirt, stroking light circles over my lower back. I whine, automatically thrusting my chest toward him.

The sound makes Declan shiver. His voice is rough velvet in my ear. "You need me, baby? Want me to make you feel good?"

I can't think, but I know there's some reason that isn't a good idea. I try to focus, but I can't even breathe. My heart is overflowing. And all I know is how good this feels.

His body is warm and smooth and so ridiculously cut. And he isn't pushing me away.

He isn't pushing me away.

As if he can read my thoughts and wants to confirm them, Declan hugs me properly, spreading his big hands over my back. "Let me touch you," he coaxes. "Get you so slick for me. I'm not so good at saying how I feel. But I can show you."

I whimper again, only narrowly resisting the urge to grab him by his sore shoulders and climb his big body. Declan moves, swiveling his stool to face me entirely. He leans back just far enough to put us face-to-face as he glides his hands around my hips, teasing the sensitive skin under my navel, dipping long fingers into the silky waistband of my lounge pants.

He hangs there. Our gazes collide, and I see that he's waiting for me to give him permission. Atoning for the last time when he couldn't.

My consent comes as a desperate whine. "Please, Declan. Touch me."

He growls quietly, wasting no time. His strong, skilled fingers skim over my bare mound, curling to feel the slick gathering along my slit.

A wide, masculine grin graces his face. "I knew you'd be

perfect," he claims. "Smooth and slick and smelling like a fucking *dream*—"

I'm already in a state of utter disbelief when Declan retracts his hand and brings it to my nape. He fists my hair gently, pulling my head back and meeting my gaze with all the calm dominance of a true alpha.

"I'm going to make you come like this," he informs me. "That's not because I don't want to be inside you. It's because Arch said I can't fuck until he clears me. And... I haven't earned you yet. I intend to. Soon. But for now, I want to make you feel good. Nod if you agree, princess."

I'm panting, my hips writhing slightly against his wrist. I nod.

He gives me his special smile. "That's our girl."

chapter
sixty

WE WIND up lying side-by-side on the living room floor, surrounded by new throw pillows and blankets. I have Meg's head cushioned on my right biceps; my arm bent to feather my fingers through her hair.

The alpha instincts swirling through me are new. Confusing and thrilling. I can't seem to stop fussing with her—making sure her hair is free of tangles, checking whether she's warm enough, listening for the hitch of her breath.

We're quiet.

That's also new—usually we smirk or snap at each other.

But I like this too. I can't remember a time I've ever laid in contented silence with another person. It feels *natural* with Meg, though.

Her perfect perfume spins through the air, the scent distinctly sated. I love that I can tell. I love that I'm the reason she's satisfied. My Alpha loves it, too. Our tortured edginess feels like a distant memory as I nuzzle my chin against Meg's temple and watch the morning light stretch over the ceiling.

I thought giving in to this would be much harder. Instead, it just feels like exhaling. Effortless relief.

She's happy, so I'm happy. I'm happy, so she's happy. There's a certain beauty in the simplicity of it.

While the rest of me is completely comfortable here, my cock didn't get the memo. He's being a literal dick—throbbing and twitching every time Meg shifts. I reach down to adjust myself and Meg tilts her head back, flashing me a tiny smirk.

"You good?"

I grumble under my breath, burying my face into her crown and inhaling to distract myself. Archer literally said, word-for-word, no sex or orgasms until he clears me. Some bullshit about blood flow? I don't know. Maybe he's just a sadist. Either way, it feels like karma I've earned. I won't push it.

My free hand reaches for Meg's, bringing it to my mouth. What starts out as a sweet kiss to her knuckles turns into me licking between her fingers, sucking the pads.

Fresh perfume swells off her body. I grunt into her hair, tucking her closer. Suddenly, it feels like I have a million things to say to her.

There's no urgency—I know we'll have all the time we want. But still, there's shit I need to know.

"When is your heat supposed to start, baby?"

I feel like the worst alpha in the world that I even have to ask. Arch probably has some color-coded chart pinpointing the exact hour her hormones will spike. I'm sure Ronan has stockpiled presents, just waiting to spoil her appropriately when her pre-heat funk kicks in. And Theo's sisters have probably given him a whole crash course on courting an omega in heat.

I'm the deadbeat who doesn't even know when she's going to need us.

Meg can sense my shame. She huddles closer and kisses my jaw softly. "Archer thinks three weeks. It's just an estimate, though. There are a lot of things that can influence it, I guess."

Her uncertainty rouses my protective instincts. I gather her body into the side of mine, holding her properly while I purr for her.

It's hard for me to imagine what she must have gone through, being alone in the world as an unbonded omega. Clearly no one ever helped her. In any way. Archer told me she went through her previous heats alone. In pain. Medicated to oblivion.

I stuff my self-loathing down, telling myself it won't help her right now. She can sense the change in my emotions, though. Her soft purr melds with mine, instantly sinking into the knot twisting my stomach.

God, this girl.

She's sexy and sweet and sassy.

Fucking *perfect*.

I swallow a swell of unfamiliar feelings and latch on to the one I know best—inadequacy.

My voice drops into a mumble. "If you don't want me in there with you, I understand. I haven't done anything to earn your trust. And you'll be vulnerable."

Meg's purr stutters. She tucks herself down into my bare shoulder, shrinking. "If you don't want to—"

Without thinking, I roll to put myself on top of her, pressing my erection into her belly. "*I want to*," I rumble, piercing her blue eyes with my own. "I want to be in that nest with you more than I've ever wanted any damn thing in my whole life. More than I want a winning season. More than I want the Championship ring. I'd walk away from everything to be there with you. But that doesn't make me worthy, baby."

Her brows arch as a shaky breath quivers out of her. "Are you sure about that? Because I'm pretty sure it does."

A slash of longing lashes my middle. I drop my forehead to hers. "You're the only one who can decide that. But I want you to know that whatever you choose won't affect how I feel. I'm all in now, princess."

I flash a grin. "I don't know if you've noticed, but I'm a pretty stubborn asshole when there's something I want."

For one brilliant moment, she smiles back, but a shadow passes through her gaze. Her joyful expression wilts at the edges. "You didn't want me," she whispers, barely audible. "I—if you change your mind, I'm not sure I can take any more rejection."

Fuck.

Physical pain grates my insides. "There wasn't one single moment when I didn't want you," I tell her, staring hard into her eyes. "Not one. I hated having you at the facility because I was terrified of you getting hurt there. I just couldn't understand the... viciousness of that instinct. It felt like hatred, but I'm pretty sure it was just love. All twisted up."

A single tear dribbles over her temple. "W-what?"

I rub my forehead over hers, scent-marking her. "I love you, Meg. I think I knew the second I saw you. At least, my body did. I had a crazy-strong reaction to you. One that made no sense to me. I dealt with it the only way I knew how to—by getting pissed." I give a rueful smirk and lean to her ear like I'm telling her a secret. "I'm sort of a dick."

Meg's laughter is watery but gorgeous. "I guess I can forgive you. I thought I hated you the first time we met, too. Well, my brain did. The rest of me was too busy melting into a puddle of slick."

My dick kicks against her, desperate. Her evil little smile tells me she's teasing me on purpose. Which only makes me harder.

I grind into her softness. "Mmm, baby. I love it when you're mean."

Our princess laughs in earnest. Her touch trails lightly over my forehead. "Does it still hurt?"

If it does, I can't feel it. Right now, I can't feel anything but her. "Not anymore."

The air between us simmers and softens. The light in her eyes makes me breathless. I roll us onto our sides, pulling her back on top of me where I can purr for her some more.

We watch the shadows above us fade while sunlight fills the house. A familiar rush of awe and gratitude runs through me. I never thought I'd have a life like this. Money, security, a real home. A family.

It occurs to me that this girl probably never expected to live like this either.

I cup my hand around her head. "Theo told me. About your mom. And the group home you had to live in."

When Meg sighs quietly, I know her thoughts are running parallel to mine. Even before she says, "All of this is crazy, right? I never imagined..."

My heart swells. Breaks and mends and fills. All in one breath.

She gets it.

I hug her tightly. "Me neither."

Meg snuggles into my side. "But we're here," she whispers. "And we're—"

Together.

She says it reverently. Like that's the thing that matters most. All of this wealth, security, luxury... it doesn't mean nearly as much to her as the guys and I do.

I understand the feeling. Because this whole place could burn to the ground, and all I would think about is Meg.

My pack.

Our family.

Which reminds me.

I grunt while I heave both of us upright. My head protests a little, but I ignore the throb and bend to scrape my teeth against her throat. She whimpers and shivers, perfuming when I suck the thin skin between my lips hard enough to mark it.

"I just thought of the perfect peace offering for Theo," I tell her, skirting a hand down her body.

She trembles, but sass fills her voice. "And that is…?"

"A soaking wet omega."

chapter
sixty-one

RONAN

Who took my omega?

ARCHER

Our* omega

THEO

My bad, Daddy.

DECLAN

Is Daddy a thing now?

RONAN

No.

*THEO CHANGED RONAN'S NAME TO DADDY IN
THIS CONVERSATION*

DECLAN

this is going to be awkward at work.

ARCHER

Declan, you shouldn't be looking at screens.

Theo, has Meg eaten breakfast?

THEO

cringe emoji technically yes?

DECLAN

pretty sure *water emoji* only counts as food during her heat big guy.

ARCHER

Put your phone AWAY, Dec

THEO

Doc is shouty now that we have an omega.

DECLAN

Can you just clear me already, Arch? I have an idea for a surprise for Meg.

ARCHER

No way I'm clearing you. You're clearly still delusional.

THEO

Aww c'mon. Clear him, Arch. We have the happiest omega in the world right now.

Actually, Meg says we will* have the happiest omega in the world. After coffee.

DECLAN

I'll get it.

DADDY

Seriously, Dec. How hard did you hit your head?

Megera

"MEG, I SWEAR TO GOD."

I grin at Declan's pout. "Aww, poor little baby. Am I wearing you out?"

A special spark lights his electric eyes. He loves it when I tease him. "Don't tempt me, princess."

He goes in for a kiss, but I plant my palm on his naked chest. My other hand waves my phone between us, reminding him of the task at hand. He rolls his eyes, doing his damnedest to hide a smile. "Do I *have to* sing?"

I mean, technically, no one would know the difference if he lip-synced. But I live to get under this alpha's skin, so I make my glare as severe as possible. "Yes. And make sure you work that sexy smile the whole time."

He flashes the exact grin I want. "No idea what you're talking about, princess. What smile?"

I grab his jaw to wave his face around. "This panty-dropper right here."

He reaches around to smooth his palm over my butt. The cut of the bikini he picked out ensures he gets a nice handful of bare ass. "Yours are the only panties I'm interested in dropping."

I bite down on my smile. It's been two weeks since his concussion, and he's gone out of his way every day to make comments like that. Almost like he wants to make sure I know there's no room in his mind for anyone but me.

Ronan strolls out of the house, joining us on the pool deck. He looks so ridiculously hot in his black swim trunks; all tan skin, swirling ink, and the threads of silver in his hair. He gives me his special half-smile when I perfume for him.

"Hi, baby girl," he rumbles, sliding up behind me and palming my belly, stroking down. Reminding me exactly where he was all night. And where Archer was this morning.

Our alpha's stubble pricks my ear while he murmurs to me. "You look so pretty for Daddy today."

"That bikini is obviously for *me*!" Theo shouts from his pool lounger. My blond mountain of muscles looks *stacked* in his short navy swimsuit. "It goes with the sunglasses I got her, right, peaches?"

He has a matching pair on top of his head and a big fruity mocktail in his hand. I grin at him. "You know I'm too smart to answer that."

They all love to jokingly one-up each other where I'm concerned. I didn't get it at first, but since I started working through all of Archer's research, it makes more sense. Until we're all bonded, their instincts tell them to fight each other for me. All this silly bickering is their way of working through their territorial impulses.

Bonded.

The word alone has my core melting.

The guys and I haven't discussed it since Declan's injury. We were all focused on getting him back on the field. Other than the game they carried him out of, he only missed one other.

But now the Ospreys are 3-2. Which is, apparently, not great.

There's a game with a division rival tomorrow. Declan's been on-edge about it all week. Theo thinks we have it in the bag. I'm not sure which of them is right, but I'll be in the box with Ronan either way. We're hosting the opposing team's owner and his wife.

The game is such a big deal, I made my very first mandate as their omega—a proper day off. Saturday afternoon relaxing at home.

The guys did me one better and put together a whole poolside spread. The grill is gassed up. Mrs. Fleming made trays of Florida-fruity drinks. The two TV monitors tucked into the lanai play college football coverage.

I plan to completely check out as soon as I get this video posted. Our alpha looks over my bare shoulder at my phone. "More *content*?"

"Leave the kids alone, old man," Arch drawls, lowering his book and smirking from the reclining chair at the pool's edge. "The team's socials have never looked better or had more views."

He is—as always—correct. He's also unfairly handsome in yellow trunks and nothing else. The bright color contrasts with his gorgeous brown skin. The sunscreen slicking up his muscles doesn't hurt, either. He religiously applies it to both of us every hour.

"Yeah," Declan says, swatting my ass while he grins some more. "We're working, Daddy."

Ronan punches his non-throwing arm, but crowds closer. I toss Declan a shit-eating smirk while I press play on the audio sample I've pulled for our vanilla alpha.

When Ronan hears the lyrics to Jack Harlow's "Lovin' on Me," he actually laughs out loud. Archer covers his face with his book, chuckling. Theo whoops from the pool, his own laugh echoing through the whole backyard. "Peaches, you are my *hero*."

Declan pouts for real, now. "No way am I singing that, brat."

I step up against his chest and beam at him. "Come on! It's funny! Please? For me? It's viral right now, and it's literally *too perfect* not to use."

It took a few days for me to realize it, but now I know—Declan is, shockingly, a complete softy. Only for me. And mostly in private. But still; I'm amazed by how my puppy-dog eyes affect him.

The tension leaks out of his posture, and he grabs for me.

"Fine," he growls against my mouth. "You owe me, omega."

His hands on me, his perfect luscious sweetness. My perfume explodes, the peach edged with pure *need*.

Uh-oh.

My pre-heat symptoms started this morning in the shower, after Archer and I made love for over an hour. So far, it's just mild cramps and an annoying, irrational neediness that settled somewhat once we were all together. I had hoped to hide everything from the guys until we got through tomorrow's game.

Of course, my body has other plans.

Half a moment later, I'm surrounded. Theo drips all over the pool deck, his wet hands sliding around my middle. "Peaches..."

Ronan clasps my hand, but steps aside to give Archer access to me. Our doctor alpha runs a palm over my brow and hums, his eyes creasing.

Declan stands next to him, frozen. The hands cupped around my ass twitch, and he grits his teeth. Fighting off a rut, I realize.

My heart pangs. I reach for his face, stroking over his jaw. "It's okay," I murmur. "You won't hurt me, Declan."

He nods. "I—I don't want to leave you, but I'm scared to stay..."

Ronan grabs Declan's nape, his touch commanding. And, I think, reassuring. "We're all here. You're not alone. Try to focus on that."

Theo only has eyes for me. Glowing green irises trace my face, looking for any hint of discomfort. When I give him a tight smile, he nuzzles his lips into my hair and starts his raspy purr.

I fall against his chest, meeting Archer's worried gaze. "It's just pre-heat. I've been more—" Images of all four of them pleasuring me constantly flit through my head. "—*needy* the last few days. And I had some cramps earlier. It's fine though. I have another couple of days."

At least, that's my *hope*. The Ospreys have a bye week after tomorrow's game. If my heat cooperates, the guys won't miss much more than practices.

Ronan keeps one hand on Dec and uses the other to softly cup my face. "Are you sure, little one? We can rearrange things for the game tomorrow. Get the second-string in there, call the back-up physician. And you don't have to go at all if you don't feel up for it."

A stab of disappoint hits my gut. "I want to," I whine. "It's a big game! And have you *seen* the passing routes the new offensive coordinator put together? It's going to be epic."

That's one of the best things about reconciling with Declan— he likes to cuddle with me while he reviews the playbook every night. After a few evenings of watching him, I started asking questions.

Now I feel like I'll actually know what's happening. Plus, he eventually confided that he doesn't get along with their coach, but the new offensive coordinator seems to have his back. It's his first game using the guy's plays. I don't want to miss that.

Theo reacts to my protest by groaning and wrapping me in bear hug from behind. "Oh my *God*. Do you guys *hear* this girl? Could she be any *sexier*?"

I laugh, patting his face. "Thanks, big guy. I have a good tutor."

Declan's drawn expression softens a bit at my praise. He still looks serious, though. "We can bail on the game, princess. I don't want to play one fucking minute if it means you're in pain."

It's been a while since I had to force a smile. I'm out of prac-tice, but I manage to paste one on, laying false confidence into my words. "I'll be fine! Seriously. How bad could it be?"

chapter
sixty-two

I **NEVER UNDERSTOOD** the phrase "the more things change, the more they stay the same" until Declan and I made up.

Because, yeah, he's incredible and I'm just as obsessed with him as he is with me.

But *oh my God*, is he an ass.

I think I love it.

"You're being impossible," I snort as we step out of the car. "I'm *fine*. And you're late."

He shrugs, slinging his solid, suit-clad arm over my shoulders with an indolent shrug. "Not as late as Theo."

"Fuck off," Theo laughs, climbing out behind me.

Ronan tosses the keys to the stadium garage's valet attendant. Just like last time, I'm grateful we don't have to wade through the fans and press gathered outside.

One day, we'll have to do the photo-op. Let them snap the money shot—the Most Valuable Pack, all rolling up to gameday as a unit. To be honest... I want the pictures as much as they do.

But today is not the day.

Despite the smile slapped on my face and my *repeated* reassurances that I'm completely fine... I actually do feel like crap.

Thankfully, I *look* okay. The outfit Declan picked is somehow badass and comfortable—a pair of shiny silver leggings with a distressed Ospreys' T-shirt and the thick-soled booties I had on at the last game.

When I nearly had a meltdown over my hair, he even stepped up to take care of that for me too. It's just a high ponytail, but still. The guy *really* tried. As a result of his hard work, I'm passable.

On the outside.

Inside? Not so much.

This is my first pre-heat without any suppressants in my system, and I'm starting to understand why the prospect of letting me go through this alone so thoroughly horrified my doctors.

I feel like I'm a little bit... crazy?

A hormonal mess, for sure. I burst into tears when I had to choose who to sleep next to in our bed last night. I wound up moving twice in the middle of the night so I could spend enough time touching each of them. This morning, when Ronan answered his phone during breakfast, I *instantly* whined for his full attention. That one was so embarrassing, I nearly ran out of the house to begin a new life.

...And then cried about how horribly sad I would be if I actually left.

You'd never know I need an exorcism, though. If anything, the guys seem even *more* in love with me. I'm touching one of them at all times—and not just because *I* want to.

While we walk toward the tunnel that leads to the locker room, I marvel at how incredibly safe I feel. Ronan is at the lead, Declan bundling me into his side. Archer holds my left hand, the grip comforting and warm. Theo looms at my back, as thick as a brick wall.

My body is going haywire—revolting against the fluorescent lights overhead, the noise of the full stadium overhead—but my Omega knows we're fine as long as they're all with me.

Unfortunately, that's about to come to an end.

Our group halts where the hall splits off. Theo wraps his arms around my middle and pulls me into big bear hug, spinning us. The familiar gesture gets me to smile a little before he sets me on my feet and adjusts the orange-heart sunglasses on top of my head.

His green eyes look serious while he traces my cheekbone. "You good?"

I know what he's really asking. And I know if I say I'm not okay, he will walk away from this huge game without a second thought. They all will.

So, I turn my smile up a notch, trying for shiny and bright. I wave at the tunnel. "Get out of here, big guy. Go kick ass for me."

His face lights up with a perfect Theo grin. "You got it, peaches."

He backs off and lets Declan at me. My moody vanilla alpha instantly pulls me into his arms and kisses me like he's dying. Or I am. Either way it's intense and it goes on until I'm a perfuming mess.

Ronan growls a warning, and Declan's chest rumbles in reply. Not wanting them to snap at each other, I carefully pull back and try to give Dec a smirk.

He isn't having it. His face is severe while he cups his hands around my face. "*If you need me, you will send someone to get me.*"

It's the only time he's ever barked at me on purpose, and he's doing it to keep me secure. The soft, urgent words hit my heart like a bolt from Cupid's bow. I sway and nod, letting Archer tuck me into his tall frame.

Declan exhales through his nose and squeezes his eyes shut as he turns away, storming off. Now I know him well enough to know he's worried, not angry. He's only stalking off because he's afraid he won't be able to leave me if he doesn't go now.

At least, I think so.

Ugh. I cannot *wait* until we're all bonded and I can feel all of these feelings *with* them instead of taking my best guess.

Archer holds me tenderly, his purr erasing any lingering doubt or worry from Declan's departure. "I'll be down there with them the whole time," he assures me. "I'll keep an eye on everything for you."

I squeeze him. "Thank you. If Declan—"

Archer frowns fiercely. "If he even *blinks* wrong, I'll pull him. I promise you. I'm going to go tape his shoulder up now."

I grab both of his hands, kissing the backs of each before I release him. "*Thank you*, Archer." I swallow a wad of emotion. "I mean it. You do everything for me and for the pack—"

His smile is brilliant. He bends to kiss my cheek, murmuring, "I always will. I love you, sweetheart. See you soon?"

I nod, going right to Ronan's side. My lungs feel tight, and my clothes suddenly itch everywhere. Watching three of my alphas walk away feels like lopping my hand off at the wrist. It seems unnatural to just... get on the elevator and ride five levels up.

Luckily, Ronan is in control. He guides me with a firm hand at the small of my back, his eyes scanning protectively as we emerge into the plush level that holds the skyboxes.

He turns to check in with me before we move. "Are you sure you're all right, baby girl? We can tell this other team's owner to go to hell."

I have to chuckle at his surliness. "Didn't you invite him?"

Ronan shrugs, doing a decent Declan impersonation with his spoiled scowl. "It's customary. Our team extends the invitation to every team we host. They all do the same for us; we can sit in their boxes when we go to away games."

Usually, the concept of traveling with the team gives me butterflies. I love the thought of seeing different parts of the country, and imagining my men taking on opponents in hostile territory turns me on.

But right now? Nope. My stomach turns. Being more than ten minutes from the pack house practically gives me hives.

Ronan misreads my face and moves to hail the elevator. "We'll go home now."

I grab the sleeve of his black dress shirt. "I'm fine. I was just —" I come up with a false source of anxiety. "Can you smell me?"

His lips twitch. "I can *always* smell you, omega. But the neutralizers are working. Even with your pre-heat and my intensified sense of smell where you're concerned, the scent is very faint. I hate it."

Some of my tension escapes on a hard laugh. "All right then. Let's do this."

------------ ♥ ------------

RONAN INTRODUCES the other team owner and leads me to my usual leather recliner in front of the box's window.

When a waitress appears at my elbow, I startle and instantly feel ridiculous. The guys warned me that the box would have catering and waitstaff for this game, because of our guests.

"Sorry," I squeak.

The girl smiles, tilting her head at me. "Can I get you anything?"

I almost order a stiff drink, but Archer would kill me. A drunk omega going into heat? *Yikes on spikes.*

"Just water, please."

She nods and fetches me a water bottle. Ronan returns,

frowning severely. He pulls me up so he can take my seat and arrange me on his lap. His lips find my ear.

"Are you uncomfortable? We can go home, but we might miss the kickoff if we leave now."

I want to turn tail, but I talk myself down again. Ronan is warm and solid underneath me; and I don't want to let Theo and Declan down by missing a single second of their big rivalry game.

We watch the kickoff. Overhead, the TV shows close-ups of Theo and Declan's faces as they arrange their offense and lead the Ospreys down the field to score on the opening drive. The other team scrambles to answer, going three-and-out before Declan jogs back onto the turf.

Mm. He looks so ridiculously *good*.

My crazy hormones hate that everyone else can see him looking this gorgeous. But what is the guy supposed to do? Wear a bag over his head at all times?

It wouldn't help because Theo is just as sexy. He has his hair up, showing off the hewn plains of his face. Pride swells in my chest at how intimidating he looks.

My big guy.

He's in the zone today. Every time the camera zooms in on him during a replay, I catch the determination in his eyes, the violent gnash of his teeth. By the second quarter, he's made a ton of stops and has twelve completions. The Ospreys lead 17-10 going into halftime.

Ronan convinces me to eat a little, pointing out that the box once again has all of my favorite things. My stomach turns after half a piece of pizza, so I set it aside. The waitress notices and brings me a fresh water. God bless her.

I need it. I'm starting to sweat.

No, I tell my body. *You're fine. You can wait two more hours.*

Ronan frowns at my uneaten food. He casts me a mild scolding look and speaks low, not wanting the others to overhear. "Baby girl, you know you need to keep your strength up. How about dessert? We have those cupcakes you like."

I sigh and agree, knowing he'll be anxious if I don't eat something else. Besides, the cupcakes look adorable.

The second all that sugar hits my stomach, I know I've made a mistake. My gut clenches, churning. I jump up automatically. "I'll... be right back."

Ronan's silvery eyes narrow at me, wary. "I'll come with you."

"No," I insist, mortified. "It will just take a minute. I'll be right back."

He grumbles directions, and I nod at the field. The second half is starting. I need him to watch so he can tell me what I miss. "Take detailed mental notes, please."

The skybox level has a large, luxurious ladies' room. I spend a couple of minutes standing over the trough of sinks, breathing deeply, convincing myself not to throw up.

I can do this.

Two more hours.

I can do this.

The wrenching pulse of pain below my navel calls me a liar. I whimper quietly, bending over the porcelain.

A sharp laugh echoes through the empty room. I try to turn my head, but a wave of dizziness has me squeezing my eyes closed.

There's a scoff, punctuated by the sound of heels hitting the tile floor. "God, what gutter did the Ash Pack drag you out of?"

Forcing myself to breathe, I finally lift my gaze to the woman standing just inside the entrance. She's small and curved—clearly an omega—dressed in a crimson dress that indicates loyalty to our rival team.

When I blink, her features come into focus. They're mean and beautiful, and *way too familiar.* As is the mane of auburn hair flowing down her back. The sickly-sweet aroma of torched bananas makes my stomach squirm.

"Katrina?"

She smiles, the curve of her lips as sharp as a scythe. "So he *did* mention me."

I fist my hands to hide their shaking, forcing every ounce of strength I possess into my voice. "Once. He told me you were a liar and a fraud. He told me he was sorry he ever met you and regretted dating you."

The amusement slides off her face, leaving a cold sneer. "And you believed him?" Her laugh is a hard, brittle thing. "After I saw you at the gala, I knew that you were trashy, but I didn't realize you were stupid, too."

I swallow the insane urge to lunge for her throat, internally talking myself down. *Don't make a scene over this bitch.* If anyone screams, Ronan's security will be on us in a second.

"What are you doing here?" I ask. "This is a private level."

Her barbed smile reappears. "It's easy to make friends with lots of money when you have something to exchange for their generosity." Her cool eyes drop down to my crotch. "But you've clearly figured out that much. Tell me, who was your in? Was it the big one, Theo?"

She sighs, inspecting her manicure. "I should have gone for him instead. Declan was a man-whore, but he turned out to be so much smarter than I anticipated. And Theo is just so *stupid—*"

All of the pain and need and aggression I've shoved down rises like a tidal wave. I dig my nails into my palms, baring my teeth in a snarl. The sound that comes out of me can only be described as a warning growl.

"You shut your fucking mouth. You know nothing—*nothing*—about my pack. Not Declan or Theo or any of them. Otherwise, you'd know they're all too smart and too honorable to *ever* go for a bitch like you."

"You sure about that?" she taunts, waving her phone like it contains some sort of evidence. "Declan did."

Her implication hits me.

And I *laugh.*

Not because she's so obviously lying to stir shit up; not even because I want to seem above her catty drama.

I laugh because the idea of Declan—*my Declan*, the man I

know so very deeply—going back to the woman who caused him nothing but shame and heartache is *laughable*.

Impossible, actually.

And the fact that my Omega and I both know it, beyond a shadow of a doubt, even while I'm half-sane from heat hormones; the knowledge sends a giddy thrill through my body.

"No, he didn't," I tell her, unable to hide my smile. "Because he's *mine*. I'm sorry for you, though. I know it must hurt, losing him. Trust me, I can imagine it better than anyone. But you hurt him, too. You almost broke my pack. And if I tell Ronan you're here..."

I imagine his reaction, his rage. A shiver moves over me. "It won't be good for you," I finish. "So, the best thing I can offer you now is advice—leave. Leave this stadium. Leave Declan alone. Hell, leave the state if you need to, but, for now, get the hell away from me and my pack."

The crazy omega across from me looks down at the phone wedged into her fist. I can see the moment she remembers she doesn't actually have any proof to back her up—because she is and always has been a liar.

With a scoffed, "Whatever, *bitch*," she strides out of the room.

But I hear her heels, click-click-clacking all the way to the elevator. When I hear the doors ding and know she's on her way out of the building, I find myself sliding down the wall.

Exhaustion rolls over me as the fight drains out of my body. The cool smoothness of the tile feels good under my legs. My arms and hands tremble, my teeth chattering even as a mist of sweat blossoms over my chest.

And I think, maybe, this is it.

I've pushed and stretched myself to my absolute limits. Dealing with Katrina is just the thing that finally depletes my self-control.

Weirdly, I feel okay with that. A stab of pain twists my abdomen, but I feel calm. Vaguely, my fuzzy brain remembers the last time I found myself on a bathroom floor—the day of my initial interview.

Then, I felt panicked and hopeless.

So... *alone.*

But this is different.

The fact that I can't get up or walk the forty feet back to the box feels like an inconvenience, not a disaster. As my eyes drift shut, a sense of peaceful resignation settles inside of me. I have only one thought.

It's okay. My alphas will find me.

chapter
sixty-three

DECLAN SEEMS DISTRACTED.

He throws an interception eight minutes into the third quarter, and I curse loud enough to startle the other owners. They're an older, polished beta couple, clearly not accustomed to tattooed alphas yelling "fuck" in polite company.

I don't care. That was a particularly stupid throw. Declan doesn't normally make mistakes like that.

On the screen overhead, I watch Theo jog up and nudge him. They share a few words and motion to the sidelines, requesting a time out. While Theo ambles over to Coach, Dec takes off like a shot.

Running toward... Archer?

I have my phone in my hand before it even rings. "What's wrong?"

"Possibly nothing." Arch sounds calm, but the background noise is deafening. He speaks up. "Is Meg there with you? Declan needs to speak to her."

I don't want to alert the other team's owner to our weakness. "Not at the moment."

Archer relays the information. The television broadcast has gone to commercial, so I have to squint down at the field to see Declan harassing him. Players aren't allowed to take any calls on the sidelines, per League regulations. Really, Arch shouldn't even be on his phone.

My oldest packmate comes back over the line with a terse sigh. "Ronan, I don't know what's going on up there, but you better put our omega on the phone or you're not going to have a quarterback for the rest of the game. His Alpha is on edge."

I stand as casually as I can and make my way to the box's door. Worry crowds in when I realize Meg's been gone for close to twenty-five minutes. "Tell him I'm going to get her, and I'll have her text you a message for him in a moment," I direct. "He has to go back out there. Remind him that she came here today to watch him play."

I click off the call and pace down the curved hallway. It's hard to hear with the roar of the fans below and the stadium's speakers pumping pop music, but some instinct inside of me trips and I break into a run.

The peach perfume soaking the air is my first clue.

Oh fuck.

Meg's perfume has saturated the air. It's so strong, I'm afraid to reach for the bathroom door handle.

Will every other alpha on this level smell her the same way I can?

Before I can think twice about it, I have my phone out again, sending Archer an SOS. He replies that he's on his way up.

Meg is on the floor when I charge into the ladies' room. I have no time to wonder how long she's been there or why no one bothered to try to help her. I'm too busy sinking to my knees and taking her head in my hands.

She whines quietly, her hips bucking. Pain creases the space between her eyes. "*Alpha*. I knew you would come."

I exhale around the urge to rip her leggings off and knot her right fucking here, focusing on carefully pulling her into my lap.

"Of course you did, good girl," I praise. "Daddy will always come for you. And Archer is on his way, too."

Meg seems to understand, nodding and nuzzling my neck at the same time. "How did you know to come find me?"

I swallow a snort. "Declan is wigging out."

Her lips twitch into a weak smile. "He always knows when I'm not safe." A pained whimper slips out on her next breath. My body stiffens with alarm.

"We're going to get you home, baby girl," I promise. "And make you *ours*."

chapter
sixty-four

THE SCOREBOARD FLASHES over Osprey Stadium, bragging so I don't have to.

34-17.

Not fucking bad. And fourteen of those points are mine.

I join the other guys on the field, rushing out to shake hands with the opposition. Even in a field of pro football players, I'm still taller than pretty much everyone. I crane my neck, scanning for my packmates.

A hand fists the back of my jersey, jerking me. "C'mon. *Now.*"

It's Dec, and he sounds pissed. I turn around to glower at him

—because, seriously? What the fuck, man; we just crushed it—but his face gives me a chill.

Shit.

He looks *freaked.*

I snap into my body all at once, instincts whirring back online.

Meg.

Something isn't right. Why else would Archer bail? And Declan may be a dick about it, but he's always known when she's in danger before the rest of us.

He holds onto my shirt while we plow through the crowded field, making a beeline for the tunnel. Ronan is there, his expression darker than I've ever seen it. He motions over his shoulder. "We're leaving. *Now.*"

"What the fuck happened?" Dec demands. "I've been three seconds away from puking for the last *hour.* Where is Meg?"

Ronan blows out a breath. It looks like he's counting internally, trying to wrestle his impulses. "Meg is fine, but she's in heat."

My mind skips like a broken record. His words don't sink in. "Wait. *What?*"

Ronan growls, leading our charge down into the tunnel, "She went into heat early. Archer says that can happen, especially with undue stress. Coming here today was clearly too much for her, but she forced herself anyway.

Declan freezes, his shoulders rising and falling on exaggerated breaths. "*Fuck.*"

Ronan runs both hands through his hair, snarling at the dark concrete ceiling. "I *know.* Listen, there will be time to talk about all this shit in the future, but we have to go. Right now."

I shake my head. As if that will help all of this make sense. "Where the hell is she? In the car?"

"Archer has her," Ronan murmurs, waving us on again. "He took her home. It's too dangerous for her to be here with her heat perfume in full effect."

Declan shouts, panicked. "I thought we had more time! It wasn't supposed to start until later this week!"

Fuck.

Fuck, fuck, fuck.

FUCK.

Desperation spears me. "I just want Meg. Where is she?"

I expect Declan to rip a chunk off one of us, but he simply nods, somber. His voice is hoarse. "I need to see her."

Ronan picks up his pace. "Let's go."

chapter
sixty-five

ARCHER

"MEGERA?"

My poor sweet girl whines, tucking her sweaty face into my chest. I tighten my arms around her and wait for the driver to open my door. It took some doing to find a female beta on the ride-haling app, but we're finally home.

I carry Meg into the house, every instinct on high alert. I watch to make sure the hired car leaves and double-check that the property's gate locks behind her. My senses are sharper than usual —I can tell that Mrs. Fleming is gone from just a cursory sniff of the air.

We instructed her to take leave, starting today. It seemed prudent given how shy our omega is about her heat. Mrs. Fleming spent the better half of the week deep cleaning everything and stocking our kitchen with pre-made meals.

I'm glad she won't see us like this. My Alpha is half-feral from the smell of Meg. God knows what Ronan will be like when he gets here. Or Declan.

I force down my fury at the thought and focus. If I get Meg into a cool bath, it should keep her lucid enough to talk to me. I want her to know she's safe at home before she loses sight of where she is and what's happening.

I also need to know if she wants us all to bond during this heat.

It would make sense if she declined, given the circumstances. But honestly, I am praying she says yes. Today was hell. If we were bonded, I would have heard her distress. She could have shown me where she was, and we would have found her much sooner.

I'm not sure how much longer any of us will last without that tie to her. Not just for safety, either.

I truly can't describe the way I *need* her.

Every day, our relationship runs deeper and deeper, like a river carving a canyon. I'm walking around with a chasm inside me. A place made just for her.

I think we all are.

In her bathroom, I strip both of us and climb into the tub with her, cupping handfuls of cool water over her limp limbs. Her lashes flutter three times before they finally fall open. Dazed blue peers up at me.

She blinks, the movement sluggish. A tremble moves through her as she stutters in a whisper, "A-Archer?"

Emotion blocks my throat. Guilt, worry, and love thick enough to strangle.

"I'm here, sweetheart," I murmur. "You're safe at home now."

She shudders in my arms, her head lolling against my bare

chest. "I-I'm sorry about the game," she slurs. "I tried to hold it off, but I think I'm in heat now."

I don't know if I'm closer to laughing or crying at the absurdity of her apologizing to us. For this. "You did nothing wrong, my love. You were perfect. The rest of your alphas will be here any minute and we'll take care of you, okay? You can relax."

I know she won't. Her biology won't allow her to until we're all together. Still, I massage her arms and hands, hoping to at least put her at ease.

The tension in her back slowly releases. She tries to look up at me, her eyes searching in the dim, unlit bathroom. "Alpha?"

My cock twitches. I blow out a calming breath. "Mmhmm?"

She lifts her listless hand to touch my cheek. "Thank you," she whispers, her eyes fluttering closed. "For teaching me. I didn't know how to do this before I met you."

My lips skim her brow. "Do what, sweetheart? Your heat?"

She fights her heavy eyelids long enough to pin me with a look of utter sincerity. "No," she murmurs. "This. Us. All of us... Before I found you guys, I didn't have anyone to teach me, so I never learned... how to love someone." Her eyes shine. "I learned from watching you."

The gravity of her words hits me square in the chest. The bridge of my nose stings, emotion rushing to fill my throat. "Me?"

She nods, the motion lazy. "Mmhmm. The way you listen. How well you know each of us and keep tabs on the things that are important to everyone. You're the very best teacher for this."

I can barely speak. "Meg..."

She tucks her face against my neck again. Her voice is soft, but firm. "I love you, Archer. So much. More than I ever thought I could."

Because *I* taught her.

Me.

Bone-deep *want* fills my body. The need to bite her, claim her, make her mine in every possible way. My muscles bunch, rebelling against my restraint.

She feels them and shifts against me, her perfume rising. The next time our eyes meet, hers are slightly less clear. "I want the bonds, Alpha," she breathes. "Please?"

I swallow past my thick throat, banishing the sting of tears from my eyes. My arms squeeze her closer. "Okay, sweetheart. You'll have them. I promise."

She sighs, the sound weary but content. "Good. Can we get in my nest now?"

My heart lurches. Pride and joy swell through me. She's *never* asked for her nest, even when she needed it. Hell, she's never so much as called it *her* nest.

"Of course we can."

A cramp takes hold of her. She winces, covering her abdomen with her hands. "I want all four of you," she whimpers. "It hurts, Alpha."

In a flash, I have her out of the tub and dry, wrapping my own towel around my hips. We're going into the nest. "I'm going to make it better, omega."

chapter
sixty-six

Megera

MY SKIN IS SWARMING.

No, I can't explain what I mean by that. But trust me, it makes sense, somehow.

Every movement is pleasure and pain. Fire snaps over my body, burning down to my nerves, lighting each one up like a Roman candle.

I hate how *aware* I am.

My quiet alpha explained that it's the final burst of lucidity before the heat pulls me under. It won't end until they're all here with me. He says they're coming as fast as they can.

I know I'm in some sort of half-haze because I can't remember anyone's names. Just their faces, their scents, and the way need bursts through my body at the thought of them.

I'm myself, but I'm also not. When the quiet alpha sets me in front of my nest, I walk right in. I can't seem to recall why I haven't done so all along. Whatever the reason was, I need to let it go.

My Omega is *adamant* about that.

The door to the nest swings open. I hear a sharp inhale, smell the way ginger and bourbon swell to spice the air. When I reach back, a large, warm hand engulfs mine.

"Omega," the alpha says, reverent. "Your nest is a dream. I love it."

I love it too. That's been the hardest thing for me to admit to myself—how much I love this round, quiet room. How much I love the alphas who gave it to me.

The quiet one takes a careful look around, his dark eyes lingering on the black velvet walls, fine gold details, and plush stack of cushions. Without a word, he bends halfway out the door and retrieves a basket.

Scents swirl from the clothing inside it. I feel my eyes widen. My body sways closer to the alpha scents.

"These are all for you," he tells me, smoothing a hand over my head. "Take whatever feels right."

He barely finishes his offer before I'm on my hands and knees, scrabbling around the padded mattress that forms the base of the nest. Some distant part of my brain reminds me that I'm supposed to be afraid of this—that I've never tried to do it before.

But it's easy.

This shirt goes over here. These sweats belong there. Vanilla with spice. Citrus with smoke. Then smoke with spice and citrus with vanilla. Smoky vanilla? Spicy citrus?

By the time I have all of the blankets and clothing arranged properly, I'm practically salivating. I roll and twist, stack and tuck until its perfection.

"Alpha. Come." The words leave my lips without permission. I can hear how weird I sound—some blend of sultry and demanding—but I can't care.

The core of my body is *melting*. Slick slips down my thighs, its sheen visible all the way to my knees.

Present.

The word slips through my mind at the exact second my body moves, shifting me into the right position. I nuzzle my cheek into the nest, inhaling the alpha scents and whining with want. My ass raises while my knees spread slightly.

He kneels behind me, his fat cock hard against my backside while he fits his thighs to mine. The feel of his skin against mine is ecstasy. Like the smoothest silk and roughest velvet, stimulating and comforting. Tingles race over my entire body.

A deep purr rolls over me, and I shiver. "Good omega," the alpha rumbles, his voice huskier. "Presenting so perfectly for your alpha. Look at how beautiful you are."

Large hands stroke firmly over my thighs. A stab hits right between my hips.

Knot. I need a knot.

I wiggle, whining again. "Alpha. Please. It hurts."

Rustling and panting distract both of us. We turn toward the cracked door in time to catch the three others rushing into the other room. They're all partly naked. A shrill keen streaks out of me.

"More skin," I beg.

The tattooed pack alpha sees me through the crack and nods, stripping off the last of his clothing. My big alpha is next, tripping out of his pants and rushing to the doorway.

"Can they come in, omega?" the quiet one asks.

"Yes." The word is half-choked. A fog tumbles over my vision. My body writhes. "Need them all. Need all of you."

The pack alpha and the big alpha come in immediately. The pride and awe on their faces as they take in my nest send a charge through my blood. I whine again.

"Where is he?" I cry, the pain fisting my insides. "I need—I need—"

Him.

The angry one. He's the last to the door, where he stands, his chest heaving and eyes wild. I watch as he steps into the nest and closes the door behind him, his focus unflinching.

They're all here.

They're all mine.

It's my last coherent thought before the haze takes me.

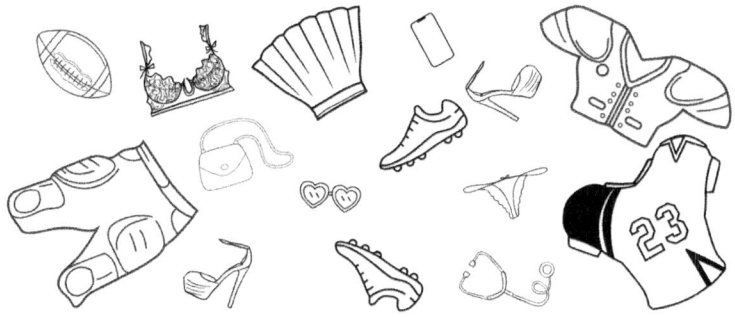

chapter
sixty-seven

WE ALL HOLD our breath while we watch the haze slip over our omega. Her eyes lose focus as her breathing accelerates, ragged and desperate.

Her succulent scent is sharp with *need*. It soaks the air, the inside of my lungs, my tongue. My cock and knot both pound. A wild whirl pulls inside of me. The urge to fuck, fight, claim.

To rut.

She pushes up onto her elbows and turns. Looking right at... *me?*

"Alpha." She crawls on her hands and knees, coming to the edge of the nest at my feet. "Need your knot. Need *you*."

I drop to my knees instantly. Our eyes meet. She's gone, but I still see her in there. *My princess.*

She wants me first because I don't think I deserve her. Even lost to her haze, she's still sassy and demanding, using her choices to make a point.

"You want me to fuck this pretty pussy, omega?"

She whines, presenting so beautifully I could fucking weep. Every bit of her is on display, perfectly bare and glistening with slick.

Gripping her hips, I lower myself behind her. My hands rub over her ass, thumbs meeting to stroke down her center. She mewls, grinding her hips back. I hook an arm around her middle and pull her up, back-to-front.

My cock kicks up against her and comes away dripping. I grunt. "Fuck, you feel perfect. You gonna take this knot like a good girl?"

Ronan kneels across from us, framing her face in his hands. Their eyes lock. It's a relief to see that Archer was right—we're all seriously turned the fuck on, but none of us seem to be in rut territory.

"Of course she is," our pack alpha rumbles, purring. "She's my perfect baby girl."

Meg pants, trying to lean forward to capture his lips. When he smirks at her, she whimpers, "Please, Alpha."

I can't take it. Without waiting a second longer, I slip into her from behind, my hips thrusting hard.

Holy *fuck*.

She feels incredible. Soaked and tight and *pulsing*. She comes almost instantly, gripping me in a slippery vice. We both moan, the sounds filling the nest.

Ronan catches Meg's cry with his mouth, kissing her while he fists her hair in his hand. She breaks their lip-lock to lick his throat. Our alpha growls, his eyes flying to Archer and Theo, brows raised.

Theo crawls over while Archer moves to the side of the nest and stretches his arms wide, half-smiling. He looks calm, but his voice is gravel. "I want to watch."

Ronan nods. When Theo gets close enough, he reaches over and grips the back of the big guy's neck. "Lick her clit, Theo."

My teammate drops to the mattress with a groan, shimmying to get up on one elbow and seal his lips around her cleft. I feel his tongue—smooth and hot, lapping around her swollen clit and the base of my dick.

Meg instantly tightens around me, gushing all over again. I curse and buck into her, rubbing the head of my cock right where my knot will press into her.

Our omega catches sight of Theo and Ronan's swollen cocks and knots, keening with need. She tries to reach for them, but she can only get to Ronan's. I lean forward to whisper in her ear.

"Want me to stroke Theo, baby? I can get that knot all juiced up for you."

Meg and Theo both squirm. I pick up my pace, pounding into her hard and steady while I reach down and grip Theo's dick. If I wasn't balls-deep in our omega, I might smirk at how ready he is; he won't need much priming at all.

Ronan snarls while Meg works him over, slipping both of her little fists over his girth. I know I won't last long, watching them lick into each other's mouths, feeling the way she flutters while Theo licks us.

"Fuck, baby. You feel so perfect. Gonna make me fill this pussy with my cum. You want my knot?"

"Alpha!" she shrieks. And I don't know which one of us she's screaming at, but it's good enough for me.

I press down and edge forward, popping my knot into her wet warmth. My back bows, and my lungs stutter as her body grips me, massaging every inch of my cock and knot with her trembling muscles.

Pleasure cracks through my blood. I fuck her hard while I still can, wringing two more climaxes out of her before my knot expands all the way.

Theo's about to come, so I leave him be, saving him for our omega. Ronan wraps one of his hands around her throat, and her pussy clenches around me as my orgasm barrels down my spine. I fill her in thick spurts, my knot locking us together.

We all fall onto the enormous, round mattress. Meg snuggles back into me, her hands frantically searching for mine. I wrap one arm around her, pressing my palm over her belly. The other finds her face, turning her head so I can kiss her.

"I love you," I pant, biting her lower lip. "You're fucking *everything*, baby."

Her body pulses around mine, already craving another fix. Another knot. I smile into her shoulder. "Should we let Daddy go next?" I murmur. "Or have the big guy give you his first knot?"

Theo's pained groan answers for her. As soon as she hears him, her eyes light up. Her hands make an adorable grabby motion.

My knot releases us quickly, adjusting to make sure she can get all she needs. I roll away from her back so Ronan can take my place, sitting against the edge of her nest with her propped in his lap. He roams his hands over her, tweaking her nipples and spreading her thighs wide.

Mouth watering, I watch while a mix of slick and cum seeps out of her perfect peach pussy. Meg catches my eye, reaching down and using her index finger to scoop up the mixture of her and me, bringing it right to her mouth.

chapter
sixty-eight

"HOLY FUCKING SHIT."

Declan seems to agree with my assessment, staring at Meg like his brain fell out his ass.

Even Archer can't control himself. He growls, biting his lip, and wrapping one of his hands over his knot, stroking himself with the other. Meg licks her lips as she watches him, another whine building in her chest.

"Theo." Ronan waves me over, his eyes following Meg's every move as she wiggles in his lap, pressing back on his erection with her luscious ass. "You ready?"

Ready? I've almost come like eight times. The only thing stopping me is the thought of not giving our omega what she needs.

"*Alpha*," she cries, reaching for me again. "Need your knot."

Well, that won't be a problem. I've never been so hard. And I have a feeling I'll bounce back three seconds after we're done, just like Declan. He's already pounding his cock into his fist, eyes transfixed on the hot fucking mess between our omega's thighs.

When she clenches around the open air, hips bucking, I lose it.

Fisting her calves, I yank her over to me and bend her knees to the sides of her torso. I want to watch the slick and cum cream while I fuck her, see her body take my knot for the first time.

Ronan bends forward to hold her head between his hands, peering at her upside down. He can't stop touching her, but that's normal for a pack alpha at the beginning of a heat. He'll be on edge, worried about all of us until we fall into a rhythm. Watching to make sure Meg has every last thing she needs.

Because he's good fucking alpha.

So is the rest of my pack.

Dec is clearly lost to the heat haze after fucking Meg so thoroughly, but he still pauses to offer me a nod of encouragement. Archer appears on my other side, his presence as calming as ever, despite his monstrous hard-on.

I'm fucking *nervous*. And horny as hell. Worried, a little bit. I've never knotted anyone before. Arch reads my face and sets a hand on my shoulder.

"You want this alpha's knot, sweetheart?" he teases, running his free hand down Meg's side. "Tell him."

She dribbles slick over the head of my dick. I grunt like I've been punched in the gut. "Want you," she pants, her touch sliding down my abs. "Need you to knot me deep, Alpha. *Please*."

The plea winds down my spine and snaps my hips forward, punching my cock into her pussy.

Oh good, sweet motherfucking—

Whatever chill I thought I possessed?

Gone.

Poof.

My head falls back, the wet squeeze of Meg's pussy ripping a deep groan from my chest.

Ronan strokes a hand over her blonde head. Our omega's eyes are unfocused but gooey with all sorts of good things when she looks up at him and then over at me.

Our alpha snarls quietly, teasing her. "You gonna give me a show worth watching, baby girl? Take that alpha cock until he knots you?"

We both moan while she pumps her hips up to meet mine. "Fuuuuck," I hiss, filling my hands with her tits. Her hips. Her perfect ass.

Mm. I can't wait for one of us to take this, too.

She's going to love being filled by two alpha cocks.

Meg's legs start to shake, another orgasm bearing down on her. Archer mumbles around his gritted teeth, "Good. When she's about to come, you'll push all the way in."

The thought makes our girl moan. My balls tingle at the sound. I buck harder, rubbing at her sweet, swollen clit with the edge of the knot pounding at the base of my shaft.

She chokes on a scream. Arch's hand squeezes my shoulder. "Now," he says, quiet. "Tilt your hips and push down. Then rock forward."

Tilt, push, rock, I repeat to myself, following the instructions before I lose my nerve. *Doesn't seem that ha—*

Holy *fuck.*

HOLY FUCK.

Wet, hot *pressure* rolls around my knot, gripping me all the way to my balls. Slick soaks them while her spread lips tease the tightening skin. My chest heaves. I stare down at the place where we're joined. My brain fucking *melts.*

Meg whines, bouncing against me. I choke on a growl at the feeling. The *tug.*

Fuuuuuuck.

"I know," Dec murmurs, hoarse. "Doesn't she feel incredible?"

Ronan pets her head again. "Beautiful girl," he praises, bending closer to her. "Perfect pussy. We love it, omega. Can't get enough of the way you were built for our knots."

I'm practically brain dead, but I manage to catch the way he skirts his gaze to mine. Some sane, far-away part of my brain tells me that he's sweet-talking her for me, trying to give her the comfort she deserves while I piece my skull back together.

It might not happen. I think my mind is permanently blown. Arch moves away from me and bends to put his lips to her neck, sucking on the thin skin.

The sight has me desperate, my cock jerking inside of her. I groan again. Arch bites the soft part of her shoulder. Hard. Barely avoiding breaking skin. That will come later.

Meg screams and comes *all over me.*

All over me.

Her inner walls massage everything I've got. I explode instantly, bucking and grinding, spurting into her so hard that my vision dips and the nest disappears.

chapter
sixty-nine

ARCHER

THE SECOND THEO'S knot releases, Meg throws herself into my arms.

"Need you," she whimpers, going for my throat. "Bite me."

I curl my fists against her back, gathering every bit of self-control I possess. We all agreed to wait until the end of her heat, when we know the bonds will have the most health benefits for her. It's only round one, and our goal already feels impossible.

We have to try our hardest, though. *For her.*

I nuzzle my cheeks against both of hers, scent-marking. "You've been such a good omega," I praise, scraping my teeth over the imprint they left on her shoulder a moment ago. "I think you deserve a treat."

Meg's hazy eyes sparkle in the low light. I can't help but smile at her eagerness, joy shimmering in my chest. I catch Ronan's eye and my smirk widens at the murderously impatient look on his face.

Tilting Meg's head back, I kiss her hard, slipping my tongue against hers before I call, "Ronan. Think our omega can take two alpha cocks at once?"

Meg's head falls back on a cry of pure longing. "Please," she begs. "Fill me up, alphas."

He bites back a fierce growl, instantly on his knees. "I want her ass," he husks out. "She's been grinding it all over my knot."

He's on the brink, but he still pauses to get her prepped, slipping her slick from her pussy back to her ass, pumping it into the tighter opening with two fingers, then three. I rub her wet clit, gently rolling it between my fingertips until she's clawing at my shoulders, pleading incoherently for more.

When none of us can stand another second, I drop onto my back and pull her over my cock, slamming her down onto the rigid length in one slick glide.

I grunt like I've been shot, my head falling back into the plush perfection of her nest. "Meg—ah God, you feel so incredible, omega. Can you ride me hard? Show your alpha how bad you want this knot."

Our sweet omega rises to the challenge—literally. Pushing up onto her knees and balancing her hands on my chest, she rides my dick harder than she ever has before.

We're usually tender with each other, both of us reveling in the intimacy of fitting our bodies together. This is dirty, desperate *fucking*... and I love it every bit as much.

When she sinks her blunt teeth into my chest, I nearly choke. She only stops before breaking skin because Ronan wraps a hand around her throat from behind, using her bent position to slip the first third of his cock into her ass.

"*Behave, omega,*" he warns, pure smoke. "Or I'll stop stuffing my cock into you."

She whines, squirming between us. "Yes, Alpha."

His free hand strokes down the curve of her spine. "Good girl."

My fingers find her clit again, thrumming as consistently as I can while Ronan works his way into her. When he finally bottoms out, she practically screams in ecstasy, thrashing back and forth between us. I can feel how much he stretches her through the thin layer separating us. I know I'm not exactly average-sized, either. She must be ready to burst.

I nod at him, and he thrusts. I wait until he pushes back in to pull out. We create our rhythm like that, alternating back and forth until I swear my knot will explode.

"More," Meg gasps. "Need more."

I'm about to go for her throat when Declan and Theo appear. They each stand at her sides, offering her their hard cocks. She slips her hands over both and begins sucking them off, turning from one to another with a starved moan.

Her body clenches hard around us both, preparing to tip over the edge. Based on the growls ripping from their chests, Theo and Dec won't be far behind.

Ronan is ready, too.

The second Meg starts to come, we both shove into her and lock deep, completely filling her body. Declan grips her jaw and comes in her mouth while Theo paints her chest.

Meg hums happily, drinking her alpha down like a vanilla milkshake. He steps back, allowing Ronan and I to roll onto our sides with our omega knotted two ways between us.

Before our bodies have released her, her eyes flutter shut, and she drifts into a dead sleep.

Theo's laugh is shaky. He lowers himself beside her head, petting her hair back. "Well," he says, grinning. "That's round one."

chapter
seventy

FOR YEARS, I lived my life in a haze of aggravated exhaustion.

Why did I work so hard?

I had so much; why push, hustle, struggle, and scrap for more?

For this. In this moment, it's all worth it. The moment I finally have what I've always wanted.

Meg's nest is perfect. For three days, none of us have left it unless we needed to get our omega food or water.

Archer is a brilliant bastard for suggesting we install that kitchenette along with a bathroom large enough to fit all of us at once. We've used both every day; although, our girl is much keener on washing than she is about eating.

She doesn't mind the shower as long as it's dark and we're all in there with her. When it comes to food, though, I've had to break out my softest bark a few times.

It helps that we have a doctor monitoring for any signs of dehydration or exhaustion. He's fanatical about getting Meg to drink enough water, and it's hilarious watching him try to persuade her.

Unlike the woman we all know and love in real life, Heat Meg is very pissy when she doesn't get her way. Declan and I have both spanked her over the last few days—though, when I do it, she moans and submits. When he does it, she fights back, and they both love it.

Theo is the epitome of a team player. He fetches things, heats up all the food, and helps Meg rebuild any part of her nest that gets mussed. He also keeps everyone in good spirits, always making Meg smile, even in the deepest part of her haze.

I've never respected these alphas more. I couldn't be prouder to be their leader.

Right now, Meg sleeps peacefully on Theo's chest, his purr filling the nest even while he dozes under her. Declan is at an angle, his head against the small of her back and his arms around her hips. They've been there for six hours. It's the longest any of us have slept since we got home on Sunday.

I'm grateful. We've fucked non-stop, in every possible configuration, and it's been incredible. I know we're all exhausted, though. And I'm not sure if Meg sleeping so much is a sign she's winding down or preparing for a second wind.

When Archer senses I'm awake, he hoists himself up, sitting beside me against the far wall of the nest so our voices won't disturb the others.

A soft smile touches his face while he watches them. "Won't be long, now, I think."

I try not to get my hopes up and fail miserably. "Until...?"

He makes my dreams come true. "Bonding. I think she'll wake up much more lucid. Her refractory periods are getting longer, and her haze seems less severe today. We probably have about twelve to eighteen hours left until her fever breaks."

I rub my palm over my chest, wondering why my heart aches. He smirks at me. "It's bittersweet," he adds. "I know. But we'll be right back here in four to six months. *Every* four to six months."

Fuck, that's amazing. These have been the happiest days of my life, and I get to have them forever.

All because of our sweet little omega.

Sometimes, I swear she can already feel me inside of her. The second I wish she were awake to kiss me, her body twitches. A moment later, two blue eyes pin me in place.

They seem clearer. When I meet her gaze, I don't get the sense she's looking *through* me. Or trying to peer through some sort of fog to look *at* me. Her smile blooms. "Alpha."

She's lucid and she's teasing me. Damn Archer for always being right about everything.

He shoots me a shit-eating grin and crawls over to her. "How are you, sweetheart?" he asks, running his hand over head. "You feel a little cooler."

She blinks, the motion still a bit laggy. She uses a variety of words she hasn't said in a while, but they're half-thoughts. "Mm. Good. Happy. Want you. Want the bonds."

Arch flashes another smile at me, this one triumphant.

Oh fuck. Is it time?

He picks up the small hand resting over Theo's heart and scrapes his teeth along her pulse. "You want my bite, omega? All of your alphas' bites?"

Perfume engulfs the nest. Her need soaks the air, my tongue, the inside of my lungs. She's everywhere and everything.

Theo and Declan instantly jerk awake, both of them already semi-hard.

"She's ready," Archer tells them, his voice quiet with reverence as he turns to me one last time. "Pack alpha has to go first."

chapter
seventy-one

I DON'T KNOW how long it's been since I had a coherent thought, but my first one is *wow it feels weird to be able to* think.

So I'm guessing it's been a minute.

Ronan is the first face I really see. His secret smile makes my stomach flip. I repeat his name to myself, relieved to be able to.

Ronan.

Just the thought of him makes me perfume, slick gushing out of me. He comes straight over, lifting me into his arms.

"Hi, baby girl," he rumbles against my lips, chest purring. "How are you?"

I don't care how I am. I care about having him in me, connecting us forever. Whining, I scrabble closer to kiss him.

He chuckles, holding me tight. "God, I love you, little one. Can't wait to be inside you. In every way."

The others agree, all of them rousing to surround me. Archer touches under my chin, turning my head to meet his bottomless eyes. "How do you want us, sweetheart? All together?"

My Omega and I are one person right now. There isn't a moment of hesitation. No worries that I'm wrong or silly. I just know what's right for us.

All of us.

I smile. "One by one."

He grins back, pride so clear on his face, I could swoon from it. He steals a quick kiss. "We love that idea, right, guys?"

Everyone agrees, each of them touching my face or hair before shuffling back and letting Ronan keep me. A twinge of discomfort pinches my core and I shift, a whine building.

I *need* him.

He doesn't make me wait. Within seconds, I'm flat on the nest, the dark-haired, tattooed pack alpha looming over me. His dominance rolls around us in waves, soothing every last drop of uncertainty, leaving me lax and at his mercy.

My eyes roam his physical perfection, his unmatched intensity soaking into my soul. My Omega preens—this is a *true alpha*. She chose well.

We chose *perfectly*, I correct, opening my arms to him.

Ronan lowers himself into my embrace, purring and rubbing his face along my throat. "Omega," he roughs out. "Need you. Have to bite you. Make you mine. Make you *ours*."

While he speaks, his body fits itself into mine. Even after days of non-stop sex, he still stretches me wide. It takes him a moment to work all the way in, but this time, he fucks me with his knot, pushing it all the way in and pulling it back out on every thrust.

The sensation makes me wild within seconds. My body has been conditioned to come when I feel their knots pop into place. The way he's using his now should be illegal—every time it goes in, I start to climax, but the peak fades away when he pulls out.

I dig my nails into his back, trying to keep him all the way in me. He just works me harder, one of his brawny hands eventually pinning both of mine over my head.

I keen and moan, bucking against him, begging for more. When I think I'll pass out, he wraps his free hand around my jaw and pulls my head back. His knot starts to grow, hindering his torture. He dips his mouth to my throat at the same second he presses into me for the final time.

His knot expands, rubbing every simmering nerve inside my pussy, tugging with perfect friction. He groans while I come, squeezing him.

Ronan's lips open over the front-right side of my neck. A savage growl vibrates over the thin skin.

And he *bites.*

Raw heat pours into my body from both sides—the spurt of his cum filling my pussy while his very soul scorches its way down my throat.

His bond is a brand. White-hot, blinding possession. I feel him sear his place in my center, a thread of brilliant, burning intensity. For a moment, I feel the tether, but it seems... loose.

When he shifts over me, releasing my face and baring the right side of his own neck, I realize why.

He needs my bite, too.

I worried I wouldn't know what to do or how to do it, but it all feels entirely natural. Brushing both of my hands down his chest, I press my palm into his heart and lean up to bite him back, pressing until I taste sweet smoke.

Ronan growls and comes again, setting off another climax for me. While we both clutch at each other, the bright white thread in my chest pulls taut.

Binding us. *Bonding* us.

Ronan exhales into my hair, his hands softening against my

face. "There you are, baby girl," he murmurs, pressing his fore-head into mine. "Right at the heart of me—where you belong."

He stays there, nose-to-nose, and pours feeling into the bond. Things I've never seen on his perpetual poker face... I can feel them now. Wonder and glee and gratitude. Then there are the feelings I totally expect from Ronan—possession, pride. And love. *So much love.*

Tears slide down my cheeks. He kisses them away, rolling us onto our sides. We both revel, sorting through each other's emotions and kissing until I'm so dizzy, I think I might fall back into a haze.

The second he senses my trepidation, he pulls back, smirking. "I was going to say I have to let you go for now. But really, I don't, do I?"

He proves his point by pulling away physically while pressing in through his bond at the same moment. We're not touching anymore, but I still *feel* him.

I smile, and he offers a rare grin. With his signature blend of roughness and reverence, he reaches over and strokes his thumb over his claiming mark.

Absolute bliss rolls through me, settling right where his release and mine seep out of me. I moan and arch into his hand. By the time he's done stroking the throbbing bite, I'm panting for another knot.

His smile holds the same blend of smug arrogance and tender amusement I feel echoing in our bond. Both feelings intensify as he says, "Proud of you, little one."

My belly flips and he feels it, grin widening. He skirts his eyes to the side. "Who's next?"

I speak without thought. "Theo."

Ronan sends me wordless approval while he finds a place to watch along the wall of the nest. I feel him give one last burst of reassurance before he slips behind that curtain Archer described, leaving me to have my moments with the others.

Theo comes over hesitantly, eyes full of disbelief. "Are you—"

He breaks off when I tackle him, his question turning into a grunt and then a groan as I situate myself over his pulsing cock. Fresh slick dribbles over him, making us both moan.

I never have to worry about Theo wasting time. His enormous hand cups the back of my head while he grips my hip and pushes straight inside me. We rock together, building while we kiss.

He pulls back. Green eyes search my face. Tears clog his voice, turning it into a gruff rasp, "Peaches, you're the best thing I've ever done. I love you so fucking much."

A whine of pure need tumbles out of me. "Please, Alpha. Bite me."

He bucks up harder, driving both of us closer to the edge, using his knot to tease my clit. The familiar move sends me hurtling into a climax within minutes.

Pleasure ignites in my body. My head falls back on a silent scream. He tugs me down and tilts his hips, knotting me effortlessly as he brings his face to my chest and sinks his teeth into the top of my left breast.

Theo.

If Ronan is white-hot intensity, Theo is *color*. Bursting brightness. Invigorating joy. An innocent kind of wonder that reminds me of a child's enthusiasm.

He's *energizing*. Sparks of life and light flow into my soul—a swirling, chaotic buzz that leaves his tether in its wake.

We're both still coming, one simultaneous climax rolling into another while I lick the side of his neck and bite him just below his ear. A snarled sob stutters out of him. Our bond pulls taut, the link lighting up like a strand of fat, colorful Christmas bulbs.

He's so *good*. The purest, happiest spirit. Boundless optimism. Confidence without one smidgen of arrogance. Utter contentment.

I hear Ronan grunt behind me. A pulse of shock and satisfaction throbs through our new connection, reminding me that he can feel Theo now, too. It won't be as strong or direct as my link to him, but still. They're bonded.

Theo's breath tickles my new bite as he nestles between my breasts and closes his eyes. He looks spent, but he's sending me feelings as fast as I can process them. I smile into the top of his head, remembering how I always expected his mind would move fast.

His emotions are a chaotic whirl. In the best way. A flurry of happiness. Explosive joy. Love. Love. Love.

He feels my answering push of adoration and leans back to kiss me. When we break apart, he cracks the widest smile, pressing his hand over this heart. "Welcome home, precious."

I feel my own face split into a grin. It will be impossible to stop smiling now. My own happiness tweaks higher at the thought, and his echoes mine until we're both laughing.

His knot releases us, but he keeps me in his lap for another minute, licking the half-moons he left on my breast until I'm writhing all over again.

"Let these other knot-heads stare at your boobs now," he mutters, jokingly petulant. "They'll just be looking at *my* mark."

I trace the bite I left on the side of his neck, right where everyone will see it whenever he pulls his hair up during games. A giddy, mischievous thrill skirts through me. *Mine, bitches.*

I must be thinking loudly because Ronan and Theo both snort. "Yours," Ronan confirms. He sends me a beat of curiosity, asking without asking. *Who's next?*

Theo feels my attention turn and tosses me one last crooked grin, along with a final burst of joy. He sets me on my knees and shuffles over to Ronan's side, where our pack alpha reaches over and squeezes the big guy's nape. They exchange a look, both of them smiling broadly.

My Omega watches, utterly smug. Dang, she's a self-assured bitch. I think I might like her.

Archer.

I meet his dark, steady eyes across the nest. He reads my face. We move toward each other without a single word.

We've been fucking for days. Dirty, raw, animalistic. Totally at odds with the way he and I normally fit together.

This time, though, he comes at me carefully. His hands shake with restraint while he lays me down and joins me, putting us on our sides, face-to-face.

We don't need words. His eyes tell me how much he adores me. I can see from the naked emotion on his face that mine beams my love right back at him.

Archer makes love to me, drawing out my pleasure until I lose track of how many times I've come. I'm reduced to a sobbing, squirming mess by the time he finally seals us together, filling me so deeply I want to cry at the ecstasy and the intimacy of it.

When we both tip over the edge for the final time, he brings the hand he's holding up to his mouth, brushing his lips over my knuckles like he has so many dozens of times. This time, though, his mouth ghosts lower. His teeth pierce the thin skin, leaving a prominent mark right over the back of my right hand.

Cool, dark calm flows into me. Soft velvet. Deep water. The moving humility of staring into a starry sky.

Archer is wisdom. Depth. Perspective. Safety. A shield. An anchor. He ties himself into my soul, a cool touchstone to ground the rest of me.

I can *breathe*.

I can *think*.

I can soar, because I'll always know the way home.

To him.

Overwhelmed by the soft rush of reverence flowing between us, I cry in earnest, tears streaking down my face while Archer tends to his mark. Euphoria glows through my body, sending it into another peak. My quiet alpha groans low as I come around him, setting off another pulse from his knot.

I hold his eyes while I tilt my head and fit my lips against the hand still holding mine. It's the perfect place to claim. How many times has he reached for me with this hand? Offering me comfort, support. And that special sort of understanding that only he possesses.

Our bond snaps into place as I pierce him. Archer comes one last time and growls, the sound fierce with feeling. It rolls into a deep purr, leaving me boneless as he takes my mouth with a worshipful kiss.

A deep river of love flows between us. Steady and refreshing. I feel his awe and gratitude, echoing my own.

By the time we break apart, he and I aren't the only ones with wet eyes. Theo sniffs openly while Ronan clears his throat. His muted thump of embarrassment makes Archer and I both smile.

My dark-eyed alpha takes my head between his hands one last time as his body slips out of mine. He traces my face as if memorizing it.

"Thank you," he tells me, sincerity ringing through the bond. "You've given me everything. I'm the luckiest alpha in the world."

Selfless to the last, Archer gives my hand one final kiss and moves aside, taking the spot beside Ronan. They sit shoulder-to-shoulder. I can feel them communicating through their new bond, and I smile.

They've been in a pack for fifteen years, and now they're finally bound. *I* did that. Three glittering strings spark in my center, responding to my pride with approval, arousal, and impatience.

That last one is Theo. He's practically bouncing in place, giddy about the final alpha who will complete our pack.

I turn to Declan. He's been uncharacteristically quiet this whole time. Unnervingly so.

Over the last few days, there was rarely a configuration he didn't partake in.

After Ronan, he was the second-most-likely to direct the others, coming up with arrangements I never could have dreamed of. And he had absolutely zero qualms about getting his packmates off when I couldn't manage another cock.

Our gazes lock across the nest. Turbulent emotions fly across his gorgeous face, drawing me over to him.

I watch as he tries to play off his uncertainty, forcing a cocky half-smirk that doesn't touch his blue eyes. "You made me wait on purpose, didn't you, princess?"

I know I did, but I'm not sure why until he says it out loud. Bolstered by the clarity of taking three bonds, the first coherent thought I've had in days fights its way to my mouth.

"I wanted you to know that it's not just me choosing you," I whisper, tracing my fingers along his cheek and nodding over my shoulder. "It's all of us, Declan. We all belong together."

Absolute silence swells for half a second.

And then he's *on* me.

Declan grips the nape of my neck with one hand and palms my ass with the other, sweeping me into his hard body. He spanks me hard, yanking on my hair while he takes my mouth in a bruising kiss.

"Perfect. Fucking. Girl," he grinds out, landing a slap to my backside with each word. Dominance and lust roll off him in waves, making my pussy clench with want.

My back bows while I moan. He cups me roughly, the motion possessive. Two calloused fingers spear into me, pumping.

God, his hands. They're so *strong*. As I cling to his broad shoulders, he kneads my ass and rubs his thumb over my clit, working it until I'm tugging on his cock, begging for his knot.

He finally grabs me, kissing me hard one last time. The motion of his lips against mine grows desperate and sloppy. Pain creases his eyes.

"I love you," he pants, chest rattling with a ragged purr. "Tell me you know that."

He wants me to believe him. Now. Before. It's important to him that I take him at his word, even though I'll be able to feel his emotions for myself in a moment.

I nod, fresh tears streaking from my eyes. "Yes," I whisper. "I know that."

He snaps his eyes shut and exhales hard. When they open again, the blue blazes with want.

"Present for your alpha," he commands.

I scramble to obey. He doesn't make me wait, sinking right into me.

Spanking me while he fucks me with his cock and his knot, he torments me the way Ronan did. It doesn't last as long, though. Within a minute, we're both bucking and shouting our release.

Declan knots me deep, ecstasy exploding through my body. As the waves crash through me, he bends and bites right above my ass, leaving his mark between the dimples at the small of my back.

Declan.

Something dark and delicious winds its way into my blood. Pounding into all of my pulse points. Bittersweet slicks my soul.

Rage and relief.

Spirit and softness.

If Archer is bottomless calm, Declan is all-consuming *passion.* Every single emotion he feeds me is the strongest I've ever felt. Deeper than I ever would have guessed.

His ferocity rips the air from my lungs. Unable to wait, I reach back and wrench his hand off my hip. Turning my face, I find the corded muscle of his right arm and bite him *hard.*

I don't care what this arm does, I think, wanting them all to hear. *I only care that the alpha it belongs to is* mine.

Declan *roars.* His cock erupts again, sending me into another orgasm. He falls against my back, his body rubbing the new claiming mark. I kiss the half-moons on his arm as I fall flat to the mattress.

A rush of pure, undiluted devotion rushes right to my heart, followed by that same desperation I felt when he first kissed me. I snuggle back into him, sending as much reassurance as I can through our tether.

He tenses, going rigid on top of me. Disbelief and pain rush through him, followed by amazement. "Meg," he moans softly, burying his face into my hair. "*Fuck*, baby."

I see everything clearly, now. The women who were supposed love him never did—so he *couldn't* believe I did, no matter how many times he told himself it was true.

But he can't deny my love anymore.

And it's crushing him.

I pour every drop of adoration I can into our bond, adding as much comforting calm as I can muster. My quiet purr starts up and he dives for it, nuzzling his face against my back to get closer.

I feel his tears through our tether before they smear across my skin. There's a quiet flurry of movement around us. Suddenly, we're surrounded.

Ronan lies back and hauls my body over his, bringing Declan with us. Theo props himself up, reaching over to put his hand on his best friend's back. Archer settles at the other side, softly stroking my hair with one hand and setting the other on Declan's shoulder, squeezing.

Purrs roll through all of them. The bonds anchored in my chest light up like a switchboard, pulsing with pride, reassurance, relief.

We're all bound, now. None of us will ever feel alone again.

A weak haze starts to creep over me. The lucidity that grew with each of their bonds fades a bit, sinking me into a languid state of bliss, melting on top of Ronan.

Declan burrows between my shoulder blades, trailing soft kisses over my skin. He sends me a rush of affection and consternation, silently telling me to rest.

Ronan catches my apprehension and meets my glazed eyes. "You did it, baby girl," he rumbles.

The hand that isn't holding my hips to his reaches up and grips the nape of Declan's neck. He sends me a fond beat of pride and possession, saying, *I've got this.*

Theo's purr deepens, forcing my eyes to flutter shut. Archer is the last voice I hear before I sink under.

"Rest now, omega."

chapter
seventy-two

IT ONLY TAKES seconds for Meg to fall asleep beneath me.

I'm relieved. The feeling echoes through me and then back at me, coming from the three other alphas stacked around us.

Because... *they're all still here.*

Even though Meg isn't, really.

Theo's hand rubs my back, his purr not letting up even though our omega is passed out cold. When he feels my confusion through the bonds, he sends me some impatient emotion that, despite feeling distinctly gruff, seems sort of like... affection?

Of course we aren't leaving you, it says. *We love you, man.*

Archer's hand squeezes my other shoulder. *You're ours just as much as she is*, he tells me, his even calm soothing.

Ronan's fist releases the nape of my neck. He shocks me by pressing his palm against the back of my hair and stroking it. *You didn't believe it before*, he realizes, his internal tone heavy and sad. A spark of hope glimmers at the edges. *I hope you do now.*

How could I not?

They all leave their bonds wide open to me, letting me poke and prod at each emotion. And I do. I give each one a deep, thorough examination. Looking for holes. Lies. A trap.

Ronan's hand never pauses. "I didn't know," he says out loud. "How hard it was for you to believe in all of this. I'm sorry."

Theo bear hugs me and Meg from the side. "Me too, bro."

Archer sends a pulse of regret. "I should have tried harder to understand."

This was on me, though.

Always me, pushing everyone away. Pulling into myself so I wouldn't get hurt. Which was bullshit because it still hurt like a bitch. And then I got mad at them for that, too.

So many layers to this thing. Archer senses my overwhelm and rubs his hand down my arm, sending his thought without words so it won't embarrass me. *I can find you someone to talk to*, he tells me. *I want to help.*

And he *does*.

He *means* it.

He isn't judging me or thinking I'm weak and wishing he'd hitched his wagon to a better alpha. He just... wants to help me.

I nod, nuzzling my forehead against Meg's back. She lets out a long sigh, her dreams sending flickers of horny happiness through all four of us. When I look back at Archer, we both smile like idiots.

His eyes warm as they drop to our omega's face, tracing her features. His thoughts are quiet and wise. He projects them to all four of us, and shares one sentence that settles into my soul. The final piece falling into place.

We have the best reason to be our best selves.
I huddle closer to Meg.
The best reason, *ever*.

———————❤———————

I HAVE no idea what time it is, but some indistinct instinct tells me it's close to dawn. I blink awake, finding myself face-to-feet with Theo's hairy toes. With a grimace, I turn my head, just as a flicker of amusement shudders through my bond.

Shit.

I'm still getting used to that. It almost gives me a heart attack.

Meg reacts to my thump of surprise with another internal giggle. She thinks my disgust regarding Theo's furry feet is hilarious and a bit melodramatic. I retaliate by reaching down to pinch her side. Her naked body squirms over mine.

The rest of the bonds are silent while the guys sleep. We all got a decent amount of rest, finally.

Archer was right about the bonding helping Meg's heat. After we all passed out, she only woke up three more times, and each round only required one or two of us to settle her down... unlike the height of her heat, when she could work her way through all four of us and then start all over again.

My cock twitches, filling at the memory. Meg glances down at it. Her wry disbelief sounds a lot like, *You've* got *to be kidding me.*

Which is fair, considering she's fucked each of us three dozen times over the last four days.

I examine her face, smiling at the clarity radiating from her blue eyes. Not wanting to wake the others, I send a thought through wordlessly.

You look good, baby. How do you feel?

She gives a bratty little huff, clearly intending to mask her real emotions when she snaps, *Sore.*

For a second, I think I'll have to ask for more. But then her internal curtain lifts, letting her feelings flow through both of us.

She feels *shy*.

Embarrassed.

Come here, baby. I tuck her right up into me, wrapping both arms around her, sending reassurance and gratitude back. She relaxes into me, keeping the path between us completely open, letting me read everything more closely.

There's chagrin and a bit of dismay—normal, I'd bet, for someone who demanded to be serviced every hour on the hour for three days—but there's also a deep sense of satisfaction. Pride. Happiness. *Awe.*

I feel all of it for myself, sending my own versions back to her. A shaky breath quivers past her lips.

I feel her disbelief before a clear thought comes through, her voice ringing in my head. *You feel everything so deeply in here,* she says, moving her hand to cover the beat in my chest. A wince touches her brow at the exact second a pang of concern hits her heart. *Doesn't it hurt?*

I look at the pack gathered around us. At this woman who loves me so much, I couldn't believe it until I felt it for myself.

And you know what?

It did, I tell her, feeling my lips pull up into a grin. *But not anymore.*

four months later

"ARE YOU READY?"

Meg stands in front of the mirror for a final second, scanning the outfit Declan picked out for her. It's way too fucking sexy. A stretchy black mini skirt that matches the lace trimming her silky orange bodysuit.

When I asked him why he wanted our omega in lingerie in front of the entire godforsaken universe, he pointed out that the low-cut, backless onesie displays all four of our claiming marks. I smile to myself while Meg fluffs out her waves, turning on her platform. Sure enough, the bastard was right. His bite—the lowest one on her body—is clearly visible—two silver half-moons glimmering just above the lacy, tapered point above her ass. Theo's is prominent, too, thanks to the bustier style of the front.

A surge of possessive pride streaks through me while I bend to skim my lips over my own claim. Meg's knees shake. A surge of pleasure rolls down her back.

I smirk, raising one brow at her though the mirror. "I'll take that as a yes," I murmur. "Though, maybe I should I avoid riling you up while the guys are trying to focus."

Theo and Declan's bonds are unnaturally quiet. I can tell our omega doesn't like it. She lets me see her anxiety, soundlessly wondering if she should reach out to them. I push as much confidence and calm to her as I can.

Because if there was ever a day for me to hold my pack together, it's definitely today.

The National Championship.

Meg turns and smiles at me, amused by the way I act like I'm not nervous. I know she knows better, but it's still a hard habit to break.

"Did the Matthews get here?" she asks, picking up her purse.

I nod. "Archer got them into our box without any issue. It's very nice, apparently. Plenty of room, and it's on the club level, so we're closer to the field than we would be at home."

It's a brilliant layout. One I wouldn't mind duplicating. I make a mental note to call an architect on Monday—that way it will be done before next season kicks off.

An image slips in through Meg's bond. Her imagined picture of me overseeing a construction crew in the Ospreys' stadium.

Damn. She caught me.

My lips twitch up. "You know me too well, little one."

With a shrug, she jaunts to the door. The light in her eyes is both mischievous and full of adoration as she reaches for me. "Hold my hand, Daddy?"

I tuck her right under my arm and wind our fingers together for good measure. "Always, baby girl."

Outside the private dressing room, the roar of the crowd fills the hallway. Security officers flanking our door fall into step, leading us out of the concrete maze.

Our bonding launched our pack's notoriety into a whole new stratosphere. Meg still manages all our social media accounts. With each of us having tens of millions of followers, it's a full-time job. She still likes to run the team's PR, too. Her creativity and trendspotting continue to blow me away.

By now, I know what to expect when she pulls her phone out. While we walk the long corridor, she pans her camera around, gathering snippets she'll use later to make something impressive.

The League made arrangements for the families of the players and celebrities. Since we're both, Meg and I are some of last ones out of the private tunnel. When we emerge onto the stadium's club level, which has been cleared for public figures, the crowds above and below us go wild. The Jumbotron hanging over the field lights up, showing our faces—featuring my aviators and Meg's favorite orange-heart sunglasses.

Typical hip-hop music pumps through the air. Early evening light slants in through the opening at the apex of the stadium's dome, gilding the air with a golden glow.

Meg jerks to a halt, her hand squeezing mine. I watch while she looks around, soaking in our surroundings. Reminding me to do the same.

I find myself grinning. Our team, our pack—*my pack*—we're actually fucking here. We did this. Together.

Our omega's deep-seated certainty bubbles through our bond. She turns and flashes me the best smile in the universe.

"We're going to win."

ARCHER

"HERE YOU GO MRS. MATTHEWS." I hand my packmate's mother the drink she requested and receive a beaming smile in return.

The small, plump woman looks nothing like our omega, but her warm demeanor reminds me of Meg. I knew they would adore each other, but I'm not sure I've ever met a mother-in-law who loves her daughter-in-law quite as much as Matilda Matthews.

Theo's whole family came to visit at Christmas time, assuming the two-month cushion after our bonding would allow us all plenty of time to work through our honeymoon phase.

Or so we thought, anyway.

The fact that one of his relatives almost walked in on us six different times would indicate otherwise.

We were on our best behavior, but when there are five people in a bond, the odds one of you will get turned on and trigger a chain reaction is a bit higher than average.

A lot higher.

Luckily, the entire Matthews family is as easy-going and good-humored as Theo. They thoroughly enjoyed teasing all of us. One of his dads even started wearing a bell around his neck as a joke.

Meg fell in with both alphas and their daughters effortlessly, but she formed a special attachment to Matilda. Once Mrs.

Matthews heard about Meg's childhood, the sweet omega made it her mission to give our omega all the mothering she missed out on.

I'm beginning to suspect she plans to do the same for me.

Matilda pats my cheek softly, raising one thin blonde eyebrow. "Now, Arch, you know you're supposed to call me Mom. Or do I need to start calling you Dr. Monroe?"

One of Theo's fathers—Pop, I think—drops down into the seat beside Matilda. "Leave the man alone, darling," he chuckles. "Tensions are high around here."

"No idea why," my favorite voice chimes. "I already told Ronan we're going to win."

I feel Meg before I see her. She's a rush in my veins. Sparks of joy in my chest. The light of my life.

I grab her through the bond and tug. She appears at my side half a second later, giggling quietly at the way I mentally yanked her over. "Miss me?"

I miss her every second. And also never. It's an endless cycle of longing and having. To think of her is to want her. Thankfully, she's always with me. *In me.*

I'm still not over the miracle of it four months later.

I reach for her hand on instinct, bringing it to my lips. She pulls away before I can get my mouth on my mark, clucking at me, "Declan and Theo are trying to concentrate."

Pops snorts and sends me a knowing wink. His packmate— the father Theo calls "Daddio"—sits on his other time. Ironically, "Daddio" is the more serious of the two. He shoots me a worried look. "How are our boys?"

They all consider Declan their son. I know that same care extends to me now, too, but I'm still processing it.

I can't feel the guys the way Meg can, but they're both quiet. Which, for Theo, is either a very good sign or utter catastrophe. For Declan, it simply means he's walling us out at the moment.

I look to our omega, and she smiles. "They've got this."

We all settle in and watch as the Ospreys charge onto the field, led our new coach—Dean White.

Ronan promoted the offensive coordinator after he fired Henshaw. The move was a great success. Dean, Theo, and Declan became fast friends, collaborating on strategies that spoke for themselves. The team went 13-3 in the regular season and absolutely crushed the playoffs.

The team looks great tonight. I feel a pang at watching them spread along the sidelines. Part of me wishes I could be down in the action like I usually am. But I know all the guys are as healthy as could be, and I want to be here for Meg and Ronan.

My oldest packmate and I end up side-by-side with our girl on both our laps. She bounces in place when she spots Theo and Declan, squealing. We all cheer and wave when they turn and look for us among the Lucite boxes lining the club level.

Meg presses her hands to the window, one for each of them. Theo thumps his fist over his heart, grinning. Declan's face stays serious, but he points right at her. Whatever he sends through their bond makes her eyes water.

"They're ready," she says, settling back with a brilliant smile. "I know it."

I wrap my arm around her waist.

How could they not be? I ask her, whispering through our tether. *They have you.*

DECLAN

ACROSS AN ENTIRE STADIUM of rabid fans, my eyes lock with Meg's. Our blues meld together. She gives a burst of pride and shows me the solid certainty sitting in the center of her.

Careful not to distract me, she only sends one other thought.

You're going to win, Vanilla.

If I do, it's because of her. Every good thing I am... it's all because of Meg.

So, I point right at her, letting every spectator, camera—the entire world—see her claim on my arm and the person I'm pointing to. I send her one thought back.

I already did, baby.

THEO CATCHES my eye across the huddle. He's panting, drenched in sweat.

They're giving us hell.

We knew it would be like this. Their defensive is the best in the League—a proper match for our unsurpassed offense.

But, damn, I want this.

The score looms behind Theo. 23-27. We trail by four with

less than two minutes on the clock. It's third-and-goal. If I fuck up this pass...

Coach White is in my ear, muttering through the speaker in my helmet. He suggests a few different options, and I pick the one I think is best. It's another running route for Theo, but he'll have to make it look like a block. I need him to really sell it if we're going to fake this defense out.

He hears the play and nods, meeting my eyes.

You good?

I've blocked my pack out for the entire game, trying to keep my head clear and spare them the inner turmoil that comes with stakes this high. For part of a second, I let him past my wall. He sees what's there, and I feel him reach for Meg as the huddle breaks.

One minute, fourteen seconds.

Thirteen.

Ten.

Meg fights her way to me, forcing one simple emotion through.

Pure, unconditional love.

She's a slant of sunlight in a dark room. The warmth, the light. Reminding me where I am. What I'm doing. Why I'm here.

I look up, absorbing the stadium full of screaming fans, the pound of my heart in my ears.

Fuck yeah.

We're doing this.

I call the play and close down my bond, focusing. Our center snaps the ball. Our line shoves against the invading defense. Theo fakes the block until I'm situated and makes a break for it.

I hold.

Hold.

Hold.

And throw.

A BUZZER SOUNDS. The sting of Declan's spiral echoes in my fingertips as confetti catapults into the air.

Orange and black.

We won.

We *won*.

The number flashes on the Jumbotron. *29-27*, it says.

FINAL.

Holy fucking shit.

Someone pulls me up. Teammates immediately slam into my sides, tackling and hugging, whooping and jumping.

Bodies flood the field. Declan gets swarmed. Fellow Ospreys —players and coaching staff—fly at me while I make my way to him.

I'm so dazed, I forget I have all my bonds locked down. The second I rip the curtain open, a flood of pride and excitement lights up my insides. Ronan sends me an image of him maneuvering Meg down to the field for us. I change course and jog to the sidelines.

Archer and Ronan emerge from the tunnel with our girl. She's already wearing an *Ospreys—World Champions* baseball hat. Ronan ordered two hundred of them as soon as we clinched the playoffs and we all thought he was insane.

Guess the fuck *not*.

I'll let him give me shit later. Right now, I can't think about anything except for getting to my girl.

She launches herself at me, jumping straight into my arms, laughing and crying. I spin her around, absorbing the swirl of joy and amazement zinging back and forth between us.

"You know what this means, right?" I shout.

She flashes her brightest grin. "Daddy is taking us to Disney World?"

"Damn straight he is," I laugh. "Pack your bags, peaches. You and me are getting matching mouse ears."

Her hands clutch my sweaty bun and my beard, holding me still for a dozen kisses. When she pulls back, her crystal eyes shine.

"Big guy—I am *so* proud of you."

Fuck.

I just won all over again.

I twirl her some more, scent-marking her while a small army of video cameras look on. Declan sees us on the screen and sends us all a hard nudge. He's on the podium with Coach, holding our trophy.

But he wants his prize.

Megera

I DON'T WANT to be that girl and say *I told you so*, but...

Who am I kidding? I am totally that girl.

It's the best kind of chaos as Theo carries me through the confetti and the crowd, making a beeline for the makeshift stage erected in the middle of the field. Archer and Ronan stride right behind him, each accepting handshakes and fist-bumps as we go.

Instead of making me wait to get to the edge of the field and climb the stage's stairs, Theo sets me on the platform. He nods, grinning. "Go to him. We'll be right there."

Declan is center stage, wearing one of our championship hats and holding the enormous trophy. The second he sees me, he opens his arms, paying the hardware in his hand no mind.

I practically climb the man, inhaling his intoxicating vanilla scent as I wrap my arms and legs around him. Stretching up, I whisper right into his ear. "I told you so."

He laughs against my temple, raising his voice to be heard. "You told me so, princess."

Holding me with one arm, Declan kisses me long and hard, sliding his tongue along mine. Our bond opens, emotions gushing through it like a river released from a dam. Joy, disbelief, pride. But his gratitude runs the deepest—and, in the end, that's what leaves my eyes wet.

He murmurs against my lips, running his nose along mine. "I have something for you. We all do."

I lower myself back onto my heels just as the guys make it to the stage. Their bonds light up, but I don't hear anything—a sure sign they're all plotting against me.

It's clear why, a moment later, when Declan turns me toward the crowd and wraps his arm around my waist. The others present me with... a box? It looks like a ring box, but maybe a bit too big.

We talked about bonding rings and decided we didn't need them. Well, I decided we didn't need them. The guys all begged me to choose one for myself, but it seemed like a waste of money that Dec and I could put toward our foundation.

My heart still stutters while I stare at the black velvet case. Declan's voice is deliciously dominant against my ear. "It's not what you think. Open it, omega."

I flip back the clasp, revealing the *enormous* ring inside. A *championship* ring. It's solid rose gold, inlaid with shining onyx and dozens of shimmering diamonds. The black stone forms our new Ospreys logo, along with the year and the words *World Champions*.

It's exactly like the ones they'll all get. They had one made for me, too.

Happy tears slip over my cheeks while Archer places it on my right hand, reverently skimming his claiming mark in the process.

Declan gently takes my fingers from him and holds up the ring for my inspection, twisting it to show me the inscription engraved along the side.

Megera Ash - MVP.

a note from ari

Oh hi!

Welcome to my identity crisis, aka Knot Her Goal!

If you've read any of my other books, you know by now that this one was completely out of my comfort zone. I have no big explanation except to say that it was 100% my best friend's fault. She lured me into a false sense of security over a pile of Mexican food and then planted the seed in my mind—a football Omega-verse novel.

It sounded just crazy enough to be amazing, so I came home and decided I'd jot a few ideas down. Two days later, I had 25,000 words of this story and I could. Not. Stop.

This is a place I never expected to find myself in creatively, but I absolutely love it. I have a few more ideas for this series and I can't wait to write them.

With Meg's story, I hoped to speak to the pressure so many of us feel to "control" or "overcome" our own natures. The prevailing notion that feeling pain or anxiety makes someone weak has been very damaging for me in my own life and I hope watching Meg overcome that narrative might help others give themselves permission to be their authentic selves.

All of this to say, if you're a new reader, thank you so much for taking a chance on my very first Omegaverse. And if you're a loyal reader who made the jump from contemporary romance to this crazy-fun why-choose universe, you have my most sincere gratitude!

xx,

Ari Wright

acknowledgments

Because this project was super top-secret and completely out of my element, I didn't share its existence with many. But here are the ones I need to thank!

Of course, I have to thank my best friend Kelly, who helped think up this universe and the alphas in it. I probably never would have read sports romance or Omegaverse—let alone written a combo—without her! Here's hoping my playlist lived up to her expectations.

A huge thank-you to my editor, Katie, who does so much more than tell me where the commas go. Her support and her opinions are invaluable. Hearing them all in her gorgeous British accent over voice notes just makes them even better!

To my Aunt Mary and my friend Katie—you love me and listen to my insanity even when it's... well, insane. Thank you for always being so supportive and treating my career with respect. I love you both for not running away screaming when I described this book (thank God we'd had plenty of champagne).

Lastly, a shout out to my husband, who makes these books possible in so many ways. I wouldn't be able to do any of this without him!

about the author

Ari Wright was once entirely sane, but then she realized sanity is over-rated and decided to write sporty Omegaverse smut.

Because life is short, you know?

When she isn't writing unhinged romances, she enjoys drinking coffee to the point of excess, kitchen experiments, raising her littles, and trying to keep her plants alive (just kidding, her husband does that). She loves really embarrassing music, moody weather, and any story where the bad guy gets the girl.

Because what's Happily Ever After without a little (or a lot of) spice?

You can follow her works in progress, favorite reads, and very pink aesthetic on Instagram!

Printed in Great Britain
by Amazon

43243568R00253